CHERNOBYLITE

MIKE DOWSETT

DowCorp Press

Published by DowCorp Press 2020.

This book is a work of fiction.

ISBN: 978-0-6488474-0-3

To my amazing wife Liz –
thank you for all the love and joy you bring
to my life and your incredible support and
belief in me.

To Michelle –
thanks for the inspiration!

PROLOGUE - THE OLYMPICS

The crowd settled.

A hush fell over the vast Olympic stadium in Bucharest, Romania. The last ten years of Thomas Taylor's life had all been leading up to this moment. He filled his lungs with a deep intake of breath, absorbing the pulsing energy that was flowing around the arena and through every part of his body. This was the Olympics! The pinnacle of his sport, the ultimate goal for the elite Judo fighters on the planet and here he was, about to battle it out for the gold medal.

The countless hours of training, the injuries and the sacrifice had all brought Tommy to this one moment. He straightened up his Judogi, the traditional uniform, adjusted the black belt tied neatly around his waist, bowed respectfully and then stepped onto the mat, instantly switching into combat mode.

He emptied his mind of all clutter and noise, gathering his energy and focusing every fibre of his being on one thing – combat. He used this technique before every training session and every competition, forming his own version of muscle memory on a grand scale, triggering his whole body into a state that was hyper-aware but calm at the same time, fluid and ready for instant action.

With a height well over two metres and tipping the scales at 130 kilograms of pure muscle, Tommy was a giant of a man, in absolute peak physical condition. He was in the heavyweight division, competing against the biggest men of the sport. He was the young buck, full of energy and vitality but lacking the experience of the old bull that he was battling for the Olympic crown. He was fighting a triple Olympic champion in his last tournament, a crowd favourite who had seen every move and technique in his long Judo career. While Tommy had a height and weight advantage over his slightly smaller opponent, he knew he would need all his skills and every reserve of strength to match it with his much more experienced combatant. Speed was on his side – for such a big man, Tommy moved surprisingly fast, quicker even than many fighters smaller than him.

The two man-mountains walked across the mat, faced each other and bowed. The referee signalled them to begin the match and it was under way. Slowly and carefully they circled each other, sizing up their opponent, arms outstretched with claw-like fingers, searching for an opening – that all important grip that could enable a throw. Twenty seconds in, the crowd was getting restless, calling for action, when suddenly the old pro launched, landed a vice-like grip on Tommy's Judogi and got him with a hip throw. The move scored a quarter point and landed Tommy on the mat. Instantly the champ was on top of Tommy, fighting for an advantage and trying to pin him to the mat. But Tommy was in a strong position and resisted the attack long enough for the referee to call time. The men climbed to their feet again to restart the action.

Tommy was behind already in just the first minute, handing the advantage to the more experienced fighter, which was something he could not afford to continue. Collecting himself, Tommy took a deep breath and prepared for battle once more. Knees slightly bent, arms outstretched, he searched for an advantage, steeling himself to land the all-important next grip, and so he did, his greater reach proving the difference. Tommy got an overhand grip and at the same instant shot out his right foot in a blur of speed and executed a perfect foot sweep that caught the champ by surprise, landing him on his side on the mat, scoring half a point. Seizing the opening, Tommy threw himself on top of his opponent, quickly flipped him onto his back and dropped his weight onto the other man's chest. Unfortunately, Tommy hadn't been quick enough to completely trap the arms, so couldn't apply the impenetrable hold-down he was searching for. After a few seconds, the slippery veteran squirmed his way out of the hold-down and the referee once more called them to their feet.

Both now breathing hard from their exertions, they circled each other once more. Again, it was the more experienced of the pair who landed the next grip, quickly stepping in and under the taller man and applying a foot sweep of his own, sending Tommy backwards towards the mat. Instantly Tommy knew he was in trouble; if he landed flat on his back it would be a full point against him and the match would be over, just like that. Judo was an unforgiving sport, always with the potential for one mistake to end a fight in seconds.

Catlike, Tommy twisted his upper body as he fell through the air and managed to change position just enough so that he landed slightly on his side, losing only half a point, and saving the match. But he was still in dire trouble, with the off-balance twisting causing him to flail his arms about, presenting an opening that was instantly seized upon. Tommy felt his neck wrapped in a forearm pincer like a bear trap, applying a choke hold with violent force. Within just a few seconds Tommy was seeing stars and could feel the blood supply being cut off to his brain. He knew that if he didn't get out of this choke hold very, very quickly he would be gone. Even though he was fading fast through lack of oxygen, he resolved not to tap out; he decided he would rather lose consciousness than lose the match by submission, forever wondering if he had tapped too soon.

Just in time, Tommy managed to get an arm free and slammed his hand up between his own neck and the imposing forearm. Instantly, he knew he had a chance when he felt a slight give in the force of the hold. Seizing the tiny advantage, Tommy used his immense strength to drive his hand further into the small gap, at the same time heaving his body, twisting with all his might to put his attacker off balance and break the grip that was bringing on the black of unconsciousness. Suddenly he felt the grip give and he wriggled free, throwing his opponent off him with a huge show of strength.

The crowd exhaled as one as they suddenly realized they had been collectively holding their breath in simpatico with Tommy. A great cheer erupted as they realized the fight was still alive between these two mighty warriors.

Move-for- move, the fight continued between the perfectly matched pair until the buzzer sounded signalling the end of the allotted time, with points tied dead level. The match instantly moved into "Golden Score", meaning it would go on and on with unlimited time until the next point or penalty. The crowd were being treated to an epic match, one for the ages that threatened to bring the house down.

As the battle raged on, the fighters became more breathless, battered and bruised, until slowly but surely the younger man's speed, stamina and endurance took their toll on the old fighter. At last with a mighty heave, Tommy in a blinding blur of speed perfectly landed the throw of his life and his opponent was on his back in a flash, dazed and confused and wondering how on earth he had gotten there so fast.

Slowly but surely through the deafening cheers of the thundering crowd, the truth dawned on Tommy as he finally realized that he'd done it – he'd won! Thrusting his arms straight up in the air, Tommy let out a thunderous roar. Ten long hard years of training and commitment had culminated in this, his defining moment; he was the heavyweight Olympic champion, king of the world!

Suddenly remembering the all-important tradition of respect in Judo, Tommy paused his celebrations, returned to his starting position on the mat, straightened his Judogi and his belt, stood up straight and waited for the referee to indicate the winner, bowed first to his opponent, then the referee and the judges. Once the ritual was over, Tommy's opponent embraced him and congratulated him on a fight well played. The excited crowd roared their appreciation of the two combatants and Tommy raised both arms above his head in victory, circled the mat and waved to the adoring spectators.

Peeking through his euphoria, a twinge of sadness came over Tommy as he remembered that he had no family here with him to share this special moment. He consoled himself in the knowledge that while his loving and supportive mother back in Australia couldn't afford the plane ticket to see Tommy's moment of glory, he knew she would be watching so proudly from the other side of the world. Tommy was a wild and crazy jumble of emotions all the way from ecstasy to disbelief at what he had just accomplished. He returned to his cheering Australian teammates, secure in the knowledge that whatever happened from this moment onwards, he would always be one of the select few people in the world who could call themselves an Olympic Champion. It certainly had a nice ring to it.

After what seemed an eternity, the time for medal presentations finally arrived. Tommy made his way to the podium and stepped up onto the tallest dais. The vanquished veteran by Tommy's side reached his arms out and delivered a warm and genuine embrace to the young warrior, congratulating him on his efforts and letting him know everything was okay, because he was ready to retire. Satisfied with his long and stellar career, the ex-champion had three Olympic gold medals and now this, his first silver medal.

Tommy couldn't quite believe his eyes as he looked over and saw the medal procession, being led by a special guest, the President of Russia, who was apparently a Judo exponent himself. In the most surreal event in Tommy's young life, he leaned forward to allow one of the most powerful men in the world to drape an Olympic gold medal around his neck.

The Australian flag was unfurled, and the national anthem filled the air. Tommy soaked it all in and was overcome by the deep feelings rising within him. Through teary eyes he saw the crowd go crazy, including his best friend Chad, a fellow Olympian, but with Team USA.

As he stepped off the victory dais, the very first thing he did was call his mum Molly back home in Sydney, who answered straight away and immediately burst into tears. It had been so hard for her being all alone, so far away from her beloved son for so long that all her pent-up emotion suddenly gushed out of her like a geyser. She had told herself she would keep her emotions in check, but then figured some tears were warranted; after all, her only son had just won a gold medal at the Olympics!

Sobbing and laughing all at the same time, Molly was so happy and proud that she felt she was going to burst. 'Oh Tommy,' she cried, 'You did it! You bloody did it! You were amazing! I could hardly watch the fight, I felt like I was going to pass out so many times I had to keep closing my eyes, I could hardly bear it. You did so well, that guy was incredible!'

'Thanks Mum. I know, I can't believe it! Yeah, that guy was tough as nails,' Tommy replied. He heard whistling and cheering in the background and asked, 'Hey, who's that with you, is it the girls from the club?'

'Yes, they decided to take some time off the stage, so they could watch their favourite boy win a gold medal! The boss says they've got to get back to stripping now to keep the customers entertained and the money flowing, so they just said a quick goodbye.'

'Tell the girls thanks for everything Mum, thanks for all the support, it means a lot to me,' said Tommy.

'I will, Tommy,' said his excited mother. On and on she went, and Tommy just sat back and took it all in, absorbing the moment and his mother's pride, with tears rolling down his cheeks. They were tears of happiness but tinged with sadness too, knowing how much he wanted her there. Tommy vowed that one day it would be different; he would make enough money for them both to live a comfortable life without the unceasing struggle that had been their constant companion for so long.

'Oh Tommy, if only your father was alive to see your fight, he would have been so proud. You meant everything to him,' said his mum sadly, the pain as fresh now as it was ten long years ago.

Tommy felt a sudden wash of pain and grief that his father couldn't experience this defining moment of his life with him. But he knew deep down that his father was always with him, held close in his heart, so in some way had been there all along and seen everything, lived it with him.

'It's a shame too that Viktor couldn't be there to see you compete. Did he say why he couldn't come?'

'No,' responded Tommy sadly. He had really hoped his old Judo coach from back home would come and watch him in the Olympics, but the man who had been what amounted to a surrogate father to Tommy had been steadfast in his negative response to Tommy's invitation. His coach, who had always been so supportive of Tommy in the past had provided no reason or explanation for not coming, which had hurt Tommy more than he cared to admit.

The next half an hour was full of rapturous conversation as Tommy described the bout for his mum in great detail, just like he used to when he was a boy and he'd been off fighting at some far away competition that his mother couldn't attend because she had to work. She'd always pressed him for more and more detail until he ended up almost re-enacting the entire fight. She was always thirsty for more and Tommy loved embellishing the story for her, so he did that again tonight, just like back in the day in the tiny rundown apartment they had shared together, despite the fact that this time she had already seen it all on TV.

Eventually they finished up their phone call and Tommy's mum went back to work at the strip club. He hung up the phone, happy that he had shared that special time with his mother, who was such a huge part of his life, his tower of strength and source of boundless love and support.

Elated, Tommy finally left the presentation area and went off to find some of his Aussie teammates who had already finished competing and were feeling rowdy and ready for a night on the town. 'Time to hit the bar, boys!' Tommy shouted as he came across a group of them in a huddle.

Turning as one, they roared, 'TOMMY! Here comes the Champ, you're a bloody gold medallist, mate!' And off they went to the nearest bar, ready to paint the town red.

Morning dawned on Tommy like some sort of blazing attack of the senses. As sleep slowly left him and he gradually stirred to wakefulness in a hazy blur, his head was pounding, and his insides were howling in protest at the abuse he had unleashed on his body the night before. Way too many beers and cocktails had made their way into him last night in what was his first taste of alcohol for exactly one year. He had been off the booze for a full 12 months in his lead-up to the Olympics, so was well short of drinking training and recovery skills.

In a sudden moment of panic, Tommy clutched at his neck and then breathed a sigh of relief as he felt the Olympic gold medal still hanging around his neck. He had heard so many stories of athletes getting blind drunk and losing their medals that he had been paranoid about doing the same, but thankfully had held himself together enough not to lose track of his. He took the medal from around his neck, reached down to the floor and stashed the medal safely in his suitcase.

With a loud groan, he rolled his massive frame out of his tiny bed and got unsteadily to his feet. He knew he had a big day ahead with media interviews and cheering on his best mate Chad, who was competing in the wrestling that afternoon. So, he dragged himself to the shower and washed away the worst of his hangover, then got moving into the day.

Since Chad had been there for him the day before, it was time for Tommy to return the favour and support Chad in his fight for the wrestling gold medal. Chad was a decorated athlete, Ivy League champion three years in a row and USA national champion for the past two years. He was hyper-competitive, always up for a challenge and a credit to his team and his family. He was overjoyed when he was selected out of a huge pool of athletes to carry the flag for the USA in the opening ceremony, ahead of so many other equally deserving competitors. It had been the proudest moment of Chad's life just a few days earlier as he led the team into the arena for the opening ceremony, a close-up of his face beamed around the world for billions of people to see.

Chad's mother Amy had been frightened about the location of the Olympics in Bucharest. She was uncertain how safe that she, Chad and her daughter Brittney would be in what she thought of as a dangerous part of the world because of traumatic events in her past. But she knew there was no way she could possibly have denied Chad the opportunity to fulfil his dreams of Olympic glory. There was no way she could stay away, and she knew that Brittney would have found some way to get there on her own, even if Amy didn't want her there. Keeping her sense of foreboding and concerns about the safety of the trip to herself, Amy had put on a brave face and embraced the pomp and ceremony of this incredibly special event in all their lives.

Chad had fought exceedingly well in his preliminary bouts and progressed to the medal rounds through tough matches that had gained him invaluable experience. He had been fighting against international opponents with skills and techniques different to those of his homeland opposition. Now guaranteed at least a silver medal in his final fight, Chad was happy, but committed to go for gold. However, he had picked up some sort of sickness and been feeling progressively worse over the past two days so was not sure how he would fare in this, the most important wrestling match of his life.

Chad looked up and saw his best friend Tommy playfully lumbering towards him with arms outstretched like Frankenstein's monster, who then wrapped him in a huge bear hug. Mouth close to Chad's ear, Tommy said quietly, 'Go get him Chad. You can do it. You can take this guy! That gold medal has got your name written all over it.'

Tommy let Chad go and then stepped back to look him over. Chad's skin was a pale-yellow colour, his eyes were bloodshot, he was shivering and had sweat dripping down his face. 'Dude, you look like shit! What's wrong?' exclaimed Tommy. 'I knew you weren't feeling well, but this is a whole new level of messed-up. Are you sure you can fight?'

Chad groaned a little but nodded and said, 'I've been feeling worse and worse since that bee sting a few days ago, but I haven't come all this way to give up now. I need to at least try – I can't not compete.'

'Mate, be careful, don't go too hard,' said Tommy, immediately worried that Chad might do himself some serious damage. He resolved to stay as close as he could to help if he needed to. He looked over to the stands, searching for Chad's mother Amy and sister Brittney. Finally spotting them, Tommy waved to catch their attention and his heart melted as Brittney saw him, smiled and gave a wave in return.

The time came for Chad's match. By now looking quite woozy, Chad made his way onto the mat, squinting at his opponent, breathing heavily but determined to put up a good fight. The referee called the start and they circled around each other, searching for an opening. In Chad's hampered state, his opponent quickly found a weakness in Chad's stance and brought him to the ground. Frantically trying to avoid the grip he knew was coming, Chad exerted himself to his weakened limit. Strong arms with thick corded muscle rippling beneath the skin enveloped Chad and flipped him on his back. The heavy weight of Chad's opponent instantly followed, and Chad immediately blacked out.

The other fighter instantly sensed something was wrong as the body went limp beneath him. The crowd collectively drew in a breath and held it, not daring to exhale. The arena was deathly quiet as the crowd willed the fallen combatant to regain consciousness, but it was not to be.

Medics rushed onto the mat and started work on the inert body. Tall white screens were rushed onto the mat to hide the grisly scene from the crowd, but everyone had already seen enough. The medics did their best but could not bring Chad back to consciousness. Behind the screens, the drama unfolded as, slowly but surely, the life ebbed from Chad and he faded away into death.

Tommy from his vantage point close-by and Amy and Brittney from their more distant location looked on, transfixed, numb with fear, desperate to know but at the same time not, what was happening behind that ominous white screen. An announcement came over the public-address system asking everyone to leave the arena, which was not a good sign.

Tommy raced over to Chad to see if he could see anything at all behind the screens and caught a glimpse of something that he immediately wished he hadn't – a white sheet completely covered Chad's body and face. His best friend was dead!

Shocked, stunned and unable to process the enormity of what had just happened, Tommy looked over to where Amy and Brittney had been sitting. With a gasp, he saw four men dressed completely in black, one on each side of both Amy and Brittney, marching them out of the stadium, pushing them along with something jammed in their back. Tommy could tell from their body language that the women were terrified and in shock.

Tommy was torn; his best friend had just died right in front of him and now the remainder of his friend's American family were being taken away! In an instant, he chose the living over the dead and launched into action, leaping over rails and setting off in hot pursuit of the women and their captors.

There would be time enough to mourn his friend Chad, but that would have to wait.

PART 1 - AUSTRALIA

CHAPTER 1

Born to a hard-working farmer and his loving wife in the tiny coastal town of Brooms Head in New South Wales in down-under Australia, Tommy had a joyous childhood full of fun and roughhousing with his mates in the country. Days were spent surfing, racing go-karts and playing endless games of cricket in the summer and rugby in the winter.

Tommy spent special time with his dad Charlie in those early years in the country; they were inseparable. Sharing so many traits and interests like their odd sense of humour and a love of fast cars and action movies, they were as thick as thieves. Many a day was spent at the movies or on the couch watching classic action movies with stars like Schwarzenegger, Stallone, Jackie Chan, Bruce Willis, Steven Segal and Jean Claude Van-Damme. They could never get enough of seeing bad guys getting an ass-kicking while the hero delivered priceless one-liners.

Tommy and Charlie spent many a weekend working in the back shed on Charlie's favourite muscle cars that he had inherited from his own father; one an American beauty and the other a home-grown favourite. Tommy particularly loved the deep blue 1965 Shelby Cobra Mark III with a massive 427 cubic inch V8 under the bonnet, while Charlie's sentimental favourite was the bright orange, race-bred 1976 Holden Torana SLR 5000, fitted with a thumping 308 cubic inch Chevy V8. In line with the rev-head interests of the pair, they used to race go-karts together and his father had Tommy driving cars around their rural property when he was too small to even see over the steering wheel or reach the pedals. Like many of his friends in the country, Tommy became a capable driver at a young age.

All through his primary school years in the tiny schoolhouse where all the students shared the same two teachers, life was good for Tommy. The first Christmas after he finished primary school promised to be the best one yet. At 12 years of age he had been one of the kings of the school, idolized by the younger students. Tommy's high school adventure would begin the next year, but right now he had five more weeks of holidays to enjoy; riding his bike, racing go-karts, surfing, fooling around with his mates and watching the Ashes cricket tests on TV with his dad, seeing Australia battle the old enemy, England.

The day after Christmas Day was shaping up to be a hot one. Tommy loved the heat. While the adults were comatose and whining indoors, Tommy would be out and about, revelling in the sunshine and spending his time at the beach with his surfboard. But today was different – he was heading out early with his dad.

'Ready, Son? Let's go see if we can shoot ourselves some dinner – rabbit stew sounds pretty damn good!' said Charlie with a smile. 'We'll jump in the ute, go pick up old Fred and then we'll take off into the bush and chase down some bunnies.'

Tommy happily jumped in the front of the ute with his dad and off they went. Tommy wasn't really a fan of hunting; he didn't like guns and he was an animal lover, so he didn't like to see them get hurt. But Charlie loved it and Tommy enjoyed spending time with his dad, so took every chance he could to go with him. Plus, Tommy was a country boy, and that's what they did in the country. Dinner was often a chicken or a young lamb from the paddock, or a cut of beef from one of the cows they had slaughtered and tossed in the freezer.

Charlie's banged-up ute pulled into the driveway of his old mate Fred's place. Tommy jumped in the rear tray of the ute to let Fred have the front seat as they headed off into the bush. Fred was getting on a bit; he'd retired long ago, and his health was fading. Fred's eyesight wasn't great, so he didn't hold out much hope of bagging any rabbits, but he enjoyed being out and about anyway. It made him feel young again.

'What do you think Fred, how does it look over there?' asked Charlie, pointing to a hillside full of holes that looked like rabbit burrows.

'She's a beauty Charlie, I reckon that'll do nicely,' answered Fred, even though he couldn't see much detail on the slope.

Charlie slid the ute to a halt with a nice sideways handbrake stop to throw Tommy around in the back, which he loved as he tumbled about laughing and giggling.

Charlie and Fred climbed out of the ute and headed over to the hillside, rifles cradled in their arms. As they walked away, Charlie called out, 'You stay up there, Tommy, safe and out of the way.'

Tommy laid down in the tray of the ute, basking in the half sun / half shadow of the trees, daydreaming as he gazed happily up at the wispy clouds drifting by on a light breeze against the intense blue backdrop of the sky beyond. 'Ah, life doesn't get any better than this,' said Tommy out loud to himself. He was happy and content in the present and looking forward with eager anticipation to the future, to see what this next stage of his life had in store.

Tommy's daydreaming was shattered by a sharp gunshot piercing the silence as the sound split the air on its headlong passage towards him. 'Hope they got one,' he said to himself.

But a few seconds later, Tommy's stomach churned, his chest constricted and his throat dried up as he heard a pained wail, full of anguish as Fred's tired old voice yelled out, 'Oh my God, what have I done? CHARLIE!'

Tommy was instantly out of the ute, racing madly towards the sound of Fred's voice, who was now sobbing incoherently. Tommy flew around a tree and witnessed a scene that would burn in his brain forever as he slid to a grinding halt, kicking up a cloud of dust.

He saw Fred on his knees, convulsing with sobs, bending over the body of Tommy's beloved father, his hero, friend and protector. A vivid crimson pool of blood was rapidly spreading over Charlie's flannel shirt, shaking loose an involuntary gasp from Tommy. He had never seen so much blood, never seen it such a bright red before.

Everything came into sharp focus for Tommy as he took in every detail of the shocking scene; Fred's still-smoking gun lying on the ground, the look of utter shock and despair on Charlie's face, and the rabbit that had escaped with its life bounding off into the distance.

Fred rolled onto his side on the ground in the foetal position, rocking himself and crying inconsolably. His poor old addled mind simply couldn't cope with the enormity of what he had just done.

Then Charlie groaned and beckoned Tommy to come over to him – he was conscious! Tommy raced over and leant down to get close to his father's face as he wheezed out, 'Son, I'm not going to make it. I'm done for – the bullet got me right in the chest, now I'm struggling to breathe. Tommy, it was an accident. Fred's eyes aren't too good, so he missed the rabbit and got me instead. He just didn't see me. Make sure he doesn't get into any trouble, that he knows it was an accident and I don't blame him.'

Tommy thought it was so like his dad to look after others, make sure they were alright, even on his deathbed. Struggling to breathe, Charlie sounded like he was slowly suffocating.

'Son, I'm so sorry I'm not going to be around to watch you grow up into a man, and that I'll miss all those special moments that I know are going to come. I'm so proud of you, Tommy, you're a great lad. You're the best thing I've ever done in my life and I know you're destined for greatness. Look after your mother and be a good boy for her. It's going to be tough, Son, but you've got to be strong. Be strong for yourself and for Molly.'

With tears streaming down his young cheeks, Tommy cried out 'Dad, Dad, don't die, please don't die! What will I do if you're not here anymore? I'm scared of what life will be like without you!'

'Tommy, you'll be okay, I know you will. You're strong and you've got a good heart. Always remember that. Never lose sight of who you are and what you stand for,' said Charlie, struggling for breath. 'Tell your mum she made a simple country boy the happiest man on the planet. I was blessed by an angel the day she picked me at the high school dance, and I treasured every minute we spent together. Tell her I've loved her always, I love her now and I'll love her forever, whatever happens and wherever she is.'

By now gasping for breath, Charlie laid his head back down on the baking earth as he prepared himself for Death's cold embrace. 'I love you Son,' whispered Charlie, and then his last breath floated out of him and his head lolled to the side.

'I love you too, Dad,' sobbed Tommy as he laid his head on his father's shoulder and wept.

After a time, Tommy realized that his father was right – he needed to be strong. He had to take control of the situation because they were in the middle of the bush, out of contact from everyone. He needed to get help. Tommy reached over and closed his father's eyes forever. It was the toughest thing he'd ever had to do, a task much more difficult than a boy his age should have to face.

Tommy got an old blanket from the ute and used it to cover his father's body, which helped to calm Fred. Soon Fred had recovered enough to stand vigil over his old friend. Tommy felt bad leaving the frail old man there, but Fred insisted that he would be okay and that it was the right thing to do. Fred couldn't drive because of his eyes and didn't have his wits about him enough to do what needed to be done, so it was all up to Tommy.

Devastated at what had just occurred, Tommy forlornly got in the car, dreading what he knew was coming but knowing that he was the one who had to do it. Slowly and carefully, he drove the bush tracks and country roads home, suddenly glad that his father had taught him to drive so young. As he pulled into the long driveway of their home, his mum smiled and waved from the front door of the house. Tommy died a little inside when he thought of the news that he was about to break to her.

As the ute got closer, Molly realized that there was only one person in it and then saw that it was her son, instead of her husband, who was driving. Her nerves instantly on high alert, she knew something was seriously wrong. Ashen faced, she raced over to the oncoming ute as it slowed to a stop and opened the driver's door. 'Tommy, what is it? Are you okay? Where's your dad?' she asked quietly, trying to remain calm.

Tommy took a deep breath, trying to keep himself together and said, 'I'm sorry Mum, but there was an accident and dad got shot. He's dead.' And then he collapsed out of the car and into her arms. Molly reeled back from the news as if she'd been punched in the stomach. Her knees buckled and then she too collapsed in shock and they both fell to the dusty ground, sobbing in each other's arms, sharing their grief.

When they were both spent, they slowly got up and went inside the house. Molly called the police and waited for them to arrive. Tommy had to take them to the body, or they could have been searching for hours. Tommy knew that Fred would need looking after too, so was glad that an adult could take over now. All he had to do was direct the police to the tragic scene.

As they rounded the bend and took in the sight, everyone was even more concerned when they saw Fred's body lying down beside a figure covered by an old blanket. They quickly got out of the car and tried to wake Fred, but there was no response. He looked uninjured and his face showed no signs of pain. The doctor who had come along for the formalities had not expected a second victim, but quickly examined Fred and proclaimed his expectation that Fred had suffered a massive stroke, guessing that his mind simply couldn't cope with the trauma and had imploded, driving a giant clot into his brain and cutting off the blood supply to that critical organ.

Fred had led a long and good life and had been very lonely ever since his darling Esme had passed away. With no children and no family left alive, Fred was the last of his line. Everyone there thought perhaps it was for the best that Fred didn't have to live with the knowledge of what he'd done to his mate Charlie.

The two bodies were loaded into the doctor's van and taken away to the morgue. The policeman asked Tommy a few questions about the accident, which he answered woodenly, as if in a daze. Satisfied it was just a terrible accident, the country policeman took the woman and her boy home and sadly watched them go in their front door, dazed and confused. He knew their lives would be forever scarred by what had happened that day.

Nothing would ever be the same again.

CHAPTER 2

Tommy and his mother were devastated by their loss. Tommy was particularly traumatized, having never experienced a loss of this scale and because of the horror of what he had personally witnessed. The weeks after Charlie's death were just a blur; they were both hollow from their loss, like their insides had been taken out. But Molly knew that life had to go on – she had to be strong for Tommy. She had to sort out the family property and get Tommy back to school.

Molly knew the farm was debt-ridden, that they owed more than what the property was worth. However, they had planned ahead and taken out a life insurance policy on Charlie when Tommy was born, so Molly thought they might be able to keep the farm going once the insurance payout came through.

Then the crushing news arrived in the mail that the insurance company had refused Charlie's payout because he was killed while hunting, and hidden in the fine print of their life insurance policy was a clause that denied payments if the person died while engaging in 'dangerous hobbies'.

With no savings and no equity in the farm, Molly had to make the tough decision to sell the property, along with her dead husband's pride and joy, his muscle cars. With no income and no immediate family to support them, Molly was forced to uproot her young son from the place he loved and transport them to the big smoke: Sydney.

They landed in the heart of the madness that was Kings Cross, the writhing underbelly of a vibrant town where nothing was off-limits. A magnet for the desperate and the destitute, "The Cross" could at the same time be an escape and a prison – famous for its night clubs, strip joints, brothels and streetwalkers.

Molly's cousin Judy ran a strip club in Kings Cross and offered Molly the security of a steady income and a roof over her head, working as the cleaner and on-site caretaker of the club. The job included a tiny apartment at the back of the venue, with a fold-down bed in the living room for Molly and a separate bedroom for her young son. Molly realized this was the best she could do. She knew Judy was a good person, hard-working, reliable and trustworthy and had been the only one to offer Molly a helping hand.

Molly would have preferred a different environment in which to raise her young son but felt that he would be okay, so long as she kept a close eye on him and stayed strong for him. She resolved to always put him first and resist the sometimes-overpowering urge to wallow in self-pity. With Tommy's role model gone and without a strong male figure in their life, Molly knew she would need to be both mother and father to young Tommy.

CHAPTER 3

From the freedom of a country primary school, Tommy was thrust into the mayhem of a tough inner-city high school. Yet to hit puberty, Tommy was a weedy whip of a kid who had no experience of bullies or gangs and was easy prey, fresh meat for the local kids. From the very first day when he tentatively wandered into the schoolyard, not knowing even one person, and having no experience of a city, he was running scared.

'Hey, who's this? Where did you come from, dickhead?' sneered a brute of a kid who was a head taller than Tommy and flanked by a cohort of snivelling disciples. Tommy looked up, dumbfounded at this unlikely welcome, and stayed silent.

'Hey!' the kid shouted again. 'Don't ignore me, you little rat turd! Answer me when I talk to you! What's your name and where are you from?'

'Um… my name's Tommy and I come from Brooms Head,' Tommy stammered in response.

'Ahhahahahahah!' roared the bully in derisive laughter. 'Brooms Head? What the hell? What kind of dumbass name is that for a town? Bloody stupid. Never heard of it. And what's wrong with you, talking like that? Are you some kind of retard, Tommmmeeeeee?' drawing out the name in a mimicking, insulting tone. 'Is that how they teach you to talk up there, you dumb country hick? You're in the big smoke now, Boy and you better get used to it. Learn to speak properly, you moron!'

'Welcome to High School,' mumbled Tommy under his breath. This was not going to be easy. He was not looking forward to spending the next six years of his life among these bullying halfwits.

'Okay, retard, let's get something straight. YOU are a piece of SHIT,' crowed the gang leader, punctuating every word with a poke of his fat finger into Tommy's chest. 'You are worthless, the lowest of the low, like the remains of a piece of dog crap I couldn't even be bothered scraping off the bottom of my shoe. Remember that and we won't have a problem. Me, I'm the king around here and these are my men. Nobody messes with us. Watch your step, dickhead, because if you get out of line you are going to cop it something terrible. Now get out of my sight before you make me throw up in my mouth.'

Tommy turned and bolted, relieved that he had escaped the confrontation without copping a beating but having the sinking feeling that wouldn't be too far away in his future. Unfortunately, he was right. The verbal abuse soon escalated into bumping and pushing and before too long, into full-on beatings. The gang would regularly lay in wait for him in the schoolyard and on his way home, taunting him and then torturing him.

It was brutal.

CHAPTER 4

School problems aside, Tommy and his mum settled into a comfortable life in their tiny, cozy but not very private apartment. There seemed to be a constant stream of knocks on the door as someone always seemed to need something cleaned or repaired or to borrow various bits and pieces. Molly was often busy with her work at the club, so Tommy shared the duties of cooking dinner with his mum, and soon built an impressive array of recipes, becoming quite the little chef. He loved to cook and surprise his mum with a new dish he had seen on TV or spotted in one of her gossip magazines that she loved to read.

One morning Tommy woke up full of beans; he'd been saving up his meagre pocket money and was planning to surprise his mum with a special dinner for her birthday, her first since Charlie's tragic passing. Tommy knew it would be a tough day and wanted to do something special for his mum.

He bounced out of his bedroom, ran over to his mum, gave her a big hug and said 'Happy Birthday, Mum! You're not getting your present until tonight – hope you don't mind. And no, it's not because I forgot to get you something, I just want to make you wait,' he said with a cheeky grin.

Molly smiled sadly, knowing that Tommy was making a special effort to try and cheer her up. She had to work the day shift today, but not the night shift as well, because Judy had given her the night off, knowing it was her birthday. Molly was glad she would be distracted at work today, but wasn't really looking forward to the long night, which would be her first birthday without her Charlie for more than 20 years. The reality of her situation hit her once more, when she realized that never again would she have her soulmate by her side to celebrate a birthday with her. A lone tear rolled down her cheek at the sadness of it all.

Being a Saturday, there was no school, so Tommy was like a cat on a hot tin roof all morning, getting under Molly's feet so much that she was glad to leave the apartment and get to work to look after things for the lunchtime crowd. As soon as she left the apartment, Tommy raced out the door and took off down to the shops. He only had a few dollars in his pocket, so he had to be creative with his menu choices and ingredient selections. Luckily, there was only him and his mum, so the food didn't have to stretch too far. He had decided to go with one of his mum's favourites – curried sausages, which was cheap but hearty fare, followed by a chocolate cake to satisfy her sweet tooth.

Happy with all his plans, he raced home and started cooking up a storm and making an almighty mess in the kitchen. Funnily enough, those cooking shows didn't seem to focus too much on doing the dishes, so he wasn't too good at keeping the place clean! By the time he was finished there was such an assortment of frying pans, pots, chopping boards, mixing bowls, utensils and trays strewn all over the kitchen that it seemed there couldn't possibly be anything left in the cupboards.

Molly walked in the door to the chaos and her heart melted as she saw her beautiful, dishevelled son beaming up at her, proud as punch of what he'd managed to put together for her, with his own money, skills and thoughtfulness.

Bursting into tears, she strode over and scooped young Tommy up in a crushing embrace, squeezing him so tight that Tommy instantly felt her need and her fear. Quietly they stood, mother and son in a moment of silence, together but alone, lost in their own thoughts. Tommy resolved to let Molly choose when to break the hug and the silence too, knowing that all she needed right now in this moment was for him to be still and receive her love in all its abundance, and to give his love in return.

Finally, she slowly let Tommy go, wiping the tears from her face as he smiled through tears of his own and said, 'Happy Birthday, Mum. I've made us a special dinner. And you know the best part? As my birthday gift to you, you get to do the dishes!' He made a grand sweeping gesture at the monumental mess he had created.

'I don't think so! Not tonight buddy, you know the rules – no doing dishes on your birthday!' she said with a laugh.

'Alright, alright, we can work that out later. Right now, you need to go over and sit down at the table. Here, let me help you,' said Tommy as he took his mum by the arm just like he had seen his dad do so many times and escorted her to the table, pulled out her chair and then pushed it in behind her as she sat down.

'Well, thank you, kind sir,' said Molly, loving the whole performance and what a little gentleman Tommy was being. Tommy poured them each some orange juice and then went and put on some of Molly's favourite old disco music. He went over to the kitchen, plated up his piping hot curried sausages just like they did on TV and then sauntered over to the table like a professional waiter, complete with a white tea towel draped nonchalantly over his forearm as he served up their meal.

'Yum! Curried sausages, my favourite!' exclaimed Molly as Tommy presented her meal with a flourish. As Tommy sat down, they banged their knives and forks on the table in unison as they roared out their favourite pre-dinner line, '2, 4, 6, 8, dig in, don't wait!' and then got stuck in to the simple but delicious meal.

After some regular chit-chat, the conversation inevitably turned to the missing member of the family on this special occasion, the first birthday for either one of them without Charlie. Somehow, enough time had passed, so for the first time since his death, Tommy and Molly talked freely and happily about Charlie without being wracked by the wrenching grief that so often had consumed them in the past when they reminisced about him.

Interspersed in the light mood brought on by the flood of wonderful memories about Molly's dear husband and Tommy's loving father, Tommy lit the candles on Molly's abundantly iced chocolate cake and brought it over to the table.

'Holy cow! Did you make a cake with icing on top, or did you make icing with cake underneath it?' said Molly with a laugh, knowing they both had the very same sweet tooth and weakness for chocolate.

Tommy gave her his most charming smile, flashed his baby blue eyes and said, 'Um… I sort of made single cake quantity but double icing quantity, then couldn't let it go to waste.'

Molly smiled and said, 'Son, it may not feel like it now, but you'll be a heartbreaker one day. All the girls are going to be after you.' She could already tell that his looks and his charm would be a magnet for the opposite sex in times to come. He had a fragile, wounded quality to him that made people like him and want to look after him.

'But you be good to them, Tommy. Never be mean to the girls that fall for you, because they're going to fall hard, and you need to be careful. Always treat them with the respect, love and care they deserve.'

'Yes, Mum, I will,' Tommy sighed, really having no idea why she was going on about it. He had no interest in girls and certainly couldn't imagine any of them swooning around him. After Molly finished two big servings of cake and Tommy three, they moved over to the couch in the living area and Tommy went off to his bedroom, retrieving the present he had prepared the week before. He carefully handed it to his mum, and she could tell by the way he was holding it that it was something incredibly special. Almost with apprehension, she slowly and deliberately unwrapped it and then couldn't believe what she saw when she opened it up, so much that tears started streaming down her face once more.

'Oh Tommy, it's so beautiful!' she said. It was a picture frame that Tommy had bought and placed within it the last ever photo of the three of them together as a family, captured in a moment of perfection, of wonderful fun. They had been at the beach, playing and laughing together in the sand, not knowing that a close friend had grabbed their camera and snapped a candid shot of the three of them, smiling with unbridled joy and with a gloriously bright sun in the background. They were unencumbered by any pose, unaffected by the presence of a lens to disturb their natural state. 'I haven't seen that photo since your father died, I forgot we even had it,' she said through her tears.

'I hadn't even looked at the camera since Dad died and I thought it was about time, because I knew you would like it and I wanted to make sure I remember that perfect day forever. I thought it was still on the camera, so I just took it down to the shop, got it printed and bought a frame with the pocket money I've been saving. I'm glad you like it,' said Tommy.

'I absolutely love it, Tommy. I'm going to put it right up there on the shelf so we can look at it always. I can't believe you've done all this Tommy, it's so special. Did you buy all the food for dinner as well?' she asked.

'Yep,' replied Tommy. 'I've been saving my pocket money for ages, planning it all. It makes me feel good to see you so happy.' He knew he'd done well and that somehow, he'd managed to take what could have been a sad and lonely time and turn it around into a big part of their healing and recovery process.

'So, what's next, my little party planner? What do you want to do now?' asked Molly.

Tommy saw his opportunity and said, 'Well... in honour of Dad, I thought we could watch Die Hard!' Molly was not really a fan of action movies; that had always been Charlie and Tommy's thing that they did together, but somehow it seemed a fitting end to the night, so she relented and agreed to the selection.

'Awesome!' exclaimed Tommy, put on the old DVD and happily plonked on the couch next to his mum. Bruce Willis delivered one of

Tommy's favourite lines of all time in this movie and he never got tired of it. He cheered as *Yippee-ki-yay, motherfucker!* was perfectly delivered and Tommy was happy, revelling in the memories of his dad that he suddenly seemed able to enjoy without that churning feeling deep in his gut.

As the bad guys were dispatched and the good guys survived, Tommy said sleepily, 'That's the way the world should be,' and got up off the couch. He gave Molly a hug and a kiss and said, 'Goodnight Mum. Love you,' and wobbled off to bed.

Molly smiled after him, feeling the best she had in months; so lucky to have such a special boy to share her life with. Then she looked over at the chaos on the kitchen bench, shrugged her shoulders and said to herself, 'The cheeky sod got away with it after all, leaving all the dirty dishes. What the hell, they can wait for the morning,' and took herself off to bed too, happy and content that her birthday had turned into such a delightful surprise.

CHAPTER 5

Tommy was sinking into a pit of despair with his bullying situation at school. He tried to hide it from his mother, because he knew it upset her and knew there was nothing that she could do about it. He was screwed.

Feeling helpless and sick of the abuse, Tommy lost his spark and his sense of fun, beginning a slide down into depression.

But Tommy had deep reserves of strength that he called on one day when he was feeling particularly down, remembering his father's words about staying strong. He asked himself, 'What would Dad say?' and Tommy immediately imagined his dad saying in his slow country slang, 'Don't let the bastards get ya down, mate – stand up and show 'em what you're made of.'

The very next day, Tommy made a decision that would change his life forever and determine his future path, at the tender age of just twelve years old. Tommy went searching for a self-defence school, to find someone who could teach him to look after himself and protect his mum from the danger that seemed to lurk around every corner and down every dark alley in their seedy neighbourhood.

On his quest, Tommy soon stumbled across an innocuous looking building with a lopsided, weary old sign proclaiming *Self-defence classes, inquire within*. Drawing in a deep breath, Tommy rapped his knuckles on the door. 'Hello?' he said in a quiet voice.

Slowly, the door creaked open and Tommy stared into an inquiring face littered with wrinkles and topped with a generous head of grey hair. In a heavy accent, the man said, 'Hello, my name is Viktor. How can I help you?'

'Um, I'd like to learn how to fight please,' responded Tommy.

'We don't do that here,' said Viktor.

'What do you mean? Isn't this a fight school?'

'No, this school is not for fighting. This school is for protecting yourself. There is a difference. Self-defence is not fighting. Here I teach much more than fighting. Here I teach Judo. If you want to fight, you go somewhere else.'

'Whatever you do, I need something,' said Tommy. 'But you look too old to do anything cool. You probably do Tai-Chi or something lame like that, do you?'

With a chuckle, Viktor said, 'Yes, something like that, among other things. Don't worry, I might look old, but I can still hold my own.'

Viktor's highly attuned senses alerted him to Tommy's troubled demeanour, and he had a feeling that he should take him in and look after him. 'Come inside and let's talk some more about what you want to do,' said Viktor.

Tommy watched Viktor move and subconsciously re-evaluated him. Viktor seemed quiet and unassuming but had a calmness, a quiet strength and catlike fluid movement that belied his wrinkled face and grey hair. Easily ignored at first glance, it was quickly apparent that you didn't want to mess with Viktor. They walked into the dojo and Viktor bowed as he took off his shoes and stepped onto the mat. Tommy, ignorant of tradition, walked onto the mat with his shoes on and with no trace of a bow.

'STOP!' snapped Viktor, and Tommy responded instantly to the forceful tone, almost powerless to resist. He continued the lesson in an easier tone as he said, 'Always respect the dojo. Shoes off when on the mats and always bow when you enter and leave the mats.'

'Um, okay, sorry,' mumbled Tommy as he stepped back off the Judo mat, removed his shoes, bowed, and stepped back onto the mat, enjoying the cushioned but firm feeling under his bare feet. It felt like home, it felt right. Tommy immediately knew this would be a big part of his life from now on.

'There's nobody here right now. The students will be arriving for their class soon. We can run through a few basics before they get here if you like and then you can join in the class,' said Viktor.

'What, now?' asked Tommy, pleasantly surprised at the prospect of getting started straight away.

'Of course,' responded Viktor. 'Now is the perfect time for you to start learning Judo.' And so, the old master and the young, fragile boy took their first tentative steps together.

The months rolled on and Tommy embraced the art of Judo with an insatiable appetite and a work ethic that impressed Viktor and astounded his mother. Tommy was totally committed and absorbed by the technique, the skill and the philosophy of Judo. He just couldn't get enough of it and became almost part of the furniture at Viktor's dojo. Before long, Tommy's constant training had increased his skills so quickly that he started helping Viktor teach the younger students the basics, which became an important part of his learning.

One day after training when everyone else had left, Viktor said, 'Tommy, now that you have learnt the basics of Judo, I think it's time for you to learn some other skills. The streets aren't like the dojo and not everyone fights fair, so you need to know what to do just in case you need to act quickly against a group of people, say if some bullies gang up on you.'

Viktor knew that Tommy had been having trouble with some local boys and had wanted to intervene but understood that wasn't the answer. Tommy needed to stand up to them on his own, under his own power in order to find a permanent solution to the problem.

'What kind of skills?' asked Tommy, suddenly extremely interested and even more attentive than usual. When it came to Judo, he was like a sponge; always eager to soak in knowledge and learn new techniques.

'Let's just say these skills aren't exactly in the Judo rule book, so you can't ever use them in competitions, or you'll get instantly disqualified,' answered Viktor.

'I like the sound of this,' said Tommy with a smile.

'These techniques could save your life out on the streets. I know the first day you came to my door I said that I didn't teach fighting, but for you I'm going to make an exception. Understand that this is just between us, we will be working privately one-on-one after class and you can't tell the other students about it. I know you've got some problems with some of the local boys, so I want to teach you some things to keep you safe.'

'Street fighting? Awesome! Let's do it!' exclaimed Tommy, suddenly excited. And so their street fighting sessions began, with Viktor teaching Tommy every dirty trick he had learned back in the day, with vicious strikes, punches, knees, elbows and head butts that would get him kicked off any Judo mat but could possibly save his life one day. Tommy loved it, revelled in the extra attention from Viktor and grew more confident by the day. Slowly but surely, he was growing in his power, saying goodbye to that scared little boy and maturing into a confident young man.

CHAPTER 6

The great thing about living in the same place as she worked was that Molly was always around when Tommy needed her; she could always find time to spend with him when he was feeling down, or needed help with his homework, which was a common occurrence. And they loved to dance! Molly loved lively music and would often have the radio on, swaying her hips and moving in time with the music. When a favourite song came on that was exactly right for a good groove, she would grab her willing partner and they would bust a move on the kitchen tiles. Tommy loved to dance, he loved the feeling of freedom and abandon and of course loved even more to make his mum happy. He knew she loved it; it was one of the special things they did together, that helped make the bond between them so strong. Tommy had good natural rhythm and couldn't help moving to the beat whenever he heard a good song.

Tommy spent a lot of time with his Aunt Judy and gained a great respect for her hard work and business sense. Tommy was slowly learning the ropes and observing what was involved in running a business and dealing with people. Judy was happy to have someone around who took an interest in her and in the business and liked teaching Tommy whatever he was keen to learn, mentoring her young charge. Having never married and with no children of her own, Judy loved having family close-by and was building a much deeper connection with Molly and Tommy than with anyone she ever had before.

Constantly surrounded by women at home, Tommy soon felt the urge for some manly activity and the smell of petrol fumes, so he started going out to the local car racing track. Phil, the track manager, noticed the young kid and slowly got to know him, casually chatting with him on his smoke breaks. Phil soon discovered Tommy's love of muscle cars and the time he had spent with his father working on the V8's back home. Tommy clearly knew his way around a toolbox, so Phil offered him a part time job at the racetrack, which Tommy gleefully accepted. Before too long Tommy was helping by cleaning garages, sweeping workshops, polishing cars and anything else that needed doing when he was on shift.

There was an incredible collection of cars kept at the track, where the rich guys from Sydney stored their cars and took them out for weekend race days. Phil would keep all the cars serviced and even had to take some out for a drive around the track every now and then for those that were away and needed their cars to get a run occasionally. One day Phil asked Tommy if he'd like to have a drive of one of the cars kept at the track, making sure it was the oldest and cheapest car on the lot. Tommy of course jumped at the chance and performed unexpectedly well for a young kid. Phil decided to give Tommy some more responsibility at the track and soon Tommy was servicing cars himself and tearing around the track under Phil's watchful eye. Tommy was in car heaven and lapped it up. Who would have thought he could get paid for doing this!

Tommy's other great escape was the beach. While Kings Cross had its bad points, it was close to the famous Bondi Beach and Tommy would make his way down there at every opportunity for a swim, a surf or just to gawk at the girls sunbathing on the beach, who were sometimes topless if he was really lucky. He picked up an old second-hand surfboard for a bargain and used to hitch it on to a homemade rack on his bike and head off down to Bondi for a quick surf after school. He got to know the lifesavers and the regulars well and fitted right into the beach lifestyle, which reminded him so much of the coastal town where he grew up.

CHAPTER 7

As Tommy's training progressed, so did his hormones, finally. After what seemed to Tommy like an eternity, puberty finally caught up with him and a monumental growth spurt transformed him from a puny weed to a mighty oak seemingly overnight. And the food! He was an eating machine, chowing down on anything and everything at every opportunity. No matter where he was or what he was doing, he was *always* hungry. His poor mother just couldn't keep enough food in the house to keep him satisfied and he was constantly on the prowl, eating everything in sight.

Tommy was a bit of a loner, who hadn't really made many friends at high school. Labelled a country hick, he was often ignored by those in the school, who had built their friendship cliques way back at the city primary school and followed them through to high school. For a while, Tommy tried to fit in and find his place in the school, but he soon gave it up as a trivial pursuit and worked out that it didn't really bother him anyway.

The bond between Tommy and Viktor quickly became unbreakable as Viktor tutored and trained his young charge five times every week, many times for hours on end. Tommy never tired of Viktor's teachings and faithfully absorbed everything that Viktor could teach him.

But there remained a personal distance between the master and the student. Viktor was a mysterious man who divulged nothing of his past. In Judo there were no limits to their conversations, but everything else was a vacuum. Tommy understood at a deep level there was some painful past that Viktor did not want to share, and Tommy of all people could understand and respect the wishes of his master to leave some parts of his life unknown.

Without really knowing how or when it happened, Tommy slowly realized that Viktor was helping to fill the void that his father's loss had left. In turn, Viktor recognized that Tommy was becoming like the son he had so desperately wanted but a cruel tragedy had stolen any chance he had for children of his own.

Tommy soon developed a strong sense of self-confidence and inner strength born from knowing with absolute certainty that he was more than a match for just about anyone. But he was most certainly not arrogant – there was no need to prove what was clearly self-evident.

With an outlook so common among true masters of the martial arts, Viktor instilled in the young and impressionable Tommy the core values of Judo such as Respect, Honour, Humility, Self-Control, Perseverance and Courage. Judo, meaning the Gentle Way, became a way of life for the young Tommy and provided an outlet to channel his abundant energy and power, focusing his attention in a positive way to benefit himself and those around him.

Tommy's embracement of Judo and its principles defused any remnants of anger he felt toward his schoolyard tormentors and removed any desire for revenge that others may have entertained. Deep down, Tommy knew that anger and revenge did not serve him and that only by putting aside the wretchedness he had previously felt about his systematic torture by the local gang, would he achieve happiness and fulfilment. But one day his hand was forced when the thugs confronted him in the local park.

Tommy was coming home from training one night, oblivious to his surroundings, his favourite heavy dance music blasting through his headphones as he jogged in time to the fast-paced beats, slipping in a few dance steps every now and then just for fun. Suddenly, something caught Tommy's attention and his whole body instantly received a shot of adrenaline as his fight-or-flight instinct kicked in. Unfortunately for the gang of youths who were about to confront what in the past had been easy prey, Tommy quickly realized that flight was not an option because he had ventured too far into their midst without noticing, and some of the boys had already circled around behind him. Tommy removed his headphones, silent and alert.

'Oi! Dickhead!' the leader shouted to Tommy. 'Where do you think you're going, faggot?' He sneered, delighted at the thought of some sport with a defenceless victim. The pathetic kid with a pumped-up ego and inflated self-belief of his own importance had long ago realized that preying on the weak gave him a sense of power and garnered respect from his band of blind followers.

'We haven't seen you for months. You've been avoiding us, haven't you?' jeered the boy. 'You've probably been too busy jerking off watching your mum get her gear off at the strip joint! Think you're too good for us, hey? Well, it's time we reminded you who's boss around here and whose territory you're in.'

Tommy surveyed the scene, calmly looking around from beneath his hoodie, which covered his head and screened his eyes. He counted six members of the gang, scattered around the park in a wide circle around him, with cigarettes hanging out of their mouths and empty beer cans strewn around the place. Tommy made a quick decision, confident he could take them on, but knowing it was dangerous and not wanting to fight. To try and defuse the dangerous situation, he said, 'Hi guys, long time no see. Look, I don't want any trouble, I just want to get home.'

'Well bad luck, shit-for-brains, coz home's a long way away and you're not going anywhere. We were just sitting around drinking, saying how bored we were, and wouldn't it be good to have some excitement, and then you came along at just the right time,' crowed the gang leader.

'Let's have some fun, boys and take this maggot to pieces!' the boy suddenly yelled, capping it off with a blood-curdling war cry. The gang whooped it up and started cheering and closing in, oblivious to what was coming.

'Look, I don't want anyone to hurt anyone,' Tommy called out. 'Let's just stop right now, I'll go on my way, forget this ever happened and none of you will get hurt.'

The gang stopped quizzically and then the leader burst out laughing, slapped his thigh and said, 'HURT? US? Are you fucking serious? Get a load of this guy! Mate, now you're really going to cop it!'

Tommy knew the time had come for action. They would not stop and there was no way he could run from it, so there was no option but to fight. Through his extensive training, Tommy knew sometimes there was no alternative but to make a stand. He didn't want to fight them, but he was sure as hell going to give it to them, because they had left him no option.

Tommy snapped into state, all senses alert and every muscle fibre firing. Slowly and deliberately, he flipped back his hood, took off his jacket and emptied his pockets. The gang members were taken aback, unused to seeing this kind of calm behaviour from their victims. Much more crying, whimpering and pleading was generally involved in their beatings, so this calm self-assurance and confidence was a new experience for them. The vaguely more intelligent ones in the group decided they would hang back a bit and see what happened when the thicker boys made their first move on Tommy, just in case.

As the sun set over the scene, an outside observer would have been seriously worried about what was about to happen to Tommy. The situation looked so dire that a hospital or even a morgue looked like the only outcome possible for him.

The first thug to make a move was the biggest of the lot, a fat, ugly, pimply-faced kid with four chins who looked like he enjoyed torturing small animals. He lumbered over like the big oaf he was and launched a violent push at Tommy's chest.

One of the fundamental principles of Judo is *Maximum Efficiency with Minimum Effort* and using your opponent's momentum is one of the key strategies. In a blur, Tommy used this principle to devastating effect as he quickly sidestepped, grabbed the meathead's extended arms, stepped back in and expertly threw him over his hip, landing his attacker flat on his back with a sickening thud. If this were a competition, Tommy would have left it at that, bowed to the referee and accepted the points and the match. But this was different; it was a street fight, not a competition. So, in a flash, Tommy leapt onto the thug's stomach and smashed the heel of his right hand square in the guy's face, breaking his nose and knocking him out cold. One down, five to go.

Suddenly, there were murmurings of concern in the crowd as the gang came to realize this was definitely not the same wimpy kid they had tormented in the past. They saw how tall he was as he stood up, how much he had filled out and how he moved, like a fighter. Settling himself again, Tommy adopted his fighting stance, knowing he did not have to hide his abilities anymore. Suddenly he cut an imposing figure with chest out, shoulders back, feet slightly apart and arms down in front joining at the middle with fists clenched. He looked solid, steady as a rock and ready for anything. The gang members quickly realized that the boy they had so enthusiastically tortured in the past would be a victim no more.

The less ballsy of the group decided this was more than they had bargained for and took a few steps backwards, but they were quickly brought back into line by their leader, who shouted, 'Hey! If any of you pricks run away, I'll come around and beat the shit out of you myself – nobody goes anywhere!' His crew begrudgingly tightened the circle and the leader ordered his next two biggest members to take Tommy together, one from each side.

Slowly and warily the attackers moved in on Tommy, who stayed perfectly still, seeming to not move a muscle. Closer and closer they came and still Tommy didn't move, until one of them drew his fist back and threw a punch. Tommy quickly weaved out of the way, grabbed the arm and executed a perfect foot sweep, taking his attacker's legs out from under him and landing him flat on his back. Tommy quickly finished him off with a crushing elbow to the head.

The remaining offender really had no clue what to do now, so without thinking he blindly charged at Tommy, hoping to wrestle him to the ground. Tommy saw the opportunity for one of his favourite moves, so he quickly dropped his weight down, reached his arms out, grabbed the jacket of his charging assailant and planted his right foot firmly in the boy's soft midsection. As the thug's momentum carried him forward, Tommy dropped down even further and then drove his foot forcefully into the stomach until the boy's feet left the ground then he launched him into the air and sent him a full two metres back over his head. The goon came crashing to the ground in a heap, severely winded and no longer a threat.

The gang leader really didn't like how this was going but wasn't ready to admit defeat, so in a panic called on his remaining troops to attack. Tommy quickly collected himself and instead of defence, reached out to attack his closest combatant, quickly stepping in, grabbing him under one arm and lifting him across his shoulders, spinning him around 180 degrees and slamming him to the ground with a mighty heave. *Another one bites the dust.*

Tommy decided the time had come to put the leader in his place, who knew by now not to rush in. Slowly he circled Tommy, seeking an opening. He flashed a right cross at Tommy who grabbed the arm, neatly sidestepped and executed a perfect hip throw, landing the gang leader on his back. Still with the arm trapped, Tommy instantly dropped to the ground, laid his left leg across the leader's neck and his right leg over the chest, pinning the body and leaving the arm protruding up between his legs, still held tightly in Tommy's grip. Tommy leaned right back and applied a brutal arm bar, hyper-extending the elbow. Normally this move would call for a submission, but Tommy was in no mood to accept a tap-out, so he applied even more force until he heard the arm break with a sickening snap.

This last move was more than enough for the remaining gang member, who bolted like a scared rabbit in a crazed run away from the carnage. Five young men were on the ground, two unconscious and others flailing about, groaning in pain. The whole scene had unfolded in less than two minutes. Tommy picked himself up and dusted off, collected his things and surveyed the scene. It wasn't something he had wanted to do, but they had asked for it and he had to admit a little part of himself was glad that the bastards got what they deserved.

Tommy smiled and said, 'Six against one? Sorry, I know that wasn't fair, but hey, you started it. Anyway, thanks for the warm-up boys, I'd better get back to training so I can have a real workout. Let's not go through this again, hey? You leave me alone and I'll return the favour.' Tommy walked away, confident that he would have no more trouble from these boys.

And so it was, with the gang developing a grudging respect for Tommy and a determination to just leave him the hell alone – he wasn't worth the hard work.

CHAPTER 8

'Slow down, release your mind, clear your thoughts and focus your attention inward. Visualize your heart, your lungs, slowing. Be motionless, like a snake on a rock, basking in the sun, perfectly still and yet alert,' Viktor whispered in a hypnotic voice to Tommy. They were ready to take Tommy's training to a new level. In a rare moment of personal reflection, Viktor had shared with Tommy that he'd spent time in a Japanese Buddhist Temple, learning from the Zen masters, training in the ancient arts including Zen Meditation. Tommy had asked Viktor to start teaching him some of these techniques because he thought it might help his fighting, plus it sounded so damn cool.

They were both on their knees on the mats in Viktor's studio. There was no sound and no other people around; they were alone and quiet. Viktor had spent three years with the Zen masters, learning their techniques, raising his consciousness, meditating and learning to control the basic functions of his body, the ones that so many people thought were uncontrollable, beyond conscious intervention. Now it was time for the old master to pass on this knowledge to his young apprentice.

'You must learn control, Tommy. Slow your heart, slow your breathing. Get into state. You can do it,' whispered Viktor. Slowly but surely, Tommy could feel his body responding to his mind as he achieved a state of calm he had never experienced before. This was like meditation on steroids!

Once Tommy started to get the hang of the technique with Viktor, he continued training every night at home. He worked and worked and steadily got better and better, extending his trancelike state until he could slow his metabolism at will, dramatically reducing his heart rate and making his breathing so shallow that he almost looked like he wasn't drawing breath at all. Soon he could quickly slip into that state, even when there was noise and distraction surrounding him. He would remain conscious and aware of his surroundings but go into a trance-like state that completely freaked his mother out the first time she saw him do it, because he looked almost dead.

Extending these techniques of control over his heart and lungs, Tommy loved to see how long he could hold his breath under water. For morning training, he would often run the eight kilometres to Bondi Beach, swim out beyond the break and then go free diving, testing and pushing himself to hold his breath longer and longer, diving deeper and deeper. Before too long, he could stay under water for 10 minutes. While this was well short of the world record free dive time of over 20 minutes, Tommy was damn proud of himself and his new abilities.

Cold water didn't stop him. Even in the middle of winter in the freezing cold water of the ocean Tommy would swim out and free dive. He felt so free out there, it was like another world, one of peace and beauty where he was on his own and could connect with the Earth's energy, forgetting the loss he'd faced in his past and the challenges of his daily existence.

It was in these formative years that Tommy developed his extremely high protectionist instinct. Seeing his mother work hard in a difficult job under sometimes arduous circumstances and seeing the women in the strip club nightly parading themselves under the leering eyes of often unsavoury clientele, it made Tommy realize that he wanted to take care of those who needed help. So, at the young age of 16 but at a size to rival most men and with fighting skills to match, Tommy took on a security role as a bouncer at the strip club to earn some extra money. This would help his mum and pay Tommy's way for his Judo training, which had been a major strain on his mother's paltry income.

While his bouncer role was in no way legal for someone not yet an adult, Tommy was so big that nobody ever thought to question it. Besides, Judy's was just a small strip club among a multitude of clubs along the street that nobody was watching too closely, so Judy felt safe with Tommy on the door.

Tommy's time as a bouncer at Judy's strip club taught him many lessons, from how to take down a violent drunk in just a few seconds without really hurting them, to understanding what women really talked about in the dressing room and of course the dance moves and stagecraft of the performers.

CHAPTER 9

Tommy always looked forward to Ladies Night at the club. It broke up the monotony of the regular routine and the crowd was a lot more fun. The women in the audience seemed to enjoy themselves much more than the mostly sleazy guys who came in on the regular nights. Plus, he liked to check out the moves of the male strippers, it always made him laugh seeing the big dance moves they pulled and the loud responses they drew from the women watching. Hen's nights were especially fun, when the lucky girl would be singled out for special attention from the guys on stage.

Tommy was still just a teenager in his final year of high school when he was on bouncer duty one Ladies Night, with Judy bringing in her usual selection of male strippers. The room was filled to capacity with a particularly rowdy bunch of women instead of the usual male clientele. Trouble came at the last minute as one of the strippers pulled a groin muscle during his warm-up while executing an overly enthusiastic pelvic thrust.

The troupe were a man down with only a few minutes to go. Judy, not one to panic at the drop of a hat, had a sudden flash of inspiration and, knowing Tommy had a few good dance moves up his sleeve, seized the moment and called out, 'Hey Tommy, bet you fifty bucks you can't get up there on stage and have the women go crazy for you!'

Tommy burst out laughing and said, 'What! You want me to get up there and strip? No way! I've never done that before.'

'Don't worry, you don't have to go all the way – you can keep a G-string on,' she said with a smirk. 'Come on, you'd be doing me a huge favour – one of those bloody useless strippers has done a groin and I've got no choice. There's no other option – this crowd of oversexed ladies will have my blood if I don't serve up a hot young stud!' Even though Judy was laughing, Tommy could tell it was a serious request.

Tommy thought for a second, then said, 'Make it a hundred and you've got a deal. And I get to keep the tips!'

Knowing she had him, Judy shot back a reply, 'Eighty bucks and we split the tips fifty/fifty.'

Before he could talk himself out of it, Tommy said, 'Okay, you're on! I'll do it. What gear do I wear?'

Judy replied, 'I'm sure I've got something out the back in the dressing room – just grab whatever is going to make you look super-hot.'

Off Tommy went, searching among the various thongs, bras, suspenders, tights, boas and leather outfits, trying to find something that he would not only be willing to wear, but that would actually fit him as well.

With his striking blue eyes and shoulder length hair, bleached blond from all his surfing, extremely tall and with muscles rippling from his constant training, Judy knew she was on a winner with Tommy. He was like some ancient Viking warrior, seemingly carved from granite with a firm jaw and chiselled features. And yet he was oblivious to his effect on women, never noticing their reactions as he walked past. He had a casual charm and easy-going personality to go with his good looks that made him instantly likeable. Judy was sure they would both score big on the tips tonight.

As Tommy emerged from the dressing room in a cowboy hat, brown leather vest over bare chest, chaps and cowboy boots with a big grin on his face stretching from ear to ear, Judy gasped and then caught herself when she realized the boy/man she was ogling was related to her! Gazing wistfully at the image swaggering towards her, Judy wondered why she had never come up with this idea before.

Tommy joined the band of strippers and introduced himself, explaining that he was just the bouncer filling in for their fallen comrade.

'A stripper virgin! What a treat – always fun to watch a guy on his first time,' said the troupe leader with a laugh. 'Thanks for filling in, mate, we appreciate it. Don't worry about the group show, we'll take care of that. You just need to fill Jason's five-minute spot near the end. Just get out there, shake a few moves, get your gear off and the crowd will love you!'

Tommy's spot arrived and he tentatively walked out on stage to a loud chorus of catcalls from the brazen audience; he took a deep breath as he stared out at the blinding lights and the deep throbbing music raised in intensity, filling the club. *Macho Man* by the Village People started up and Tommy let the music take him, moving and gyrating his hips, slowly getting into the swing of it. With a smile, he thought of his mother and that she wouldn't have expected her dance lessons would prepare him for stripping on stage.

The calls from the audience grew louder as they cheered and demanded he start to strip off. As his nerves settled, Tommy lapped it up, strutting around the stage, collecting the tips being shoved down his pants and loving the attention and the response he was getting from all the women in the crowd. A true showman, he was born for this.

When it seemed the noise from the crowd couldn't get any louder, Tommy whipped off his cowboy vest, exposing his rippling chest muscles and he proceeded to do his trick of flexing each pec muscle alternately in time with the music. Laughing to himself, he thought of how many times he had practiced this very move in the mirror at home, but nobody had ever cheered him for it!

Next to go were the chaps. As he ripped them off in one smooth move, the Velcro sides came apart with a satisfying rip. He threw them into the audience and the girls went wild.

'Oh my God, Judy, you've created a monster!' said Molly, who was watching from the back of the room.

With a huge grin spread from ear to ear, Judy crowed triumphantly, 'I'm such a genius. I know talent when I see it and I knew Tommy had it in him. He could be a star!'

'Hmmm… I don't mind him being on stage, but I want more of a career for him than a life in the clubs,' said Molly.

The show continued, with the crowd going crazy, calling for more and throwing money at Tommy. Standing there in just his cowboy boots, a cowboy hat and a bright red G-string, Tommy egged them on, cupping his hand to his ear as if asking for more. The girls responded with an even louder roar of cheers and whistles, so Tommy pulled off his boots and dropped them off the side of the stage. With music thumping and crowd cheering, they called out for even more, so in a quick flash, Tommy flicked the strap off his G-string and in the same movement brought down his cowboy hat off his head to cover his freshly exposed junk. The crowd went nuts as Tommy turned and swaggered off the stage, flashing his bare ass to the audience. Then, with his back still facing the crowd, he put his hat back on his head and danced off the stage.

'Wow!' said Judy. 'I need to book him for next month!'

Molly smiled ruefully, shaking her head about her showman son.

'Better go pick up all those tips – half that money's mine!' said Judy with a laugh as she raced off to pick up all the money that was strewn over the stage and the floor after Tommy's naked exit had left nowhere to stash his cash.

Tommy walked backstage to clapping and cheering from the other strippers. 'Dude, you killed it out there! You sure you've never done this before?' the leader said. 'If you're interested, I'm sure we could make room for you in our troupe.'

'Thanks mate, I appreciate the offer, but this was just a one-off to help out my auntie. I still have to finish high school!' said Tommy with a laugh as he put on his jeans. 'Maybe next Ladies Night we can do an encore performance.'

'You're on Bro, we'll definitely share the stage with you when we come back next time!' the leader replied.

'Awesome, thanks mate. Catch you next time,' said Tommy as the group made their exit.

Shortly after, a loud knock came at the dressing room door. Curious, Tommy bounced over to the door, opened it up and was pleasantly surprised to see one of the girls from the club smiling back at him. 'Hi Candy, what are you doing here on your night off?' asked Tommy with a big grin, suddenly acutely aware that all he was wearing was a pair of jeans.

'I was at a loose end, so I thought I'd check out the action and see how the boys handle the stage,' replied Candy with a wink and a smile and an admiring glance at Tommy's impressive bare chest. 'Imagine my surprise when I saw young Tommy up there strutting his stuff! Not too shabby, not too bad at all, I have to say.'

Candy was an athletic 20-year-old brunette and an expert on the stripper's pole. She was just a few years older than Tommy but much more experienced. Tommy had never got up the courage to say much more than a couple of words to Candy because he thought she was out of his league. Despite his performance on stage, Tommy was still a virgin and not confident with the ladies, and Candy had never given Tommy a second look until now, after seeing him up on stage in an entirely different light. Suddenly she was seeing him as a strikingly handsome and well-built young man rather than just a boy. With a glint in her eye, she looked down at Tommy's enormous feet, then stared right into Tommy's eyes and asked, 'Hey Tommy, is it true what they say about a guy who has big feet?'

The naïve Tommy replied, 'What, big shoes?'

Candy burst out laughing at the endearing response, leaned over close to the confused lad and whispered in his ear, 'No. Big dick.' She then lasered him with a stunning smile that lit up her whole face.

Tommy suddenly blushed bright red as a beetroot and looked down at his feet. The poor boy was like a deer in the headlights. But Candy had a feeling Tommy was a virgin and she resolved to be gentle with him for his first time. She handed him his shirt to put on, took him by the hand and led him out of the club, then walked him to her tiny, run-down apartment just around the corner. Tommy numbly complied and followed her without resistance; he was surprised, excited and terrified all at the same time. He was only glad his mum hadn't been around to intervene when they left the club.

Candy was experienced enough to know what she wanted and was not afraid to go and get it. She had an itch that needed to be scratched and Tommy was just the right treatment. She even thought of it as a community service; helping some lucky girls in the future by teaching the young stud the ropes and how to look after a lady properly.

'Do you want a drink, Tommy?' purred Candy as she looked at him standing self-consciously in the middle of her lounge room. Tommy was freaking out inside and almost shaking, he was so nervous, but he tried to calm himself down, wishing his Zen training had covered this situation.

'Um, yes please, thanks Candy,' replied Tommy. This was way out of his comfort zone, but he wanted to escape that comfort zone so bad!

Candy smiled and then sashayed her sexy walk out of the kitchen and back to Tommy, handing him a soft drink, not wanting to corrupt the young lad with alcohol that she knew would not be okay with Tommy's mother. She chuckled to herself at the oddity of the thought but didn't let it stop her; she was committed now and eager with anticipation.

Tommy had a sip of his drink and then Candy took it out of his hand, had a drink herself and then put it down on the table next to her. 'Have you had sex before, Tommy? It's okay if you haven't because I have. I know what to do and I'm happy to show you what to do and teach you. It'll be fun.'

'Um, no, I haven't done this before, but I do like to learn new skills,' replied Tommy with a cheeky grin.

Tommy gazed down at Candy with the full force of his charisma and his ridiculously vivid blue eyes peeking out from behind his long wavy blonde hair. Shocked, Candy felt a little quiver and went a bit weak at the knees. This never happened to her; she was always the one in control!

Collecting herself again, she smiled up at the impossibly tall young man standing in front of her, reached up and pulled his head down towards her. As their lips came together, Tommy fought for control, already feeling like he was going to burst. He couldn't believe what was about to happen, with this woman who seemed so much older than him and was oh, so sexy.

Calm down Bro, you've got this, you can do it, thought Tommy. Then everything was okay, all was right with the world as he lost himself in the exquisite feeling of their first kiss that was so deep, so filled with longing and the promise of what was to come.

The kiss gained in intensity as they pressed their lips harder against each other, the passion rising with every flick of their tongues. Tommy's hands searched under Candy's clothes, feeling womanly curves he had never touched before, sending shocks of feeling like electricity through every part of his body, right to his core.

Candy raised her arms up and Tommy pulled her dress up over her head, then stepped back to admire her firm but voluptuous body standing in her underwear. He had seen her naked plenty of times on stage, but somehow this was different. Now, in this moment, she was here only for him. They were sharing a special moment where nobody was getting paid and nobody was working; just a mutual, freely made choice to enjoy each other's bodies.

Tommy then raised his arms up above his head, stretching them out way above him and laughed as his fingers were now touching the ceiling. 'Your turn,' he said with a smile, 'but you might need a ladder!'

Laughing, Candy jumped up, linked her arms around Tommy's neck, then quickly swung her legs up and around until she was suddenly sitting on his shoulders, ducking her head to not bang it on the ceiling. 'You might be big, Tommy, but I've got some skills!' she said with a sexy grin as she looked at him in the mirror in front of them.

The moment had lightened the mood and allowed them both to relax a bit and for Tommy to get more comfortable, knowing it was okay to be himself and not feel too much pressure. He put his giant hands under her armpits and lifted her off from around his neck. He was so strong and lifted her so effortlessly that Candy felt lighter than she ever had before. Carefully, Tommy swung her around until he was cradling her in his arms across his massive chest and kissed her hungrily on her mouth, which was open, panting and ready for him.

Tommy laid Candy on the couch and sat down next to her. She moved around in front of him, grabbed his shirt and pulled it up over his head. She smiled when she saw his body up close. While only a teenager, he was huge for his age, with powerful muscles firm from the endless hours of training. She ran her hands over his chest and arms, revelling in the feel of him, wanting to explore every part of him. Candy's hands were like jolts of electricity running over Tommy, sending shock waves deep into his body at her every touch and caress.

Candy's hands went downtown, and Tommy was suddenly terrified by this next stage, as Candy expertly undid the button and fly of his jeans and gently pulled them down as Tommy wriggled around on the couch to help. Candy stood up in front of Tommy and under his watchful gaze, she gently removed her bra, letting her full round breasts loose with a flourish as she flicked it away. Tommy was transfixed at the scene unfolding before him, unable to breathe for fear that this was all just another wet dream and soon he would wake up in a moist patch on his sheets.

But Tommy stayed in the moment, absorbing every detail of Candy's incredible body, watching as she slowly and deliberately tucked her fingers into the waist band of her G-string and pulled it down to her ankles, bending forward, but still looking up at Tommy, with her dark, long, lusciously wavy hair cascading over her face as she reached down towards the floor. Tommy's gaze was held like a laser beam on Candy as she stood up, exposing all her gloriously naked womanhood to him. He drew in a deep breath, wanting to freeze-frame this moment and etch it in his memory bank forever.

Then he said with a smile, 'I don't think I've ever wanted to go to Brazil as much as I do right now.'

Momentarily puzzled, Candy paused and then laughed as she looked down at her naked body without a scrap of hair anywhere. 'If this is how you're handling your first time, Tommy, you'll do alright with the ladies, I'm sure,' she replied.

Then, it was the moment of truth. Candy looked over at Tommy and could see his bulging erection trying to burst out of his jockey shorts. She reached down inside his jocks and gently took hold of his rigid member as Tommy strained to keep control of himself. 'Wow,' he breathed softly, 'That feels so much better when someone else does it.'

Candy gave a knowing smile and pulled his underwear off him, then pulled his hands to get him up off the couch.

'Impressive package you've got there, Tommy,' said Candy with a smile. 'Let's go to the bedroom. You first, I want to check you out.' She pushed him ahead of her and gazed at his tall, muscular body walking away from her. 'Tommy, you really do have the cutest ass.'

'You're not so bad yourself,' Tommy said as he looked back over his shoulder at Candy in all her naked glory. He climbed onto the bed and Candy directed him to lay on his back.

'Now, I know this is going to be quick and that's okay, it always is when it's your first time. But we'll just take it slow and whatever happens, happens and that's ok,' said Candy.

Tommy said, 'Are you sure? I want it to be good for you too.'

'That's fine Tommy, it will be good for me too. And then after a while we can do it again and it will be even better,' she said with a smile.

Candy laid down on top of the strapping young lad, enjoying the feel of his hard muscles beneath her, like she was lying on a firm but pliable rock. Again, they kissed, their passion instantly rising again as they explored every part of each other's bodies.

'First things first,' said Candy as she reached into the bedside drawer and pulled out a condom. 'Rule number one – always have protection, no matter what, no matter who.'

'Thanks for the tip,' said Tommy with a smile.

'No, thank you for the tip,' replied Candy, as she tickled the tip of his penis and then stretched the condom over his proud erection.

Candy moved up the bed until her breasts were swinging over Tommy's face. He gently took one breast in his hand and then suckled the nipple of her other breast, taking it deep into his mouth. Candy cried out as his touch set off a response deep within her and suddenly, she wanted him inside her. She moved back down, straddled him and grabbed his throbbing penis then guided him into her warm, wet depths. As she took him inside her, Tommy couldn't help himself and suddenly exploded in a spasm of ecstasy that he had never imagined could be so intense, crying out as he came.

Candy lay still on top of Tommy, panting her pleasure but still not complete. Slowly, she pulled Tommy out of her and then lay down in the crook of his arm, looking up at him with a smile. Ashamed, Tommy said, 'Sorry, I didn't mean to be that fast, I just couldn't control it.'

'That's okay. Don't worry about it, I knew that would happen. It's like that for everyone the first time. It doesn't matter, we've got all night.'

And so, Tommy's learnings in the ways of the world continued into the next morning, except this time under the bed covers instead of on top of the Judo mat.

CHAPTER 10

Tommy's time at high school rolled on, and while he applied himself diligently in his studies, he was never much more than an average student. He made the grade, but did not set the school world on fire, because his mind was always on the mat, his passion always Judo.

Viktor always encouraged Tommy to test his strength and skills against bigger and better opponents, entering him in as many competitions as possible. Always fighting in older age groups and against bigger fighters, Tommy quickly progressed through the ranks and at the tender age of 17, he was fighting for the open age championship against much more experienced Judoka fighters when he was noticed by a nameless observer in the crowd, scribbling furiously in a notebook and surreptitiously videoing Tommy in his match-ups. After his win and filled with joy at being crowned the youngest ever Australian national champion in the light heavyweight division, Tommy was oblivious to the feverish activity of the cagey observer.

One day towards the end of Tommy's final year of high school in Kings Cross, a very official looking letter stamped with an international postmark arrived for Tommy. Bursting with curiosity, he excitedly tore open the letter, itching to discover the contents. All at once he was filled with excitement but a sense of dread at the same time. He had been offered a full scholarship to an American college; Columbia University wanted him in New York!

Tommy didn't realize just how privileged he was, managing to be lucky enough to score a scholarship to one of the most prestigious schools in the world, an exclusive Ivy League college with very selective entry criteria and an extremely high price tag to attend. For Tommy, this was a one in a million chance.

Tommy's offer for Columbia was highly unusual. A member of the elite Ivy League comprising eight colleges in the north-east USA, Columbia was desperate to improve its wrestling results. The new wrestling coach was eager to expand the skills of his wrestling team and so had targeted young national champions in Judo and Jujitsu to supplement and support the training of Columbia's wrestling team. Tommy was one of six international competitors in Judo and Jujitsu who had been awarded scholarships by Columbia, for the purposes of training with the wrestling team.

Tommy of course didn't understand how controversial this scholarship offering was, as it went against the policy of Ivy League schools offering athletic scholarships. However, they got around this by applying the financial aid rules for scholarships and so for the first time in his life, Tommy was thankful for his state of poverty.

Tommy was faced with a tough decision. He began his life as a naïve country boy, who had since been hardened by circumstance but nurtured by strong people and role models in his life. He was at a crossroads; he had never been anywhere except the remote country town of his birth and his adopted city of Sydney. He didn't even have a passport and he had no clue about the world outside his bubble, what to expect or even if he was afraid of flying!

Molly sat Tommy down and read the letter again, quickly grasping what a chance this represented for her special young man. This letter could deliver Tommy a life of which they had barely dared to dream, one full of new experiences, great challenges, wonderful people and a wide expanse of opportunity. University in Australia hadn't even been on the radar for Tommy, and Viktor had reached the limit of what he could teach him; the student had surpassed the master some time before.

Tommy, Molly and Viktor all knew that the end of high school was a pivotal time for Tommy. He was ready to ascend to a new level, whatever and wherever that was, but none of them could see how that was possibly going to happen. And then fate intervened, in the form of an anonymous talent scout from the other side of the world. Tommy knew that he had asked the Universe to provide him a solution to his 'What Next?' conundrum and now it had been delivered, he couldn't turn it down.

In a heartbeat, his decision was made. He turned to his adoring mother with tears in his eyes and with one glance silently asked her permission to go. She smiled, threw her head back and let out her delicious, delightful, infectious laugh and with tears streaming down her face said, 'Of course you can go, Tommy. How could I ever refuse you? Your father would be so proud of the man you've become. He would want you to take life by the scruff of the neck and give it a bloody good shake!'

The deal was sealed with a huge bear hug from Tommy that almost crushed his poor mother, but she loved the strong embrace so much that she couldn't protest.

The next challenge was working out what Tommy would study. One of the conditions of his scholarship was that he must achieve a minimum academic performance judged by Grade Point Average in order to maintain his scholarship funding. He knew he had to do something interesting, because he didn't want to be bored out of his skull for the next four years. Plus, he would have to like what he was doing if he were to keep his scores up.

Tommy ran through the list of courses offered at Columbia, shaking his head at the confusing array of options available, from Anthropology and Anatomy all the way through the alphabet to Women's Studies and Yiddish. He was completely bamboozled.

Seeing Tommy's confusion, Molly said, 'Let me look. You just sit back and take a breather, Son.'

Slowly and methodically, Molly ran through the plethora of options on offer until suddenly she struck gold and exclaimed, 'Film school!'

'Say no more! Sign me up,' said Tommy, and so the unlikely combination of a Judo fighter from Australia and the Ivy League Columbia University School of the Arts in New York was born.

The course was set, and the planning began. There were passports to organize, clothes to buy, research to do and farewells to make. In just a few short months, Tommy would be off on his new adventure. He was full of wonder and trepidation at what lay ahead.

PART 2 - CHECHNYA

CHAPTER 11

It was a crazy time in a crazy place.

Embroiled in the aftermath of the dissolution of the Soviet Union, Chechnya had been torn apart by rebellion and war. The region was full of treacherous areas and dangerous people.

A wild and rebellious teenage girl only just turned 16 was yearning to escape the iron rule of Communist government and her overprotective parents. She took to the streets of Chechnya to break free of her life of rules, limits and constraints.

Young Tatiana thrust herself into the heaving maelstrom of Chechnya's underworld, where she quickly started running with an adolescent street gang. It was there that she met Nikolai, a much older man who was charming and enigmatic but with a constant palpable tension like a coiled spring ready to violently unravel, a bomb seemingly always on the verge of explosion. This barely contained power was exciting to the young girl, immediately drawing her to the man who was building his own army of impressionable and gullible youths searching for a strong leader to follow in those uncertain times.

This period would see the building of an empire for Nikolai, forging organized crime connections with the Russian Mafia, also known as the Bratva or Brotherhood. Nikolai enforced his iron will on those around him and became the Pakhan, or Godfather, of his crime unit.

Tatiana was quickly entangled in Nikolai's web and was soon sharing his bed, going everywhere and doing everything with him. A whirlwind romance culminated in a wedding only months after they met.

To her detriment, Tatiana soon realized that the dangerous strength and fear that Nikolai inspired in others and had so attracted her in the beginning, put her in mortal threat when it was directed at her. It started slowly, first with harsh words and emotional blackmail, but soon escalated to physical violence.

At the tender age of 18, Tatiana discovered to her horror that she was pregnant, carrying Nikolai's child. She knew then that she would be forever in the grip of his almost demonic possessiveness. She realized what a fool she had been and the mortal danger she had put herself in when she had left the comfort of her family home and the parents who cared for her.

Time seemed to slow for Tatiana and her world shrank into a blur of violence until she was literally a prisoner in Nikolai's fortress. The baby came, a beautiful bouncing boy whom they named Anatoly, after Nikolai's grandfather. The young boy was the light of Tatiana's life, full of innocence that she knew she had to somehow preserve as a symbol of purity in her world of darkness.

With nobody to help her and only impassive guards for company, Tatiana filled her days with Anatoly and plans of escape. She knew she would have only one chance to break away from her brutal husband and it would have to be handled with absolute precision, planned down to the finest detail. But circumstance played its hand and soon after Anatoly's birth, Tatiana once again fell pregnant. She knew she could not escape in that condition, so resolved to remain in Chechnya for the birth and then implement her plan to flee as soon as she was able after the delivery.

For a successful escape, Tatiana knew that she had to completely disappear forever, because she was certain that Nikolai would never stop searching for her. She resolved to flee the country and start a new life with her children in America. They would become Americans, blend in so that nobody would ever know her past; she would be a ghost.

In preparation, Tatiana taught herself English from a small Russian /

English dictionary and learned the American accent by watching endless television shows and movies. Her plan was clear, and she was a diligent student who quickly learned her new language in secret.

Tatiana knew that she would need help to complete her escape from Nikolai. With virtually no contact with the outside world, she had to work from within. Unfortunately, most Nikolai's men were thick brutes, incapable of independent thought and fiercely loyal to Nikolai. Tatiana despaired that she would ever find the man she needed to help her escape, until one fateful day Nikolai dealt the pregnant Tatiana a particularly fierce beating in full view of Nikolai's right-hand man, Pasha.

Pasha was a man of violence, a tough fighter who grew up on the mean streets of Odessa in Ukraine, a bustling port on the shores of the Black Sea, surviving with his fists and his wits. Pasha had demonstrated a fierce capacity for enforcement and a sharp mind for money. A chance meeting with Nikolai years before had eventually resulted in Pasha being elevated to the role of Kaznachey in Nikolai's organization.

Pasha was the money man, the intermediary between Nikolai and his army. Pasha had done many things he was not proud of. He had hurt and killed so many people that his soul was wounded, almost dead except for his one shining light, his young wife Katerina, who deep down knew there was some good in him. Pasha thought of his link with Nikolai as a means to an end, as he collected and saved all the money he could so that he and Katerina could escape the madness and buy a place of their own where they could start a family.

Pasha strained at the yoke of Nikolai's brutal rule, but his years as a boy and a man of the streets had taught him well; keep your head down so it doesn't get taken off.

As the beating continued, Nikolai smashed his fist into Tatiana's face and Pasha's hatred of Nikolai grew to epic proportions. He vowed that somehow, he would help Tatiana get away from her cruel and vicious husband.

After the beating, Pasha took every opportunity to spend time with Tatiana, creating reasons and making excuses for being in the house near her. Slowly, they developed a bond and then trust soon followed. When she finally knew she was safe with Pasha, Tatiana made the first move and one day broached the subject. She said, 'Pasha, I'm so terrified of that bastard Nikolai, I know one day he'll go too far in one of his beatings and kill me! Then there will be nobody to protect my children. For my sake and that of my young son and unborn child, I need to escape this madman! I only have one chance and I can't do it alone.'

Tatiana silently pleaded with every part of her being for Pasha to agree to help her, and was overcome when he responded, 'I'll help you, but only on my terms. You do as I say and nothing else, or we'll both be dead.'

Pasha knew he was taking a terrible risk, but he could no longer stand by and watch Tatiana's body and soul be crushed by a brutal monster. He knew his darling Katerina would want him to help Tatiana, and that was all the motivation he needed.

CHAPTER 12

A few short months later, Tatiana's unborn child announced its impending arrival, demanding to see what this new world had to offer. Pasha raced her and Anatoly to the hospital and he knew the time had come to execute the meticulously planned escape. Pasha had enrolled the services of a doctor who owed him a life debt from when Pasha had saved him from a knife fight when he was a wild boy growing up on the tough streets of Odessa.

The doctor was a key part of Pasha's plan. He delivered a vibrant and healthy baby girl into Tatiana's loving arms and then announced that she had some after-birth complications and needed two weeks recovery in the hospital. This would be enough time for Tatiana and her baby to recover from the birth and gain the strength to travel the long and arduous journey that lay ahead. Key to the plan was her being free of the confines of Nikolai's fortress for an extended period.

Pasha had made all the arrangements, carefully planning the entire escape down to the last detail. He had called in many favours and even dipped into his own savings for her. On the night before Tatiana was due to be released from hospital, a nondescript Russian Lada sedan silently glided to a stop at the side entrance of the hospital. Tatiana vigilantly watched her minder, one of Nikolai's Byki, his personal bodyguards and a hulk of a man, as the powerful sleeping pill she had slipped into his drink finally took effect and he dozed off to sleep in his chair.

Tatiana quietly snuck down to the waiting car and it silently spirited her away into the night. In tow was her young son Anatoly, her new baby daughter Valentina and a suitcase of essentials. She held her future in her pocket with her family's new identities, American passports, money and plane tickets leaving from Moscow.

The drive was an endless blur, more than 1,800 kilometres through harsh countryside and terrible roads, fearing for her life all the while and still recovering from the recent birth. At the halfway point, her silent driver swapped duties with another who took the wheel to complete the difficult journey, travelling all through the day and night.

With every mile they put between her old life and her psychotic husband in Chechnya, Tatiana grew stronger and started to transform into her new life. Still, her driver stayed silent, both knowing it was better that neither of them knew anything of the other, not even their names. This was no ordinary situation and not knowing was the safest way to survive.

In the midst of Tatiana's escape, Pasha was back in the lion's den with Nikolai, making sure he was fully occupied and sharing a copious amount of their favourite vodka before passing out to sleep the night away, oblivious to the drama that was unfolding so far away.

The morning dawned grey and drab and through the blur of Nikolai's hangover, he realized that today his family would return to his fortress and he could once again hold them tight in his iron fist. After a solid breakfast and a piping hot Russian coffee with a dash of vodka to shake his addled brain into focus, Nikolai ordered his driver to take him to the hospital and settled in for the journey.

Nikolai knew something was wrong the minute they arrived at the hospital. Staff were running around madly; police were milling about in a confused state and the trusted man who had been guarding his family and was supposed to meet him out front was nowhere to be seen.

Nikolai's stomach turned and his brain almost exploded as a red mist of rage engulfed him. Flying out of the car even before it stopped, he raced up the stairs to Tatiana's room and saw her minder getting groggily to his feet, finally waking from his drug-induced sleep. Instantly, Nikolai rained blows upon him and raged, 'Where is Tatiana? Where is my family?'

Fearing for his life in a quivering mess, the henchman meekly said, 'I don't know Pakhan, she must have drugged me, I just woke up this morning and they were all gone.'

Suddenly calm and with blue ice running through his veins, Nikolai drew his Russian pistol from its holster, brought it up between the man's eyes and casually pulled the trigger. A splattering of brains, blood and gore sprayed over the hospital wall behind the now lifeless victim.

Nikolai thundered down the stairs of the hospital, pulling aside one of the stunned policemen and through clenched teeth said to the man, 'Get on your radio right now and talk to Detective Ivanov; tell him Nikolai has called in his favour and to meet me at my house in 20 minutes. Go on, do it now!'

As the baffled cop rushed off to do his bidding, Nikolai leapt back in the car and ordered his driver to race back to the house.

When the car came screaming into the compound and Nikolai flew out of the car with a dark look of fearsome rage on his scowling face, Pasha knew the escape had gone to plan and that Tatiana was safely on her way, away from this hellish life. But Pasha knew that he was now in mortal danger and he would have to tread very carefully to avoid being on the sharp end of a switchblade.

Thankfully, Nikolai was not immediately suspicious of Pasha and did not direct anger or questions to him. Instead, he called a meeting of his Russian Mafia cell. First on the list was his Sovietnik, his closest councillor and advisor, who also happened to be his older brother Vladimir, a singularly unpleasant individual. A brute of a man, he had a cruel streak even longer than Nikolai's, and a perverse brutality to match. A well-concealed streak of jealousy of his younger brother's power and success coursed through Vladimir, which made him even more dangerous.

Also called to the meeting were Nikolai's four Brigadiers, his captains in charge of his army of Boeviks, the soldiers. Everyone soon arrived, eager to not keep their Pakhan waiting, knowing the mood he was in and understanding the danger of pissing him off when he was in this frame of mind. A key attendee of the meeting was the police chief; he was Nikolai's crooked connection to the world on the right side of the law and one of the major reasons Nikolai had managed to keep himself out of prison all these years.

Nikolai was of course the one most concerned about Tatiana's disappearance. The others were almost relieved that she had escaped, knowing how Nikolai treated her and recognizing what a distraction she had become. Nikolai had become so obsessed with his wife that it was starting to affect his focus on the business. They all agreed to circulate word among their underworld contacts to find Tatiana and the police chief would put out an alert on the police channels that Tatiana was wanted as a suspect in a serious crime. The group had no idea where she was, except for Pasha and he sure as hell wasn't going to speak up.

The meeting disbanded. Nikolai was like a tiger in a cage, full of anger that Tatiana had run away from him and taken his precious son and daughter with her. He felt furious but impotent at the same time, powerless to immediately find her, bring her back and punish her for daring to defy him.

Nikolai vowed he would never again give Tatiana the freedom she had so flagrantly abused. Searching for answers, Nikolai sat in his elaborate mahogany office and selected his favourite Stolichnaya vodka, poured himself a generous serve and sat to settle his frayed nerves and think through how Tatiana was able to betray him so completely.

As Nikolai pondered his betrayal, there were other machinations proceeding in his fortress among those who he thought were his most trusted advisers; Pasha and Vladimir, each of whom were lost in their own private thoughts. Pasha, now that the escape plan had been executed with such precision, knew that Nikolai was no fool; he hadn't risen to the rank of Pakhan, the Godfather, without a sharp mind and an almost uncanny ability to analyse situations and understand human nature at its most basic level. Deep down, Pasha knew that Nikolai would soon figure out that Tatiana had help in her escape and that he would not stop until he found out who it was. Pasha quickly concluded that he needed to execute his own escape from Nikolai.

In another section of the compound, Vladimir too was pondering this turn of events and how he could turn it to his advantage. All through their childhood together, Nikolai, the younger brother, was always the centre of attention, the golden child, always favoured by the adults in their lives. More likeable and charming than his sullen older brother, people were drawn to Nikolai and generally ignored Vladimir, who more and more became a bystander and observer in their lives together. Vladimir progressively became more jealous of Nikolai as they grew up together. While he naturally drifted into the role of councillor and adviser to Nikolai in his criminal empire, Vladimir resented his role as second-in-command. He believed that the role as head of the family was his right to claim as the older brother.

In recent times as he saw his younger sibling build his power, his empire and his wealth, Vladimir's resentment had morphed into a festering obsession, driving him mad with jealousy. More and more he struggled not to show this to his brother, who was so attuned to the possibility of betrayal from within his private army.

Somehow, Nikolai had been blind to the betrayal from his wilful wife and Vladimir saw this as his opportunity to pounce on Nikolai's empire while he was distracted by this latest turn of events. Vladimir put his devious mind to work, formulating a plan to turn the situation to his advantage, strategizing a bold move that would overthrow his brother, whom he felt was so undeserving of his success. Vladimir, completely unaware of Pasha's role in Tatiana's escape conspiracy, decided that any plan to eliminate Nikolai must also include his apparently faithful and committed Kaznachey, Nikolai's right-hand man, the controller of the Brigadiers and therefore also the foot soldiers and assassins.

Vladimir formulated a devious plot to take out both Nikolai and Pasha in one deft move but knew that he did not have the power and support of the Brotherhood's leaders to implement this plan openly. He knew he must work quickly and under a cloak of complete secrecy.

CHAPTER 13

Tatiana's headlong rush to Moscow went on and on in a haze of tiredness, worry and fear. She struggled to stay alert and focused and to care for her young son, a rambunctious and restless toddler, along with her tiny daughter, barely two weeks old. As they finally approached Moscow more than 24 hours after the harrowing ordeal of her initial escape, Tatiana now faced the enormity of the task that lay ahead. She needed to transform into a worldly American traveller, who had visited Russia late in her pregnancy on a business trip accompanied by her young son and unexpectedly went into an early labour. Having recovered from the birth, it was time for her to return home to the States.

This would be the first real test of Tatiana's English skills and her American accent, on the most important stage imaginable; she had to fool the Russian Customs Officers at Border Control, deny her heritage and embrace her new persona. All this came with the crippling fear of knowing what would come if she failed in her subterfuge; a life of abuse, misery and potential death for her and a prison for her innocent children.

The anonymous Lada sedan slipped inconspicuously into the carpark of Moscow's Domodedovo Airport and the driver silently dispatched his live cargo, without a word spoken between them. As she entered the potential sanctuary of the terminal, Tatiana was full of equal measures of hope and fear. She made her way into a public toilet and prettied herself up after the long and arduous journey. As she did her hair and applied her makeup, she quietly examined the beautiful face that gazed back at her. She was still so young but at the same time there was an ageless quality to her, a steely resolve and inner strength that came from knowing what she had endured at the hands of her violent aggressor and yet still had the fortitude to make her escape.

Knowing what she was capable of, Tatiana knew she had the will and the training to do what was to come. With a final steely gaze in the mirror, she suddenly transformed into a brash American with a bright and flashy smile and a plunging cleavage, expanded by her recent birth and breastfeeding. They were about to leave behind their old life, names and identities.

Tatiana casually sauntered out of the public toilet holding the hand of her young son happily waddling along beside her, carrying her babe in a sling close to her chest and towing a suitcase behind her. This was her entire world, everything she knew and cared about was wrapped up in this bubble with her.

Tatiana approached the check-in counter full of American confidence and in her best impersonation of the combined characters of Rachel, Monica and Phoebe from the sitcom Friends, who had been her American teacher for so many long hours, she let out a loud, 'Hey, how you doin' today? I came to Russia with only one kid, now I got another one to take home with me. Momma's sure gonna be surprised when I come on back home to the States with my second one!' She flashed the man behind the counter a brilliant smile and a generous look down her cleavage and said, 'Can I check us all in please?'

Hurdle number one went off without a hitch as the helpless check-in attendant was hit by the full force of the beautiful, glamorous, leggy and busty American blonde who had just dazzled him into a wondrous silence. He didn't know what had hit him, slowly blinking as he watched her walk away from him with a delightfully suggestive wiggle of her backside that was beautifully wedged into a tight red miniskirt.

The next step was Customs, always a much tougher task than the check-in counter. Hoping for a man she could dazzle, Tatiana unfortunately ended up with a tough old bird who had been beaten with the ugly stick and had a demeanour to match. This would not be easy.

Tatiana toned down the brashness because she didn't want to raise the hackles of the witch behind the counter. As she looked down the row of blank Customs officers, Tatiana idly wondered why it seemed that having a personality lobotomy seemed a prerequisite for the job. 'Focus!' she admonished herself to bring her back to the present moment. She knew she needed all her wits about her and couldn't afford this kind of drifting idle thought.

Tatiana knew her only chance was to play it straight and trust that Pasha had done his best and sourced forged passports that would stand up to the closest scrutiny. She admired the work as she handed it over, seeing the slightly worn edges and the stamps of other countries in it already and her entry stamp into Russia dated weeks before. The documents stood up to the impassioned gaze of the grumpy Customs officer and as she handed them back, Tatiana smiled and said, 'Thank you so much. Have a nice day now!' and walked through the gates towards the next stage of her life.

Hurdle number two complete, Tatiana had only one final hoop to jump through; American customs, but this wouldn't be for another 12 hours. She settled in at the gate lounge and got food and drink for her bouncy son, who was so incredibly excited about all these amazing events that he was jumping around like a jack-in-the-box.

CHAPTER 14

Activity had climbed to fever pitch in Chechnya. Nikolai's crooked police chief had marshalled his forces and put out alerts, and the whole Chechen underworld and its network of informants were searching for details of what had happened and the whereabouts of Tatiana. Pasha was executing his plan to extract himself and his wife safely from his nightmare, and Vladimir was planning his secret coup.

Pasha resolved to make the difficult call to his wife Katerina. She had some idea what Pasha did and who he worked for but did not truly understand just what he did and how dark his past really was. Pasha had always tried to protect her from this part of his life, not wanting to worry her or sully her innocence with the filth that he dealt with every day. Katerina was his secret garden, his safe haven, and he did not want her to think less of him because of what he did. But he knew the time had come because they were both in grave danger.

Pasha called Katerina and quietly explained the seriousness of the situation and that they needed to run away. While initially hurt and worried, once Pasha explained the reason for the danger and that he had saved Tatiana and her two young children, Katerina's heart melted, and she agreed to do whatever was necessary for them to be together. They would fulfil their dream of getting away and starting a family of their own.

Pasha instructed Katerina to pack some essentials. He would quietly sneak out of Vladimir's compound and stop at the bank to empty the safety deposit box that he had been filling with cash and valuables for so many years. They agreed they would take Katerina's car because it was nondescript, and nobody knew the car like they did Pasha's.

Unfortunately for the pair, Pasha did not realize that Vladimir in his scheming was eavesdropping on his conversation. Suddenly everything became clear to Vladimir and his plan fell into place with this final piece of the puzzle. Vladimir called in his only conspirator and instructed him to immediately go to Pasha's home and rig Katerina's car with a bomb, linked with a trigger set to go off 30 seconds after the ignition was turned.

A vital part of Vladimir's plan was to fake an attack by a rival gang, so it would look like they were the ones who had taken out Nikolai and Pasha. Vladimir went to Nikolai and told him that he had been approached by a representative of a rogue cell of the Brotherhood that had been giving them troubles over the past few months in the drug trade. Vladimir said the rival gang had approached him personally about him joining forces with the rogue cell to betray Nikolai and take over his business.

Furious and in no mood for such things, Nikolai did exactly as Vladimir had hoped and immediately decided to launch a surprise assault on the rival gang's headquarters, a seedy bar in a nearby district. Nikolai was feeling powerless about Tatiana's escape and being the man of action that he was, this attack gave him a sense of control and power over his own destiny.

Vladimir in his role as Sovietnik, or chief adviser, did not get involved in such direct assaults, so he took his leave of Nikolai, saying he had something he needed to take care of, which was not unusual or unexpected, and disappeared out of the compound. Pasha also was not a necessary part of the attack, as he was too valuable to risk in such a frontal assault. Nikolai made up his own rules and had a thirst for blood that would not be satisfied by hiding in his home while mayhem was afoot.

Nikolai gathered his Brigadiers and they quickly assembled a small soldier force to take up the attack and off they flew to their rival's headquarters.

Once the assault force had left, Pasha headed off in the other direction to the bank and then his home and Katerina, oblivious to the risk that lay in wait for them that had been orchestrated by Vladimir's scheming.

Little did the assault force know, but Vladimir had stationed himself opposite the rival gang's headquarters on the top floor of a three-storey building, peering out a window with a perfect view of the bar across the street. Armed and ready with his trusty Kalashnikov AK-47 assault rifle, Vladimir would watch the action unfold and take his shot when the time was right.

Three jet-black Mercedes wagons tore up the street and screamed to a halt outside the bar. As soon as the first soldier jumped out, the alarm was raised by the lookout inside the bar and then all hell broke loose! Shots were fired from the attacking force with the benefit of surprise on their side and they gained an initial upper hand. But they were attacking from a point of weakness against an armed group with cover inside, so the odds quickly evened up as the rival gang got themselves together and returned fire.

In the maelstrom of flying bullets, Vladimir saw his chance; he took careful aim at his brother's head and calmly fired off a quick burst. Lost in the chaos of the surrounding action and noise, the shots from a different direction went unnoticed. Nikolai's head exploded in a mist of blood and brains and he slumped to the asphalt, well and truly dead before his body hit the ground.

Gasping in disbelief, Nikolai's remaining troops could not comprehend this sudden development as they looked at their fierce, indestructible leader lying on the road in a rapidly widening pool of blood, with half his head blown away. Without their boss, the gang quickly disbanded, jumped in their cars and tore off down the street in a cloud of smoking rubber.

As the smoke cleared and the vista opened before him, Vladimir was triumphant in his moment of glory. There was no trace of remorse about killing his own brother as elation took hold. He quickly and quietly packed up his gear and stole away down the back stairs to the rear exit where he had hidden his car. He inconspicuously drove slowly away down the street, with not one person any the wiser about what had just occurred. As far as any observers were concerned, the dead bodies were just the result of yet another turf war that seemed all too common in their neighbourhood. The police didn't care, and nobody would be investigating – as far as they were concerned the gangs could wipe each other out as much as they liked.

As Vladimir was driving back to Nikolai's compound, the second part of his plan was about to unfold. Pasha had stopped by the bank and retrieved the contents of his safety deposit box – his life savings garnered from all his nefarious activities over the years. This money would soon be transformed into something good and pure as he and Katerina put this dark chapter in their lives behind them and started a family of their own. They would have a fresh start in a new place far away from Nikolai and the Brotherhood.

These thoughts raced through Pasha's mind as he quickly drove home to collect Katerina and take her safely away. He knew time was critical now and that every minute counted. He had no idea what had just happened to Nikolai or of Vladimir's plans to take over the gang, but Pasha knew he would never again be safe in Chechnya.

Pasha pulled into his driveway, relieved to see his darling Katerina coming out of the front door of their tiny, drab apartment trailing two suitcases behind her, moving towards her car. He parked and raced over to her, feverishly kissing her, hugging her so tightly she could hardly breathe.

'Pasha, what is it?' said Katerina as she felt the desperation in his embrace.

'Nothing, my love. I'm just so happy to see you safe and that we're leaving this hellhole behind us. I'll put these suitcases in the car, then we'll go inside for one last look before we say goodbye to our old lives and leave this dump of an apartment for good.'

Pasha put the luggage in the car, then they went inside and looked around, reflecting on the times they had spent there and knowing that together they were strong and good, but when they were apart Pasha was drawn into his old ways of crime and violence. He decided then and there that no matter what happened, whatever his future held, never again would he go back to his old ways. Pasha committed to himself that he would live a good, full life in a way that would make his Katerina proud. Fifteen years his junior, Katerina was a sweet, quiet, bookish librarian who knew some of Pasha's violent history but loved him anyway. They had met through Pasha's habit of seeking solace from his brutal life in the library among the giants of Russian literature. This was the Pasha who Katerina grew to know and love, not a key man in a Russian Mafia cell.

Pasha and Katerina held hands as they walked out of their apartment, which even though it was dreary had been theirs together and did hold special memories for them. On the threshold they shared one last tender kiss before they started on the next phase of their lives together.

Pasha normally drove, but Katerina knew how exhausted he was, so she insisted she would drive so that he could rest, and she would look after him for a change. As they climbed into the car, Pasha shuddered, feeling a premonition that something terrible was about to happen. He shook it off as a stupid superstition, something he had never suffered from in his life, and settled back into the seat as Katerina turned the key and started the engine.

A chain reaction started the very instant the electrical impulse fired the engine, activating the 30-second timer attached to the block of C-4 plastic explosive that had been planted under Katerina's car. From that moment, their fate was sealed.

As Katerina put the car in gear and started to reverse out of the carpark, Pasha suddenly remembered he had forgotten to collect a wad of bills he had stashed in a cupboard in the apartment. Briefly he hesitated, wondering whether to leave it there, but he knew they would need everything they could get their hands on to start their new life together.

'Wait Katerina, I just need to quickly get something from inside, I'll just be a few seconds,' said Pasha. As Katerina brought the car to a halt, Pasha took off his seat belt, opened the door and turned in his seat to get out of the car, just as the timer delivered its jolt to the detonator, instantly firing the deadly pack of C-4 in a massive fireball that engulfed the car.

Katerina was killed instantly, as she was directly above the C-4. Pasha received a huge blast so powerful that it launched him out of the car like a human cannonball, landing in a broken, bloody, burning mess in the middle of the street, 10 metres away from the shattered remains of the car.

In the aftermath of the explosion, a motorbike coughed into life and the black-clad rider raced away into the distance, comfortable in the knowledge that his task was complete.

Vladimir was content. He was ensconced safe in the compound, having taken control over Nikolai's organization. Everyone knew he was the logical choice and with Pasha gone, there was nobody else with the skills or the leadership to take over the group. Vladimir had brokered a peace deal with the rival gang to smooth over the troubles, established their boundaries once again and was sure everything would soon return to normal. The only difference would be that he was now rightfully the one in command, befitting his birthright as the older brother. Vladimir was also happy that Tatiana was out of the way, with no Anatoly to worry about taking over in the future or for Tatiana to make trouble for the Brotherhood. He and everyone else was happy to see the back of her, knowing she would never return.

Vladimir called off the dogs and cancelled the search for Tatiana. Word spread quickly about the new regime and everyone just kept their head down, knowing that Vladimir could be just as dangerous as Nikolai.

To make sure his plan was complete and be certain of Pasha's fate, Vladimir checked with the hospital and was informed that the bomb victim was pronounced dead on arrival, the injuries sustained during the explosion being too severe for anyone to survive.

Vladimir vowed to expand his criminal empire even further, building something of which even his dead brother Nikolai would never have dreamed.

CHAPTER 15

Tatiana was breathless and exhausted. She was having trouble keeping herself together after the previous tumultuous 48 hours. She was so close! She was on American soil, but on the wrong side of the gates. She had just one last barrier to her new life – it all came down to these next few minutes. If she could get through US Customs and Border Patrol, she would be safe, and her children's lives would be assured. If not, she would be cast back into the hell of her previous life, with danger lurking at every corner.

Once more she collected herself but couldn't help looking somewhat dishevelled. She was exhausted, nearly spent, with bags under her eyes from not having slept properly for almost three days. Her son was very tired and grumpy, with the novelty of a long flight having worn off many hours before. Her daughter was cranky and fussy and constantly harassing her mother for attention.

While this was all exceedingly difficult for Tatiana, it worked in her favour. For her entry into the USA, Tatiana was lucky enough to draw an elderly gentleman for her customs check who as it happened had recently become a grandfather for the first time and was sympathetic to her plight. Tatiana breathed a sigh of relief when she saw a smile come across his face as he said, 'Welcome to the United States. You look very tired and you've got your hands full, so let's see if we can get this out of the way quickly for you.' He quickly looked over the papers, which were all thankfully in order and he said, 'Welcome home madam, best you go on and get some sleep.'

Dumbfounded, Tatiana mumbled a thank you to the kind gentleman and staggered through the gates into freedom. An unbelievable sense of relief washed over her as she passed through the gates, like a cool breeze wafting over her whole body. She gathered her things and corralled her son under way as they trudged to collect her suitcase.

As she stepped out of the airport and into the American sunshine, the enormity of what she had just achieved suddenly hit her full force and she burst into tears, sobbing as all the pent-up tension and pressure came bursting forth in a gush of emotion. After a few minutes of this, an elderly lady came up to her and asked if she was okay. Tatiana replied yes, she was just exhausted and needed a cab to take her to a hotel. When the kind lady heard her perfect American accent, she said, 'Welcome home dear,' then hailed her a cab and sent her on her way.

PART 3 - USA

CHAPTER 16

I was beside myself, freaking out at what was about to happen. I was with Mum at Sydney Airport, about to leave Australia for the very first time in my life and embark on a life-changing experience at just 18 years of age. Suddenly I panicked and my 12-year-old self tearfully said, 'Mum, I know this is stupid and the timing could have been better, but I think I've changed my mind. I don't want to go. I want to stay here with you.'

Through tears of her own, Mum craned her neck as she looked up at me, now a strapping young lad, powerful on the outside but vulnerable on the inside. With love in her eyes and a depth of feeling in her voice that I'd rarely heard, she put both her hands on my cheeks and pulled my face down towards hers so that we were almost eye-to-eye and she said, 'Tommy, since your father passed away, it's just been you and me against the world. We've had nobody to look after us and we've been through some incredibly tough times together. It hasn't been easy for me and God knows it hasn't been easy for you, but we got there. You're an adult now and it's time for you to spread your wings and build a life for yourself. My mission was to get you this far and I reckon I did a bloody good job, but now it's up to you. It's time for you to shine, so get out there and do what you love. Make a name for yourself. Make me proud.'

Wow. What a speech. It looked like it was hard for Mum to say that, because I'm sure a little selfish part of her really wanted me to stay home with her, so we could be together always. She knew I would do it if she asked, but I think she knew it wasn't the right thing for either of us. As a parent, it was time for her baby to leave the nest, spread his wings and fly on his own magnificent journey of self-discovery.

Mum always had a way with words, she always knew just what to say to cheer me up or show me the right thing to do and now she'd done it again, propping me up just when I needed her. One day I would be able to do the same thing for her, but right now she was the parent and I the child, even though I couldn't have looked anything less like a child in that moment, with my towering height and enormous frame. I resolved then that I would get on the plane and embrace whatever was coming my way now and in the future. With one last tearful hug and a kiss, I bent down to say goodbye to my loving mum.

Suddenly there was a raucous cheer and I looked up to see a gaggle of stunning women running towards me, all big hair, big boobs and high heels; the strip club had gone off the reservation! The club had paused the live shows and resorted to video for an hour, so the girls could send me on my way. Mum and I burst out laughing at the sight, and the whole crowd at the airport looked on in astonishment as eight scantily clad women swamped me in one big girl-crush of an embrace. I was in heaven and certainly the envy of every bloke in the building!

I finally extracted myself from the delightful embrace of womanliness, gave Mum one last hug and walked through the departure gates with a nonchalant smile and wave. I was back! I was 18, indestructible and ready to take on the world; *Bring It On!*

CHAPTER 17

Jesus Christ, it's cold enough to freeze the balls off a brass monkey! I really should have brought a jacket. As I stepped out of the terminal and stood around with a bemused look on my face, I shivered in the freezing winter conditions that I really hadn't planned for. Leaving Sydney in the height of summer, I just hadn't expected it to be so cold.

I guess I should have listened to Mum when she said I should "pack something warm, because it's winter there". Yeah, no worries Mum. I laughed and dug another jumper out of my bag and threw it on, bringing the hood up over my head in a pointless attempt for some extra warmth. More than a hoodie was needed to keep out this biting cold.

In my broad Australian accent, I asked a local guy if he knew where to find a taxi. In response the guy looked at me and in his New York drawl said, 'What are you, retarded? What does that sign say?' pointing to a sign nearby that said TAXI STAND in big bold letters.

Oh yeah, thanks, *mate*. Welcome to New York, asshole. I walked over to the sign and waited to hail a cab.

After a few minutes freezing my nuts off, I finally got a cab and then jumped into the front seat. 'Dude, what the hell are you doing?' asked the cab driver angrily in his thick New York accent.

'What? This is a cab isn't it? I pay you to drive me somewhere. Isn't that how it works?'

'Yeah, but what the hell are you doing in the front seat?'

'Uh, that's where I always sit. That's how we do it back home.'

'Well, nobody does it that way here. It's plain weird,' the driver said, shaking his head.

'I can move if you like, but I can see more from up here,' I pleaded.

'Okay, whatever. Where to, buddy?'

'Columbia University, thanks mate,' I responded. I really do like the sound of that.

'You want the quick way, or the tourist drive so you can see some landmarks and the famous heart of the city?' asked the cabbie.

'Let's take the scenic route' I replied. Despite the tiredness that engulfed me after my long flight, I was desperately excited to fill my eyes with all on offer and experience as much as I could for my first time ever on foreign soil.

I was transfixed as the cab took me through Brooklyn, over the East River and across the iconic Brooklyn Bridge. Then we headed north through Tribeca, Soho and Greenwich Village along Seventh Avenue with Madison Square Garden on our left and the Empire State Building on our right. I was struck dumb as we went past Times Square and veered onto Broadway past the famous theatres and then Central Park, which seemed to go on forever. I couldn't believe I was here, in New York! I was seeing for real so many famous landmarks and scenes that I'd admired in movies and on TV my whole life and now I would be living in the very heart of it.

'I am one lucky sonofabitch,' I said to the taxi driver.

'You sure are, man. New York's the best place in the world; you couldn't pay me to live anywhere else.'

The sights, sounds and smells of New York filled the cab, as we rolled past steam clouds rising through vents in the footpath, police sirens wailed and the scent of bagel bakeries wafted in through the window; even though it was cold, I'd left the window open to experience as much as I possibly could of my first exposure to the Big Apple.

We turned off Broadway and travelled through Manhattan's exclusive upper West Side along the banks of the famous Hudson River until we reached Columbia University, which would be my home for the next four years. Steeped in history, the campus was full of amazing architecture and historical old buildings that presented an imposing façade to a simple country boy from Australia.

For me this was a one-in-a-million chance and I was reminded again just how out of my depth I was.

CHAPTER 18

After what seemed like an age of aimless wandering around trying to find out where I was supposed to be going, I finally found my dorm room and knocked gently on the open door.

'Hey Brother, how are you? I'm Chad, pleased to meet you,' called out a short, stocky and powerfully built young guy as I wandered into the room that would be my home for the next four years.

'Owyagoin' mate, awright?' I said in my usual friendly greeting that I had used all my life back home in Australia.

Chad stared blankly back at me and responded, 'Uh... what language are you speaking, dude? Is that English?'

I laughed and said with a smile, 'Sorry mate, I'm an Aussie. Just landed and haven't learned the local lingo yet! I just asked how you're going. And the name's Tommy.'

'Man, you are a big unit, what are you, six-foot-eight, maybe 220 pounds?' Chad asked, looking up at my full height stretching a couple of heads above him.

'Mate, good guess, you're pretty close. I think I've just about stopped growing up, but now I need to fill out and put some meat on my bones if I'm going to be fighting those big bastards in the heavyweight division!'

Chad smiled enthusiastically and asked, 'So, you're a fighter too? I'm a wrestler. What's your specialty?'

'Judo,' I replied. 'But I don't think you guys over here know how to do that do you? I think you dudes just oil each other up and then roll around on the floor with your shirts off trying to hug each other and then call it a sport instead of a love-in, right?'

Chad burst out laughing and said with a smile, 'Piss off, you big oaf. I think we're gonna get on just fine, roomy.'

Chad extended his hand and as I wrapped my big bear paw around his much smaller hand, I felt a steely strength in his grip and quickly realized that Chad would be a tough competitor on the mat.

As we sized each other up in that brief moment of human contact, I realized we would be firm friends. I was glad I'd found a good roommate, especially a fellow fighter on the team. Suddenly I was relieved of one of my great worries, that I would have to share a room with a total dickhead for the next four years. I'd been a loner through high school, struggling to make any friends of substance because I was such an outcast, so I looked forward to establishing a firm friendship with my roommate.

Chad immediately took me under his wing. A native New Yorker all his life, Chad was in his element at Columbia. His mother Amy had built an extremely successful import / export business and had used her street smarts to mix it with the big boys in a male-dominated industry. Chad's father had died when he was very young, and his mother had never married again or had a serious relationship. Amy was a self-made millionaire who lived in a large apartment in an exclusive part of town close to the iconic Central Park, just a stone's throw from Columbia University on the banks of the Hudson River.

Chad also had a younger sister called Brittney who he said was 16 years old and just as feisty and independent as her mother. Like Chad, Brittney was very athletic and a fighter too, training in Mixed Martial Arts, MMA. She was a Junior at high school, with two years to go until she too would apply for college. Apparently, they were an extremely close, tightknit family.

Chad was studying business at Columbia, in preparation for working with his mother in the family business. Apparently, Amy was in the prime of her life, not yet 40 years of age and at the peak of her business prowess. She wasn't planning to retire anytime soon but was looking to build a family dynasty and was keen for Chad and maybe even Brittney to join her in the business.

I had never really cared what I was studying in the past at school. I'd never been particularly academic and all I wanted to do since the day I met Viktor was Eat, Sleep, Judo. As a result, I had just gone through the motions at high school. But since I had the opportunity for an advanced education at one of the best colleges in the world, I thought I'd better make the most of it. Plus, I needed to maintain a minimum level of academic performance to keep my scholarship funding, so I knew I really had to pull my finger out and study if I was going to be able to stay at college and train with the best of the best. So, I resolved to really knuckle down and apply myself to my studies as well as my physical training.

For me, the unique training program developed by the college's innovative wrestling coach was exactly what I needed. I'd been doing Judo for six years now with the same coach. For all of Viktor's expertise, I needed variety and exposure to different training techniques and expert opponents with different skill sets to really catapult my learning to a whole new level.

The rounded approach of different skills covering other fighting disciplines, with different grappling, throwing, striking and submission techniques would be a vital tool in my Judo development. The constant training on campus, close to the dorm where I would be living would also dramatically accelerate my learning. This was a challenge that I was really looking forward to. It was a daunting prospect that would no doubt be difficult but fun at the same time.

I was ready and raring to go to take it on.

CHAPTER 19

'Don't you just loooooove film school?' cooed the exceedingly attractive and perky young brunette next to me. I was reminded once again how glad I was that I had chosen film school as my course of study, because it seemed to attract an inordinate number of hot babes to the student body. Much better than the engineering school or the mathematics department.

'Ab-so-bloody-lutely!' I responded with a smile, in my broadest Australian accent. I had learned through delightful experience that young American women seemed to be particularly attracted and interested in me when they found out I was from Australia.

'Uh... excuse me?' the girl replied with a puzzled frown across her brow, making her even more alluring.

I flashed her a smile and said, 'Sorry, I mean I definitely agree with you, film school is totally awesome.'

'Oh, are you an *Ossie*? How cute!' she squealed.

'Yep, I'm from Australia. My name's Tommy and I'm very pleased to meet you,' I said and stuck out my hand in greeting.

Gingerly she took my hand and said with a giggle, 'Oh my God, you're huge! Sorry, I've seen you across the room before, but I haven't been this close to you, so you kind of took me by surprise. I'm Randy.'

Am I glad to hear that! Being randy back home meant something much more than a name. I said, 'Don't worry, I might be big but I'm not scary. Under this tough exterior I'm a complete marshmallow, a real Momma's Boy.'

'Does that mean you melt when it gets too hot?' she cooed as she looked up into my eyes and batted her eyelids at me. I let out a huge laugh that broke the sexual tension of the moment that had built up so quickly.

'Yeah, that can happen sometimes. Do you want to go and grab a drink somewhere? We've finished classes for the day.'

'Oohhh, that sounds awesome. There's a great place around the corner where me and my gals go. Let's see what's happening there.'

As the night rolled on, it seemed like an instant replay of so many other nights I had already had at college. Not that I was complaining, I enjoyed the chase and certainly enjoyed the sex that was the usual outcome, but it was all so fleeting and meaningless. I could feel myself wanting more than casual encounters. Since my first time with Candy I'd had a succession of enjoyable one-night stands but now felt like I was ready for something more serious.

Just like Mum had taught me, I was always caring and respectful and was never mean to the girls I bedded. It just never went any further than the bedroom, and mostly that was okay from the girls' point of view as well. None of them really fell for me, they too knew it was just casual.

The girls were indeed great, but that was just a bonus. Film school really *was* awesome. I loved all aspects of the college and the course. My early love of movies developed with my dad had evolved into a genuine interest in the craft and I found myself absorbed in learning film history and elements of producing, editing and directing. I could see myself making a career of this film caper. Coupled with the technical side of movie making, my love of performance, my height and looks made acting a logical addition to the craft, so I took acting classes to round out my education.

'Okay, class,' announced the acting coach as the day's lesson started. 'Today's exercise requires everyone to think of the silliest character they could possibly play that goes completely against your physique.'

Bookish girls chose assassins, nerds chose body builders and me with a brilliant sense of the absurd chose Little Bo Peep for my character.

With a little styling, I already had the long blonde curly hair for it, so the wardrobe department just supplied me with a tiny pink dress and a shepherd's hook, and I was all set. Getting into character and playing a role had quickly become second nature to me. My sessions on stage at Judy's strip club had prepared me well to take it to the next level with my acting performances. The whole class loved my outrageous performance as the poor little girl who had lost her sheep. A muscle-bound giant of a man prancing around in a little dress and crying about her little lambs brought the house down. Of course, I lapped it up.

Still laughing, my acting coach afterwards said, 'You know what Tommy, I really think you could make a career out of this. You've got the look, the skills and the attitude, not to mention the dance moves I've seen you pull off in class. Once you work out what you want to do with your life after college, look me up and I'll see if I can put you in touch with the right people.'

'Brilliant!' I replied. 'Thank you so much! I can't think of anything else I'd like to do more after college than be in the movie business.'

CHAPTER 20

'Hey Chad, guess what! It's official; I'm going to be a *Star*,' I said to my roomie and now best friend.

'Ah get over yourself Tommy, what bullshit are you making up now?' was Chad's rather unkind response.

'Fair dinkum mate, totally legit. After seeing my Little Bo Peep performance, my acting coach says I've got what it takes to be a star!'

'Give it a rest man, he's just pulling your chain, all these movie people are full of shit, he's just blowing smoke up your ass, trying to get you to pay for more acting classes!'

'What, you reckon he's just pissing in my pocket?'

'Dude, what is wrong with you? Where do you come up with these expressions?'

'Seriously? You're having a crack at me about stupid sayings straight after pulling out the *blowing smoke up your ass* line?' I replied.

Continuing the joking around, I said to Chad, 'So what are you doing tonight, mate? You going to try and get a root?'

'Again, what the hell are you talking about right now, what do you mean *root*?' asked Chad, incredulous at my Aussie turn of phrase.

'You know, Do the Horizontal Tango, Bump Uglies, Fornicate, Lay, Screw, Bang, Bone, Bonk, Nail, Ride, Pound or whatever else you want to call it. Root – that's what us Aussies call it when you get lucky.'

'No, I don't think I'll be doing any of those things tonight.'

'Oh, I get it – bit of DIY tonight, hey? Spending some alone time with Mrs. Palmer and her five daughters?' I said with a laugh, winding him up even more.

'Dude, you are seriously retarded,' said Chad with a shake of his head at me and my somewhat manic chuckling.

'Look, I think I need to give you an education in some Aussie slang, and then you can return the favour and teach me some American slang, so I won't sound like such a dickhead when New Yorkers talk to me.'

'Okay, deal. For starters, the expression *Blow smoke up your ass* is a real thing – doctors used to do it to their patients!'

'What? No way!'

'Yep. Doctors used to do it to people to try and resuscitate them, especially for drowning victims.'

'Dude, that is seriously weird. I'm glad I wasn't around when those idiot doctors were making shit up like that!' I replied. 'Okay, let's play this game that I've just invented. I'm calling it the *slanging match*. Get it? We each say a piece of slang and the other person has to guess what it means. We'll have fifteen turns each and whoever gets the most points wins. You get a point for each correct answer.'

'Okay, I'm in. Let's do it. You first,' said Chad, suddenly interested now that his highly competitive nature was engaged.

'Alright, here's number one: He's got a couple of kangaroos loose in the top paddock.'

'Uh… the farmer lost some animals?' guessed Chad.

'Wrong. It means someone's a bit crazy, not all there. The lights are on but nobody's home; he's a couple of sandwiches short of a picnic. Okay, number two: Crack a fat.'

'Drop some kitchenware?'

'Wrong. It means to get an erection.' Chad really shook his head in amazement at this answer. 'Number three: She was wearing a thong.'

'Ah, I know this one – she was wearing a G-string.'

'Nope. She had a sandal on her foot. Thongs are like sandals, flip-flops, jandals. You wear them on your feet. Number four: He's a two-pot screamer.'

'Jesus, I don't know! Somebody in the kitchen who yells a lot?'

'Nah, someone who gets drunk really easily. Number five: Stone the bloody crows.'

'Kill some birds?

'No again! Mate, you really suck at this. We're a third of the way through and you haven't managed to score a point yet! That one means you're surprised about something. Okay, here's number six: It's going off like a frog in a sock.'

'Going crazy?'

'Hallelujah! We have a winner! That's one point. Number seven: It's cactus.'

'Is this a trick question? Surely it means the plant that grows in the desert.'

'Nope. You're back to your normal state of being wrong. It means broken or stuffed. Number eight: Sparrow's fart.'

'Dude, I cannot even guess at this one. Tell me.'

'Early in the morning, the crack of dawn. Number nine: Budgie smugglers.'

'More birds! What is it with you Aussies and birds? Does this mean a criminal who works the black market in tropical birds?'

'Nope. It means a guy's swimming costume, trunks, Speedos. Number ten: Piece of piss.'

'Hmmm… a urine sample?'

'Ha! Nice one! Wrong again. It means something that's super-easy. Two-thirds of the way there and you've got one lousy point. Number eleven: Mad as a cut snake.'

'Someone who's really angry or crazy?'

'Woohoo! Another point. Correct. Number twelve: Dead horse.'

'Uh… a dead horse?'

'Don't be stupid! Why would it mean that? It means ketchup, tomato sauce. Number thirteen: Fig jam.'

'Um... jam made from figs?'

'Nope, wrong again! It means someone who thinks they're really good, they've got tickets on themselves, think they're shit hot, as in *Fuck I'm Good, Just Ask Me.* Number fourteen: Flat out like a lizard drinking.'

'Lying down, relaxing?'

'Nope, in fact that's so wrong that I should deduct a point because it's the total opposite of what you said. It means someone's really busy, hard at work. Number fifteen: Map of Tassie.'

'I know this one! It's got to be a map of Tasmania, the island state off the bottom of Australia.'

'Sorry, wrong again. It means a woman's pubic hair. Chad, that was a disgrace! You only got two points out of fifteen. We've got some serious work to do on your verbal education, my friend.'

Chad just shook his head, completely flummoxed and said, 'I seriously don't know how you guys even communicate with each other. All that makes absolutely *no sense.*'

'Okay, my turn – hit me with your best shot,' I said.

'Okay, here we go. Number one: Fanny.'

'Easy! Vagina.'

'Nope. The other side, man – it means your butt. Back bum, not front bum. Get that right, or it could get you in a lot of trouble! Number two: Go Dutch.'

'Hmmm... visit Holland?'

'Wrong. It means to split the bill. Number three: Jock.'

'A guy's underwear?'

'No again. Not that easy, is it Mr. Smartass? It means someone who's into sport, an athlete. Number four: Stoop.'

'Bend over. That's got to be right doesn't it?'

'Wrong again. Stairs in front of an apartment building. Number five: Bodega.'

'A town in South America?'

'Ha! Incorrect. It means a corner store. Number six: Plead the Fifth.'

'Oh, I know this one. To not answer so you don't get in trouble.'

'Finally! Your first point. Well done, Einstein.'

I flipped him the bird on that one.

'Number seven: Drinking the Kool-Aid.'

'Drinking soft drink?'

'Nope. It means you believe something without proof. A bit soft in the head. It's actually a terrible story, a whole bunch of people in a cult killed themselves by drinking soft drink laced with cyanide.'

'Geez, thanks for bringing down the vibe. This was supposed to be fun.'

'Sorry. Okay, number eight: Kicks.'

'Kicking, like with your feet?'

'Sorry, no. It means sneakers, or shoes. Number nine: Ice.'

'Easy. Methamphetamine.'

'Huh? Dude, what planet did you get that from? That's so wrong it's not even funny. It means jewellery. Number ten: Rack.'

'Boobs!' I exclaimed, convinced I had this one right.

'Correct! There's another point. We're even now at two apiece. Number eleven: Wack.'

'To hit someone or something?'

'Nope. It's a bit like you right now – bad, terrible. Number twelve: Flying rat.'

'Hmmm… a rat you throw off a building?'

'Nope. It's a pigeon. Number thirteen: Cheddar.'

'I suppose you're going to tell me it's not cheese?'

'That's right, sucker, wrong again. It means money. Number fourteen: Benjamins.'

'A group of guys all with the same first name?'

'Nope. It's a hundred-dollar bill. Number fifteen: Grill.'

'I suppose you're going to tell me it's not a barbecue?'

'Ha! There are a few options for this. I would have accepted teeth, mouth jewellery or even a stare, but definitely not barbecue. It's a tie! Two points apiece. Looks like you've got some work to do on this game too, Bro.'

'Jesus! We finished level. I can't believe it,' I said, frustrated at my complete inability to beat Chad at this game I had just invented. 'Dammit! I thought I was going to beat you for sure, but you pulled out some weird sayings too, Chad. Alright, let's call it a night – you've still got that date with your own right hand and I wouldn't want you to miss out!'

'Up yours, pal!' Chad retorted as he flicked the light out and jumped into bed with a laugh.

CHAPTER 21

'Oh, my GOD! Who is *that*?' my brain shouted.

Something amazing had just happened, like a bolt from the blue. I was dumbstruck and instantly infatuated. I HAD to meet that girl!

I had just wandered into an MMA tournament. I'd walked in, checking out the action among the crowd and then spotted the cage. The fight in the metal fenced octagon had just started and the crowd was beginning to get into it. As my eyes focused on the cage, I'd realized the fighters were two young women. Curious, I got closer to the cage and saw an extremely hot blonde rip out a blindingly fast roundhouse kick to the head of her opponent, sending her down to the canvas. Stunned, the fallen girl took a moment to recover before she groggily got to her feet, shook her head and prepared to continue.

The blonde was a powerhouse, built like the proverbial brick shithouse. She looked super fit, extremely strong and had a take-no-prisoners look and attitude about her that aroused my interest immediately. I'd never seen a girl quite like her and was instantly attracted to her strength. I'd always seen myself as the strong one, the Protector, and seeing such obvious power, strength and independence in a woman who was at the same time so attractive, was incredibly alluring. She was a vision of power and beauty; I was transfixed.

Chad could wait, I'd meet up with him later. The Bro-Code could bear a bit of a delay where a girl like this was concerned. I didn't want to miss a moment of this bout, so I grabbed the closest vacant chair to the cage and felt my way into it without taking my eyes off the action unfolding before me. The blonde dynamo was raining a flurry of punches, elbows, kicks and knees on her hapless opponent.

Mesmerized, I silently observed the action and then gasped along with the rest of the crowd as the blonde fighter dropped her opponent with a left jab and a right cross, then leapt on top of her in a flash and applied a ruthless arm bar. But her opponent had no will to tap out, as she was already unconscious, so the referee stepped in and stopped the fight, declaring a win by knockout.

I let out the breath I didn't realize I'd been holding and soaked in the aftermath of the fight. She was a goddess! Her face flushed from the exertion, with strands of her long blonde hair escaping from the tight plaits and sweat glistening on her hard-muscled body, she was a wild, exciting woman. I knew I *had* to meet her, somehow. This had been the first fight on the night's card, a junior bout for young, up-and-coming fighters to get some experience in the cage. Clearly this girl had a big future. Her opponent perhaps by now had different thoughts about her outlook in the sport after her first competitive fight.

Finally, I regained my senses and checked my ticket for my reserved seat, which was way over the other side of the octagon and made my way over. Seeing three empty seats, I wondered where Chad was, but figured he would turn up soon enough, so settled in to wait for him as I watched the action on the next fight.

'Hey Tommy, good to see you man,' I heard Chad call out. As I turned to greet him, my eyes opened wide and my mouth dropped open in a look of stunned surprise as I saw who was next to Chad walking down the stairs. It was the blonde bombshell from the first fight!

'Dude, what is wrong with you? What's with the goofy look on your face? Close your mouth, I can see what you had for breakfast in there!' joked Chad. I quickly clamped my mouth shut and recovered some semblance of a normal expression.

'Tommy, this is my baby sister, Brittney. Brittney, this is Tommy, the big dope I was telling you about.'

'Oh, shut up Chad! I'm not your 'baby' sister anymore, I'm 18 for God's sake!' exclaimed Brittney with a smile and a solid punch into Chad's midsection.

'Ow!' complained Chad with a laugh. 'I have to remember to stop teasing you now that you're a lethal weapon! Man, you really wiped the floor with that girl, that was awesome.'

I could see the obvious love and camaraderie between the pair as they joked around and talked. Clearly, they were close.

Brittney was looking a bit the worse for wear, with a fat lip and a half-closed right eye that would no doubt develop into a full-blown shiner, but she didn't look fazed at all. I swear I had never seen a girl quite so hot before, even with a face that looked like it had come off second best after smashing into the back of a bus.

'Man, I've never heard you this quiet before Tommy, what the hell is going on with you?' Chad said as he turned to Brittney. 'Normally I can't get this big oaf to shut up and he hasn't said a word to you.'

I gave my head a quick shake and let out a big laugh, recovered my composure and said, 'G'day Brittney, great to meet you. Chad's told me lots about you. How was your gap year?'

'Oh, it was amazing! Six months in Thailand learning Muay Thai kick boxing and six months in Brazil learning Brazilian Jiu-Jitsu, it doesn't get any better than that!'

'Chad told me you were into MMA, but he didn't say how bloody good you are!' I said.

'Well thanks, I sure do appreciate that. I felt pretty damn good out there, I was really happy to do so well in my first cage fight,' responded Brittney. 'I can't believe I haven't met you after all this time. Chad's talked a lot about you, but we've never managed to get together. I'm really glad to finally meet you.'

'Okay you two, that's enough,' said Chad as he stepped in between us, defusing the sparks that he could see were starting to fly. Chad had told me before that he was extremely protective about his little sister and had always been awfully hard on potential boyfriends. We all sat down to watch the rest of the fight card and I was happy to be sitting next to Brittney with Chad on her other side. The conversation continued and I quickly realized there was much, much more to Brittney than the cage fighter I had seen when I first walked in. There was obviously a soft, fun side to her as well that I was already yearning to get to know better.

'So, have you decided where you're going to college yet?' I asked Brittney, hoping she would say Columbia.

'Looks like I'm going to California, baby! I got into a Sports Science course out there.'

'California? Geez, you couldn't get any further away from New York and still be in the States, could you?' I replied, trying to keep the disappointment out of my voice.

'Well, they're one of the top sports institutions in the country and I wanted to make sure I was learning from the best. I love competing in MMA, but I know I need more than just trying to be a pro fighter. Plus, I love all kinds of sports and want to make it my career. If I do make it in MMA, I'll only have a short career so need to have something else to do after that part of my life is done.'

'Sounds like you've got it all worked out,' I said, impressed. Brittney really was the whole package; tough, beautiful and smart. I was smitten.

After we dropped Brittney off on the way home from the fight night, Chad turned to me in the car and in a very serious tone said, 'Man, I love you like a brother, but you *cannot* date my sister. I saw what was going on tonight between you two and I need to put a stop to it right now. We're roommates and I've seen what you're like with the ladies, full of one-night stands and casual relationships. I know the string of beauties you've bedded, one after another and the constant booty calls. Good luck to you Tommy, that's cool and I've never judged you before, but I won't let you do that to my sister, not to Brittney.'

I was silent. I had nothing, no snappy one-liner, no funny comeback. As much as I hated to admit it, Chad had a point. I had built a well-founded reputation as the Chief Ladies Man on campus, a Casanova who was great for a bit of fun and a roll in the hay but not serious boyfriend material. I had never let any girl get close to me and didn't really know why. Was I scared to lose someone close to me so always kept everyone at a distance? I was just so used to being alone and independent that I found it difficult to let anyone get too close.

I wanted to protest to Chad and say that it would be different with Brittney, but how did I really know? Deep down I was certain that I had never felt this way about any girl I had met before, but Chad was my best friend and I had to respect his wishes. Plus, Brittney would soon be leaving to go to the other side of the country for the next four years and a long-distance relationship was just all too hard.

'Okay, fine. I understand. I'll stay away from Brittney,' I said, not realizing how difficult it would be to keep my promise.

CHAPTER 22

'Okay fellas, it's decision time. We're two years out from the Olympics and you two need to decide whether you're going to go for it or not,' stated our coach, as if he was talking about a walk down to the corner shop, not the pinnacle of sport on a world stage watched by billions of people.

Chad and I stared back at our coach, lost for words. 'Really?' we said in unison.

'Yes. I've seen an awful lot of fighters in my time and I know that you've both got the potential to be world beaters. Chad, pound for pound you're one of the best wrestlers I've seen for your age and Tommy, with your size and speed you're a beast on the Judo mat. I think you should both go for it, but you need to absolutely commit 100% for the next two years.'

Chad and I turned and looked at each other and said, 'Absolutely! We're in! Tell us what we need to do, and we'll do it.'

'First, we need to increase your training loads. You've been working hard, but we need to take it to a whole new level now. You need to stop drinking and partying and we need to more closely monitor your food intake. Coaching-wise we're okay with Chad because I'll be doing that, but Tommy, we need to get in a specialist coach to work more specifically on your Judo. You've been doing a lot of wrestling and Jujitsu, so we need to refocus on Judo. A friend of mine was an Olympic gold medallist in the heavyweight division, and he said he's willing to work with you three times a week, so that will be on top of your regular training.'

'Awesome, let's do it!' we chorused.

The head coach's radical experiment of bringing in exponents of Judo and Jujitsu into his wrestling team to train with his athletes had been a runaway success. Columbia had taken out the Ivy League wrestling championship the year after the program started.

We had been working hard before, but it was nothing compared to this. The days went past in a blur of early morning training, a full day of classes followed by more hours of training and then study back in the dorm room before collapsing into bed and then doing it all over again the next day. It was tough, but it was worth it, and we loved every minute of it. Being best friends and going through it together with a laser focus on our common goal made it bearable. When one of us was flagging, the other was always there to keep us going.

As we settled into our new routine, we both realized we had been ready to take the next step in our sporting lives. We'd had a couple of years enjoying college life to the full, partying hard, chasing girls and having fun, but now fresh into our twenties we were primed for the challenge.

One night late in our dorm room while we were kicking back and relaxing with a protein shake, I said seriously, 'Chad, I've come to a decision.'

'Sounds serious, Bro. Tell me.'

'I'm taking myself off the market.'

'Really? Tell me more.'

'I've decided to stop chasing girls. I'm going to set myself a challenge to be celibate for the next year.'

Chad burst into a fit of laughter. 'Bullshit! You're pulling my chain.'

'I'm serious, mate. I reckon I need something like this to shake me out of my habit of one-night stands and casual sex. I need to prove to myself that I can do it and hold out for something more meaningful. Plus, I want to focus on my Judo and nothing else right now.'

'Dude, there is no goddamn *way* you will be able to pull that off. You'll be pulling something else off, that's for sure. You won't last a month! In the last two years, what's the longest dry spell you've had?'

'Hmmm... good question. I haven't really thought this through in that much detail.' With a furrowed brow, I was deep in thought, counting on fingers and mumbling to myself, then came to an answer.

'Shit. I don't think I've gone longer than a week without a root in all that time. That's a lot of women! No wonder you wouldn't let me date your sister!'

'See? I told you man, there's no way you'll be able to do it. In fact, let's make it interesting. I'm so confident you won't be able to do it, I'm willing to make a bet on it. A big one.' After a long pause, he said, 'I've got it! I tell you what, if you can pull it off, I'll let you date Brittney. But if you can't finish the job, you never get to go out with her. Ever.'

'You're on! Agreed,' I responded quickly, before either of us could change our mind. I stuck out my hand and we shook long and hard on the sudden, unexpected deal.

The first month was the hardest. Booty call after booty call came through to my phone and I turned them all down. The first few weren't too difficult but after a while I would look longingly at my phone as my favourite girls came up on Caller ID. The abstinence was really starting to hurt. The news spread quickly, because apparently my cohort of lovelies were known to chat among themselves about me and my prowess in the sack. Somehow the news of my celibacy commitment made me even more alluring and they redoubled their efforts to break me. Seems that my girls loved a challenge.

All sorts of promises of sexual fun and glory were made to me at all times of the day and night. In the end it got so bad that I changed my phone number, sharing it only with Chad and Mum.

My three points of availability had been my phone, my nights out on the town and around on campus. With the first two points now out of action, the sexual guerrilla warfare took to the campus. As time went by, news of my continued commitment to the challenge spread to women even outside my course and normal social circle, resulting in me being accosted by a bevy of lovelies at the most random of times, all of which I rebuffed with a rueful thank you.

The situation got so problematic that I even got a couple of T-shirts printed up with big, bold lettering stating, *Sorry Ladies, but I'm off the market*. Man did that backfire! It stirred up an even greater frenzy of renewed efforts by my female pursuers. After just a few outings, the printed T-shirts were retired.

The pursuit gradually slowed and finally stopped after a few months as the chasers realized that I was resolute in my commitment to my mission. Sad at the waste of my hunk status, I heard through the grapevine that some girls secretly admired my quest, with some of them rethinking their position on me not being boyfriend material.

CHAPTER 23

Well, the first year of my Olympic training was over, along with my successfully completed celibacy vow. Time for review. The Olympics were looming on the horizon like Mount Everest. Chad and I had been training like men possessed and were in the absolute peak of fitness and ability. Nobody on the team could even come close to us on the mat, we'd been honing our skills, focusing on the one-percenters that make all the difference, that separate the merely excellent from the truly elite.

Our coaches were pleased with our progress and confident we'd both be highly competitive against the best in the world at the Olympics. They'd mapped out the next 12 months of our training regime and competitions and now we just had to work the plan.

Judo: tick. Now, to other matters. 'Hey Chad, it's time, man.'

'Time for what, Tommy?'

'Tomorrow it'll be one year. 365 days without a root. Mission accomplished; I've cured myself of casual sex. You know what this means don't you? Remember our agreement?'

'Hmmm… I was wondering when you were going to bring that up! Suddenly I regret ever making that deal. Well, I can hardly go back on it now, can I? Although you do realize it's not up to me, don't you? Brittney's a big girl, strong willed and independent and makes up her own mind about who she dates. You're on your own there, pal. So, what's your plan?'

'She'll be coming home for Thanksgiving soon, right? I thought I'd make sure I'm around at your place and launch the charm offensive.'

'Ha! Offensive is right. You'll turn her off in no time.'

'Don't you worry about that Chad, just leave it to old Tommy here,' I said, sounding more confident than I felt.

Finally, Thanksgiving arrived. I'd never been so happy about the arrival of that American holiday, which had never meant anything to me before. This was harder than I thought – the last few days had been killing me. Brittney was special, not like the other casual relationships I'd had. I care deeply for her, so it was disturbing my mojo, disrupting my usual game. Had I lost the ability to be smooth and charming after so long out of the saddle? I hadn't been this nervous about a girl since before my first time with sweet Candy. I felt like a goddamn scared little teenager again.

I didn't realize how hard I'd fallen for Brittney until the prospect of us being together, or much worse, *not* being together, had been on my mind. What if she doesn't like me? What if she doesn't want to be with me? What if she already has a boyfriend? What if she says yes, but there's no spark between us? All these damn questions were making my head spin.

'Happy Thanksgiving!' Brittney shouted to Chad as she ran through the airport gate and into Chad's arms with a huge embrace. 'Great to see you, Bro. How's things?'

'Awesome, Brittney. Training's going well, Coach is happy and I'm getting better, fitter and stronger every day. I'm loving it! How about you?'

'Fantastic! I loooooove California, the lifestyle is amazing, the beaches rock and the weather is *epic*. School's great, I'm loving my course, learning heaps and have made loads of cool new friends. And my fighting's going well too; getting better all the time, loving training and getting a few small bouts in here and there.'

Brittney extracted herself from Chad's embrace and glanced over at me. I felt different and she seemed to sense something had changed too, somehow, or was I just imagining it? There was a slight pause in the conversation as she looked up at me, then smiled and said in her best terrible Australian accent, 'Well g'day mate. What's the matter? Cat got your tongue?' God, she is so beautiful.

'Um, uh, h-h-hi Brittney,' I stammered like a fool. Jesus Christ, I don't think I've ever felt as nervous as I do right now. Snap out of it, dickhead!

'Since when have you started stuttering, you big oaf? Come over here and give me a Thanksgiving hug.'

My legs felt like jelly as I took the two steps over to her and bent way down to give her a hug. A shot like electricity went through me as my cheek touched hers and then I felt her breath on my neck while she gave me a big squeeze, holding it longer than necessary. My heart jumped a couple of beats as she let me go and we looked deep into each other's eyes as we pulled away. So much for no spark! Quick, bring out the tinder and the kindling and let's fan those flames! Maybe she does like me.

'It's… nice to see you again Tommy, it's been months. You seem… different somehow,' said Brittney, appearing surprised and disconcerted at what had just happened.

'Yeah, I've been working hard on my handsomeness and it's finally paying off,' I said, with one of my best smiles.

'Still as humble as ever, I see.'

'Ah, you have to work with what you've been given.'

'I hate to interrupt you two,' chimed in Chad. 'But I should get you home to see Mom and get this holiday season started.'

We grabbed Brittney's bags and headed out to the car. This was going better than I could have hoped and I was starting to relax a bit now, thank Christ.

'Shotgun!' called Brittney with a laugh.

'Damn it! You beat me to it, you sneak. I'm a bit off my game.' I opened the front door of Chad's sporty but tiny two door coupe and squeezed myself into the back seat, head hunched down and legs stretched sideways across the seat. 'I feel like some sort of giant pretzel!

I hope you two are nice and comfortable in the front seats.'

As Chad pulled out into traffic for the drive home, I thought I should keep the conversation flowing. 'So, how long are you staying on this trip Brittney? Do you have much planned?'

'I'm here for a week. Not much planned, just chilling with my gal pals and spending some time with Mom and Chad. What about you?'

'Well, as usual I can't afford a trip back home and Mum can't make it out here, so I'm kind of at a loose end. I'll just be hanging out, doing some training, staying around the dorm.'

'What? You can't spend Thanksgiving all on your own! You *have* to come and spend the weekend with us. Did you ask him Chad, you slacker?'

'Yes, I told him he could spend Thanksgiving with us, but he wasn't sure if he'd be intruding.'

'Well that's stupid, Tommy, it's settled. You'll spend the holiday with us. Mom won't mind, she likes you; I've seen her checking you out before when you're wandering around with your shirt off on a hot day!' she said with her outrageous laugh that I adored.

'What? Stop it, you're making me blush,' I said, feeling the heat rising to my face.

'Oh, don't get all shy on me now Tommy, I haven't seen that side of you before.'

I settled into the banter as it continued throughout the drive home, feeling more comfortable and hopeful as time went by. I had known Brittney for quite a while but hadn't spent much time with her because she'd been away at college. She seemed so much more independent and grown up now and somehow even hotter than when I had first met her.

Chad parked the car and we made our way up to Amy's apartment and knocked on the door. As Amy swung the door open, Brittney squealed, 'Hi Mom, it's so good to see you!' as she wrapped her in a big hug. I love Brittney's enthusiasm and her energy; she's always so *on*.

'Oh, Brittney, I've missed you so much, it's really hard now with neither of you living at home anymore and me rattling around in this huge apartment all on my own. But it's so good to see you both. Hello, Chad darling,' said Amy as she gave her son a warm hug. Then it was my turn. I really liked spending time with Amy and even though I knew it was wrong to think of my best friend's mother like this, Amy was super-hot. A leggy blonde with big boobs and still not yet forty years old, she was an exceedingly attractive package and independently wealthy into the bargain. I couldn't understand why she was still single. She flashed her brilliant green eyes and a big white smile at me and reached up to give me a hug. Finding it hard not to look down her top from my significant height advantage, I bent down and she gave me a warm hug. As attractive as she was, I knew I would never ever go there. It was hard enough contemplating dating my best friend's sister, let alone his mother – that was just too weird!

'Hello Tommy, it's wonderful to see you again, it's been way too long since you've shared a family meal with us. Are you joining us for Thanksgiving this year?'

'Well, if it's not too much trouble, that would be a bloody ripper!'

'Hmmm… Tommy, you still confuse me with your Ossie slang. Is that a good thing or a bad thing and a yes or a no?' said Amy, shaking her head.

'Sorry, I still manage to confuse people, especially when I get excited. 'Bloody ripper' is most definitely a good thing and yes, I would love to join you all for Thanksgiving. Thank you so much for looking out for a poor holiday orphan.'

'Well, any friend of Chad's is welcome in our home, especially when they're as cute as you are!' said Amy with a wink.

'Mom! Stop it, you're making him blush! Tommy, that's twice in the last hour, what is going on with you today?' teased Brittney as she grabbed my arm.

Then Chad stepped in and saved me as he said, 'The women in this family seem to be making him nervous, that's what. Let's cut it out now. Tommy, let's get some drinks organized.'

The night rolled on with plenty of drinks, good food and great company until we all fell into bed at midnight, tired and happy. I was tossing and turning, struggling to sleep knowing that Brittney was in bed just down the hall. But this wasn't just another conquest. I needed to pace myself, take my time and not rush things. There were another two days in close quarters with Brittney, I just needed to let nature run its course.

The next day dawned a crisp, cold but sunny morning on Thanksgiving Day. I needed to work off some excess energy so decided to go for a run and was overjoyed when Brittney said she'd come along, but then not quite so happy when Chad said he would come too. But at least we were together and enjoyed a good workout.

The day progressed with the whole shebang of a ridiculously huge roast turkey with all the trimmings and lots of fun and games. Amy and Chad had done most of the cooking, so after the huge meal, Brittney and I volunteered to do the dishes and banished Amy and Chad into the lounge room to chill out.

We put some music on and attacked the disaster area formerly known as the kitchen with gusto, happy to be in each other's company and sharing the chore.

Trying to work out how to ask the question to which I was so desperate to know the answer, but trying not to sound like it, I casually asked, 'So, it sounds like college is going well for you and you've got a good group of friends there. Is there anyone especially close?'

Seeing through my pathetically obvious question in an instant, Brittney laughed and said, 'Tommy, if you want to know if I have a boyfriend, just ask me!'

Feeling sheepish but relieved at the same time, I said, 'Well, do you?'

I don't think I've ever been so relieved to hear a 'no' in my life when she delivered those magical two letters to me.

'Okay, good to know, thanks,' I said with a smile. 'Well, these dishes aren't going to do themselves, let's get back to it.'

As the dishes task continued, I found myself unconsciously moving to the music as per my usual habit, without even being aware of it until I heard Brittney say, 'You got some moves there, Mister. I didn't expect a big guy like you to actually have rhythm and be able to move like that.'

'You ain't seen nothin' yet Brittney. Wait until you get me on a real dance floor with some real music. Or maybe even up on a stage,' I responded with a wink.

I could tell she was interested in where this was going, especially when she said, 'Well, let's put on some real music and see what you've got right now.'

'Bring it on, I'm up for that if you are,' I replied. I'd never been out with Brittney and never seen her dance, so I wasn't sure if she had any moves, but was certainly keen to find out. She went over to the music player and selected her dance tracks playlist and got some beats going. I liked where this was headed!

As the music beat ramped up a notch, I flung away the tea towel and started busting a few moves. 'Nice work Tommy, you *have* got some groove,' said Brittney as she came over and joined in. We got closer and closer, moving together with the music and getting lost in each other's eyes and bodies. I put my arms around her waist and pulled her in towards me, still gyrating with the music. She was getting into it as much as I was, so I took a chance and leaned in, getting closer and closer, slowly moving my mouth towards hers. She didn't pull away, so I kept moving in, slower and slower, still moving in time with the music until I finally paused with my lips almost touching hers, in a moment of delicious anticipation, waiting for her to take the final step.

After what seemed like an age, Brittney finally closed the gap, bringing her lips to mine in the most exciting and wonderful kiss I'd ever experienced. As her lips parted and our tongues explored each other, I felt a surge in my groin that suddenly developed into an ache that hadn't been released for more than a year. The sweet joy of this moment was indescribable. The torch that I'd been carrying ever since that first moment I had seen Brittney fighting in the octagon had now magnified itself into a goddamn bonfire!

Finally, we parted lips and Brittney looked up at me through eyes wide with desire, face flushed and mouth slightly parted and said, 'Jesus, Tommy, what took you so long? I've been waiting for you to let me know how you feel since that first time we met! I've been hot for you since I first laid eyes on you.'

'I'm sorry Brit, but I didn't know how you felt and Chad's my best mate and then you went away to college, so it just seemed like something always got in the way. I've wanted you so much ever since the first time I saw you pounding that chick in the ring, you were just so awesome.'

'Well, I've been waiting a long time for you to make a move and I'm glad you did, because that was the most amazing kiss I've ever had. From what I hear, you haven't seen too much action in the bedroom lately, so you must be feeling pretty desperate about now!' she said with a laugh.

'What? Oh shit, I can't believe Chad bloody told you about that, the bastard!'

'No, don't worry, it wasn't Chad, so don't blame him. I have my sources; I've had one of my besties at Columbia keeping tabs on you. I was worried when I heard what a man-whore you were, but I've got to say I was impressed when I heard about your celibacy vow and was hoping like hell you would make it,' she said and then reached up for another kiss.

'What the hell? Looks like I can't leave you two alone for a minute! Having fun *doing the dishes* are we?' chuckled Chad as he walked into the kitchen. As we pulled away from our clinch, I looked over at Chad, hoping he would be okay with this latest development, but he seemed fine. He went over and grabbed a drink from the fridge and said, 'So what now? How's this going to work?'

'Geez, calm down Bro, we only just had our first kiss, it's not like we're going to get married tomorrow. Let's just see how things develop, shall we?' replied Brittney with a laugh.

And develop they did. Brit and I were joined at the hip for the rest of her week in New York, knowing we were on borrowed time. Two days after our first kiss, we shared a bed together for the first time. One of Brittney's friends had a tiny apartment in the city and had gone home to her family for Thanksgiving, leaving a key with Brit in case she wanted some time on her own. I cooked Brittney an Aussie roast lamb dinner with mint sauce and all the trimmings, followed by pavlova for dessert. She was suitably impressed, and we revelled in each other's company, alone together for the first time.

Lots of talking, laughing, a few drinks and some cozy time on the couch soon led to me carrying Brit over to the bed in the corner of the little apartment. For the very first time in my life I made love with a woman, instead of just having sex. It was an incredibly intimate experience that made every previous casual conquest pale into insignificance. I was hooked, totally and completely head over heels for this girl.

Saying goodbye felt like the hardest thing I had ever done, harder even than saying goodbye to my mum in Australia. That's when it suddenly dawned on me that this is what love feels like! That gut-wrenching feeling when you know you must farewell someone but just can't bear the thought of not seeing them for what feels like an eternity.

'Oh Tommy, I can't believe I have to go *already*,' moaned Brittney through tear-filled eyes as she looked up at me and the tears that were rolling down my own cheeks.

'I know Brit, it's not fair! I waited so long to be with you and now you're leaving already, it's too soon!' I picked her up and gave her a huge hug that squeezed the air out of her lungs and we shared one final urgent kiss, mashing our lips together until it hurt, trying to fill each other up and get as close as possible while still standing up.

'Okay, you'd better go now, you don't want to miss your plane. Have a good flight and call me as soon as you land!' I sent her on her way with a slap on her gorgeous bum in her tight blue jeans and watched her delightful wiggle as she walked away from me, looking back over her shoulder and waving.

Man, I really got lucky here, I cannot believe this week happened! The feelings washing over me were the most powerful I'd ever experienced. I had literally never felt this way about a girl before. I didn't know whether to smile, cry, laugh or chase after her and plead with her not to go, so I just stood there rooted to the spot with a dopey look on my face and waved goodbye to the girl that had well and truly captured my heart, wrapped it up and taken it on the plane with her.

I came to the realization that ever since Dad had died nine years before, I had built a wall around my heart and my feelings, hiding behind a façade of casual relationships that never went any deeper than the surface, protecting myself by not letting anyone get too close. But now that I had let Brittney in through my hard shell into my soft inner core, I realized that life is for living to the full, not for hiding away. I resolved then to be completely open to this new experience with Brittney and to give us every chance of building something special and long-lasting together.

She turned one final time as she walked onto the plane, blowing me a kiss as she boarded. In one of those cheesy moments lifted from a movie, I caught it in my outstretched right hand, brought it to my lips and then blew her a kiss of my own and we both laughed at our corny antics.

The following months flew by in a blur as Brittney and I managed our long-distance relationship, with long phone calls, texts, video chats and holiday visits. We loved every minute we spent together, and our relationship grew stronger every day. Mixed in with this were studies in my final year of film school and my last months of training in the lead-up to the Olympics. It was total chaos, but I loved it. My training was going well, I was really hitting my peak, winning all my bouts and qualifying in the trials. Everything was on track as we prepared for the Olympics.

PART 4 - UKRAINE AND ROMANIA

CHAPTER 24

The noise in the control room was deafening!

The bleary-eyed technicians tried to function despite the cacophony of sirens wailing and warning buzzers blaring, as just about every sensor in Reactor 4 at the Chernobyl Nuclear Power Plant went haywire. What started out on the day shift as a planned experiment to test a new safety feature, dragged through the evening and into the night as problem after problem and operator error after operator error combined to create a highly unstable situation in the reactor core. The automatic system that activated the control rods, a critical safety feature of the plant, was disabled and nearly all the control rods were manually removed, leaving the reactor core dangerously susceptible to an out-of-control chain reaction.

By the time the experiment was ready to run, the nuclear reactor was highly unstable, and the experiment was a disastrous failure, triggering an emergency shutdown procedure. What happened next caught the inexperienced night shift operators completely unaware; the graphite tipped control rods descended into the reactor core to interrupt the feedback loop and stall the impending chain reaction, but they instead triggered a catastrophic chain of events. The reactor core immediately created a huge power spike that superheated the cooling water, generating a massive volume of steam so desperate to escape that it exploded, destroying the reactor casing and tearing off the 2,000 ton upper plate, blasting it through the roof of the reactor building.

Just a few seconds after the first reactor explosion, an even larger explosion occurred. This mercifully stopped the chain reaction but caused more damage to the reactor enclosure and launched superheated lumps of radioactive graphite into the air and exposed the reactor core.

The reactor fire raged out of control and fire fighters and emergency workers raced into the maelstrom of certain death from sources seen and unseen. The blazing heat of the inferno was an obvious risk familiar to the fire fighters, but the invisible deadly blast of radiation was a ruthless killer, slower than fire but just as certain. The radiation levels were so severe inside the building that a fatal dose of radiation was delivered in little more than a minute.

The fire and explosion spewed nuclear fuel and deadly radioactive waste into the air, creating a radioactive cloud that spread over Ukraine, its neighbours and great swathes of Europe. Four hundred times more radioactive material was released from the Chernobyl reactor than from the atomic bombing of Hiroshima.

The fire inside the reactor core blazed for weeks, eventually being extinguished using helicopters dropping more than 5,000 tons of boric acid, clay, sand and lead onto the flaming reactor. The basement below the reactor became a collection point for the deadly waste material, with the smouldering nuclear fuel and other material superheated at more than 1,200 degrees mixing with molten concrete to create corium – radioactive lava.

Eight months later, the monumental task of sealing off the reactor was finally complete. More than 250,000 workers were involved in the clean-up, under incredibly arduous and dangerous conditions. The whole reactor was encased in a concrete sarcophagus, sealing it off from the outside world.

At the completion of the clean-up, a team of nuclear scientists entered the reactor building to investigate the high levels of heat still emanating from the reactor core. Eventually they found the source, which they called the Elephant's Foot, an intensely radioactive pile more than two metres wide and weighing hundreds of tons, formed by the radioactive lava flow. The mass of complex radioactive crystals they discovered was named *Chernobylite*.

The worst nuclear accident in history, Chernobyl was the first Level 7: Major Accident nuclear event, which directly killed more than 50 people, caused an estimated 4,000 cancer victims and triggered the evacuation of the town of Chernobyl and the nearby city of Propyat in Ukraine.

An exclusion zone with a 30-kilometre radius was established to become the *Chernobyl Nuclear Power Plant Zone of Alienation*, with restrictions on public access and habitation due to the high levels of radioactivity.

After the Chernobyl disaster, the remaining three nuclear reactors at the power plant continued to operate, progressively being decommissioned until the generators finally fell silent many years later.

Decades after the meltdown, the Chernobylite in the basement of Reactor 4 remained untouched, still emitting intense heat and deadly radiation.

CHAPTER 25

'Hiroto, it's great to see you again,' called the young medical student as the Japanese academic entered the busy restaurant. 'Please, have a seat. I'm glad you could fit our dinner into your busy schedule.'

The two men shared a common educational institution, both being stationed at the Taras Shevchenko National University of Kyiv in Ukraine.

With a polite bow to his dinner companion before taking his seat, Hiroto replied, 'It is my pleasure to see you once more, Dmitri before I leave to return home to Japan. My sabbatical visit to the Faculty of Philosophy has been most illuminating. It is truly one of the most historic educational institutions in the world and I feel very privileged to have furthered my research in its halls. I am sorry I must leave so soon.'

'Well, at least we have one more opportunity for a traditional Ukrainian meal before you depart and to celebrate our friendship in the three months of your posting. I think it was lucky for us both that we met at the faculty party so early in your stay in Kiev.'

'Agreed. And *Kanpai* to our continued friendship in the future,' said Hiroto as the somewhat unlikely pair raised their glasses in toast.

The evening passed with diverse conversation on a range of topics, delicious food and fine wine until it was time to depart. The usual argument over who would pick up the bill ensued, with the local Dmitri insisting on paying for Hiroto's farewell dinner. As Dmitri paid the restaurant owner, he heard the front door of the restaurant open and close and smiled as he figured Hiroto, as per his usual habit, had stepped out to enjoy the crisp night air.

The long-haul trucker rounded the bend, slewing his machine from side to side as he fought off the exhaustion that was the inevitable result of his 14 hours of driving in demanding conditions on rough Russian country roads. The quiet bliss of sleep finally enveloped the driver as he rounded the turn but did not straighten up, sending 40 tons of steel careering towards the restaurant at high speed.

Hiroto was oblivious to the wheeled behemoth bearing down on him as he gazed up at Ukraine's night sky, which seemed so different to that of his homeland. Finally, his attention was wrenched from the sky as the truck mounted the curb, suddenly jolting the driver awake, who reacted instantly with a sharp turn of the wheel. Thankfully, this manoeuvre saved the restaurant and its occupants, but unfortunately did not help Hiroto.

The corner of the enormous steel bull bar mounted on the front of the Russian beast struck the slight Japanese man a glancing blow in the upper body, instantly breaking his collarbone, wrenching his shoulder from its socket, crushing his windpipe and knocking him unconscious. The limp body was flung away from the impact like a spinning top. The truck and its now suddenly very awake driver roared off into the night, never to be seen again.

The young medical student came tearing out of the restaurant, fearing for his friend's life in all the commotion. He quickly evaluated the scene and his years of training took over. Racing to his car in the parking lot, he grabbed his medical bag and returned to the unconscious body lying on the pavement in front of the restaurant, as some of the patrons came out to see what all the disturbance was about.

A quick examination revealed that the crushed windpipe represented the biggest risk to his Japanese friend, who was not getting any air into his lungs and would soon expire without major intervention. After a few seconds of deliberation, Dmitri decided that an emergency tracheotomy was required. He pulled a surgical scalpel out of his bag and extracted it from its sterile wrapping. Quickly and expertly he cut a hole in the man's throat, below the crush site. He then inserted a plastic tube into the incision and breathed into the tube with two quick breaths.

Relieved to see Hiroto's chest rise and fall firstly with his help and then on his own, Dmitri was satisfied that the breathing situation was under control. As he looked up, he became aware of the small crowd that had gathered around him and registered that someone had already called for an ambulance. Dmitri continued his examination and was content to find no other life-threatening injuries. Hiroto was extremely fortunate that he was dining with someone who had almost completed his medical degree and was only a few small steps away from becoming a practicing doctor. Without that good fortune, Hiroto would have died on a cold Kiev street that night outside the restaurant.

Fifteen minutes later, with a blaring of sirens and flashing of lights, the ambulance pulled up to the curb and bundled Hiroto into the back, accompanied by Dmitri, who wanted to ensure that his patient received the best possible care. He stayed with him every step of the way, through emergency, admission, operation and recovery.

When Hiroto finally woke up, he saw Dmitri sleeping in a chair beside his bed, looking unkempt and dishevelled. Dmitri stirred when a nurse came in to check on Hiroto, having registered his change in vital signs.

Hiroto signalled he wanted to speak but the bandages around his neck and the tube down his throat proved an insurmountable hurdle for his vocal cords to overcome. With questioning eyes, he looked at Dmitri, clearly searching for an explanation.

Dmitri said, 'You're okay Hiroto. You were hit by a large truck, moving fast, when you were on the footpath outside the restaurant. The driver mounted the curb, clipped you on your side and flung you clear. You're lucky to be alive. Just a few more inches towards the middle and you'd be dead for sure.'

Hiroto nodded in understanding, so Dmitri continued his

explanation. 'You have a broken collarbone and had a dislocated shoulder, which has now been reset. The worst injury was your crushed windpipe. I had to do an emergency tracheotomy out front of the restaurant to get you breathing again, then we operated on your trachea to repair it. Right now, your body is still getting over the trauma, so you're breathing through a tube in your throat. Before too long, you'll be able to breathe again normally, but until then there is no chance of speaking, so don't even try.'

Hiroto blinked his eyes in thanks to Dmitri and gave a slight bow of his head before he grimaced in pain. Dmitri was glad to see his friend conscious again and promised to check in on him regularly. He excused himself to go and collect his car from the restaurant and get home for some real sleep in an actual horizontal position, followed by a shower and a good meal. He was exhausted after the long ordeal but happy that he had been there to save Hiroto's life.

Days later, Dmitri visited a nervous Hiroto as the time came to remove the tubes from his throat that had been providing air to his lungs. Since the swelling had gone down and his throat had continued to heal, the tubes were slowly extracted from the patient with a gurgle and a gasp, with attentive doctors and nurses ready to act if he couldn't breathe on his own. Thankfully, they were an unneeded precaution as Hiroto drew his first breath from his mouth down into his lungs and back out again. Breathing was looking good but speaking would have to wait some more.

Finally, the day came when Hiroto had approval from the medicos to try for some speech. Dmitri on his surgical rounds arrived to check on his favourite patient and smiled as he saw Hiroto standing and offering him a deep bow when he entered the room. 'Hi Hiroto,' said Dmitri, 'you're looking well. Are you ready for your speech test? Just nod if you are, don't say anything yet.'

Hiroto nodded in return and Dmitri progressed with his instructions. 'Okay, we're just looking for a soft whisper to start with. It will be rough, raspy and sore, but that will improve over time, so don't worry if it's difficult to start with, it will be a long process. When you're ready, just softly whisper one word, anything you like.'

'Giri,' croaked Hiroto in a soft voice, almost too low to hear. It sounded rough, but clear enough.

'Excellent! That's wonderful Hiroto, a very good sign. Let's just leave it at that for now, we don't want to overdo it. You can talk some more tomorrow. I'd better get back to my surgical rounds. See you later.'

Curious about the meaning of the word that Hiroto had chosen to utter, Dmitri at home that night looked up 'Giri' and discovered it represented a traditional Japanese value describing one's sense of duty or burden of obligation that one man has to another. Clearly, Hiroto felt he owed Dmitri his life.

The day of Hiroto's discharge arrived; Dmitri visited for the final time and said, 'Well, goodbye my friend, it is time for you to leave the hospital and Ukraine, for you to return to Japan. It has been a pleasure having you as my friend and I look forward to many more conversations with you in the future. I'm glad you have recovered your voice so well; it is such an important part of your academic life.'

In a voice still somewhat croaky and changed forever in tonality by the trauma, Hiroto replied, 'Thank you, my friend, for saving my life. I will be forever in your debt. Anytime you ever need something, do not hesitate to ask me, no matter how big or how small. I will be ready to do whatever is in my power to repay the life debt that I owe you.'

'Thank you Hiroto, I appreciate you saying that, but it is truly not necessary. I am studying to be a doctor and I will take the oath to save people's lives with no expectation or obligation in return.'

'I know, but it means everything to me. It would be my honour to serve you.'

CHAPTER 26

War is the very definition of Hell on Earth for many people, but for some, it represents opportunity. There are a select few, a special breed who thrive on the chaos and mayhem of conflict and make money in the process. Vladimir found his niche in warmongering, making his mark and expanding his fortune, reach and reputation in a string of conflicts, including the Chechen Wars in his very own backyard.

Supplying weapons and military paraphernalia to rebels and separatists the world over, Vladimir was constantly building his wealth and expanding his power base. He became an arms dealer in the true sense of the word, supplying a range of weapons to insurgents across the globe. Humans seemed to have an insatiable thirst for conflict and there were always battles of one description or another going on somewhere in the world, which Vladimir was only too willing to supply.

Vladimir saw opportunity on his borders in the Ukrainian Crisis, which became a flashpoint for renewed East/West tensions invoking memories of the Cold War. Ukraine was straining at the yoke of Russian rule and interference in their affairs; Vladimir saw these escalating tensions and wanted to be at the heart of the chaos. He had been working on plans for a bold new weapon and, knowing the time was right, had moved his headquarters from Chechnya to Kiev, the capital of Ukraine and only a short drive to Chernobyl.

Once established in Ukraine, Vladimir visited his Chernobyl base for the first time to check on the progress of his latest weapon. Greeting his man on the scene, Vladimir said, 'Hello Aleksei, it's good to see you again. Give me a full briefing and tell me the latest news from your doctor; is my chief scientist and resident genius going to survive long enough to see his plan through to the end?'

His gaunt, precise, lab-coated technician replied, 'They've given me only three months to live, so we need to accelerate the program if I'm going to see results.'

'Only three months? I'm sorry to hear that, Brother. Can we do it?'

'Yes, I think we can achieve our goal before the cancer eats away so much of my brain that it kills me,' replied Aleksei.

The technician proceeded with his briefing, explaining to Vladimir how the extraction of the Chernobylite was progressing; a team of four workers masquerading as clean-up crew had stationed themselves close to Reactor Number Four, gained access inside the sarcophagus in the main hall and set their robots to work beneath the reactor core. Their heavily modified bomb disposal robots were fitted with radiation shielding and tungsten drill coring attachments and were proving effective in extracting Chernobylite from the Elephant's Foot.

They were now mining a full load of radioactive material in the robots' lead-lined storage chambers every three days and transferring that back to their processing plant. The old military facility in the heart of the exclusion zone was ideal; the portable storage chambers were removed from the extraction robots and placed on the automated assembly line. The Chernobylite was retrieved from the chamber, ground up using stone wheels and then the crystalline powder was mixed with a resin and set into tiny slivers that emitted enough radiation to kill a man from the inside in less than a week.

Once Aleksei had completed his briefing, Vladimir said, 'It's lucky you know the power plant so well after spending so long working there in your younger engineering days, my friend. Except, of course it's not so fortunate that the plant dosed you with enough radiation to give you brain cancer.'

'Yes, and now it's time to take revenge on Mother Russia for what they did to me and my beautiful Ukraine when they screwed everything up at Chernobyl. It's time for those bastards to pay for the carnage they rained down on my homeland!'

For Aleksei, the highly radioactive Chernobylite was the perfect symbol of the worst that Russia had done to his beautiful country when the Chernobyl nuclear reactor was destroyed. In his eyes, Russia had nearly killed his motherland, poisoning the earth, the water and the food and was still slowly killing thousands of people, including him.

Vladimir now turned his attention to his faithful general and weapons master, Borys; an ex-member of the Spetsnaz GRU, the feared Russian special forces unit. An enormous individual, Borys had a sick brutality so severe, it had gotten him kicked out of an organization that generally welcomed such traits. An expert in both armed and unarmed combat, he was a highly trained killer with no conscience, which made him a uniquely qualified enforcer who was feared by all inside Vladimir's criminal organization. Borys' reputation outside of Vladimir's Russian Mafia cell was formidable and growing.

'Over to you now, Borys. How are you progressing with development of the ammunition casing and the pistol to deliver the Chernobylite to the victim?' asked Vladimir.

'The development of the gun is almost complete; we are now ready for trials,' responded Borys. 'The guns are simple; they are made of plastic and are a hybrid of paintball guns, BB guns and the air guns designed for tranquilizer darts. They use a powerful manual compression technique using a revolutionary hand pumping action. The gun is basically silent, with no explosion, just a whoosh of air that most people wouldn't notice unless they are close to the shooter.'

'Excellent,' said Vladimir. 'What about the chances of detection?'

'Being high strength plastic with no metal components, the guns are immune to metal detectors and won't set off weapon scanners,' said Borys. 'If the authorities find one of these guns on a person, they feel so small and light they would think it is just a toy, nothing serious.'

'Well, it sounds like the pistol is okay. What about the ammunition?'

'Okay, here's where it gets a bit more difficult. We've spent a long time developing the ammunition, but I think we're just about there. It needs to be small enough and sharp enough to pierce the skin but without making so much of an impact that the target realizes they've been shot. About the worst anyone can tolerate without asking too many questions is something like a bee sting. They swat it away, rub the entry wound and think there is nothing too serious. We also need to protect the shooter by having enough radiation shielding around the Chernobylite sliver. We've developed a hard bio-soluble plastic that can be sharpened to a fine point, like a tiny dart.'

'Do you have a prototype I can look at?' asked Vladimir, intensely interested in this latest development and so excited that all his years of planning and putting the right team together was coming to fruition.

'Yes, I have a sample pistol and bullet here to show you,' said Borys as he handed them over to Vladimir. As he took the pistol, Vladimir was surprised at how light the small pistol was and how innocuous it looked, like a toy, with no indication of the deadly cargo destined for its firing chamber. He was fascinated by the deadly Chernobylite sliver encased in its bio-soluble plastic; he held the tiny dart up to the light and admired the glistening black and yellow core through the clear protective housing. It was so light he could hardly feel the weight as he held it delicately between his finger and thumb.

'Pass me the Geiger counter Borys, I want to check the levels,' said Vladimir. He waved the detector across his hand but there was no response other than the usual background radiation. Satisfied, he handed the probe back to Borys and said, 'The shielding is good. But are you sure this will work? It's so light; it doesn't seem like it can fly through the air fast enough and straight enough to pierce the skin.'

'Yes, we've done many trials on pigs and we're confident we have the right balance between weight, sharpness and accuracy. The problem is the range. Because the dart is so light, we must be quite close to the target, no more than 15 metres away, or the accuracy drops off too much. The plastics engineer did a great job with the outer casing, we can hone the point to extreme sharpness, almost like a syringe. And the bio-solubility is outstanding, the casing starts to break down after only six hours in the body, exposing the highly radioactive core of the Chernobylite sliver.'

'What about the sliver? It looks so tiny, is it enough to kill a man?'

'From the inside, definitely. From the outside, no. The time for death to occur depends on where the sliver is ingested and where it goes once it gets inside the body, plus the size and health of the target. If the sliver sits in the muscle below the skin, it could take up to a week to kill. But if it makes its way into the bloodstream and then lodges in a vital organ somewhere like the heart, lungs, liver, or kidneys, it will be much faster, maybe three days or so. Wherever it ends up, the sliver poisons the victim with deadly radiation.'

'Great work brothers, we are certainly on track. Our buyers are going to be pleased with these developments and will pay top dollar for what we produce. Are we ready to demonstrate the weapon?'

'Of course, Vladimir,' responded his weapons master. He signalled to one of the assistants who had been standing in the background with a juvenile pig on a leash, weighing in at around 70 kilograms, close to that of the average human.

Borys wandered over to the unfortunate swine and painted a small target on its side, then paced 15 metres to Vladimir, who was holding the pistol loaded with its lethal cargo. Vladimir cocked the pistol by pulling back on the air charging lever, took aim and gently squeezed the trigger. With only a slight whoosh of escaping air, almost no trace of a recoil and a projectile that was too small and fast to be visible, Vladimir almost wondered if the shot had been a dud. But he did notice a flicker of response from the pig and realized his dart had made an impact.

With what seemed the porcine equivalent of a shrug of the shoulders, the pig went back to ruminating about whatever had been on its tiny mind before it had been injected with a lethal dose of radioactive material formed decades before in a nuclear reactor meltdown.

Vladimir went over to examine the pig, who did not seem at all perturbed about what had just happened to it. Peering close to the target painted on the side of the pig, Vladimir could just make out a small red welt slightly off centre of the target, marking the entry point. It looked like nothing more serious than a pimple and clearly there was nothing left of the dart hanging outside the skin. It had fully penetrated through the thick skin of the animal.

'Excellent, excellent, this is all going very well. What happens to the pig now?' asked Vladimir.

'We observe and monitor it but if it's anything like the others, it'll be dead within the next few days, then we toss it in the high temperature incinerator and give it a nice pork barbeque send-off,' laughed Borys.

'So… next step is a human trial, correct?'

'Yes, that is the next stage of the program. We're almost ready for that, we just have some final adjustments to make and then we'll be ready. In the meantime, we'll keep stockpiling the Chernobylite, processing it and manufacturing the darts. We've got the production line running quite smoothly now. Let's go and have a look.'

The control room was an innocuous looking office, just a security room with two desks and four video monitors mounted on the wall. The images on the screens could have been just about any small manufacturing facility, with a conveyor belt slowly feeding a robotic production line that took raw material in one end and spat out tiny darts at the other end.

Except the product of this assembly line was horrible, festering, torturous death.

CHAPTER 27

Vladimir was back in his Kiev headquarters and enjoying a shot of his favourite vodka to toast his success. Close to pulling off the biggest arms deal of his life; he was in a celebratory mood. But as usual, he had no one to share it with. His own betrayal of his brother had fed his paranoia that everyone was out to get him and had driven him to a life of solitude. His only company was the occasional visit from one of his favourite prostitutes, whom he knew without a doubt would not betray him through fear of not only their own death, but that of their families too.

Tonight, Vladimir was on his own. He sat down on his favourite recliner with his vodka and his traditional Russian dinner of Veal Orloff prepared earlier by his housekeeper and turned on the enormous wall-mounted television.

Sifting through the slim pickings on his television, Vladimir's interest was mildly piqued by a rerun of a Eurovision song contest, but he continued flicking through the channels until he noticed the Parade of Nations being beamed from the Opening Ceremony of the Olympic Games, which was just getting underway in Bucharest; the action beamed into his Kiev lounge room from just over the border in Romania. Mildly interested, Vladimir decided this was the best of a bad lot and settled down to his dinner in front of the Ceremony.

Country after country filed through the stadium entry, each with a close-up of the country's flag bearer.

Suddenly, Vladimir almost choked on his mouthful of veal pie, coughing and spluttering as he ejected the wad of half chewed meat and pastry halfway across the room. Reaching for the remote control, he paused the broadcast on the close-up of the flag bearer of the United States of America and collapsed back into his chair, gasping for breath.

The steely eyes of his long dead brother Nikolai stared back at him, seemingly piercing through the screen and boring into his very soul, silently planting the words *Killer, Killer, Killer,* into his brain. Vladimir couldn't control himself when confronted by the scene that was placed before him like a distant call from the grave finally catching up to him.

Something snapped inside Vladimir as he struggled to understand the enormity of what had just happened and was still on the screen in front of him. The resemblance was uncanny, it was *Nikolai incarnate!* Vladimir's paranoia suddenly slipped into psychosis and he became convinced that his long-dead brother had returned from the grave to wreak his revenge. Vladimir panicked, and quickly decided he must kill his brother all over again.

Vladimir picked up his phone, dialled Borys and snapped, 'Collect four of your best men, right now. We're going on a trip. Bring the new pistol and some Chernobylite. We're going to do our human trial. We've got a long drive ahead of us, so bring supplies. We'll need three cars. We leave in an hour. Go.'

Vladimir quickly packed a bag, then paced the room back and forth like a caged lion. He stopped and stared at the incarnation of his dead brother on the TV and snarled, 'Karma's a bitch, Nikolai, but it will be you feeling it's wrath all over again, not me.'

A loud horn blast rang out from the sleek black SUV out front of Vladimir's house. Vladimir grabbed his bag, raced outside and climbed into the front seat of the lead car alongside Borys. Off they sped into the night, shadowed by two identical black SUV's, each with two thugs in the front seat.

'Where are we headed, boss?' asked Borys.

'Bucharest,' responded Vladimir in a quiet, menacing tone that Borys knew all too well, 'And make it fast. We need to be there by morning.'

CHAPTER 28

Bucharest was in chaos; security was at an unprecedented level for the Olympics as the procession of black SUV's rolled quietly into town. Vladimir turned to Borys and said, 'We'll need a base to work from, somewhere close to the security perimeter. Head for Ferentari, it's an industrial area close to the city – we can take over a factory. It'll be quiet there, lots of businesses will have closed down for the Olympics.' Tired after their long overnight drive from Kiev, the men all needed a break and a debrief before the next stage of their mission.

Ominously cruising down the main street of the industrial borough, the three large black SUV's raised the eyebrows of some of the locals. Looking down the side streets as they went, Vladimir finally selected a quiet street on the edge of the neighbourhood and the convoy drove all the way to the end, then parked outside an innocuous looking factory announcing itself as a mechanic's garage. 'Let's use this. Borys, go check it out,' ordered Vladimir.

Borys exited the vehicle, grabbed some tools from the back of the car, strode up to the locked gate, cut the chain and casually wandered up to the front door of the garage. Noticing there were no lights on inside, Borys didn't bother knocking, but just took out a heavy screwdriver, inserted it in the barrel of the lock and punched it with a large hammer. The heavy blow launched the barrel out the other side of the door and Borys walked in, alert and ready for whatever lay inside. It had all taken just a few seconds.

After a quick look around to confirm there was no alarm and the place was empty, Borys opened the large garage doors, came back outside then drove in, followed by the support vehicles. Borys closed the gate and draped the chain back so a cursory glance would indicate all was in order.

Vladimir addressed his troops; 'Brothers, we have an important mission to complete. This is the day we test our new weapon. We're going to make a statement and kill a Russian traitor masquerading as an American. You all need to be on high alert because the eyes of the world will be upon us. You can all have a short rest, freshen up in the bathroom, do whatever you need to do. Borys, see if you can find some food and coffee in the kitchen of this dump. We'll need to hide the weapons in the cars so we can get through the security checkpoints. Use the under-floor smuggling compartments, the guards will never look that closely.'

Borys found supplies in the kitchen and summoned the men in. While they ate the stale biscuits and drank the foul coffee, Vladimir outlined the details of the plan. 'Okay, first we need to get into the Games area, through the security checkpoints. We'll split up so we don't draw so much attention when we go through. We don't want to arouse any suspicion from the guards. Once we get through the checkpoints, we'll meet up again inside the zone. I did some research on the way here and have identified the traitor. His name is Chad Wilson and he's an athlete on the American wrestling team. It will be too difficult getting close to him in the Athlete's Village, so we'll need to get him at the venue. I've checked the schedule and he's competing later this afternoon. We need to get to the stadium before he arrives, then follow him into the marshalling area and take our shot before he gets on the mat.'

'Then how long will it take for the Chernobylite to kill him?' asked one of the men.

Borys replied, 'It depends where the sliver ends up, but it should take around three days. If it lodges near his gut, he'll be vomiting but if it stays around near his brain, he'll be getting dizzy and having headaches. Either way he'll be dead from radiation sickness. We'll need to keep an eye on him as much as we can in the meantime. We'll take shifts following him; when he competes, we'll make sure we're all in the stadium.'

'What about tickets? How are we going to get in?' asked one of the other men.

'We'll just find a friendly usher and pay them to sneak us in. It won't be hard to find one willing to make some extra money,' said Vladimir.

Refreshed and with plans set, the team of six set off in their three separate directions and made their way to the rendezvous point in the parking lot of the stadium.

CHAPTER 29

'You want *how* much?' exclaimed Borys.

'Like I said, five thousand Lei. Hey, I could get in a lot of trouble for letting you into the athlete's area, so you have to make it worth my while,' replied the usher, knowing he had the upper hand but at the same time the murderous look on the giant's face told him not to push *too* hard.

'Look, I don't have that much Lei, but I can give you eight hundred Euros,' said Borys as he pulled out a fat wad of notes.

'Okay, you drive a hard bargain, but you've got a deal. Take these Access All Areas passes; they'll get you everywhere you need to go.'

Vladimir, Borys and one of his goons took the passes and entered the stadium, wary and on the lookout for any trouble. The others stayed behind, one in each vehicle. As the expert marksman and weapons master, Borys had the air pistol and Chernobylite deep in a secret pocket of his jacket, immune to metal detectors and light enough and cushioned enough to pass a cursory pat-down.

Walking purposefully like they were meant to be there and wearing their passes prominently around their necks, the three men strode through the bowels of the stadium, conscious of the activity above them. The crowd were busily milling around and finding their seats, eager to see the action unfolding before them on the mats. Taking their position near the athlete's entrance as instructed by their co-conspirator usher, they lay in wait for their prey to arrive.

Before too long, the athlete's buses began to arrive and the competitors filed in, eager to pursue their quest for glory. After what seemed an interminable wait, Vladimir nudged Borys from within the shadows and nodded towards Chad as he wandered past, joking and laughing with his fellow teammates. Vladimir went weak at the knees as he saw up close for the first time in more than 20 years what he thought of as his own flesh and blood whom he had so brutally murdered many years before. It was almost more than he could bear, being so close to the resurrection of his long-lost brother, raised from the dead to wreak his revenge upon his attacker. Borys nodded, he had laser-like focus on his man and smoothly slipped into the stream of athletes, officials and coaches as he followed Chad's trail.

The group of athletes dispersed as they went to their designated areas and ran through their warm-up routines of massages, strapping, taping, exercises, stretches and last-minute tactical advice from their coaches. Borys calmly bided his time and waited for his opportunity, peering unobtrusively from a dark corner at the end of a bank of lockers. Eventually, the competition began above them and some of the athletes filed out, leaving behind just a few men doing their final preparations, including Chad, who was going through his last stretches. Borys knew his time was right, carefully raised the pistol, took aim, and gently squeezed the trigger from a range of five metres across the room. Making no impact on its surroundings as it exited the muzzle of the pistol in a whoosh of air, the tiny but deadly projectile sped its way through the air across the room, undetected until it pierced the skin of Chad's neck, going all the way through and lodging into a blood vessel, sealing his fate.

'Ouch! What the hell was that? Jesus Christ, that hurt!' Chad exclaimed, vigorously rubbing his neck to ease the sting. With the pain easing, he walked over to the mirror and carefully examined his neck, which had already come up in a tiny red welt. He felt fine and the pain was settling, so he figured, 'Just a bee sting. I've had them before. I'll be fine,' and continued on with his final stretching.

The tiny foreign body in Chad's bloodstream made its deadly way deeper into his body, dissolving its bio-soluble plastic outer covering as it went, progressively reducing the separation between Chad's fragile innards and the intense radioactivity of the pure Chernobylite sliver.

Chad's competition day progressed well as he made his way through his preliminary bouts. Quickly he became one of the early favourites to take out the competition and was identified early as one of the men to beat for the gold medal.

By the end of Chad's wrestling bouts for the day, the last remnants of the protective outer covering of the Chernobylite dart finally dissipated into Chad's bloodstream. By this time, the deadly cargo had made its way up towards Chad's brain and lodged itself in the area that an ear, nose and throat specialist might refer to as Kiesselbach's Plexus, part of the nasal septum where four arteries converge behind the nose.

The human heart is an amazing machine, beating around 100,000 times per day and circulating the body's entire blood supply every minute, traversing the journey from heart to brain in only eight seconds. The Chernobylite kept pumping out its deadly ionizing radiation, energetic enough to knock out electrons from the delicate cells in Chad's body. With every passage of blood past the deadly radiation source, more and more of the 75 trillion cells in Chad's body sustained greater and greater damage.

The carnage spread through Chad's body like tentacles on an insidious march of microscopic destruction at a cellular scale. Like a deadly virus taking over its host, the black tentacles left a trail of irreparable damage that would lead steadily to a painful and horrible death.

CHAPTER 30

'He's looking really sick; I think today will be his last. He certainly won't be winning a gold medal in this fight,' said Borys to Vladimir.

'I think you're right Borys, he's nearly at the end. One bit of strain in his fight will be enough to tip him over the edge. This is my first time in the stadium. You've been tracking Wilson for the last three days. Who are the people that have been with him?' replied Vladimir.

'He has a big friend who is a Judo competitor from Australia; he won the gold medal yesterday. That's him over there,' replied Borys as he pointed over at Tommy, who was talking with Chad and looking concerned.

'Okay, nothing to worry about there, just another dumb athlete. What about family or supporters in the crowd?'

'There they are, over on the other side of the mat, about four rows back, two blonde women, mother and daughter,' said Borys as he pointed them out.

Vladimir's face blanched white and he buckled at the knees. It was Tatiana! In a sudden flash of insight, Vladimir put the pieces together and realized that Chad was in fact Nikolai's son, not some revengeful ghost of his dead brother. The women sitting in the crowd were Tatiana and her daughter Valentina, who had escaped two decades before.

Vladimir realized he had now murdered not only his brother but also his nephew, across 20 years and a journey halfway around the world that had brought Nikolai's son back into Vladimir's sphere of influence.

Vladimir immediately resolved that he must capture the two women. With Tatiana's history, she could make real trouble for him. Plus, she was still an extremely attractive woman. Vladimir had never married or had a family and now he saw the opportunity for the ultimate victory over his favoured baby brother – he would take what was left of Nikolai's family and make it his own, achieving something that was beyond Nikolai in his life. Tatiana would complete Vladimir's life and conclude his destruction of Nikolai, by taking the very thing that his brother had yearned for so desperately – his wife and child.

'Borys, we must take them; they need to come with us. When the boy dies, chaos will break out. Kidnap the two women in the uproar of the crowd. I'll take the car and go ahead with one of the men to prepare. I can't be seen in the crowd around them. You take both the women in the car with you and have the other car as backup. Meet me in Odessa at our wharf shed. We'll keep them there until we're ready to move onto Kiev.'

'Are you sure, Boss? Why are they so important? It would be much easier just to leave them here.'

'Trust me, they are too important to leave behind. They *must* come with us. No excuses, no failures,' Vladimir said as he fixed Borys with an intense stare.

'Okay, we'll get it done,' replied Borys as he moved off into the crowd with three goons in tow, explaining the plan as they went. Vladimir and the remaining man went out to the parking lot, got in their car and took off on the long drive to Odessa, leaving the chaos to unfold behind them.

Vladimir travelled in silence, thinking about what he had done to his family. First, he had killed his only brother and then 20 years later his only nephew. A pang of remorse prickled his conscience as they ate up the distance on their journey to Odessa.

CHAPTER 31

'Mom, look, there's Tommy,' said Brittney with a smile as she waved across the mats at her big hunk of a man. 'It's so exciting, I still can't believe he won the gold medal yesterday. He was so happy when we were out last night. He really celebrated hard and it looks like he's paying the price now; he doesn't look too good. Hey, is Chad okay? He really doesn't look well.' Brittney was suddenly concerned at the health of her older brother. 'Tommy looks worried too, he's really talking to him closely now. I hope he's alright. Should we go over there?'

'No, I think we should stay here,' replied Amy. 'Chad wouldn't want us interfering. He's done well so far and has been okay. He said he just got stung by a bee a couple of days ago and has been feeling a bit funny ever since. If it were really bad, I'm sure he would stop and see the doctor.' Despite the reassuring words to her daughter, Amy was concerned; Brittney was right, Chad really didn't look well.

'It looks like he's going to compete. Tommy's finished talking to him now and is going back to the athlete's area,' said Brittney. 'Oh, I hope he's going to be alright.'

The match started and the two wrestlers came at each other in a flurry. Clearly, Chad was in trouble and just couldn't compete at the level required. His opponent quickly got the upper hand and didn't relinquish it. Suddenly, Chad was flipped on his back and his body went limp. A hush descended on the crowd as they stared at Chad's unnaturally still form, lying on the mat.

'NO! Chad, get up baby, please!' cried Amy as she reached out in a panic to clutch onto Brittney.

'Mom, what's going on? Why won't he get up?' implored Brittney, struggling to come to terms with what was unfolding before their eyes.

The medical staff rushed over to Chad's motionless body, quickly examined him, and then called for the tall, white emergency screens to put around them while they worked on Chad.

From his position close to Chad on the mats, Tommy looked on, unable to move and helpless to act. Amy and Brittney in the stands were numb, staring at the scene, their eyes boring into the white screens as if they could penetrate and uncover the activity behind.

The public address system crackled into life and blared, 'Ladies and gentlemen, everyone please leave the arena. The competition for the rest of the day has been postponed. Please make your way in an orderly fashion to the nearest exit.' Pandemonium broke out when the crowd rose as one in their effort to exit the building.

'Mom, we have to get down there, let's go this way!' shouted Brittney and they started their hopeless move against the surging mass of people. Then suddenly she cried out, 'What the hell? Get your hands off me buddy! Mom, look out, this guy is making trouble!'

'Be quiet girl and you won't get hurt. You're coming with us,' snarled Borys as he pulled out the sinister air pistol and jammed it into Brittney's ribs.

'Ouch, you're hurting me!' exclaimed Brittney.

'You'll get a lot worse than that if you give us any trouble,' barked Borys as he grabbed Brittney roughly with his free hand and started frog marching her up the stairs along with the crowd, flanked by one of his goons. The other two men took care of Amy, manhandling her roughly up the stairs.

'Hey! Amy, Brittney, STOP! Somebody stop them, they're taking them away!' shouted Tommy as he looked over at the most important person in his life being forced away at gunpoint to God knows where, maybe out of his life forever. He had to stop them! 'Wait, I'm coming,' he shouted, unheard in the crazy scene as he took off after them.

'Quick, dose them up and get them in the back. Hurry!' ordered Borys to his henchmen. They administered the strong tranquilizer using the auto-injector, fiercely stabbing one end into the thigh of each woman. Within seconds, the women lost consciousness and were tossed roughly into the back of Borys' car. He took off with a screech, followed closely by the second car with the two thugs in the front seat.

CHAPTER 32

I raced out to the parking lot after the kidnappers, seeing Brittney and Amy getting thrown into the back of a sinister-looking big black SUV. I had to get moving!

I quickly scanned the carpark and spotted a thing of beauty, the perfect machine; an old BMW M3, precision German engineering at its best. It was smaller than I would like for my enormous frame, but it was light and powerful, with more than 300 horsepower crammed under the hood. It was manoeuvrable, bloody fast and best of all, it was old enough for me to be able to hotwire it. I smashed the front passenger window with a big elbow strike, reached in among the glass, unlocked the door and wrenched it open. Somehow, I squeezed myself into the small car, grabbed under the dash, extracted the right wires from under the steering wheel and had the car started in just a few seconds.

As the car roared into life, I gunned the engine, jammed it into first gear and dropped the clutch, pulled a massive burnout and launched off in pursuit in a flurry of noise and clouds of smoke. The crowd that had come streaming out of the wrestling venue looked on in wonder at the chaos in the carpark, wondering what the hell was going on outside now, after what had just happened inside. Hundreds of heads turned as one as I expertly peeled out of the carpark like a mad racing car driver, thrashing the car through the gears as I tore off down the street.

Thankfully the two black SUV's stuck out like dog's balls, so I could still just see them in the distance even though they had a head start on me; I had some serious ground to make up. Redlining the engine through every gear, within seconds I was tearing through the suburban streets at over 120 km an hour. I snuck a glance down at the speedo and flicked my gaze left and right, keeping an eye out for any obstacles. All senses on high alert, I was at one with the machine, just like when I was racing go-karts back home in country New South Wales and tearing around the racetrack in Sydney.

Approaching my first major intersection, I quickly ran down through the gears, hitting second but still doing 90 km as I flew through the stop sign, judging a tiny gap down to the millimetre and scaring the pants off a little old lady trundling through the junction in her old Russian clunker of a car.

As I looked up at the stately, historic buildings of Bucharest, they seemed to frown in disapproval on the unseemly activity tearing through her quaint streets. Having stood the test of time through hundreds of years of history dating back to the Ottoman Empire, Bucharest seemed too regal to witness such mayhem on its roads.

Stiff shit, history, my girl's in that car and I've got to get her back, so I don't give a toss about your frowns.

Slowly but surely, I was gaining on my targets, making ground through a combination of superior driving skills and desperation to save the woman I loved. As I left the city streets behind and headed out of town, my speed increased even more, and I soon closed the gap to within spitting distance of the car in front. I knew I had to get past the trailing support vehicle if I was going to get to the car in front and save Brittney and Amy.

As if knowing what I was thinking, the trailing car suddenly slowed down, blocking my path and allowing the lead car with its valuable cargo to pull away from me. I slammed the car down into third gear, hitting the redline as I floored the accelerator and shot out to the left in a doomed attempt to overtake the car in front. With not enough room to move and an oncoming car looming ahead, at the last second my prey suddenly swerved to the left and gave me a nudge. I jumped on the brakes with both feet, washed off loads of speed in a flash and pulled back into the right lane. Simultaneously, the engine of the big SUV barked as the driver floored it and put some distance between us.

'Bastards!' I shouted, as I realized the failed manoeuvre had cost me valuable seconds and distance. I had to be more careful; I was no use to Brittney and Amy if I died in an exploding fireball of a BMW. Fighting against the shot of adrenaline coursing through my already hyper-charged circulatory system, I shook off my fear and rage, calmed my breathing and regained my focus.

I squinted my eyes in concentration, flexed my hands on the steering wheel, downshifted and mashed my foot hard on the accelerator, almost putting it through the floor. With the engine screaming in protest at the abuse I was dishing out, the car leapt ahead like a cheetah launching itself on the hunt. I quickly recovered my lost ground and was soon within striking distance once more of the support vehicle. In a sudden panic, I realized I could no longer see the lead car; Brittney and Amy were getting further and further away from me and I feared I might never get them back.

Realizing that I was the better driver in a faster car, the men in the SUV knew they couldn't outdrive me in my M3, so they decided to resort to a primitive but highly effective means of discouraging pursuit; the man riding shotgun took the role for which his position was named, wound down the window and poked out the menacing black muzzle of a huge handgun. My target slowed down a fraction to give me just enough room for another overtaking move. I saw my chance, decided to take the risk, floored the accelerator, and pulled out to go around the SUV.

FUCK! The muzzle flashed and I heard a sharp crack as a bullet smashed through my windscreen and slammed into the B-pillar of the car, right near my ear. Jumping on the brakes, I washed off speed again and swerved back in behind them.

Jesus Christ, I hate guns! They have a bad habit of killing people. I heard another sharp retort and once again a bullet pierced my windscreen, this time burying itself in the headrest of the front passenger seat. Bloody lucky we're not in Australia now, or that would have been the driver's seat and my head would have exploded like a bad watermelon.

Planning and strategizing took a back seat as instinct took over. I knew I was stuffed unless I took these guys out, so once again I pounded the accelerator into the floor but this time instead of swerving out to go around, I lined them up and rammed into the back corner of the car in front. My rearwards attack hit at just the right angle and at a speed of over 170 km an hour, the SUV wobbled, then swerved, and the driver in a moment of panic over-corrected, sending the car lurching into an uncontrollable sideways skid.

Physics took over and the tires fought against the inevitable, but the enormous forward momentum pushed the rubber beyond its limit and sent the car into a death roll, spinning and bouncing like some crazed machine, launching shards of glass and bits of plastic and metal into the air as it rolled. I could see the cockpit was a crazed maelstrom of airbags exploding and flying debris as the two doomed occupants were flung to-and-fro in their seatbelts, suffering crushing blows at every impact.

I slowed behind as I observed the mayhem playing out in front of me like some lunatic slow-motion video, with the big SUV rolling over, and over, and over again. Finally, the car came to a halt with one last roll, the hulking mess settling back on its wheels with a mechanical groan of exhaustion accompanied by wisps of smoke.

Holy shit, that was intense! I hope one of those bastards is still alive, or I'm screwed. I came to a halt and leapt out of my now sad and sorry BMW. I went around to the passenger side first and almost vomited the instant I looked in, averting my eyes and grabbing my stomach, trying to stop myself from retching.

What I saw hardly resembled a human head anymore. It lolled at an unnatural angle, clearly with a very broken neck. There was a bloody imprint of a pistol on the man's face, marking where he had been holding the gun in front of him just as the air bag fired its explosive charge, slamming the gun at breakneck speed straight against his nose, smearing it across his face, knocking out teeth in the process with the butt end of the handle. Finishing the grisly picture was the outline of the muzzle plastered across his left eye socket. To complete the carnage suffered by the man's poor cranium, his head had slammed into the side pillar, crushing his temple and spreading a lurid purple bruise across half his face.

Clearly, this guy was not going to tell me anything. I crossed my fingers in the hope that the driver was in better shape, ran around to the other side of the car and looked in through the smashed driver's window.

Without the hazard of a large handgun being propelled into his face by an airbag exploding at over 300 km an hour, the driver was marginally better off than his unfortunate passenger. But he was faced with an entirely different condition that had my insides churning once more. I was hit with the confronting sight of the man's left eyeball hanging out of its socket, retained only by the optic nerve that was still attached to his brain. After being popped out of the eye socket by one of the car's many impacts, the solitary eyeball had succumbed to gravity's pull and was pointing down, bouncing on the stalk like a pair of those crazy glasses on a spring.

Severely bruised and extremely bloody, the driver was at least semi-conscious, intermittently groaning and pleading for help in a language incomprehensible to me. I realized I had zero chance of getting the driver's door open and it would be a challenge pulling him out of the mess of a car, which had the roof squashed down and who knew what was going on with his legs under the steering wheel and the dashboard. Not to mention the tiny detail of a *fucking eyeball* hanging out of its socket, resting ungainly against his left cheek.

Hmm… conscious is good, but incomprehensible language is not a good sign for effective interrogation. 'Hey! Hey mate, do you speak English?' I shouted at the man as he struggled to stay conscious.

'Yes, I speak a little English,' said the unfortunate driver in a thick Russian accent. 'Help, get me out of car!'

'First you need to tell me who your boss is and where he's going with my girlfriend. Tell me that and I'll get you out, I promise,' I responded.

'No! Out first, talk later,' said the man, clearly resolute in his demand. 'What is going on? Why can I see ahead out front and down into car at same time?'

'Don't worry about it, you'll be *fine*,' I said, somehow keeping a straight face. 'Just a little issue with your eye, we'll fix that right up in a minute. I'll get you out. But it's going to bloody hurt mate, I can tell you, sure as shit.'

I tried the door, but it was jammed shut, so I reached in through the window and unbuckled the wretch's seat belt and checked his legs to see if they were stuck under the steering wheel. I was careful to avoid the macabre spectre of a bloody eyeball dangling out of its dark and empty socket by a dripping tendril of an optic nerve.

The man's legs seemed to move okay, so I grabbed him by the shoulders and turned him sideways in the seat with his back to the window, accompanied by screams of agony at every shuffle until he passed out. Feeling a need to talk, perhaps as a distraction from the crazy scene, I said to the unconscious man, 'Dude, you are seriously messed up. I don't know what the hell is going on in there, but you are in bad shape. Serves you right for trying to kill me, you prick. Probably just as well you're out cold for this next bit, because you are gonna be a human pretzel when I drag you out of there.'

I braced myself against the side of the car, grabbed the guy from behind under the armpits and heaved him up and back towards the window. With much grunting and groaning from me and unconscious moans from my hapless victim, I eventually extricated the driver from his vehicular prison and deposited his limp form on the ground.

After a few minutes, I gave him a shake and a gentle slap on the face to rouse him from his stupor. The man's eye bounced a crazy dance in response to the slap, finally settling in a hideous position down the side of his face. Best I don't do that again, seeing the response of his unrestrained oculus.

With a groan, the driver came back to some semblance of life and through his remaining eye that was in its rightful orifice, he looked up at me and with labouring, rasping breath said, 'Hospital. Quickly.'

'Hey, you said you would tell me what I need to know if I got you out of the car. We had a deal,' I said, knowing full well that a hospital would not help this poor bastard. A morgue would be his next stop, but I had to give him enough hope of survival so he would tell me what I so desperately needed to hear.

'Take me hospital,' groaned the dying man, who was by now blowing blood bubbles out of his mouth. Clearly there was some serious shit going on inside this guy, with internal bleeding and probably a punctured lung. I would have to work fast.

'Okay, I tell you what. You tell me what I need to know, and I'll take you to a hospital myself, quick smart. We'll go like shit off a shovel.'

'Alright, I tell,' he spluttered as another blood bubble popped on his lips. 'My boss Vladimir Zhukov. He has women. Take to Odessa.'

'Okay, Vladimir Zhukov,' I repeated, committing it to memory. 'Odessa. Where in Odessa? Where is he taking them?'

'To our headquarters in port, Wharf Shed 17. Now take me hospital,' the man said, wheezing and gurgling through his blood-filled lungs.

'Thank you. Thank you for telling me that,' I said, as a huge wave of relief washed over me, knowing I at least had the next step on the road to recovering Brittney and Amy. 'I'll go and get the car and we'll go to the hospital.'

I knew it was hopeless and the man would likely be dead inside of a minute, but I wanted to follow through on my promise of help, not wanting betrayal to be the last emotion on the man's mind when he did give up the ghost.

In a moment of clarity, the dying man finally realized that no hospital on Earth would help him and that his fate was sealed. 'Wait,' he croaked as he feebly lifted his hand towards me.

'What is it, mate? Do you want me to hold your hand?'

'No. I want you go *fuck* yourself for killing me, you bastard,' he spat, as his outstretched hand somehow curled the outer fingers down, leaving the middle one up in a crooked, but unmistakable gesture of flipping me the bird.

'And do me favour. Find ex-wife Julia Marova and give her message. Tell her last thought before I die was how much I hate her,' spouted the broken man in a last vitriolic moment of anger as he expelled his last breath with a sagging depression of his chest. His head lolled to one side, with his good eye still open and staring and the other eye still dangling like a yo-yo on its string on the other side of his face. A stream of blood oozed from the corner of his mouth and made its way down to the ground beneath his head.

Wow. Someone's got some issues, haven't they? So much for feeling guilty about my responsibility for him dying and everything. What an asshole! Something tells me I did old Julia a favour with that one.

I collected myself and looked around at the carnage, realizing that just a few short minutes had passed since the accident. The SUV was still smoking and creaking with metallic noises as the car cooled and the body's lifeblood of coolant, petrol and hydraulics created a spreading pool over the road. There was a trail of shrapnel behind the car that had been shed in the death roll, a dead body in the vehicle and another one lying on the side of the road; it was like some sort of surreal war zone.

I couldn't believe that I had been not only in the middle of it but had personally caused the death and destruction. This was not little Tommy from Brooms Head in New South Wales, nor was it Olympic Gold Medallist Thomas Taylor. This was a whole new level of weird and I needed to get my shit together and get out of here, fast. I certainly did not want to be trying to explain all this to a bunch of pissed-off Romanian cops. I had to move; I needed to be free from any authorities and do everything I could to get Brittney and Amy back.

I turned on my heel, leaving the devastation behind me and strode over to my poor Beemer, which had served me so well on my mission. I jumped in, started it up and roared off down the road, leaving everything in my wake.

CHAPTER 33

Slowly, the effects of the tranquilizer were wearing off.

One by one, her senses were coming back. First was her hearing. As if through a thick fog, she thought she could make out the sounds of water lapping, machinery humming, her own blood pumping in her ears.

Next was touch. She felt cold and damp on her back, with hard stone edges grinding into her shoulders and neck, tight cords binding her wrists and cutting painfully into her flesh. A sudden, urgent need to go to the toilet joined the clamouring for attention.

Next was smell. Diesel fumes and the unmistakable stench of nesting vermin assaulted her nasal passages, rousing her further like smelling salts would.

Taste came next, like furry mothballs on her tongue.

Finally, came sight. Slowly, cautiously she opened her bleary eyes, blinking rapidly as she stirred from her long, drug-induced stupor. The dim light made its way into her retinas as she registered her surroundings and her condition.

The brain fog lifted as Brittney opened her eyes fully, then painfully sat up and looked around.

'What on *earth* is going on here? Where the *hell* am I?' muttered Brittney quietly, somehow knowing deep down that caution was required here. The last she could remember was the stadium. Chad! What had happened to her brother? She had no idea if he was alive or dead; the last she had seen were the ominous white sheets surrounding his body and then... the thugs! She had been taken away at gunpoint, marched out into the parking lot and that was all she remembered.

'Mom! Mom, where are you?' called Brittney in an urgent, strained whisper, desperately looking around as she got her bearings. The dim room was strewn with various equipment and materials; she was in a big shed, maybe down on the docks or something. A dark shape in the corner caught her eye and she decided to take a closer look. Too quickly, she stood up, not registering that her feet were also bound and immediately toppled over and collapsed back down on the hard stone floor.

'Shit!' she exclaimed as the stinging pain radiated up from her elbow where it had slammed into the floor. Her head spun and she fought a wave of nausea as her system struggled against the after-effects of the heavy tranquilizer.

'Okay, slow down, regroup and go again,' said Brittney to herself with a quick shake of her head and some deep breathing. She drew her knees up to her chest, rocked forward and up, straightening her legs smoothly to bring her to a stable standing position.

'Step 1; done,' said Brittney quietly, now vertical at least. 'Step 2; hop. Just like back in high school, except on two feet and with a fucking rope tied around my ankles by a couple of psychos!'

Hop, hop, hop, she went across the room, occasionally stopping to steady herself against a packing crate or stack of pallets. Finally, she reached the crumpled mess on the floor and realized that what looked like a pile of rags was in fact her mother. Amy was extremely pale, with no trace of consciousness.

Dropping her backside and bending her knees, Brittney tucked and lowered herself down beside Amy. Gingerly, Brittney reached out and put her hands on Amy's chest and breathed a deep sigh of relief as she felt the steady rise and fall of the body. Brittney gave her a little nudge, which elicited a groan that further alleviated Brittney's concern.

Figuring that Amy was close to wakefulness, Brittney stayed by her side, leaving her to come to her senses on her own rather than trying to hurry the process. After a few minutes, Amy went through a similar procedure as Brittney had done moments earlier, although this time she had the benefit of a familiar face close by. As soon as Amy had properly woken from her forced slumber and sufficiently recovered her faculties, she leant on Brittney, who spread her bound arms far enough to get them around her mother's neck and they shared a deep, long and desperate hug. At least they had each other in this moment of madness.

With a start, they were both shaken from their brief moment of comfort by a sinister jangling of keys in a metal lock, followed by an ear-splitting screech as rusty metal hinges protested their straining movement when the heavy steel door was pushed wide by a brainless oaf of a man. He barked harshly at the pair of them in a language incomprehensible to Brittney.

There was a long silence, followed by another stream of guttural utterances from their captor. Brittney responded, 'I'm sorry, but I don't know what you're saying. I don't understand. What do you want from us?' she pleaded.

The heavyset guard responded with a grunt and an upturned nod of his head in Amy's direction, clearly indicating he wanted her to speak. 'She can't understand you either. We're Americans, we only speak English,' said Brittney.

Amy put her hand gently on Brittney's arm and said, 'It's okay, Brittney, don't worry. We're going to get out of this. Here, help me stand up.'

Brittney gracefully got to her feet, then reached down with her bound hands and helped her mother stand up. Amy put her shoulders back, raised her head, defiantly stuck out her chin and unleashed a fluent tirade of what seemed to Brittney to be abuse, but in a language that she had never heard her mother speak before!

What the hell is going on here and who is this strange woman speaking in tongues next to me? thought Brittney.

The simpleton chuckled, turned and closed the door behind him, locking it with a solid clunk as the key drove the lock home.

In the ensuing silence, Brittney slowly turned to her mother and said, 'Ah… Mom, what the *hell* was that? You've got some serious explaining to do! Since when do you speak another language, for God's sake?'

'Brittney, there's something I need to tell you. I'm sorry, but I haven't told you the truth about your heritage.'

'*Heritage?* What heritage? What on earth do you mean? I'm Brittney Wilson from New York, born and raised. I've got the passport and the birth certificate to prove it!'

'I'm sorry, Brittney, but there's a lot more to your life than that. And mine too. I didn't think I'd ever need to tell you the truth about your history, but I think I need to do it now. I was nervous when Chad said he wanted to come here; I should have listened to my gut, but I didn't have the heart to tell him he couldn't come, and he wouldn't have listened anyway. I thought we'd be safe, it's been so long; it's been 20 years, I thought I'd left all that behind me!'

Amy's voice had grown in volume and raised in pitch as she spoke, finishing with a sob as tears streamed down her cheeks, clearly traumatized about whatever it was she had to tell her daughter.

'Oh, God,' said Amy suddenly, as she blanched white as a sheet and put her hand over her mouth. 'What about Chad? Is he okay? Do you think he's… dead?'

'I don't know, Mom. We need to be strong and hope he's still alive until we know for sure. Right now, we need to focus on us and getting out of here. Who the hell are these people and why have they taken us? Does this have something to do with my father?'

Amy steeled herself to break the news to her daughter that she had fought desperately for so long to keep from her and said, 'I'm so sorry Brittney. And yes, it has *everything* to do with your father.'

CHAPTER 34

My geography sucks.

I have no clue where Odessa is, so I need to get a look at a map and I need to ditch this car; after what I've just been through with it, it's so hot it will be on every police alert in the country. My phone has no signal out here and is just about flat, so my GPS is no good to me.

After 30 minutes of driving at top speed, I figured I had enough distance between me and the crash site to slow down and not draw *quite* so much attention to myself. I passed through two small towns and lots of farmland and decided to ditch the car on the outskirts of the next town. As I crossed a bridge over a river, I saw a village just ahead of me and figured this was as good a spot as any to lose my conspicuous vehicle.

I pulled off to the side of the road after the bridge, checked around to make sure nobody was in sight, slipped the trusty machine into neutral and gave it a push down the embankment. It slowly rolled down the hill towards the river, coming to rest nicely hidden under a large, low-hanging tree. Nobody would see it from the road, and it would only be discovered if someone were really poking around down there, by which time it wouldn't matter, because I would be long gone.

With a pang of regret, I said goodbye to that beautiful driving machine, precision engineered and built so long ago by expert German hands that had delivered me the information I needed to continue my search for Brittney and Amy. God, I'm so worried about what she must be thinking and feeling right now and what might be happening to her. And Chad! Jesus, I couldn't believe Chad was gone! He had only died that morning but already it felt like a lifetime ago.

'Focus!' I said to myself. 'Snap out of it! You can't dwell on this stuff yet. Get yourself out of this mess right now and take the next step.'

My self-talk worked; I got back to reality and the perilous state of my current situation, I had to get my shit together and find cover. My face and name had been all over the TV yesterday when I won my gold medal and there was security everywhere at the stadium, so I knew that someone, somewhere would have seen what happened and I would most definitely be a *person of interest* in the investigation. I had to go to ground.

I wandered nonchalantly into town, pretending it was a completely normal thing for someone who resembled Thor the Norse God to be making his way on foot into a small town in the Romanian countryside, without luggage of any description. Needless to say, there were a couple of glances from curious locals, but thankfully none of them made a scene.

I wandered into what looked like a general store and had a look around. Spying a rack with books and magazines on it, my eyes fell on a tourist map of Romania and the surrounding area, so I grabbed that. Suddenly my stomach let out a growl as it protested the lack of attention that I had given my appetite so far that day and I immediately realized I *really* needed food.

Spying what looked like roast pork sandwiches behind the counter, I pointed them out and held up three fingers to the shop owner's questioning gaze. I tossed the map on the counter and handed him some crumpled notes extracted from my pocket. Wordlessly, he handed me some change and I walked out of the store with my bounty. The whole exchange had taken place in surreal silence.

I sat down in front of the store and wolfed down my three huge sandwiches as I consulted the map. A passer-by wandering down the street stopped to look at me through squinting, untrusting eyes and said in broken English, 'You not from here. You lost?'

Glad for the assistance, I held out the map and said, 'Yes, I'm lost. Can you tell me where I am on this map?'

'You here,' the man grunted and stabbed a thick, stumpy finger down on the map, way past the western outskirts of Bucharest.

'Great, thank you very much,' I said. My gruff helper continued on his way, seemingly satisfied that he had sent an interloper on his way out of their peaceful little town.

Well, that's one problem solved. Don't suppose you can recommend the best place for me to steal a car, can you? Guess I'll need to take care of that one on my own. But that's something I can do well.

Scoping out the town from my vantage point in front of the general store, I spied the local pub, or whatever it was called in Romanian, and figured that was a pretty good spot to try for my next mode of transport. I wandered across the road and into the carpark out the back of the hotel and had a look around. Slim pickings, that's for sure.

Then I spotted it, tucked away over in the corner, an old, boxy, plain grey Russian looking car that would blend in like a snowflake in a snowstorm. It was perfect. Nobody would look twice at me in that thing. I snuck past the dumpster out the back of the hotel and retrieved a piece of wire that was hanging off a packing crate, then walked over to the car, surreptitiously keeping an eye out for any watchful observers.

It only took me a few seconds to fashion a hook out of the wire, slip it down inside the gap between the window and the door sill, catch the locking mechanism and pull it up with a quick tug. With one last glance around, I opened the door and slid into the spongy driver's seat, reached under the dash for the ignition wires and got the engine started into wheezy life.

I casually pulled out of the carpark and onto the main drag and drove myself out of town, headed for the coast.

Two hours into the drive, my eyes were getting heavy and every part of my body was begging me to stop. Time for a recap; I'd had a brutal, draining Judo fight the day before against a guy who was every bit a match for me, I'd gotten completely hammered out on the town last night, woken up with a ball-buster of a hangover, seen my best friend die on the wrestling mat, my girlfriend and her mum get kidnapped by four goons, stolen a car, had a long high-speed chase, been shot at, caused an enormous car crash, killed two men, stolen another car and then finished off with a long, tense and draining drive to make my escape in a country that was a complete mystery to me. No wonder I felt like shit.

It had been a seriously heavy-duty day and I really needed to stop for the night. After what seemed like an eternity, I finally found a seedy hotel by the side of the road and pulled into the carpark at the rear of the *establishment* in what I considered the loosest possible interpretation of the word.

I went in, struggled through negotiations with the innkeeper, who spoke no English at all. As for me, I was completely clueless about the language, not even knowing whether Romanians spoke Romanian or Russian or something completely different. I really need to get better educated on geography and other cultures. I'm just a simple Aussie lad, but that's no excuse for not learning at least the basics about countries that I visit. Something to work on when I'm not fighting for my life and on some half-baked rescue mission against impossible odds, I guess.

I wearily made my way to my hotel room, trudging up four flights of stairs because the elevator was busted. As I opened the door, I was greeted with a pungent waft of cigarette smoke and some foul odour I simply couldn't recognize, and in fact didn't want to; it seemed better not to know. And what was that movement? Oh, awesome, I won't be alone tonight, I've got some roommates in the form of two freakishly large cockroaches and a giant spider dangling from the grungy light shade hanging from the brown-stained ceiling that I'm sure must have been the height of fashionable décor a century ago when this godforsaken place was built. But at least my room was quiet, out of the way, inconspicuous and warm.

I sat on the bed and for the first time in this completely weird and messed-up day, I could finally settle down and take stock of my situation. It was grim. All I had were the clothes I was wearing, my phone, a credit card and a small amount of cash. Everything else was back in my room at the Olympic Village.

I'd seen enough movies to know that using my credit card was a complete no-no at this point, because for sure my face would be plastered all over, from one end of the country to the other, and both the right and the wrong sides of the law would be after me. The first thing they would do would be to track my credit card.

Shit! The second thing they would do would be to track my phone signal. I pulled it out of my pocket and for the first time in history I was relieved to see a blank screen staring back at me, knowing that the battery had run out of juice some time back. Just to be sure, I removed the SIM card from my phone as well.

I was pretty much off the grid.

CHAPTER 35

'Mom, you're really scaring me, what is going on? Tell me!' pleaded Brittney.

'I'm so sorry honey, I was really hoping that we would never have to have this conversation, but clearly we do now,' responded Amy.

'Is it about my dad? Or about the fact that you can speak a foreign language I've never heard before?'

'Well… it's all that and quite a bit more, I'm afraid. Come, sit down and make yourself comfortable. Well, as comfortable as possible I guess,' said Amy with a wry grin as she held up her bound wrists and looked down at her bound feet. They shuffled over to a packing crate, but before they sat down Brittney was reminded of her pressing need to urinate.

'Wait, sorry Mom, but I really need to pee. I'll go over in the corner way over there.' She hopped off across the room, returning a few minutes later feeling a whole lot better.

'Okay, Mom, now start at the beginning,' said Brittney as she looked expectantly at her mother, very curious but also apprehensive about what was coming. She had never known her father and Amy had always just said he was a good man who had unfortunately been killed before Brittney was born. She'd said he was killed in a tragic accident when their home had burnt down and that the fire had taken all their possessions including their photos, erasing their history completely. Brittney had never even seen a picture of her father and had daydreamed as a child that she would somehow, someday find out something about him. Now, she wasn't so sure that she wanted to know the truth.

'What I am about to tell you will seem incredible, like something out of a movie. In fact, it seems so strange that even I struggle to believe it really happened to me all those years ago. But being in this part of the world has brought a lot of memories flooding back to me,' said Amy.

'I'd better start with the big shocks, to get them out of the way,' she continued. After a long, pregnant pause, Amy took a deep breath, leaned in close to Brittney, looked her right in the eyes and quietly said, 'You and Chad weren't born in New York. You were born in Chechnya, in Russia.'

Brittney was struck dumb. Her jaw dropped down slackly and stayed there. When no sound came from her mouth, Amy decided to continue.

'And Brittney isn't the name you were born with. You were named Valentina.' Amy finished the sentence with a flourish, pronouncing Brittney's real name with a beautiful Russian intonation so suited to the exotic name, bringing forth images of Tsars, the Kremlin and Russian dolls.

Brittney/Valentina's jaw dropped even further on hearing this latest bombshell, but still she made no sound.

'Actually, none of our names are the ones we were born with. My name was Tatiana and Chad's was Anatoly.'

Silence. Amy/Tatiana resolved not to break it, knowing that Brittney needed to process the first shocking news before she could continue.

Brittney's whole life as she knew it had just come crashing down around her. She was torn, her gut was wrenching, her head was swirling with worry and confusion, all of which quickly progressed to anger. Then the silence was shattered by Brittney's hysterical cry of, 'WHAT? What do you mean? My whole life is a lie! How could you do this to me? And to Chad? Why? What possible reason could you have for lying to us for so long and keeping this a secret for my entire life? Especially when you know how desperate I've been to find out things about your past with my father. How could you do this to me?' she cried out, as the tears streamed down her face.

Amy's eyes welled with tears of her own as she watched her only daughter in so much pain. Sadly she shook her head and said in a voice full of anguish, 'I'm so sorry Brittney, I never meant to hurt you, but I was in such a desperate situation and I did what I had to do to protect myself and you kids from a monster who would have killed me and imprisoned both of you to a life of hell. I had no choice but to escape our lives and change all our names, give us new identities and a new life in America. I kept saying to myself that I would tell you the truth one day, when you were old enough to understand. But then, so much time had passed, and we were all so happy that I couldn't bring myself to tell you everything. I'm so sorry, my love.' Amy reached up her bound hands to touch Brittney's cheek and wipe her tears, but Brittney recoiled from her touch.

Brittney was torn between wanting to know the truth about her life, especially her father, but at the same time wanting to avoid the pain of knowledge that she was sure was yet to come. She did not like at all where this conversation was headed.

'What did you mean when you said *monster*?' asked Brittney in such a cold, dead voice that it shocked Amy to her core.

Steeling herself with another deep breath, Amy raised her head to look again at Brittney and said, 'Your father's name was Nikolai. He was a brutal Russian gangster. At first, he was so charming. He was such a strong, handsome and powerful man. I was young and impressionable, and he was much older, more experienced and a leader of men. We had a whirlwind romance and married just a few months after we met. But I soon found out he was possessive, violent and jealous. He had a savage mean streak and was so quick to violence that it was uncontrollable. He had a temper and used to enjoy taking it out on me. He used to beat me, keep me locked up in his big house like a prison. Then to make things worse, I got pregnant with Chad, when I was much younger than you are right now.'

Brittney had again been stunned into silence, suddenly horrified at the ordeal her mother had been through and feeling guilty that she had been so hard on her. But she had still lied to her all these years! Why couldn't she have just told her the truth earlier? But she wondered if she would have been ready to hear it before now.

'I was so helpless. Nikolai was so strong and would explode at the slightest provocation. I had to be so careful not to make him angry for fear of what he might do to Chad. He would beat me senseless and rape me, force me whenever he felt like it. Then I got pregnant again, with you.'

'Oh, Mom, I'm so sorry,' wailed Brittney. This was too much to bear. The thought of her mother going through all that, scared and alone, when she was younger than Brittney was right now, was horrifying.

'It's okay, baby, it's alright. I was strong and I had help. From a wonderful man named Pasha, one of Nikolai's most trusted lieutenants. Pasha saved my life but paid the ultimate price for it. He was killed the day after I escaped. But remember, something good did come out of my ordeal. I got you and Chad, the most special gifts a woman could hope for. I've had a wonderful life and I am so proud of you and Chad and the people you have become.'

'What happened to Nikolai? Did he come after us?'

'No, he never pursued us, thank God. It took me months to find out what had happened in Chechnya. I was so scared of being discovered, I didn't want to try and find out what happened after I escaped. When nobody came after us, I didn't want to rock the boat because it might have brought someone chasing us. Eventually I got up the courage to do some digging, just to be sure we were safe. I had a job in New York and worked hard, saving up enough money to pay an investigator in Chechnya to find out what had happened. Nikolai was killed the day after I escaped; his head was blown apart when he got shot in a fight with a rival gang. Nikolai had an older brother named Vladimir, who had always been jealous of Nikolai's success. I always had my doubts about Vladimir; he was just as much of a psychopath as Nikolai, if not worse. Nothing was ever confirmed, but there were stories that Vladimir had arranged to have his brother killed, if not pulled the trigger himself, so he could take over Nikolai's empire.'

'Holy shit!' exclaimed Brittney incredulously, engrossed in the story, which so did not sound like something in which her New York 'soccer Mom' and active member of the Parent Teacher Association would be embroiled. 'So how did you escape?'

'It was you that helped me get away, my love. I planned it for more than a year. I secretly taught myself to speak English, including how to speak in a New York accent. I watched all the American TV shows I could, especially ones set in New York. Seinfeld, Friends, The Cosby Show, Law and Order, anything I could find. Rachel, Monica and Phoebe were my favourites. One day Nikolai beat me to a pulp in front of Pasha, while I was pregnant with you. That changed everything. From that moment on, I had an ally, someone who could really help me. We planned my escape for when I would be out of the house to give birth to you. Pasha had a good friend at the hospital, a doctor who helped us. He made me stay in the hospital for two weeks while I recovered from the birth and then Pasha arranged through his contacts for me to be taken out of Chechnya and driven to Moscow, where I got on a plane to New York. Oh, Brittney, it was so scary, but I knew I had to be strong, I knew I had to do it for me, for you and for Chad.'

'Oh God. Chad! I can't stand not knowing what's happened to him! I hope he's okay,' cried Brittney with a whole new set of tears.

'Let's wait and see Brittney, there's no point getting upset when we don't know what's happened,' Amy said as she reached out for Brittney again and this time found a willing recipient, as her daughter rested her head onto Amy's shoulder.

'Oh, Mom, I can't believe you had to go through all that by yourself, when you were still just a teenager! How did you do it?'

'I just did it. I knew I had to give you and Chad the life you deserved, not one run by a madman.'

'So, did you ever hear any more of my uncle Vladimir?' asked Brittney.

'Not for more than 20 years, until our simple friend the guard told me a few minutes ago that Vladimir was here and would be coming to see us soon,' responded Amy with a shudder, as a feeling of cold ice running through her veins wracked her body with a deep shiver.

CHAPTER 36

With a huge sigh, I collapsed on the bed. I was devastated. Alone in a foreign country, just a simple country boy from Australia, I couldn't speak the language, had no idea what to do, my best friend, in fact my only true friend, was dead and the love of my life had been kidnapped by psychotic Russian gangsters.

Finally, I gave myself permission to grieve. I'm not ashamed to admit that I broke down sobbing on the bed. It had just gone ten years since my dad had died but it still felt like yesterday, as Chad's death brought all those old feelings back to the surface. All the pain, anger and grief gripped me in an overwhelming sense of loss that turned me into a quivering mess, curled up in the foetal position rocking back and forth on the mattress.

Finally, my training took over, arresting my downward spiral and kicking in to cope with the stress. My years of Zen meditation training allowed me to focus inwards and slow down, just like Viktor had taught me. Viktor! Maybe he would know what to do. Plus, I needed to call Mum and let her know I was okay. And I needed a plan, a strategy to rescue Brittney and Amy. As my mind started working again, I realized that while my situation was pretty messed up, it wasn't completely hopeless. If I could keep my shit together, the girls had a chance. The realization that I was their *only* chance gave me the strength and the will to pull myself together.

First step was Mum. I had to let her know I was alright. She would have seen what happened to Chad on TV a few hours ago and would be worried sick when she hadn't heard from me. After that, the next step would be Viktor. But I had no way of calling them with a dead phone that would be tracked anyway and not enough money to pay the ruthless innkeeper the extortionate rates he would no doubt hit me with for an international call. Then it struck me; the wonder of the internet could save me. But first – a shower! Then some food. I needed fuel to keep this massive body running and I was beginning to feel light-headed because it seemed like an age since I'd last tossed anything down my gullet.

The dribble that masqueraded as a shower in my bathroom eventually served its purpose, although this was somewhat negated when I put my same dirty clothes back on again. However, I did feel marginally better as I stepped out of my room, down the stairs to the lobby and out into the fresh night air. I spied a homely looking restaurant across the road that looked like it would have something in my price range, which right now was somewhere down at the beggar end of the scale. I had to stretch my cash to last as long as possible.

The restaurant was not exactly a hive of activity. A total of three customers glanced up at me as the little bell on the door clanged when I entered, then immediately turned their attention back to their evening meal. Clearly, I was of no consequence or interest to them in their night of barely restrained frivolity.

As soon as I entered, a waiter greeted me with something completely incomprehensible and I stared blankly back at him and said, 'Sorry mate, but I don't speak whatever lingo you're laying on me. Do you speak English by any chance?'

A smile came across the waiter's face as he responded, 'Yes Sir, I do speak a little English. My girlfriend is from England, I met her when I was travelling last year. She is living in London now and we talk every week over the internet, so I improve my English all the time. My name is Dragomir and I'll be your waiter tonight.'

'Fantastic! What a relief, I'm so glad we can understand each other.

My name's Tommy; pleased to meet you. I'm just after a big hearty meal that's filling and not too expensive.'

'Mother has made her special Transylvanian Goulash tonight. I'll do an extra-large serving for you with some big slices of homemade bread to go with it.'

'Awesome. Is Count Dracula going to be dining with us tonight?' I asked, but clearly, he was immune to my sad attempt at humour or had just heard so many jokes about vampires and his homeland that he just didn't respond.

I took my seat and waited for my new friend the waiter to put my stomach out of its misery. By this time, I resembled one of Pavlov's dogs, salivating at the prospect of chowing down on whatever was generating the delicious smells that were emanating from the kitchen. My hunger had hit me like a freight train, embedding itself deep in my gut. Aside from a couple of sandwiches, I'd been running on adrenaline all day and ignoring my body's demands for fuel, but now it was having its revenge. My stomach had taken over my body and my brain would just have to wait until it could be in command again.

After what seemed like an age but was really only a few minutes, Dragomir came out of the kitchen with an enormous bowl full to the brim with a steaming stew that had my name written all over it, accompanied by a dinner plate with three slabs of bread topped with lashings of deliciously rich looking butter. I swear some drool leaked out of the corner of my mouth and ran down my chin.

'Here you are Sir, enjoy your meal,' said the waiter as he placed the glorious feast in front of me.

'Thank you Dragomir, you're a champion. This looks amazing!' I said and then hoed in. The next few minutes were a blur of dipping, spreading, slurping, chewing, spooning and swallowing as I tucked into what was the most amazing stew I had ever eaten in my life. My table manners took a back seat to my enjoyment of the meal and the need to recharge my batteries. Finally slowing towards the end of the meal, I was beginning to regain my humanity and my consciousness as the hearty stew did its job and calmed my screaming hunger.

As my stomach was sated, my brain stepped back into the picture again and started to do its thing, running through the logistics of what I needed to accomplish next. The big requirement was a sensible means of communication that wouldn't cost me the earth and couldn't be traced back to me. Then it hit me! Duh, it had been staring me in the face, but my neglected gut wouldn't let my brain make the necessary connections to arrive at the solution that now seemed so obvious; Dragomir! Time to cement the friendship before I hit him up for a favour.

'Hey, Dragomir,' I called over to my waiter, who was not exactly run off his feet since I was the only one left in the restaurant.

'Yes, Sir? Is everything okay with your meal?' he asked as he came over.

'Well clearly, yes. As you can see, your dishwasher won't have to work too hard on this,' I said, proudly displaying my enormous bowl that had been wiped clean of any trace of Transylvanian Goulash with the last of my bread.

'Excellent, my mother will be happy to see her food enjoyed so much. Would you like some dessert, Sir? We have an excellent traditional Romanian apple pie that I can prepare for you.'

'Absolutely, sounds perfect. But only if you join me and have a piece yourself. You've got no more customers and it's getting late. You deserve to sit down and enjoy some of your mum's cooking.'

'You know what? I think I will have some with you, it has been a long day and my feet are killing me. I'll make your slice on the house.'

'You little ripper Dragomir, that's awesome, thanks,' I said as he went off to the dessert cabinet and served out two huge slices of scrumptious looking apple pie, topped each of them with a gigantic blob of whipped cream and brought them over to the table. This was exactly what the doctor ordered; I was feeling much better now, and this apple pie would finish me off nicely.

As we tucked into our desserts, we chatted about various things and I asked Dragomir about his travels and his girlfriend. He was helping the family in the restaurant business, saving up enough money so he could travel again and go back to be with his girlfriend. I saw my opening and weaved it into the conversation with the subtlety of a house brick. 'So, how do you communicate with your girlfriend?' I asked smoothly.

'Easy,' he responded. 'I just use an app on my phone, and I can talk to her for free as long as I have an internet connection.'

'What about calling regular phones through the app? Can you talk to other people if they don't have the app?'

'Yes, I can call anyone, even internationally, for just a few cents a minute,' he said, which was music to my ears.

Okay, there's the opening, let's drive the truck through it. 'That's awesome!' I said. 'Don't you love the technology we've got? We're a lucky generation to have all this stuff at our fingertips. Look, I know this might be a bit much, but could I ask a huge favour? Do you think it would be too much trouble if I borrowed your phone to make a couple of calls using your app? My phone's dead, plus I don't even have international roaming set up on it.' I left out the part about the police, not to mention trained killers, watching my every move and probably tracking my phone.

Dragomir was obviously a bit taken aback by this bold request from a total stranger, but it seemed that in his time as a young traveller he had adopted the Backpackers Code, so after a moment's deliberation agreed to help out a fellow traveller in need. He directed me to the office at the back of the restaurant and told me to take my time with my calls, since he had to finish up for the night and get ready for the next day anyway.

'Thanks, Dragomir, you're a legend mate. I owe you, big time,' I said as he left me in the office, closing the door behind him.

I fired up the app on Dragomir's phone and punched in Mum's number, wondering how the hell I was going to explain all this and just how much to tell her. I decided that a white lie would be best so she wouldn't freak out. After just a few short rings, she picked up and said, 'Hello? Who's this calling? The number came up unlisted.'

'Hi Mum, it's just me, Tommy. The number's showing as unlisted because I'm calling through an app on someone else's phone.'

'Oh Tommy, I'm so happy to hear from you, I was so worried about you! I saw Chad on the TV and he got hurt, but they didn't say anything, it's just terrible! Is he okay? I tried calling your phone but couldn't get through. Are you alright?' said Mum, sounding extremely concerned.

'Yes, I'm okay, Mum, but I'm afraid Chad is dead. It was terrible, but I'm a bit better now. Sorry you couldn't get through on my phone, but I was a witness, so the police wanted to talk to me and then my phone went flat. I can't talk for long, I just wanted to let you know I'm okay. I'll be staying until the Closing Ceremony as originally planned.'

If only she knew the truth, she would understand that the Closing Ceremony of the Olympics was absolutely the last thing on my mind right now, but I didn't want her to worry, so just left it at that.

After a few more minutes, Mum and I finished our brief chat and I signed off, reassuring her that everything was fine. I hated lying to Mum, but I knew she wouldn't cope with the truth right now.

With Mum sorted, my next step was Viktor. After much deliberation, I decided to come clean and tell him everything. If I was going to ask him for advice, I needed to be fair and give him as much information as possible. With more than a touch of trepidation I dialled his number.

'Hello. Who is this?' Viktor's familiar deep, thick voice with its heavily accented intonation came through the phone.

'Hi Viktor, it's Tommy, calling from Romania,' I responded, trying to keep the emotion and stress out of my voice.

'Ah, Tommy, it's so good to hear from you!' came the response from

Viktor, who was obviously delighted to hear my voice. I chided myself for not ringing him yesterday after I had won my gold medal. I really should have shared that moment with him as well as Mum – after all, he was the reason I was here, but I had neglected Viktor a bit in the last 12 months in my lead-up to the Olympics. I had just been so busy that I hadn't made as much time to keep in touch with him as I should have.

'Congratulations on your gold medal Tommy! I am so proud of you. You fought well. Your opponent was strong, skilled and experienced. You did really well to beat him.'

'Thanks Viktor, that means a lot to me. I owe everything to you. All of your training and guidance over the years won it for me.'

'No, that's not true Tommy. You did it yourself. It was you up there, not me. I am one of the parts that make up the whole, but you are the champion Tommy, only you. You put in all the work, you listened, you learned, you trained hard and you did what needed to be done to win. You deserve all the credit for your win, not me and no one else. How are you feeling?'

'Uh, I'm okay. I'm sorry I didn't call you yesterday, things have been crazy here and I'm sorry I haven't been in touch with you much over the past year. All the training in the lead-up to the Olympics has been pretty intense.' My voice was cracking, and I was having trouble keeping it all together. It was all I could do not to just blurt everything out in one big mess.

'That's fine Tommy, there's no need to apologize. I've been busy myself with the dojo and training and everything. I don't expect you to call me constantly; you have your own life and I have mine. I'm happy to be a part of your life, but you don't need to call me every five minutes.'

Clearly sensing something was up with me, Viktor said, 'Tommy, tell me the truth. Are you okay? You sound strange. I've known you for a long time and we've been through a lot together. I get the feeling there's something you're not telling me.'

'Well, actually there is something. Did you see Chad's wrestling match or hear any news from the Olympics today?'

'No, I went out for a run this morning and then I was busy after that in the dojo. What happened?'

This was going to be tough. He had no idea what had gone on, so I would need to lay it all out for him. 'Well, to say the day has been dramatic would be the understatement of the century. I saw Chad this morning and he really didn't look well. I didn't think he should fight, but he was insistent. He started his fight but was clearly no match for his opponent because he was so sick. After just a few seconds he was flipped on his back and then just laid there without moving, it was terrible. The medics came over, put up some screens around him, examined him and then I saw him with a sheet pulled up over his face. It was so hard. He was my best friend!' That was all I could get out before I began blubbering like a baby, sobbing down the phone to Viktor, who was the closest thing I'd had to a father since my dad had died so many years ago.

'Oh, Tommy, I'm sorry to hear that. I know you and Chad were close. I can understand why you're so upset; it must be hard for you. How is Brittney, is she there with you?'

After a long pause while I collected myself, I finally responded 'Well, that's the other problem. Brittney and her mum have been kidnapped by some Russian thugs!'

'What! What do you mean? How did that happen?' asked Viktor, incredulous at this news.

'These thugs just grabbed them at the stadium. I had just seen the sheet over Chad's head, then I looked over at Brittney and Amy and saw them being taken away at gunpoint, so I took off after them. I knew the cops and security guards would be too busy with the crowd chaos, so it was all up to me. I saw the goons drug the girls and toss their bodies in the back of a car and take off, with another car following, so I stole a car and chased after them. I managed to take out the support car and question one of the men who took the girls, to see who was responsible for it and why the hell they wanted them.'

'So, you asked the kidnapper who was responsible. What did he say?'

'He said it was someone named Vladimir Zhukov.'

There was a long silence on the other end of the phone, then in a quiet, menacing tone that I'd never heard before from Viktor, he said coldly, 'Don't go anywhere, don't call anyone. Now that you've chased after them, they know what you look like and that you're a friend of Chad. They probably saw you compete, so you can't go out in the open again, you must stay in hiding. Stay where you are. I'm going to come straight to you. Tell me your exact location.'

Whoa. Hold the phone. Who was this stranger talking down the phone? I had never heard Viktor speak like this before; it was like he'd transformed into some sort of killer spy or something. But I must admit it was very reassuring. Somehow, I knew that Viktor would help, and we would have some sort of chance.

'I'm in a town called Medgidia in Romania, a couple of hours from Bucharest on the way to the Black Sea. My hotel is called Pension Iliescu and the address is Strada Poporului 34.'

'Okay. I've got it. Stay there. Whatever you do, don't leave your hotel. I'll come to you. I'll pack now and go straight to the airport to catch the first plane out of Sydney tonight.'

I was so overwhelmed; I couldn't believe it. My friend and mentor was coming to help me! Maybe there was a chance to save Brittney if Viktor were here to help me. 'Um, I don't know what to say Viktor, except thank you,' I stammered down the line.

'You may not thank me after this is all over. Are you sure you want to go through with this? I can tell you right now that it's going to get very messy.'

'Hey, I'm all in Viktor, all the way. I'm already in this shit up to my neck. I must be a wanted man by now; I've already killed two people in a car crash and fled the scene. The woman I love and want to spend the rest of my life with has been taken away by some psycho for God knows what reason, so I don't care if it gets messy. In fact, bring it on, because I want to get the bastards that took Brittney, especially if they had something to do with Chad's death.'

'Okay, I just wanted to make sure. Now, one more question. What happened to Chad? Do you know the cause of death?'

'No, I've got no idea. I left the stadium and followed the girls straight after Chad died and I haven't heard any news since.'

'We need to find out what's going on there. Is there anyone you know connected to Chad or his family who could be an official liaison with the local authorities?'

It took me a few seconds but then I suddenly thought of the perfect person for the task. 'George! He could do it. He's Amy's head of security, I've met him a couple of times at Chad's place. He's an ex-New York City cop, a real tough bastard. I'll call him as soon as we finish. Amy gave me his number as her emergency contact before we came to Romania. I'm sure he'll be able to help.'

'Perfect,' responded Viktor. 'You call George and get him to Bucharest. Tell him to make some waves with the local authorities, make them take notice of him and give him some answers. Tell him not to call you, that we'll get in touch with him.'

'Okay, will do. Anything else?'

'No. That's it. Just stay strong Tommy, we'll get them back. I'll be there soon to help you. Stay out of sight, stay in your room, don't let anyone see your face, don't use the phone, don't use credit cards, use only cash for whatever you need. I'll be on my way to you very soon.'

'Thank you so much Viktor, you don't know what this means to me.'

'Actually Tommy, I know exactly how much this means. Someone once helped me a great deal, in fact he saved my life. And I have some experience in kidnap and escape, so I know how you're feeling right now.

But like I said, be strong, we'll get through this together. See you soon.' The line went dead.

Okay, what just happened? What the hell does all this mean? What on Earth is Viktor's story? So many questions, but no time to answer them. I brought myself back into focus, dug out my phone and fished out the note I had written and stuffed in my phone cover in case my phone died, and still needed my numbers. I was thankful I'd thought enough to be prepared and write this shit down.

I spotted George's number in my tiny handwriting and made my third and final call. It only took two rings before an urgent voice in its distinctive New York accent snapped 'Hello, who's this?'

'Hello George, it's Tommy. I'm calling about Chad.'

'Jesus Christ! I'm glad to hear from you. I've been trying to work out what the hell is going on, but nobody is telling me anything. I saw Chad's fight on the TV hours ago and have been calling him and Amy and Brittney ever since but can't get through to anyone! I've called the police, the hospitals and the Olympic officials but nobody will tell me jack-shit. I've just booked a flight to Bucharest and I'm on my way to the airport now.'

'I'm sorry George, but Chad's dead. He died on the mat today.'

There was a slow exhalation of breath on the other end of the line as George absorbed the news. 'Damn, I'm really sorry to hear that. He was a great kid. Amy will be devastated. What a loss for a mother to bear. Well, I sure appreciate you calling me. So, are Amy and Brittney with you? Why aren't they answering their phones?'

'Well, see that's the thing. They've kind of been kidnapped.'

'What!' George exploded at the other end of the line. 'When? How? Do the police know? Why are you only calling me now?'

'Whoa, slow down George. I've been kind of busy here, so I haven't exactly had time to bring everyone up to speed, but I know you want to know what's going on.'

I laid it all out for George from beginning to end, including my part in the death of two men, which had likely resulted in me being a person of interest with the police, Viktor's impending arrival and the name of the man responsible for taking Amy and Brittney.

'Alright, understood. So, what can I do?' asked George. 'I'll be in Bucharest tomorrow.'

'Viktor and I will handle the unofficial pursuit, but we need you to handle the official side. We need you to be the liaison with the local police, hospitals, Olympic officials and media. We need to know how Chad died, what the authorities know and who this Vladimir Zhukov is.'

'Ten-four. Understood. I'm on my way. How do I get in touch with you?'

'You don't. I need to stay off the grid, so you can't call me. I'll call you, check in for updates when I can. Just make sure your phone number works when you land in Romania. When I get myself together, I'll see if I can arrange a local pre-paid phone that can't be traced back to me. Until then, just wait to hear from me. Thanks George, it means a lot to me knowing you'll be close-by and on our side.'

'Absolutely, Tommy. We need to do everything we can to save Amy and Brittney. I'll be all over it when I get there. Bye.'

'See you George. And thanks again.'

The line went dead. Mission accomplished. Correction – mission started. I felt much better knowing I had reinforcements coming and that I wasn't completely alone in my quest to save Brittney and Amy.

Just then I heard a quiet knock on the door of the office. It was Dragomir. 'I'm finished up out here. Are you all done with your calls?'

'Yes, thanks so much mate, that was awesome. You've really helped me out of a bind here. How much do I owe you?'

'No, no, there's no need for any payment. Don't worry about it, it's only a couple of dollars.'

'You sure? You really did me a big favour, Dragomir.'

'Yes, of course, it's fine. That's what travellers do; they look after each other, they give rides to hitchhikers, they let you sleep on their couch and they give you internet access when you need it. It's the backpacker's code. You repay the favour next time you help someone else. Kind of like Karma, but in your current life, not the next one.'

'Mate, that is brilliant and so are you. I won't forget this. Thanks again. I'd better go now and let you get some sleep.'

'Okay, thanks Tommy, it was great to meet you. Good luck on your travels.' We shook hands and I headed out into the darkness, back to my hotel.

It had been a successful night; I had washed, eaten and called in reinforcements. All that was left now was to get some sleep. I was completely shagged and in serious need of some shuteye. Back in my room I stripped off my clothes, collapsed on the bed and within seconds was out like a light.

Thankfully, my subconscious left me alone for the night and I slept like the dead. I woke in the morning after 12 solid hours of sleep, feeling much better than at any period over the past two crazy days and their emotional highs and lows.

I knew all I could do was wait for Viktor to arrive. I had nowhere to go and nothing to do except eat, rest and prepare myself for the chaos that was to come. First order of the day was food. After such a long sleep, my giant frame and high metabolism that was accustomed to a ridiculously high calorie intake (more than double that of most people), was sounding the alarm via my stomach that I needed some fuel. I decided I would stock up on supplies that I could prepare by myself and just eat in the room so I wouldn't have to go out every few hours to buy food and risk being identified.

The night before at dinner I'd spotted a grocery store down the street, so I headed out the door with the last of my cash. I slipped the hood of my black jacket way down over my face, stuck my shoulders back, puffed out my chest and stood up tall to my full height above two metres. I must have struck an imposing figure because nobody gave me even a first look, let alone a second, as I strode purposefully down the street. I did my rounds of the grocery store, stocking up on staples like canned meat, bread, fruit and instant noodles, paid my money to the bored cashier and was back safe in my hotel room in less than 30 minutes.

After a solid breakfast in my hotel room, the next order of business was some physical activity. I was feeling stiff and sore after the exertions of the last two days and I needed to work out the cobwebs, big time. I stripped down to my jocks and pumped out sets of star jumps, burpees, push-ups and sit-ups until I'd reached 300 of each and then cooled down with a long stretching session and a cold shower.

With the physical taken care of, it was time for the mental and emotional. I got myself into the lotus position and settled in for an hour of Zen meditation. More than ever, I needed the calming effect that meditating always provided for me. I emptied my mind and thought of nothing, slowing my breathing and my heart rate until it was almost imperceptible, achieving a plane of stillness that was incredibly rejuvenating for the mind and the spirit.

With my ritual complete, it was now time for the long wait until night-time and Viktor's arrival sometime the next day. I figured it was the right time to honour Chad and say goodbye properly. I decided to write him a eulogy, committing to myself that I would deliver it for him at a memorial service in his honour, back in New York in front of his friends and Brittney and Amy. I formed this image clearly in my mind, focused all my energy and attention to it, as if by sheer force of will that I could manifest this outcome. I formed this bright, clear vision in my consciousness, knowing it would give me the strength I was sure to need to recover my beautiful Brittney.

Over the course of the next few hours, I meditated on Chad, searching my memories for all the times we'd spent together and everything we'd done for each other, the countless hours we'd spent pushing each other on the mats to be our best, him taking me under his wing and making me part of his family, being the best friend a man could ever hope for. The eulogy basically wrote itself, the words forming as if by magic as the dodgy hotel pen scribbled across the ancient notepad I'd found tucked away in a dusty drawer. By the time I had finished my tribute to the only truly close friend I had ever had, tears were streaming down my cheeks and dripping unchecked onto the desk below as I finally mourned my loss and properly said goodbye.

Once again emotionally exhausted, I prepared a solid dinner and then fell into bed. However, this night my subconscious was not quite so kind to me. It took me an age to fall asleep and I spent the night in a fitful slumber, with images of Chad's lifeless body and Brittney and Amy locked up in some dank dungeon constantly flashing before my eyes. When dawn finally broke, I was in a cold sweat on clammy sheets and felt like crap. I was antsy and restless. I wanted to be on the move and the wait for Viktor to arrive was killing me. I felt like every moment I was sitting here doing nothing, Brittney and Amy were getting further and further beyond my reach. Every fibre of my being, every nerve ending was pulled taut like piano wire.

I wanted, no, I *needed* action.

CHAPTER 37

Once again, keys jangled against the metal door and the rusty hinges screeched in protest, just like last time. Although Amy and Brittney now felt a much greater sense of dread in anticipation of being in the presence of the ominous Vladimir. The door swung open and Amy let out an involuntary gasp as her eyes set upon the grey visage of her brutal brother-in-law, who set his steely gaze upon her through squinted eyes.

In deep, sonorous tones, he greeted her in Russian, to which she immediately responded, 'English please Vladimir, so my daughter can understand us.'

'Very well Tatiana, as you wish,' he replied in perfect English. Glancing over at Brittney, he said with a smile, 'So, this must be Valentina, the babe who triggered all that madness so many years ago. You have certainly grown into a beautiful young woman.' He shot her a leering look as he appraised her carefully.

Brittney felt a chill at the creepy gaze that seemed to go right through her. They say that the eyes are the windows to the soul, and Vladimir looked dead inside. Struggling to keep herself steady and in control, Brittney replied in a deadpan tone, 'Hello, Uncle.'

A loud, deep and throaty laugh erupted from Vladimir at this greeting from his niece. 'She has spirit, Tatiana, just like her mother. You know, I admired you very much for what you did to my brother. He was not an easy man to live with and certainly not easy to escape from. You did well to get away with your life and those of your children.'

'I can't say I was sorry to find out that Nikolai was killed after I escaped. I was glad he couldn't come after me. What happened to him?'

Vladimir rubbed his chin thoughtfully and said, 'His head had an unfortunate encounter with a large calibre bullet, fired from a weapon by a still unidentified but unquestionably expert marksman. Sadly, I have not been able to have my revenge on his killer even after all these years. One day, the truth will come out.'

'I'm sure it will,' responded Amy. 'So how do we come to be here imprisoned by you? What do you intend to do with us and what did you do to my son?'

'So many questions Tatiana, so many questions. But never mind, they will be answered in good time. You know, I'd forgotten how beautiful you were all those years ago, but you were much too young for me then. Seeing you again in the flesh has reminded me of your beauty. Age has been kind to you, you have more experience, more confidence and greater presence than the scared little girl you used to be. You are so much more beautiful now than you ever were before,' crooned Vladimir in his silky smooth but sinister and menacing voice.

Vladimir felt a stirring that he had not had for many years; an attraction for a woman that went beyond the sexual dalliances he had with his many whores. The thought of a companion, someone to share his life with, was something that Vladimir had long ago dismissed as fantasy. But here she was, his brother's wife, standing before him, large as life. Could he? Would she?

Amy and Brittney squirmed under the unblinking gaze of the cold, ruthless killer standing before them, wondering what on earth could be going on inside that twisted mind.

Suddenly, he blinked, shook his head, smiled, barked an order in Russian to the two guards, turned and marched out the door as the guards made their way into the room. 'No!' shouted Amy, clearly understanding Vladimir's instructions. 'Stay away from me!'

'Mom, what's going on?' shouted Brittney, suddenly concerned about what was coming next.

'Vladimir said the guards must take me with them to Kiev, but you are to stay here in Odessa.'

'No way! They can't separate us. Not if I've got anything to do with it,' said a determined Brittney. 'Jesus, I really wish I wasn't tied up right now or I would really kick the shit out of these two halfwits. Guess I'll just have to make do with what I've got.'

In one fluid movement, Brittney jumped off the packing crate, extended her arms out in front of her, whirled around spinning her clubbed fists in a 360-degree arc and smashed one of the guards squarely on the side of the jaw as he moved towards her. The man's head snapped around with a violent twist of the neck. Out cold, he dropped to the floor like a sack of potatoes.

Brittney knew the element of surprise only went so far, and she had just used up all her advantage. Eyeing the next guard coldly, Brittney sized him up, got in range and then jumped straight up in the air, tucked her knees up to her chest and then at the peak of her leap exploded out horizontally, slamming her extending feet into her attacker's chest and sending him flying backwards with a loud whoosh of air escaping from his lungs. She twisted her body in the air, knowing the fall was going to hurt when she hit the deck, but boy was it worth it to see that dumb oaf go flying!

Crash! She hit the hard stone floor with a thud. 'Obviously should have practiced some break-falls with my hands and feet tied up,' she thought ruefully. Momentarily stunned from the impact, she looked up with surprise into the dark muzzle of a gun pointing straight at her head from close range, by a giant of a man every bit a match in size for her man Tommy. Clearly, this guy wasn't as hapless as the other two losers she'd just taken out. She quickly figured she would be no match for him.

'Very impressive, little girl, but that's all for now. One more move and I'll blast your brains out,' sneered the beast. 'The boss doesn't care about you, so I've got no instructions to keep you alive. Vladimir has given you to me, so you and I will be having some fun later. You get to stay here in Odessa with me and we can have our own little party,' he growled, accompanied by a lurid sneer, his nostrils flaring wide and his lip curling up at one corner of his mouth in anticipation. His tongue snaked out of his mouth and he licked his lips in just about the creepiest gesture imaginable. Brittney's skin crawled and her stomach curled into a cold, tight knot of fear at what lay in store for her from this brute.

Borys glanced over at Amy, pointed the gun at her and waved it towards the open door, past the guards lying on the floor, one unconscious, the other groaning and holding his solar plexus, struggling for breath.

'No! I'm not going anywhere!' shouted Amy, a mix of rage and panic in her voice. 'I'm staying here with Brittney!'

'The boss wants you in Kiev and that's exactly where you're going, whore,' sneered Borys. In two giant strides he was at Amy, reaching out his hand and grabbing her by the hair, violently dragging her off the packing crate. Amy cried out in pain, feet scrambling beneath her, trying to stay upright and prevent a scalping.

'Hey, stop it you bastard!' shouted Brittney as she leapt to her mother's defence. But Borys was much more of a challenge than the other two bozos Brittney had dispatched so easily. In all his years as an elite soldier in the Russian Spetsnaz special forces unit, Borys had faced combatants much more difficult than a young woman with bound hands and feet. With about as much effort as swatting a fly, Borys unleashed a huge backhand with his gun arm, catching Brittney at full speed across the right side of her face and knocking her senseless.

Down on the ground, the last sight Brittney witnessed through closing eyes before she passed out was Borys dragging her mother out of their prison cell by the hair, kicking and screaming in protest.

CHAPTER 38

'What the hell is going on here?' muttered the radiographer. 'My X-ray machine is really playing up today. The last three people I've had in here, I haven't been able to get a clean image!' He grabbed the phone and called the hospital technician to come and investigate. 'Leonid, have you checked my X-ray machine recently or recalibrated it or something? It's messing up all my images today and I've got a huge backlog of cases to get through!'

'No,' came the laconic response from the other end of the phone. 'I'll come up and check it out. Calm down and go and get yourself a coffee while I look at it.'

After an impatient caffeine hit, the radiographer was greeted with a puzzled expression from the technician, who said, 'Well, everything seems fine with the machine. Maybe it's excessive background radiation from some other source. You haven't left any radiation sources lying around, have you?'

'Of course not, don't be ridiculous!' replied the indignant radiographer. 'I know how dangerous that stuff can be, and I wouldn't leave it just anywhere.'

'Maybe the problem is with the X-ray plates rather than the machine. Did you leave the new plates somewhere else before you brought them in here?' asked the technician.

'I did stop, but only in the corridor near the morgue after I got some new plates from the storeroom. I put the box of new plates down for a minute while I grabbed something. Do you have a Geiger counter we can use to check the radiation levels?'

'I've got one down in the basement, I'll go find it and come straight back up. I want to get to the bottom of this,' said the technician as he went off down the stairs. The radiographer retreated into his office to bide his time catching up on some paperwork.

The technician soon returned with his radiation detector and together with the radiographer they began their sweep of the hospital, starting with the X-ray room, where they noted the levels were somewhat higher than normal.

'Where is it coming from?' asked the radiographer.

'I'm not sure, I've only just turned it on,' responded the technician. 'Let's see if we can track it down.' He started a methodical sweep of the X-ray room and quickly identified that the source was strongest at the open door of the room. The technician and the radiographer made an odd couple as they stepped out into the hospital corridor, walking stiff-legged and staring intently down at the chattering device, which had increased its tempo as they moved out of the X-ray room.

The bizarre game of hide and seek steadily directed them to the morgue and then to their utmost surprise a body bag! 'TICK, TICK, TICK, TICK, TICK, TICK,' rattled the angry staccato of the Geiger counter as they placed the detector close to the body bag.

The self-appointed radiation detectives had expected the source of the radiation to be a machine or a rogue medical radiation source, certainly not a body. The radiographer and the technician looked concerned as they stared down at the Geiger counter, hardly believing their eyes as they observed the radiation levels.

Left in the anteroom of the morgue, the body bag was emitting high levels of radiation that were extremely unusual for a human body. 'No wonder he's dead,' mumbled the technician.

'We can't just leave him here; he's soaking the entire area with dangerous levels of radiation. We need to isolate him now and call the authorities in Bucharest. For now, let's put the body in the X-ray room and shut the door. It's one of the most heavily shielded rooms in the entire building.'

They alerted the morgue and the hospital supervisor to the dangerous and unprecedented situation, and wheeled the anonymous body in the thick plastic bag fitted with heavy duty zippers into the X-ray room, shut the door behind them and stuck a hastily scribbled 'No Entry' sign on the door. A mobile refrigeration unit was hustled into the room to keep the temperature cold and slow the normal decomposition process. But this was no normal body hidden inside the ominous black body bag.

As one of Ukraine's neighbours along with Belarus, Poland, Russia and Moldova, Romania had entirely too much experience with the detection and management of nuclear radiation as a result of the Chernobyl nuclear power plant disaster. With their own nuclear power station in Cernavoda and their fair share of knowledge in Bucharest, Romania was not lacking in nuclear experts to call for assistance. The hospital was instructed not to do anything with the body until the experts came to investigate.

CHAPTER 39

George was a grizzled veteran of the New York Police Department. After 40 years of service all the way up from beat cop to Assistant Chief, he bled blue. He had seen it all in his time on the force until finally at the age of 60, he had retired from duty. After a year with his feet up, he decided retirement wasn't for him, so in a bid to keep himself sharp and stay active, he had taken on the role of Amy's head of security at the recommendation of a mutual friend. After three years in the job, he had become a trusted confidant of Amy and proved himself to be more than capable of handling a multitude of situations.

As he stepped out of the airport and onto Romanian soil for the first time in his life, George summoned all his reserves of strength and prepared himself for what was to come. He went straight from the airport to the stadium where Chad had died and discovered there had still been no official announcement of Chad's status. A total media blackout had been enforced around that day's events and nobody knew what was happening. Speculation was rife among officials and the media, but no one knew the truth. Clearly George would need to run the story down himself and get to the source – Chad's body.

After much interrogation and bluster, George eventually extracted the name of the hospital where Chad had been taken. After a long and difficult process of negotiation, he was finally standing behind a lead-lined shield, observing the scene on a remote monitor in the X-ray room. A formal identification of the body was required.

'The radiation levels in the room are dangerously high and they seem to be getting worse, which is extremely concerning,' explained the radiographer. 'The body in the bag may be decaying, which could be exposing more of the radiation source. This suit will give you some protection against the radiation, but you'll still only be able to be in there for a maximum of five minutes. The doctor will go in with you to inspect the body also.'

George had fought physical assailants and visible dangers his entire working life but had never experienced the invisible killer that was radiation. While not visible to the human retina, George almost convinced himself he could see the deadly rays waving through the air as he walked into the room, clad in a full body suit.

They stepped over to the sinister looking body bag and its dangerous contents. The doctor reached out for the heavy zipper and pulled it down, revealing the shocking contents to the two men and those watching and recording the scene on the mobile camera mounted on the headpiece of the doctor's suit.

What had sometime before been Chad hardly even seemed human anymore. The skin and the flesh beneath it, particularly around his face, appeared to be dissolving in some hideous cellular decay. His nose had completely disappeared, leaving a dark empty cavity behind with a creepily glowing, pulsing yellow ember where his nose used to be. The cheeks were sunken, and the flesh seemed to be flowing like liquid, succumbing to gravity's pull, and filling the body bag with a gelatinous mess of cellular ooze.

'What the fuck!' exclaimed George as he saw what remained of Chad's unrecognizable face. Luckily, he was made of stern stuff from his years on the beat, busting crack houses and meth labs and seeing the state of the addicts within, or he might have thrown up inside his radiation suit.

'I can't tell if that's Chad or not by his face. Let's look at the rest of him,' said George. The doctor pulled the zipper down further, exposing all of Chad's body to the room and the camera. Clearly the source of whatever was dissolving Chad was located at his head, or more specifically around his nose. The damage was radiating out from this point, so the extremities of his legs and feet were not as severely damaged.

Oddly, the body was still clad in Chad's wrestling uniform, having just been dumped in the entry foyer of the morgue but not yet processed. The name 'Wilson' emblazoned on the uniform was a strong indicator, but the always-thorough George wanted more confirmation. 'Well, the uniform is right, and the body sure looks like Chad, it's about the right height and weight. Check his right ankle, he got a tattoo of the Olympic rings there a few months ago when he made the Olympic team,' said George to the doctor.

'Yes, there is a tattoo of the rings here. Based on the chain of possession of the body from the stadium to the hospital by the ambulance, our identification tag and your corroborating evidence, I am sufficiently convinced to our required standard that this is in fact the body of Chad Wilson. Do you concur?'

'I do,' replied George with a heavy heart, his voice full of sadness.

CHAPTER 40

Finally! A knock at the door! I'd been going crazy in my hotel room all by myself with no company except my addled brain running at hyper speed. I obviously hadn't quite mastered this Zen business, but in my defence, I don't know if the old masters had quite as much to deal with as I had on my plate right now. I jumped up off the bed and bounced over to the door. I was full of nervous energy, wound up like a coiled spring ready to rapidly and suddenly unwind with the flick of a switch. I peered through the hole in the door and to my great relief I spotted Viktor looking back at me impassively from the dreary grey corridor, with furtive glances right and left.

I ripped the door open and Viktor quickly stepped out of the corridor, into my hotel room and back into my life. I had only seen Viktor once in the last four years. He had never visited me in the States and I'd only been able to afford one visit back home to Australia during my college years.

'Viktor, I'm so glad to see you! I was so relieved when you said you would come and help me,' I said to my old master and wrapped him up in a giant bear hug as only a man of my size can truly deliver.

'Tommy, my young friend, I'm very happy to see you too,' said Viktor as he returned my hug in spades. Belying his age, Viktor had a steely strength about him developed from years of committed training. Despite his wrinkles, his grey hair and more than 60 years of age, Viktor still had it. Knowing what I did of Viktor and his capabilities, even I would think twice about taking him on. Feeling his hard muscles in our manly hug I was suddenly reminded that you did not want to mess with Viktor.

'How was your trip? I know you don't like to travel, so I was surprised when you decided so quickly that you would come to Romania to help me get Brittney and Amy back. What made you come all this way?'

'I knew you needed help, that's all. My trip was fine, thanks.'

Communicative bastard, as usual. Viktor never was one for small talk. He really could be infuriating sometimes. Unflappable, quiet, supremely capable and wouldn't tell you shit if it didn't suit him.

'So, what's the plan?' I asked my old coach, unconsciously slipping back into the mentor and student roles we had established some ten years before back in Sydney. Viktor was a natural leader and he really seemed to have it together on this one, so I was happy to let him take the lead.

'I have some clothes for you, a map, an untraceable pre-paid phone with a local SIM card, a rental car, plenty of cash and some useful local knowledge about where we're headed.'

'Wow! Impressive,' I said with a smile. 'Looks like the old dog has still got a few tricks up his sleeve, hey?'

'Yes, I may be a bit slower than I used to be, but what I lack in speed I make up for in experience,' he responded with a chuckle.

'What did you mean when you said, *local knowledge*; are you from around here?'

'Oh, here and there. Never mind. There's time for that later. Here, put your new clothes on.' He pulled a rolled-up wad out of the bag that he'd tossed on the bed as he walked in the room and handed it to me.

It was only then that I realized what he was wearing. I was so used to seeing him wearing a Judogi uniform or else a simple tracksuit, I hadn't noticed that he was all in black, dressed like some kind of Ninja. Viktor was certainly full of surprises and I was sure as hell glad he had volunteered to come and help me in this crazy rescue attempt.

I pulled out my clothes to find they were a matching set to Viktor's all black getup. We would be a weird matching Ninja pair. Better than Viktor's favourite fluorescent green and orange track pants, I guess.

Eager for more information, I tried slipping in a few more questions as I stripped off, chucked my old clothes in the corner, and got changed into my stealth outfit, including matching black sneakers. But Viktor wouldn't have a bar of it; he was a closed book. This whole secrecy thing was making me very curious, but he wouldn't come clean. He clammed up completely and totally cut me off from any more questions when I asked him about Vladimir and what the story was with him. I had obviously touched a nerve there, so I decided to leave it alone, accepting that Viktor would tell me what I needed to know, when I needed to know it and not before.

Viktor pulled out his map and summoned me over. 'Okay, we're here,' he said, stabbing a craggy old finger onto the map, pointing out Medgidia, not far from the Romanian coastline on the Black Sea. 'You said that Amy and Brittney were being taken to Odessa. That's in Ukraine. We don't want to cross the border over land; we don't want any trouble with the border guards, and we don't want any record of us entering Ukraine. We're going to enter Ukraine by water, over the Black Sea.'

My eyes narrowed as I looked at Viktor with an even greater level of respect than I already had for him. This was a whole new side to my second father, which I'd never seen before. 'What is your story? How do you know all this stuff? Were you a spy or something?'

Viktor exploded with an uproarious laugh that bounced around the walls of my tiny hotel room. 'Ha! Spy? I don't think so. More like the complete opposite. Never mind about that. Focus, Tommy, we need to be sharp and absolutely on point if we are going to save your women. Eyes back to the map!' he barked as he snapped his fingers in front of my eyes.

'Okay, okay, keep your shirt on, I'm focused already.'

'We're going to drive to Constanta, which is a big port in Romania. It's not a long drive from here. We'll find a boat at Constanta and then head out this afternoon into the Black Sea. We'll head out away from the coast maybe 15 klicks and then travel around to Odessa,' said Viktor as he traced the route on the map for me.

'How far is it? How long do you think it will take?'

'It's probably about 300 klicks. The time will depend on how good our boat is, but we can probably do it in less than 12 hours, depending on how hard we push. We'll come into Odessa under the cover of darkness.'

'Alright, I'm in! Sounds like a good plan. Let's go. I've been sitting around here like a stale bottle of piss for too long now, time's been wasting. God knows what Brittney and Amy are going through right now.'

I grabbed my meagre collection of belongings, my last remaining shopping bag (hey, who knows when I might get hungry next, a man's got to eat), checked out of the hotel, paid the innkeeper the remainder of my bill and jumped into Viktor's nondescript Skoda sedan. We took it easy on the drive, careful not to raise any attention. I took the wheel so Viktor could get some shuteye to recharge after his long trip and get ready for the journey ahead. My passenger would soon become Captain Viktor on the boat, so he needed his beauty sleep in preparation.

I gave Viktor a nudge as we pulled into Constanta. With a grunt and a rub of his eyes he was soon wide awake. 'Pull into the carpark over there,' he said as he pointed to a corner of the lot. 'Leave the keys in and lock it. After a few days someone will report it but by then we'll be long gone, and it won't matter anymore. Now let's see if we can find a boat for us. We want something sturdy but not too flashy, not too expensive. We'll tell them we want to hire it for a few days to do some fishing.'

After only about 15 minutes of scouting, we found the perfect boat. A crusty old salt was sitting on the deck chomping on a cigar and nursing an extremely generous glass of whisky. A rusty old sign adorned with an untidy jumble of writing that Viktor informed me meant *For Rent* advertised his pride and joy, a serviceable boat that looked like it could sleep two people and had fishing gear on board.

Then it happened again. The *Viktor Enigma*, as I was beginning to think of him, just became even more complex. He started spouting a language that I'd never heard before and of course could understand absolutely nothing of what he was saying. The old sea dog grimaced, squinted his eyes distrustfully and shook his head. Then Viktor switched to a whole new language! Weirder and weirder. The boat owner cracked a toothless grin that sunk his cheeks way back into his mouth and nodded his head, apparently approving of Viktor's new choice of language.

After a few minutes of haggling, they reached an agreement, money was exchanged for keys and that was it. We had our transport to Odessa and were one step closer to Brittney.

We set sail (can you still say that if you've only got an engine? I don't know) and made our way out into the Black Sea. Viktor gave me some Captain's boat driving lessons, anointed me with the honour of First Mate, gave me a compass reading and went below to get some more sleep, resurfacing a few hours later. By this time, it was dusk, which to me meant dinner time, so we polished off the rest of my meagre food rations and then I headed down to try and push some Z's myself.

After some fitful rest filled with images of Brittney and Amy locked up in their dungeon (I really watched too many action movies as a kid), I resurfaced up in the cabin. It was pitch black outside and Viktor had all the lights off, running by the GPS mounted on what I thought of as the dashboard but didn't know what to call it on a boat. 'Are we there yet?' I said in a whining tone with a smile as I channelled my inner six-year-old, but the humour was lost on Viktor, who was absolutely in the zone.

'Almost. Maybe one more hour and we'll be in Odessa. We must be careful now, stay quiet and show no lights. There will be patrol boats, cameras and people watching. But I know these waters very well. I lived around here; I know where to go to stay out of sight.'

'What? You lived around here? Are you Ukrainian?'

'Yes, I was born in Kiev and spent the first 12 years of my life there before moving to Odessa. I spent many years working these waters.'

'What do you mean, working these waters?'

'Never mind. Time to concentrate,' he said with finality, turning off the conversation tap once more. We sat in silence for the next hour until Viktor cut the engine speed down to not much more than idle. Eerily we glided along the surface of the water, making hardly a ripple but unable to see a bloody thing. I sure was glad Captain Super Sailor was at the wheel because I can guarantee I would have managed to hit something by now. But Viktor seemed to know exactly what he was doing and exactly where he was going, as if he was navigating by some weird marine psychic power. Suddenly, he turned the key and cut the engine completely, allowing our momentum to carry us the final few metres to our destination. But our stealth was to no avail.

In the silence I heard as clear as day the unmistakable double-click of a pump action shotgun loading a cartridge into the breech. Quick to follow was a bright light bursting into life, shining through the windscreen and right into my eyes that were completely accustomed to the darkness, blinding me out of my night vision. The visual assault was soon followed by an auditory one as a harsh voice barked in a foreign language.

As my eyes started to recover, I looked across at Viktor and was dumbfounded to see a happy smile break out across his face.

CHAPTER 41

'Hey idiots!' shouted Borys as he exited the makeshift jail, still dragging Amy by the hair. 'Somebody get in there and drag those two morons out and lock the door behind you.'

Two of his men quickly extinguished their cigarettes and leapt out of their chairs to carry out their task. Peering into the cell, they shook their head in wonder at the three figures lying on the floor. They quickly dragged out their two comrades and locked the door behind them.

Borys tossed Amy roughly into the back of his car and instructed two of his men to accompany him to Kiev. Borys understood his psychotic boss all too well and knew that there could be no mistakes with this precious cargo. He resolved to take no chances and decided to drive Amy to Kiev himself. He would make the drive up today, stay overnight at their headquarters in Kiev and then return to Odessa the following day.

Amy struggled helplessly against the iron grip of the huge man as she was bundled into the car. She was joined in the back by one of her captors, who reached across and strapped her in. The other man slid into the front seat, closely followed by Borys as he climbed behind the wheel. Amy's heart sank as she realized there was no escape. Her whole world and her entire family were in desperate trouble, her darling son possibly dead, her wonderful daughter lying unconscious in a prison cell facing a terrible ordeal with the monster before her in the driver's seat, and Amy herself heading into the heart of a madman's lair.

As Borys expertly piloted the car out of the port of Odessa, he smiled in anticipation at what awaited him back in the wharf shed, looking forward to his return the next day.

CHAPTER 42

'Viktor, what the hell is going on here and why on earth are you smiling when we've got a loaded shotgun pointing at us from the dock? Do you know these guys?' I asked, stunned at this latest development. I really was seeing a whole new side to Viktor that I hadn't witnessed before; he was certainly full of surprises.

'I'm smiling because it's good to see the old organization has still got good security in place. If they're monitoring this landing it means that it's still active, which means the old group is still in charge,' replied Viktor.

'Have you been here before or worked this area?' I asked hopefully.

'Yes, I used to help with smuggling operations here. We used to bring in black market goods like alcohol, tobacco, drugs, firearms, fuel, gold, electronic equipment, diamonds, high-end consumer goods from the West, whatever we could get our hands on.'

'Smuggling? Black market? What the hell are you on about? Who are you and what have you done with my Judo teacher?' I said incredulously.

I couldn't believe this latest development. Clearly, I would just need to accept whatever was coming and stop being surprised, or my eyebrows would end up somewhere on top of my head.

With a casual shrug of his shoulders, Viktor said 'What can I say? I was young and growing up on the streets; it was a natural progression.'

The voice from the dock barked again, accompanied by a vigorous waving of the torch light. Viktor looked at me and said, 'He wants us to come off the boat and join him on the dock. Let's go, follow me. Put your hands up and don't make any sudden moves. We don't want to spook him.'

'Okay, you're the boss,' I replied. Apparently being herded off a boat at gunpoint in the middle of the night was completely normal and all part of the plan. I dutifully followed Viktor off the boat onto the dock.

There was a lengthy, animated discussion between Viktor and our gun-toting guard, who was initially aggressive but appeared to be calming down in response to Viktor's explanations. After a few minutes, the man pulled out a phone and had a short conversation with someone, presumably one of his superiors. With a nod to Viktor, he hung up his phone and waved his gun at us, indicating the direction he wanted us to travel. Carefully we walked around him in the direction indicated, heading towards a small warehouse at the end of the dock.

We walked into the building and headed straight for a kitchen in the back corner. Still holding the shotgun but not looking quite so threatening, our guard nodded towards the coffee machine and the fridge, apparently inviting us to help ourselves. He took a seat in the corner and kept a watchful eye on us, settling in to wait for whoever was coming. We made ourselves a coffee and sat down at the kitchen table to wait.

About 20 minutes later, the kitchen door opened and a grey and grizzled man, still bleary-eyed from sleep, stopped dead in the doorway, gaping at Viktor. Then his face broke into a delighted smile as he strode across the room toward us with arms spread wide and exclaimed, 'Pasha!'

CHAPTER 43

The body was burnt and broken almost beyond repair and recognition.

The ambulance picked up the almost-corpse and loaded it into the back of the van, not holding out any hope that the patient would survive the trip. Upon reaching the hospital, the shattered victim was desperately holding on to life only by the thinnest of threads. The emergency room doctor examined the newly arrived patient. While the man's face was damaged, the main force of the car bomb blast had been to the back; he must have been facing out of the car when the bomb went off, which had saved his life. The doctor recognized the victim, quickly put the pieces of the puzzle together and immediately knew what he had to do. He started formulating a plan, of which the first and most important thing was to make sure that the men who had set the car bomb were sure that Pasha was dead.

After what appeared to the attending staff to be a thorough exam, Doctor Dmitri pulled the white bedsheet over the man's face and pronounced him dead on arrival. He calmly dismissed the other staff and quickly administered a powerful sedative to keep Pasha unconscious, then filled out paperwork that consigned Pasha to the morgue. He strode out of the room to the admissions desk and when the nurse's attention was elsewhere, swiped a new patient admission form and filled it out in the name of Viktor Davydenko; a factory worker who had been seriously injured in an industrial explosion. He re-entered Pasha's room and while nobody was looking, removed the bedsheet from over Pasha's head and swapped the paperwork at the foot of the bed, creating the first step in the chain of Viktor's new identity; Pasha was born again.

Dmitri took the paperwork of the now-dead Pasha out to the nurse's station and dropped it in the tray. The small issue of what to do about Pasha's body was a bit of a problem, but Dmitri had seen what went on in his Chechen hospital and thought there was a good chance it would all work out. Bodies had gone missing before and with no family to claim Pasha, Dmitri thought he might just disappear in the system. The doctor was particularly fortunate that night because the orderly who was supposed to look after the body came in to work on the evening shift drunk after being out at a bar and didn't want to make a fuss because he didn't want to get in trouble. Both the orderly and the doctor simply hoped that nobody would ask any questions about the small matter of a missing body.

The next two weeks were particularly busy for Dmitri; he constantly checked on Pasha, who would have been delirious and in unimaginable pain from all the burns and the bone breaks, so was kept in a drug-induced coma for protection. Meanwhile, Dmitri was working on the next stages of his plan. He had solved the immediate problem of Pasha's attackers resurfacing by pronouncing Pasha dead, but there would always be a risk for Pasha if he stayed in Chechnya or the surrounding region. Further complicating matters, Dmitri knew, was Pasha's ingrained sense of honour and justice, which would fuel an insatiable thirst for revenge once he found out that his Katerina was dead. Dmitri knew that Pasha would absolutely go after his attackers in a suicidal attempt that would surely end in his death, drowning in a sea of hate. It would hand ultimate victory to those who had killed Pasha's wife and wounded Pasha so severely.

Dmitri reached out to his underworld contacts and discovered that Nikolai had been killed and that Pasha and Katerina had been blown up in a car bomb. There were some rumours that Vladimir had set the car bomb, but there was nothing conclusive and nobody was willing to talk openly, for fear of his life.

Dmitri knew that if he was going to save his friend, to whom he owed his life, that he needed to get Pasha out of the country. So, he used Pasha's contacts just like they had so recently with Tatiana's escape, to forge papers and documents for Pasha's new life. Dmitri pulled some strings and arranged for a special medical mercy mission with an airline, saying that Pasha was a terminally ill patient who wanted to fulfil his dying wish of peacefully seeing out his last days in Japan among the Buddhist monks. Dmitri travelled all the way with Pasha, keeping him in a coma for the whole journey. Pasha was oblivious to everything lying in his coma, as his broken body slowly continued the healing process.

Dmitri was dreading what was about to come, the news he would soon have to break to his old friend, but he felt that this was the only way.

Finally, their journey came to an end as they landed in Tokyo and Dmitri's old friend Hiroto picked them up from the airport in a van with space for the still horizontal Pasha. Hiroto was happy to finally be repaying his debt to Dmitri after all these years, to rebalance his Giri obligation.

Hiroto had many friends and was well respected in Japan among the old traditionalists, who recognized that Hiroto had the utmost respect for his country and its long history and traditions. Hiroto's life was deeply entrenched in and influenced by the old traditional Japanese way of life. He knew and understood at a very deep level the healing power of Buddhism, meditation, personal reflection, and focused physical activity. After Dmitri had explained the severity and circumstances of Pasha's injuries, Hiroto knew there would be extensive physical, mental and emotional healing required.

Hiroto arranged to have Pasha cared for in the same Zen Buddhist temple he had attended himself and was still supervised by the same Zen master who had taught Hiroto. The temple had been established many years earlier, following the traditions of Jigoro Kano, the inventor and founder of the martial art of Judo. Kano had founded the very first Judo school in a Buddhist temple in Tokyo in 1882, calling it the Kodokan, or *Place for expounding the way.*

The temple would be the perfect place to erase the remnants of the old Pasha and create the new Viktor. It would be a long and difficult process, but the Zen masters had the time and the will to help rebuild the broken man. They knew that every life was precious, and they would do everything they could to help Pasha recover and heal.

With Pasha safely hidden in Japan in a remote Zen Buddhist temple, Dmitri finally breathed a sigh of relief. He decided it was time to administer the drug to bring his patient out of his coma so that Pasha could discover the truth and begin the enormous task of rebuilding his life.

A pain-filled groan emanated from the bed as Pasha finally stirred from his long, deep slumber. Gingerly, he opened his eyes in the dim light, trying to focus and work out what he was seeing. Dmitri said gently, 'Pasha, it's okay, it's me, Dmitri.'

'Dmitri! Where am I? What happened? Where is Katerina? Is she here?' groaned Pasha, still groggy from the after-effects of the coma.

'Slow down, Pasha, be patient. You've been through a lot and you need to recover,' responded Dmitri in a voice tinged with deep sadness.

Pasha faded in and out of consciousness for a few minutes while his body tried to free itself of fatigue but at the same time try and cope with the screaming nerve endings that were crying out in protest at their raw exposure to the outside world. Finally coherent, he was able to focus and said, 'Dmitri, I'm okay now. I hurt all over, but I'm okay and can talk now. Tell me what happened, from the beginning.'

Dmitri laid the story bare for Pasha, telling him all he knew and leaving out nothing. Pasha was silent, still as a rock, with tears running down his cheeks as he mourned the loss of his poor Katerina. For a long time, Pasha had felt that someday his life of violence and bloodshed would come back to haunt him, but this was cruel and unusual punishment; his sweetheart Katerina killed for Pasha's sins and his own life being spared instead. If only he'd insisted on driving the car like he always did, maybe everything would have been different, and Katerina would have been spared instead of him. Pasha was so still and quiet it was like he was still in his coma. Dmitri left him to his thoughts when he could see there would be no response.

Pain. Pain like he had never felt before washed over Pasha. Every nerve, every fibre of his being and even the depths of his soul felt like it was on fire. But he welcomed it, embraced the pain that washed through him in never-ending waves. This was his punishment, his suffering, his repayment that the Universe had demanded for his sin of killing his beautiful Katerina as surely as if he had put the bomb under the car himself. He resolved he would take no drugs or alcohol to numb the pain, that he would manage the pain with his mind, every day a reminder of what he had done and was paying for now in this life instead of the next. This was his Hell on Earth, living without his Katerina.

Dmitri returned to his life in Chechnya leaving a sad, bitter and lonely Pasha behind; but one who had no thoughts for revenge on anyone except for himself. Slowly, Pasha and the monks adapted to their new environment together and Pasha started to learn about Buddhism, meditation and Karma, the concepts and practice of which struck a deep chord with the broken man.

As Pasha's body slowly healed, so too did his mind as he spent more and more time with the monks. His many hours of meditation awakened his soul and allowed him to entertain the idea of second chances, that somehow, he might be able to forgive himself one day. Deep down, he knew that Katerina would want it that way. So, he embraced his new persona, became Viktor, and resolved to devote the rest of his life in service to others, living a good life to make amends for the wrongs he had done in his early life.

Viktor had forever been a man of action, always on the move, but his enforced convalescence had drained him of his old power. Although his body would be horribly scarred forever, he was healing slowly. As soon as he was able, he resolved to move just a little bit more each day. Starting with just a shuffling walk, he was soon striding around the compound and then progressed up to jogging. One day, he came upon one of the monks practicing some very deliberate and focused martial arts moves on a padded area that he hadn't noticed before. Curiosity got the better of Viktor and he knocked at the open door to see what was going on. 'Come in,' beckoned the old monk and Viktor walked into the dojo, taking care to leave his shoes at the door as custom dictated.

'Are those Judo moves you're practising?' asked Viktor.

The old monk replied, 'Yes, Judo. Have you tried it before?'

'I've seen it before, but never tried it. Is it effective?'

'Come, let me show you,' said the old monk. 'Try and strike me.'

Viktor laughed and said, 'No offence old man, but I don't want to hurt you. I've fought many men in my time far bigger, stronger, younger and faster than you.'

The old monk shrugged and said with a smile, 'As have I, Viktor. Come, try and strike me.'

'Okay, but don't say I didn't warn you,' said Viktor. He approached the monk, set himself and launched a fast right-cross at the man's face. In an instant, Viktor was on the floor, staring up in amazement at the smiling face and sparkling eyes of the old monk.

Viktor was a street fighter with a deadly combination of power, speed, strength and brutality that was unmatched in a one-on-one contest by anyone he had ever come across. But Judo was something completely different, a way of moving and a philosophy based not on brute strength but on the principle of maximum efficiency for minimum effort, making it possible for a physically weak competitor to beat a stronger one by using their opponent's own momentum and strength against them.

Viktor and the Judo Master quickly became teacher and student and then firm friends. Viktor's intense application of meditation, Zen studies and Judo provided exactly the physical, mental and emotional healing that he so desperately needed, not just to recover from his horrific injuries but also to create a new life for himself as Viktor. He truly had a second chance at life, an opportunity to erase the memory of Pasha's wrongdoings.

Viktor spent three years in the Zen Buddhist monastery, continuing his learning and gaining his black belt in Judo. One day, the masters said they had been contacted by an ex-student of theirs who was no longer able to run his Judo school in Australia, to see if the masters knew anyone who might want to take it over. Feeling that Viktor's healing was complete and that it was time for him to leave the safety of the monastery's four walls, they put the idea to Viktor, who agreed it was time to start the next phase of his new life.

Viktor soon arrived in Kings Cross, putting him on a path to meet Tommy that would eventually bring him full circle, back to where it all began.

CHAPTER 44

Finally, the nuclear experts from Bucharest arrived at the hospital. Four of them turned up in two unmarked white vans, unloading a huge array of materials, equipment and tools from the back of the vans. They stationed themselves in an area next to the X-ray room that contained what was left of the unfortunate Chad.

'Who's in charge here?' asked the leader of the nuclear crew.

'That would be me, I'm the chief of staff,' said a portly man in a suit and tie, puffing out his chest and looking rather self-important.

'Well, you're not anymore. This case, this area and that body belongs to us until we get to the bottom of what's going on here,' responded the man.

'On whose authority?' blustered the doctor.

'By government decree,' said the nuclear expert, handing over the paperwork authorizing his charge over all things nuclear.

'Very well, we are at your service,' said the chief of staff, secretly relieved that someone else was taking over this mess. They were welcome to the headache.

George looked on intently at this latest development. Maybe now he would get some answers.

The nuclear crew suited up, prepared their equipment and entered the X-ray room to inspect the grisly contents of the body bag.

Looking ominous in their high-tech radiation suits, the crew moved across to the body and the leader carefully unzipped the bag. Almost as one, they recoiled at the initial sight of what was left of Chad, particularly his face. After their momentary shock, the crew leaned back over the corpse with interest, studying the radiation levels on their monitors.

'Well, we see an awful lot in our line of work, but we've never seen anything like this, have we?' said the leader over his suit radio.

'Certainly not,' agreed the rest of the crew.

'Clearly this man has somehow ingested a high intensity radiation source, which has been attacking him from the inside. With the high exposure and proximity of the radiation to his cells and his brain, the damage has been much worse than the usual effects of radiation from outside the body.'

The group intently studied the dark nasal cavity of the body and the glowing yellow sliver buried within it, steadily pulsing its deadly radiation. 'Pass me the forceps,' said the leader. 'It's time to see what this thing is.' One of his assistants passed him the surgical extractor and the leader reached in and expertly gripped the small, deadly, radioactive sliver, pulling it from the man's skull cavity.

He carried the sliver across to the bench and placed it under a microscope. Each of the team inspected the sliver under the microscope, forming their own initial opinions of what it might be.

The deadly object was removed from the microscope and a sample was prepared for further analysis. Placing the sample in the portable mass spectrometer, the operator said, 'Okay, let's see what we've got here.' They stepped through the process and intently inspected the results as they came on screen.

Traces of sand, concrete, carbon and most importantly, Uranium and other radioactive elements showed up in the analysis of the material. 'Corium,' said the leader as their analysis coalesced into a complete picture of the sample. 'Material that is only formed during a nuclear reactor meltdown! It's been harvested, processed, formed into this tiny deadly sliver and then deliberately injected into this man. This is incredibly serious. We need to inform the authorities in Bucharest immediately!'

Meanwhile, one of the crack nuclear team continued poring over the analysis, then looked up and announced to the team, 'Better tell them to contact Kiev too, it looks like Ukraine will need to get involved. We must check the atomic signature carefully, but it looks like it might be Chernobylite.'

CHAPTER 45

'Uri!' said Viktor happily, rising from his seat and spreading his arms wide; they hugged warmly, and it went on and on amid animated conversation in their own language. Finally, they stepped back from each other, smiling widely.

Viktor said in English, 'Uri, you crazy Cossack, it's so good to see you again my old friend!' With a nod of his head to me he said, 'Would you mind if we talk in English so my friend can understand? He doesn't speak Ukrainian.'

'Of course, Pasha. I'm a bit rusty but I can still get by,' Uri responded in heavily accented English. 'We have a lot of catching up to do my old friend. I heard you were dead! How long has it been since we've seen each other? It must be close to 30 years; I can't believe it's really you standing here in my kitchen.'

'Yes, it's been about 30 years since I left Odessa and about 20 years since my unfortunate death,' responded Viktor with a smile.

I'm so glad I had already decided to suspend disbelief, because this was just off the charts! Unfortunate death? And who the hell was Pasha?

'Viktor, what is going on here? What are you talking about?' I asked.

'Viktor? Is that what they call you now? I guess you were reborn after you died,' said Uri, smiling and obviously intrigued. 'It sounds like there really is a long story in there somewhere!'

'There certainly is Uri, but we do have a bit of a time issue that we need to get around. And we could do with some breakfast, it will be morning soon and my large friend here has a big appetite,' laughed Viktor.

Uri looked at me and said, 'Excuse my manners, I haven't greeted you yet. I've been too astonished to see my old friend Pasha come back from the dead! I am Uri.' He strode over with his hand extended in greeting.

I pushed back my chair and stood up to my full height, extending my hand in return. Uri stopped in his tracks, looked up at me and whistled, turned to Viktor / Pasha and said, 'He's a big lad; what is he, your bodyguard?' He turned back to me and we shook hands. Like Viktor, despite his age this man had a strong, vice-like grip. His hand was like a slab of meat, tough and raspy from decades of hard work and he was obviously not afraid to get his hands dirty. He moved with economy and efficiency, with no effort or energy wasted.

'Hi, I'm Tommy. Pleased to meet you,' I said.

Finally, the handshake ended. Uri's eyes bored into mine, looking deep into me, then he looked me up and down, seemingly evaluating me and judging my suitability to be in Viktor's company. 'He looks capable enough. Is he as strong as he looks?' Uri asked Viktor while still looking at me as if I wasn't even there. Uri was clearly a leader of men, accustomed to command and skilled at sizing up people and judging them in just a few seconds.

'Yes, the lad is strong and tough too. He just won a gold medal in Judo at the Olympics in Bucharest,' Viktor said proudly.

'Really? Interesting. But the streets are different to the competition mats. Can he fight for real?' asked Uri.

Viktor laughed and said, 'Yes. I taught him a thing or two from the old days. Just like we used to!'

'Okay, that's enough of the formalities. Clearly, we're all friends here,' said Uri. Then, turning to our guard in the corner he said, 'Thank you, Ilya, you did a good job tonight. Very well done.' Turning to Viktor, Uri said proudly, 'That's my grandson Ilya. He's a good man. He will make a strong leader one day.'

Ilya smiled and nodded his head in thanks to his grandfather and exited the building, returning to his watch on the dock.

'Alright, let's go and see if we can find some breakfast for you. Let's go to my mother's place. The old Babushka will be extremely happy to see you, her second son, and she still has a well-stocked larder.'

CHAPTER 46

The smells emanating from the kitchen were hypnotizing. I *love* the smell of bacon in the morning! My stomach was growling like an extremely pissed-off grizzly bear woken up too early from his winter hibernation. After many meals of bread, instant noodles and canned food that looked more suitable for canines than humans, I was craving some *real* food. Judging by the sights, smells and sounds coming from the cavernous kitchen in this traditional Ukrainian house on the shores of the Black Sea, my prayers were about to be answered.

I still couldn't believe where I was and what I was doing. Just a few short days ago I had been fulfilling my destiny of winning an Olympic gold medal, and just a few minutes ago I had been greeted by an old Ukrainian Babushka. The old grandmother was hunched over from a lifetime of hard work, had deep lines etched in her face and wizened arthritic hands curled into claws, but she welcomed me with a broad, toothless smile and sparkling eyes. Her whole face, body and persona portrayed a long life of grindingly tough work but one full of history, love and more than a little mischief thrown in.

The old Babushka's whole face had lit up like a Christmas tree when she saw Viktor, who wrapped her up in a fierce embrace, both shedding a tear in the process. This truly looked like a homecoming. Her greeting was accompanied by repeated urgings to 'yisty, yisty, yisty'. How fitting that the first Ukrainian word I learned was *eat*. Despite the early hour, she was soon cooking up a storm. She seemed to have waved some sort of magic wand, bringing into existence enough food to feed a small army. My love for cooking and of course eating piqued my interest.

As I settled in the comforting warmth of the big kitchen around a huge old wooden table that I'm sure had seen many large and noisy family meals I said to Viktor, 'That was no ordinary greeting – it looked more like a homecoming. How well do you know this wonderful old lady?'

Viktor said with a smile, 'Ah, this is just like the old days. It's a long story that I might tell you properly one day when we have the time, but the short version is that my mother died when I was very young and my father was a drunk who beat me. So, I ran away from home much too young and was out on my own on the tough streets of Odessa, living in the Catacombs. That's where I met Uri; we became friends and he used to bring me here to the comforts of his mother and his home. They looked after me like a son and became my family.'

'Wow, no wonder she was so happy to see you. It must have been tough when you were dead.' Ouch! That was a bit harsh. I instantly regretted saying it as I saw Viktor's smile disappear, replaced by a flash of pain and regret across his face.

'Yes, it has been difficult, hiding all these years. But I needed to put my other life behind me. Again, that is a much longer story than we have time for right now.'

'Sorry, I shouldn't have said that, I have no idea what you went through. I'm sure you had your reasons for doing what you did, and they must have been big ones.'

Desperate to move off what was clearly a sensitive subject, I changed the topic to food. 'So, tell me Viktor what do Ukrainians eat for breakfast? This looks pretty damn good to me!'

Relieved at the change of direction in the conversation, Viktor said, 'What you probably think of as bacon is called *salo* – cured pork fatback. For sausages we have Kovbasa and Sosysky and eggs, of course. Ukraine is famous for its breads and wheat products. This morning we're having Bublik, which is kind of like a bagel, and Paska, a beautiful rich and sweet

Easter bread. Babushka knows it's my favourite. And if we're lucky we might finish off with traditional Ukrainian buttermilk pancakes and strong Ukrainian coffee.'

'Now *that's* what I call breakfast!' I said, a huge grin breaking out from ear to ear across my face. I was really going to enjoy this feast.

'Make sure you eat a lot. It's considered good manners to eat your fill. Babushka will be disappointed if you didn't come with your appetite.'

'Don't worry, my appetite is well and truly here! I'll do my best to eat my share; I wouldn't want to offend anyone.'

I turned to Uri, who had been following the conversation with interest. 'Uri, I heard Viktor call you a Cossack before. Are they the guys with the big furry hats and the crazy dancing?'

Uri responded with a dry chuckle and said, 'Well, there's a little more to it than that, but yes, you're right about the hats and the dancing, it's called *Hopak*. We're also known, respected and feared for our military skills, our toughness and our loyalty. We have military traditions dating back hundreds of years that we still follow today. Our family are direct descendants of the original Ukrainian Zaporozhian Cossacks.'

Viktor chimed in with some more information, 'And Uri is the Hetman, the boss of his group, which last I remember numbered in the hundreds. Uri has served his people with distinction for more than 30 years. He was appointed leader just before I left Odessa for Chechnya. He took over from his father, who took over from his father before him.'

'Yes, my time as Hetman is almost finished. I'm getting too old for our line of work and should have handed over the leadership already.'

'I thought you might have handed over responsibility to your son already; what happened?' asked Viktor.

A dark look of anger came across Uri's face, turning it black as thunder. Clearly there was pain cut deep in this man. 'I had been grooming my son his whole life to take over. He was ready, a good man and an excellent leader. I was just about to appoint him Hetman a few years ago, but he was taken from us. He was killed in an ambush one night by a rival gang.'

Viktor blanched at the news of his friend's loss, stood up from the table, embraced Uri and said, 'I'm so sorry brother. No father should have to go through that.'

The silence hung in the air like a heavy blanket, nobody willing to break it. Finally, the old Babushka broke the silence, making the breakfast call and serving up the huge spread, almost covering the table with enough food for ten men. They looked expectantly at me, leaving me slightly puzzled. Was I supposed to say Grace or something? That would be a challenge because I certainly missed that lesson at school and at home. Finally, Viktor gestured to the feast and said, 'Guests first – make your choices so the rest of us can dig in.'

'If you insist!' I responded with a smile and hoed in. I was in heaven. Time to move to Ukraine, I reckon!

Once I'd filled my plate, the others did the same and we ate quietly, the food taking place of voice until our hunger eased.

After a time, I said to Uri, 'I'm sorry to hear about your son. Do you have any other children? Or will your grandson take over as leader?'

'I have two daughters, but they're not in the family business. It's men's work, tough and dirty. My girls went to university and now have jobs and families of their own. My son's widow is the mother of my grandson who stopped you at the dock tonight. He'll take over as Hetman one day. I just need to last long enough to teach him what he needs to know.'

'That's good, so the tradition continues. What happened to the people who killed your son?'

'They're gone now. All dead. Nobody crosses a Cossack and gets away with it. We avenged my son's death and more,' he said with a cold, hard edge in his voice. I would certainly not want to get on the wrong side of Uri.

'Pasha, now that we have had our breakfast, tell me what brings you back from the dead and home to Odessa after all these years?' said Uri. 'And why have you come in under the cover of darkness, smuggling your large friend into port? Not that I'm not glad to see you my old friend, but I like to know what's going on in my territory.'

'Tommy competed in the Olympics in Bucharest just a few days ago. He won his gold medal and then the next day his best friend died on the mat while he was fighting for the wrestling gold medal. Then the victim's mother and his sister, who is also Tommy's girlfriend, were kidnapped. Tommy called me so I came to help. We're going to save the girls.'

Viktor's words hung heavy in the air like lead as he recounted the story to Uri, each utterance like a stab in my heart. With all the chaos going on around me and the need to focus, sometimes I pushed those thoughts so far into the recesses of my mind that it was like a jolt of electricity through my brain when I was reminded about what had happened.

'How do you know they're in Odessa?' queried Uri.

'Tommy chased after the girls when they were taken. He managed to catch the trailing car and forced it off the road, which killed one of the men. Tommy questioned the other one and got answers before he died too. The kidnapper said the girls were being taken to Odessa.'

Uri's head snapped around towards me and I felt the full force of his penetrating stare. Unblinking, he sized me up, seemingly with a new respect as he learnt this piece of news about me, filing it away in some dossier in his head.

'Interesting,' replied Uri, cryptically. 'Odessa is a big place, full of people who don't want to be found.'

'We have a name and a location,' said Viktor, hopeful for some recognition from his friend and former leader. 'Vladimir Zhukov, Wharf shed 17.'

'Ublyudok!' spat Uri, glaring at Viktor. I had no idea what that meant in Ukrainian but knew it couldn't be good. 'That bastard moved in after we wiped out the gang that killed my son. They're animals! Stirring up trouble with the police and customs inspectors. They have no respect for the criminal code, there is no honour among thieves with them. We've had nothing but trouble since they came to Odessa.'

'What can you tell us about them?' asked Viktor, eager for information on our adversaries and glad to hear that Uri knew something about them.

'I've heard their main business is smuggling weapons. They're a crazy bunch. You can't reason with them. You'll need to strike hard and fast if you're going to have any chance against them. They have many men. You'll need help.'

Viktor looked hopefully across at Uri, who smiled in return. 'Yes, of course we'll help you, Pasha. That damn gang have been a nuisance to us ever since they got here. It will be a pleasure to teach them a lesson about how things are done on our waterfront. I'll need to get the men organized and to plan our attack. We'll go tonight. In the meantime, you both need to get some sleep. But I do have one condition to the offer of our help. My poor mother thought you were dead and so did I. We've grieved for you all these years. You owe us an explanation.'

'I'm so sorry Uri to have put you through that pain and your mother too. But it was a really difficult time for me. As you know, I left Odessa more than 30 years ago and went to Chechnya to make my own name and build my own business. I was young and ambitious; I knew I had a place here with you, but I am no Cossack and would never have been completely accepted by your group. After a few years in Chechnya, I met a young man named Nikolai, who was an up-and-coming member of the Chechen underworld. He offered me a senior position in his organization, which I decided was a good opportunity with a potentially high payoff, so I took it. But Nikolai was an evil man, much worse than he needed to be. Some of the things he made us do in the name of his

Russian Mafia cell were horrific, too much even for me and you know Uri that I've never had a weak stomach for violence.'

'That's a laugh, coming from you,' said Uri, then he turned to me and said, 'Pasha is the toughest man I've ever known, Tommy. You should have seen him in his prime, he was totally without fear – no man could stand up to him.' I stayed silent, fascinated at Viktor's story, his secret past, the life he had kept hidden from everyone for all those years in Australia and even from me, his closest friend. Viktor really *was* an enigma.

Viktor continued his explanation to Uri, 'Nikolai was slowly desensitizing me, dragging me down to his depths of depraved violence, I was losing myself and my sense of right and wrong. Before Nikolai, I could honestly say I never killed a man who didn't deserve it, but that is a claim I can no longer make. This knowledge that I will take to my grave fills me with shame.'

Viktor paused long and hard, deep in thought and reflecting on the story he was laying out before us. Clearly, he had not spoken of such things in many years.

'But everything changed when I met Katerina. She was a librarian. That's where we met, at her library. She'd seen me come in a few times, then we started talking. She was much younger than me, incredibly beautiful and so sweet and gentle. She was so fragile, I just wanted to take care of her. Somehow, she saw something in me that Nikolai had not yet destroyed, some remnant of the young man I once was, here in Odessa.'

It was then that I noticed the tears in Viktor's eyes as he was speaking of his darling Katerina, the one who saw through the outer mask and deep into his soul. It was the first time I had ever heard her name. Viktor had never told me about anything in his past and I was intrigued, desperate to know how Viktor had gone from here to Chechnya and then to Sydney.

'Katerina knew something of what I had to do for Nikolai but did not judge me for it. We decided we would escape Nikolai and our life in Chechnya as soon as we could save up enough money for our future. We wanted enough to buy a small farm for us to go and live a quiet life in the country together. But something happened, I needed to help someone; Nikolai's wife Tatiana and her two small children. They were in a desperate situation, severely abused by Nikolai and in fear of their lives. So, I helped them escape from Nikolai and his brutality.'

Uri and I were transfixed by Viktor's story and prompted him to continue.

'The escape went according to plan and Nikolai's family got out safely, but then something went terribly wrong. I didn't know it at the time, but Nikolai's insane brother wanted to take over Nikolai's crime business; he wanted all the power and money for himself. I discovered afterwards that he set up a fake conflict with a rival gang, then lay in wait to kill his brother. He shot him in the head with an AK47, then ran away. He blamed everyone else, but rumours soon started circulating that Nikolai was killed by his own brother.'

Silence descended as Viktor paused with tears forming in his eyes and he gathered himself for the next painful instalment of his traumatic tale. He drew in a deep breath and finally continued.

'While Nikolai was being murdered, I was trying to make my escape. I went back to my apartment to pick up Katerina and collect our money and our things, ready to finally fulfil our dream of moving to the country and having a place of our own. But we never made it. A car bomb had been planted under our car, triggered by the ignition on a delay switch. Katerina was driving, I was in the front passenger seat. At the last second, I started getting out of the car to get something else out of the apartment just as the bomb went off. My poor Katerina was killed instantly.' By this time Viktor was a mess with tears streaming down his cheeks.

'But what about you? How did you survive?' I asked.

'I was thrown clear by the blast. I was facing outwards and had the car door open, so my back caught the impact and I was thrown out of the car, broken and burned. Somehow I survived long enough for the ambulance to collect me and take me to the hospital.'

'But what then?' I asked, on the edge of my seat.

'Lucky for me, I had a good friend at the hospital. Uri, do you remember Dmitri? The one who went to Kiev to train to be a doctor?'

'Yes, of course I remember. You saved his life one day when a group of boys ganged up on him in a knife fight. He got stabbed and they were about to finish him off when you jumped in and took all four of them by yourself, sent them on their way and then brought Dmitri here to get patched up by my mother.'

'Yes, Dmitri and I kept in touch all those years and became friends when we were both living in Chechnya. He recognized me in the hospital and knew what he had to do. He pronounced me dead to kill the trail, then had new papers and a new identity made up for me and shipped me off to Japan to recover in a monastery. That's where I found peace and eventually some enlightenment. I knew Katerina would want me to leave my old life behind and not seek revenge that would only end in my death. After a few years there, I decided to move to Australia and that's where I met Tommy.'

'Well, that is an amazing and terrible story Pasha, I can't believe you survived all that and now here you are in my mother's kitchen. But you left out one piece of information. Who was Nikolai's brother, the man who killed your Katerina and nearly you too?' asked Uri, beating me to the punch.

Viktor replied in solemn tones, 'His name is Vladimir. Vladimir Zhukov.'

CHAPTER 47

Despite her struggles, Amy couldn't keep her eyes open on the long trip from Odessa to Kiev. Borys was a machine, an automaton that somehow didn't need to stop for food, water or even to take a piss for the entire journey. Amy tried to stay alert but was exhausted from her imprisonment and succumbed to sleep, only woken by her urgent need to pee. Her companion in the back seat stared vacantly at her as he had for the entire journey, gun held casually in hand but apparently ready to move if required.

'Hey, when are we going to stop?' called Amy. 'I need to go to the bathroom.'

'Bad luck sister. Hold it or piss in a bottle. Your choice,' growled Borys.

'Fuck you, asshole,' snapped Amy back to the implacable driver. She decided to hang on, not wanting to suffer the indignity of peeing in front of these animals.

'How long until we get there?' asked Amy, still seething at the powerlessness of her situation.

'Less than an hour,' grunted Borys in response.

Amy settled back down in her seat to wait, staring out the window at the Ukrainian countryside flashing past, taking her back to her childhood in Chechnya so long ago. With the wisdom of age and experience gained through her difficult life, she thought back now to her parents with some regret. They had done the best they could under the circumstances, trying to deal with what Amy could now admit was a difficult and rebellious teenager. She reflected on her decision to run away and what it had cost her, but also on what she had gained. She had created two wonderful children, lived in a beautiful home and ran a successful business. But all that now seemed a lifetime away. Here she was back in desperate times, somehow sucked back into the vortex that was her life with Nikolai all those years ago and worse still, her children were now embroiled in it too.

Amy was snapped out of her thoughts by the words of Borys from the front seat talking to an armed man through the open window of the car, who quickly waved them through. Finally, they had reached Kiev. Amy's nerves rattled like a wind chime in a hurricane at the prospect of seeing Vladimir again after 20 years. The guy was seriously deranged, he had always given her the creeps back in the old days with the way he looked at her through his dead eyes, like a fish on a hook out of the water too long. He had always been jealous of Nikolai, jealous of his power and the fear and respect he inspired in his men.

'Out!' snapped Borys as he opened Amy's door and motioned her to exit into the enormous garage.

'Take me to a goddamn toilet right now before I piss all over the fine leather right here in the back of your car!' said Amy, with all the venom she could muster.

'Fine. Over there,' muttered Borys with a flick of his head. Amy staggered painfully from the vehicle, her bladder fit to burst and waddled over to the toilet followed closely by Borys who clearly wasn't taking any chances. 'Leave the door open,' he said as he ushered her into the bathroom.

Amy was beyond caring by this stage and accepted the door-open condition without protest. The gushing that came out of her the instant she sat down was just about the sweetest relief she'd ever felt. Finally, her stream stopped, and she fixed herself up and made the most dignified exit possible when you've been forced to pee in public by a man pointing a gun at you.

'Let's go,' said the impassive Borys to Amy. 'Vladimir wants you to be comfortable, so he's arranged for you to clean up, have a shower and put on some fresh clothes. You'll be joining him for dinner.'

'Pretty messed up way to ask a girl on a date. What happened to flowers and chocolates?' said Amy, her voice heavy with sarcasm that was unfortunately lost on the humourless Borys.

'Just do as you're told and don't do anything stupid. What you do here has a serious impact on whether you ever see your daughter again.'

'You leave Brittney out of this; she's done nothing wrong and has nothing to do with this!'

'Don't worry, I'll take good care of your daughter for you,' sneered Borys in return.

'Bastard! Leave her alone!' cried Amy, feeling a hot burst of tears flushing her eyes.

'Enough! Shut your pretty mouth and get moving,' said Borys as he pushed her roughly towards the exit door of the garage. A guard opened the door, revealing a menacing, dimly lit corridor. Amy panicked at the thought of another prison cell and started screaming, 'No! No! Let me go, you bastard! I won't go in there!'

Suddenly Amy felt a jolt like a hammer come down on the back of her neck, squeezing her tight like a vice on a workbench. *Jesus Christ, he's so strong!* she thought. There was no way she could resist Borys as he propelled her forward like a crazed puppet dancing on a string to the commands of its master.

They came out of the corridor into a house and Borys pushed her up some stairs and along a hallway until they came to a heavy steel-clad door, which Borys opened and then thrust Amy inside, saying, 'This room has a bed, a toilet and a shower, you'll find this much more comfortable than your accommodation in Odessa. It has no windows and the only way out is this door, which doesn't open from the inside. You are very secure here, so don't bother trying anything. You'll find fresh clothes in the cupboard; I believe in your size. You should shower and change and then someone will collect you for your private dinner with Vladimir. Enjoy.' And with that, he was gone, slamming the heavy door behind him.

'I am so screwed,' said Amy to the deafening silence of her cell.

CHAPTER 48

George was used to waiting. Things hadn't always happened quickly in the New York Police Department and he understood that samples had to be analysed, people had to be contacted and information needed to go through the right channels. But that didn't necessarily mean he was a patient man. He wanted answers, Goddamn it!

After the nuclear team had completed their third analysis of Chad, George figured it was time to step it up a notch. As the team leader came out of the X-ray room once more and took off his protective suit, George realized the man had a very worried look on his face, so decided not to go in all guns blazing just yet. Keeping his powder dry for when he really needed it was something George had learnt well through all his years on the force. *Softly, softly George*, he thought.

'How are your investigations coming along? Do you have any updated information yet?' asked George.

'Please Sir I can't give you anything official yet, it's an extremely sensitive situation,' replied the investigator.

'I understand,' responded George, 'But Chad was like a son to me, I've worked very closely with his mother for a long time. She deserves to know the truth.'

The leader of the nuclear investigation team was visibly shaken, apparently concerned at the outcome of their investigation. 'I can tell you, but you must promise to keep it to yourself. The news must not get out yet, not until we are ready to release it.'

'Yes, of course. I was a cop for 40 years. I know how to keep my mouth shut.'

'The man's body contained a foreign object, a small sliver that had been put inside him, into his circulatory system somehow. It travelled through his bloodstream and lodged just behind his nose. The material is *intensely* radioactive. It released extremely high levels of radiation inside his body, which caused extreme damage to his cells, his blood, muscles and brain. He died of severe radiation sickness.'

George was dumbstruck. In all his years on the force, he thought he'd seen everything. But not this. He'd never even *heard* of anything like this happening, let alone seen it firsthand.

'How do you think this happened? And why?' asked George.

'We examined the body closely and found what looks like it could be a tiny entry wound through the skin of his neck. The radioactive sliver could have been injected with a large syringe, or perhaps shot like a tranquilizer dart. That explains the How, but we really have no idea of the Why. That's a whole other investigation that I will leave to the Romanian police. This is an international incident, possibly even a terrorist threat. The victim was a US citizen, so I assume your authorities will also want to get involved.'

George had so many questions and he wanted to ask them while the investigator was in the mood to talk, so asked, 'Can you identify what the radioactive material is and where it came from?'

'Yes. Our last test just confirmed our preliminary analysis. The material came from the Chernobyl nuclear power station meltdown. It's called Chernobylite.'

CHAPTER 49

'Ah, my dear, you look ravishing,' crooned Vladimir in his silky voice as Amy was ushered into the room by two of his robotic thugs. It had taken every ounce of Amy's resolve for her to cooperate with the request to clean herself up and put on the new clothes that had been provided for her. Part of her wanted to tear the clothes to shreds and stay in the grimy state she had been in, but she wanted to do all she could to help Brittney stay safe and to find out any news about her boy Chad, of whom she had almost lost all hope.

The Tatiana persona of Amy had been in this situation before. She was made of stern stuff and resolved to give the impression of cooperation and subservience but knew that she wouldn't hesitate to act at the first opportunity for escape that presented itself. She figured washing and dressing up gave her the best chance of staying alive, so had put on the flimsy dress that had been selected for her, which highlighted her voluptuous figure more than she would have liked under the circumstances.

Vladimir filled his eyes with the sight of her as she walked across the room, a vision in her red dress. He was immediately taken back two decades to when he had seen Tatiana as a young woman after she met Nikolai. She had always been beautiful, but now in her prime she was stunning. Vladimir had never taken a wife, had never even had a serious relationship. All the women he knew were vacuous, twittering whores there for only one purpose. Could this be the woman he hadn't even known he wanted? Suddenly he was infatuated with this older, more mature Tatiana who had reappeared from oblivion. The life he had taken from his brother and made his own could now be complete, it had come full circle. Now, Vladimir could fill the gap that was missing from Nikolai's life at the end when Tatiana had run away from him.

'Come, have a seat. You must be hungry. I've had my staff prepare a special meal for us tonight. It will just be the two of us. We have all night together.'

Amy shivered at the meaning behind Vladimir's statement, her skin crawling at the prospect of spending a night with this horrible creature. 'I really am very tired. I don't think I'll last long. I am hungry so would like to eat some dinner, but then I really need to get some sleep.'

'As you wish. I just want to make you comfortable.'

'Comfortable? The last few days have hardly been comfortable!' snapped Amy angrily.

'The situation is… regrettable, but it had to be done. I apologize if my men have hurt you or not looked after you properly. They had instructions to treat you well.'

'Kidnapping is hardly treating us well. Why did you do it? And did you have anything to do with what happened to Chad? Do you know if he's okay?'

The lies came easy to Vladimir after a lifetime of experience. 'I don't know anything about what happened to your son, we had nothing to do with it. I'm not sure how he is now, I've heard nothing, there have been no reports in the media, so I assume he's okay. As for my reason for bringing you here, I was at the Olympics, in the stadium watching the wrestling when I saw you in the audience. It was simply a coincidence. It was such a shock to see you after all these years and since you had run away from my brother, God rest his soul, I just knew I needed to see you, to talk to you. I knew you wouldn't see me voluntarily, so I asked my men to bring you to me. It seems they got a bit too boisterous, so I am sorry for that.'

'Boisterous? Are you out of your goddamn mind?' screeched Amy.

She'd tried to keep a lid on her temper, but Vladimir's bullshit was just too much. 'Your gorilla out there kept us locked up in a concrete box with no food, water, toilet or place to sleep, with our hands and feet tied up and then he beat both of us. That's a hell of a lot more than boisterous, you arrogant prick,' she finished with a snarl.

'I can see you're upset Tatiana. Perhaps you need to calm down and get some rest. Let's leave it for now, you can go to your room and I'll have your dinner sent to you. We'll meet again tomorrow when you've calmed down.'

'My name is Amy, you asshole.'

CHAPTER 50

Ah, I love siestas.

The Spanish were right on the money when they came up with the idea of an afternoon nap. I had just stirred from my peaceful slumber and felt better for my much-needed rest after our long night out on the boat.

After this morning's huge breakfast, we had done some strategizing and gone over the planning for tonight's raid. Some of Uri's men had gone over to Vladimir's wharf shed and checked it out to see what was going on. There wasn't much to see from the outside and there was no cover to get any closer. We would need to wait until nightfall to get more of a look inside. Uri left a man stationed at the wharf to keep an eye on things and report back any movements. For now, all was quiet.

It was time to call George and get an update on the investigation into Chad's death. I grabbed Viktor's untraceable burner phone and dialled George, who answered in only two rings. 'Hello? Is that you Tommy?' asked George, in a concerned tone.

'Hi George, yes it's me, Tommy,' I replied.

'Jesus am I glad to hear from you Tommy. There's been a major development that you need to hear. They brought in specialist nuclear teams from Bucharest and Kiev.'

'Nuclear teams? What the hell for?'

'Because Chad was fucking radioactive Tommy! Seriously radioactive, like sending the Geiger counter off its head.'

'Shit, no way. That's messed up.'

'Well, that's not the half of it. The team just finished their analysis of

Chad's body and they said that Chad had been deliberately injected, somehow, with a radioactive sliver, which killed him from the inside. He died from goddamn radiation sickness, Tommy!'

I was deeply shocked at this news; it just didn't make any sense. 'You mean he was actually murdered? Why would anyone want to hurt Chad? He didn't have any enemies! Everyone loved him,' I said.

'Yes, he was definitely deliberately killed. They know where it got in, but not how. They found a small entry wound in his neck. They think it might have been injected with a syringe, or maybe shot with a tranquilizer dart or something.'

'Holy shit! The bee sting!'

'What? What the hell are you talking about?' asked George, suddenly very confused.

'A few days before he died, Chad said that he'd been stung by a bee in the neck. He didn't think anything of it, so just ignored it.'

'He obviously felt it then. It must have been a tiny dart shot from a tranquilizer gun or something. He would have noticed a syringe, for sure.'

'Damn it! If only he'd gotten himself checked out, he might still be alive.'

'We'll never know Tommy. Unfortunately, he didn't.'

'What's the stuff that he got shot with and do they know who did it?'

'The stuff is called Chernobylite. No prizes for guessing where it came from. The clever bastard who named it should get an award for stating the bleeding obvious. It came from the bowels of the Chernobyl nuclear power plant, produced during the reactor meltdown that happened years ago.'

I was silent for a moment as I digested this startling piece of news, then said slowly, 'Okay, well do they know how the hell this deadly radioactive poison made its way from goddamn Chernobyl into Chad's neck in a totally different country? Magic?'

'Apparently some crazy bastard has been mining the radioactive material and making weapons out of it! Somehow, they've been extracting it from beneath the reactor, processing it and forming it into these tiny radioactive bullets, all somehow without giving *themselves* radiation poisoning in the process. As for who did it, they currently have no idea. They're looking into it now.'

'Okay, let's leave it there, thanks George. We're on a mission tonight to rescue Brittney and Amy, so I'd better get ready. Thanks for everything mate, you've been a huge help. Having someone there with Chad is really comforting. I'll try and call again in a day or so and we can update each other with the latest. See you later.'

'Okay, thanks Tommy. Be careful man. Bye.'

This was beyond weird; it was getting seriously scary. Now the findings proved that someone had deliberately killed a US citizen on foreign soil using a previously unheard-of murder method and a highly radioactive material sourced from a supposedly secure facility in Ukraine, surely things would step up a notch. Official intervention should finally come, but I knew it would be too late for Brittney and Amy. We were so close and needed to act now.

Bloody Vladimir! The authorities didn't know it was him that was responsible but surely he had to have something to do with it. If he was the one who grabbed Brittney and Amy, then surely, he was the one who killed Chad. Vladimir was most definitely at the top of my most-wanted list now. I was even more restless for action now after talking to George.

By now it was late afternoon and the old Babushka was in the kitchen cooking up a storm. I had slept through lunch so was more than ready for dinner already. Apparently, we were being treated to a traditional Ukrainian meal before we headed off on our crazy mission. Hopefully this wouldn't be our version of the Last Supper!

Viktor and I walked down to the dock and spied Uri out the front of the shed. 'Hi Uri, how are the preparations coming along?' called Viktor, as we made our way over.

'Excellent. We're nearly ready. Come in and have a look and I'll give you a briefing,' said Uri.

I let out a low whistle as I entered. The unassuming façade of the rundown old building disguised an impressive operation. There must have been 50 men inside the cavernous space, all dressed in dark clothing including hoods or woollen beanies. Everyone was engaged in all manner of deadly looking activity, such as checking rifles, cleaning pistols, loading ammunition into clips, peering at grenades, untangling ropes, pulling at grappling hooks and assorted other nefarious tasks. 'Very impressive, Uri. Just what, exactly, are you expecting to do tonight?' I asked our host, who up until now I had not fully appreciated.

'Tommy, if there's one thing I've learned since my first crime well before my tenth birthday, it's that you should always be prepared. The one with the bigger balls and more weapons wins every time and that's exactly what we plan to do tonight. We're going to teach those bastards a lesson and get your women back at the same time.'

'Mate, I am so glad you and Viktor have history together, I really appreciate you helping us out here.'

'The way I look at it, it's a win-win. You get your ladies and I get their dock. There's something in it for both of us. Gentlemen, it's time to choose your weapons. Pasha, I assume you still favour the Makarov pistol and the Saiga shotgun? We have plenty of those.'

Viktor smiled and nodded and said in response, 'Just like old times Uri, just like old times.'

What the hell these two got up to in their younger days, I had no idea!

'What about you, Tommy?' asked Uri, turning towards me.

'Um... I kind of have this thing about guns. I hate them. I've never shot one before. My father was killed in a hunting accident when I was young, so ever since I've never wanted to fire one,' I replied.

'Well, that's a problem isn't it?' said Uri. 'How are you going to protect yourself? What will you do if someone points a gun at you?'

'Well, I guess I'll just have to work something out. I tell you what, give me a bulletproof vest, the biggest, scariest knife you can find, and a couple of axe handles. I saw some in the workshop on the way in.'

'Hmm… axe handles, eh? I like your style, Tommy,' said Uri. He got them out of the workshop and handed them over. I hefted them, one in each hand, trying them for weight and balance, swinging them around in wide arcs and rotating them around my wrists, practicing strikes just like I had done in the past, mucking around with wooden staffs on the mats with Viktor. Uri gave me a nod of approval when he saw I could handle them comfortably without knocking my own head off.

Uri pulled out a map and some photos and continued his briefing of tonight's mission. Our target was heavily fortified, with many armed men inside. It was Vladimir's coastal headquarters, his main way of getting supplies into Ukraine and shipping weapons out to buyers. There was a lot of military hardware in the shed and they wouldn't be afraid to use it.

Uri pointed out a photo of an enormous individual with a clear nasty streak and said, 'We've been keeping an eye on this gang for a while. Vladimir's weapons master and commander of his forces is this man, named Borys. He is particularly dangerous, both armed and unarmed, so we need to be careful of him. He used to be a Spetsnaz solider, Russian Special Forces, but they kicked him out for being too good at the torture side of his job. He's a key target, so take him out if you get the chance. The rest of the gang are just hired guns, paid workers who are ruled by fear and money, not by family and history like us Cossacks.'

Uri completed his mission briefing by appointing roles and responsibilities. His ten best men would form the vanguard, the advance party who would take out Vladimir's outer guards and quietly find a way into the shed. The rest of the group would provide cover and then follow the vanguard into the building, keeping the element of surprise for as long as possible. We would quietly take out Vladimir's troops until someone noticed, then all hell would break loose. Once inside, Viktor and I would focus on finding Brittney and Amy and leave the Cossacks to their mayhem.

'One important detail Tommy, we need to know what Amy and Brittney look like. Do you have a photo you can show us?' asked Viktor.

'Yes, I've got one on my phone, but it's gone flat. Uri, do you have a charger I can use?' I said. Uri chatted to his men and quickly procured a charger to match my phone, so I fired it up and accessed my photos.

'Here's one I took recently of Brittney and Amy together.' I handed the phone over to Viktor, who studied the photo intently, even zooming in for greater detail. For a full minute he studied the photo in silence, with a very strange expression on his face, completely lost in thought.

'Um… Earth to Viktor? Are you still with us?' I said.

Viktor looked up at me with glazed eyes, blinked and gave his head a quick shake as if to clear his mind.

'Are you okay, Viktor? What's the matter?' I asked.

'Never mind. Long story. I'll tell you later,' he replied.

I shrugged my shoulders at this not unexpected lack of communication from Viktor and just moved on, figuring that as usual he would tell me whatever it was that was on his mind only when he was good and ready.

With the briefing complete and nearing the end of daylight, we headed back up to the house for dinner, and what a feast it was! There was even more food than at breakfast. Uri's mother had outdone herself – we feasted on an amazing selection of traditional local fare that Uri informed me included the famous Ukrainian Borsch soup, Vereyky dumplings, Holubtsi stuffed cabbage leaves, Kruchenyky pork rolls, Chicken Kiev and Deruny potato pancakes, all finished off with Pampushky sweet dough and a traditional Kyjivskyj torte cake.

Sitting back after the feast I was seriously considering smuggling Babushka back home in my suitcase – this sure beat a couple of snags thrown on the barbie!

CHAPTER 51

The last strains of the day's light shone weakly through the small window up high in Brittney's prison cell. She was in serious pain from the blow to her head from Borys that had knocked her senseless sometime the day before. She reached up the side of her face and could feel the bruise already formed, her eye half closed and cheek puffy with swelling. She was tired, sore, confused, worried about her family and *extremely* pissed off.

So much had happened in the last few days that Brittney hardly knew what to think anymore. At least she now had some idea about what was going on and some new information about her past, but she was particularly worried about her mother and what that psycho Vladimir was going to do with her, not to mention the gorilla that would soon be returning.

'Dammit! Goddamn sons of bitches!' shouted Brittney in a moment of anger.

The guards outside her cell heard the muffled strains of her yelling through the thick metal door and smiled at each other. One guard said, 'She'll be yelling louder than that when that crazy bastard Borys is through with her. He must be due back pretty soon.'

'Yes, anytime now. Did you feed the woman before?'

'Yes, I gave her something to eat and drink and a bucket for a toilet. She's been taken care of. She looks like shit though – the whole side of her face is blowing up like a balloon where Borys smashed her yesterday.'

The crunch of tires on gravel outside Brittney's window sent a chill through her veins. All senses on alert, she dreaded the prospect of what might be coming. She was alone and bound at hand and feet and with nobody to help her, but she steeled her resolve. No matter what, she wouldn't go out without a fight. If this bastard wanted to torture her, she would do whatever she could to make it hard for him.

Brittney continued her constant efforts on the ropes binding her feet. She couldn't get any leverage on the bindings around her wrists, but at least she could get her fingers to work on the ones around her ankles. Slowly, slowly she had been prying at the tough knots with her fingers, then grinding and levering her ankles to increase her range of movement. Desperate now that the brute may be returning any moment, Brittney redoubled her efforts on her leg ropes. Millimetre by millimetre, she increased the play in the knots until finally with one excruciating effort she managed to wrench one foot past the other – her feet were free!

She was still locked in her cell and her hands were bound but she now had two weapons at her disposal, and she knew how to use them. She draped the ropes carefully back around her ankles to disguise her freedom of movement, enough to satisfy a cursory inspection. She leaned back, closed her eyes and settled down to wait for her assailant, mentally preparing herself for battle. In her mind, she entered the Octagon.

The harbinger of pain rang out again as the steel door creaked on its hinges. 'Wakey, wakey, girl. I hope I'm not disturbing you. My name is Borys and I'll be your host this evening,' came the guttural voice, accompanied by a low, evil chuckle.

'I'm tired. Leave me *alone*,' whined Brittney, in her best impression of a 13-year-old who doesn't want to get out of bed.

'Sorry, it's playtime now and you're part of the fun. I love what you've done with your face. That purple really suits you,' said Borys, laughing. Who said he didn't have a sense of humour?

'What *you* did to my face, you mean,' snarled Brittney.

'You've got spirit, girl. I like that in a woman, when she plays hard to get and makes it a challenge for me. We've got plenty of time for fun tonight, actually we've got all night, just you and me,' said Borys as he walked over to where Brittney was lying on the floor.

Brittney prepared herself, tensing every muscle in her body, gathering her strength for what she knew would be her best chance of saving herself from the leering monster that was bearing down on her. As he crouched down towards her, Brittney leaned back further, shifting her weight back until her shoulders were touching the floor beneath her and then suddenly exploded both her legs out, driving them straight into the face of her attacker.

Borys' nose erupted in a spray of crimson as his broken nose spewed its bloody contents across his face. Brittney capitalized on her chance and immediately separated her legs, wrapped Borys' head between her thighs, hooked her feet together and squeezed, squeezed harder than she ever had in her life as she executed the pincer lock.

But Borys was a huge man of immense strength and his arms were free. He recovered his composure, reached up to Brittney's ankles and brutally applied pressure points to both legs, eliciting an involuntary whimper of pain from Brittney and a release of her grip around Borys' head. Brittney was skilled and strong for her size, but simply no match for her much bigger and more powerful assailant.

Borys looked at Brittney and grinned, baring his white teeth through the curtain of blood raining down over his mouth. 'Seems like I underestimated you, girl. I didn't expect that. But as I said, I like it when they play hard to get. You're going to pay for that.' He unleashed a fearsome backhand strike across the unmarked side of Brittney's face, which responded instantly with a large red welt as the blood rushed to the impact site.

Stunned from the blow, Brittney was laid out on the floor. Borys stood up, grabbed a rag that was lying on one of the packing crates and wiped the blood from his face, blowing his nose and spitting blood in the process to clear his orifices of the offending red fluid. He looked down at Brittney, who was shaking her head trying to clear it to come back from the latest assault.

'Alright, that's enough foreplay, you've got me in the mood now,' Borys said grimly as he dropped his full weight on top of Brittney, pinning her completely under his massive bulk and knocking the wind out of her. He stretched Brittney out to her full length, spreading her legs beneath him as he pushed his knees into hers, moving them out sideways and locking them into position. With his left hand he pinned her bound arms to the floor above her head and then with his right arm reached down to her face, cupping her chin. Slowly and deliberately he leaned down over her, bringing his stubbled face close to hers, his mouth getting closer and closer to her lips, so close that she gagged on the foul stench of his sour breath. Brittney struggled and strained against the brute on top of her but to no avail, he was simply too heavy and too strong for her.

Borys extended his tongue and licked the side of her face from chin to eyebrow, leaving a trail of slobbering saliva behind. The revulsion that Brittney felt for this horrendous man was so strong that she responded in kind and snarled up a collection of mucus from the back of her throat and spat in his face, launching a wad of spit that landed right in his eye.

The animal above her simply laughed, as if this was all just a game. Then he paused for a moment, looked down at Brittney's breasts, then back into her eyes and with his free right hand ripped her top down the middle, exposing her bra and her heaving chest. Brittney let out a blood-curdling scream, like something out of a horror movie, writhing around beneath her attacker in a renewed burst of energy. She had to escape, had to get out of here!

Borys laughed again. 'Scream away girl, it won't do you any good. My men are well trained, they know not to disturb me, no matter what noises they hear coming out of here.'

Brittney continued her struggle because that was all she had left. Borys reached down his right hand and grabbed her bra, pulling it off her until the straps gave way and her breasts came loose, exposed to Borys' eyes and searching hands, roughly rubbing and squeezing her.

The reality of Brittney's plight was scarily apparent to her and she made one last effort to free herself before Borys could go any further. She fiercely kicked out both her legs and managed to get her right leg free in a moment of imbalance from her attacker. She pounced on the advantage and instantly drove her right knee up and into the soft groin of the man on top of her, making full contact with him right in the balls. It was the most satisfying strike she had ever delivered.

Borys roared with pain and rolled off his victim, who scurried away from him. On his knees and recovering his breath, he pulled out his gun, aimed it right at her head and snarled, 'Don't move bitch, or you're dead. I'll put a bullet right between your eyes and then still fuck you after you're dead.'

'Go ahead, asshole. I'd rather be dead than have to spend another minute with you, you fucking pig!' shouted Brittney defiantly.

A silent standoff ensued as each of them recovered their composure and considered their next move.

Then the brief silence was shattered by the sharp retort of a gun discharging outside the room, quickly followed by another! Borys looked up, distracted, confused. Then the sound of rapid gunfire erupted from the main warehouse and Borys headed for the door, snarling, 'This isn't over, bitch. I'll be back for you later. You're going to regret that.'

He left a dishevelled but relieved Brittney shaking as he locked the door behind him.

CHAPTER 52

As darkness fell across Wharf shed 17, Uri's Cossack crew made their move. The scouts had been keeping a close eye on things, with the only significant action being the arrival of the troop commander Borys half an hour before.

The team was well trained, and everyone knew their role. The vanguard moved in as the first wave, silent in the night. The zing of a crossbow bolt traced its deadly path, landing with a satisfying thud in the chest of its unfortunate recipient. A throwing knife whizzed through the air, lodging in the throat of its unsuspecting target. Both men fell silently to the ground, well and truly dead.

With the outdoor sentries duly dispatched, the vanguard continued their advance. A frontal assault was too noisy, too obvious. Stealth was required for this phase of the attack to retain the critical element of surprise. Lightweight ladders were deployed beneath high-level windows on each of the east and west sides of the shed, with three men each quickly scaling their heights. Lax security on these forgotten upper windows meant locks were old, broken or simply not used, allowing easy access for the six men. Slowly and quietly they made their way through the windows and then down the inside walls to the disused side entrances of the shed.

A crack of light emerged from each side of the building as the doors were opened simultaneously. The rest of Uri's gang moved in, followed by me, Viktor and Uri bringing up the rear. Two more of Vladimir's men had been taken out in silence, again with the deadly combination of crossbow bolt and throwing knife.

As we were skulking around in the shed, I swore I heard a noise, like a cry or a scream coming from the other side of the building. I nudged Viktor and pointed in the direction of the sound. He nodded in agreement and we made our way over to the other side.

There are only so many people you can kill before someone notices. In this case it was nine.

Finally, one of Vladimir's men called out in surprise as he turned at just the right moment to see his compatriot drop to the ground, victim of a bullet fired from a silenced gun, a puddle of red now spreading grimly across his chest. The man called out to raise the alarm and the madness began.

Shots were fired from both sides, machine guns clattered, the noise was deafening! Men were dropping like flies, others scurried for cover, searching for high ground and the best vantage points to continue their assault.

Seconds after the gunfire started, I noticed the massive troop commander coming out of the doorway where the screams had come from. He looked in serious trouble, with a smashed nose, blood smeared all over his face and doubled over in pain as if he'd just copped one in the nuts. He was holding a gun out in front of him and raced out into the fray.

'Viktor let's check it out, maybe the girls are over there,' I said, pointing to where the big commander had appeared. Viktor nodded his agreement and we increased our speed over to the doorway. We stopped outside the corridor and peered in. Boom! Crack! A shot was fired from the depths of the corridor and the bullet lodged in the door frame just above my head.

'Shit, that was close! Bloody guns, I hate those damn things!' I said to Viktor.

'Don't worry, leave this to me,' said Viktor as he dropped down and laid full length on the floor. He poked his handgun around the corner, down low, and sprayed three quick shots down the corridor. Then he rolled over fully into the doorway, bringing his shotgun around, cocking it in one fluid movement and unloaded the shot down the corridor. The noise was like an enormous cannon going off!

As the smoke cleared, we spotted a body lying on the floor of the corridor. 'Nice one, Viktor. Still got some moves, I see. That's one less scumbag we need to worry about. Let's go see who he was guarding.'

We carefully made our way down the corridor, alert for any more men, but they were all occupied with the mayhem outside. We grabbed the large ring of keys off the guard and after three attempts found the right one that opened the door.

'Wait, be careful Tommy. We don't know what's behind that door, it could be anything or anyone.' Slowly we swung the door open and recoiled as it squealed like a banshee. Tentatively, I peered in but couldn't see anything.

'Piss off you bastard! Don't come back in here, you prick, or I'll give you another beating!' rang out a woman's voice from inside the room. It was Brittney!

'Brittney, honey? It's me, Tommy, where are you?'

'Tommy? Oh, Tommy!' she shouted and ran over to me, threw her arms over my head and squeezed me in the fiercest hug I'd ever had. She started sobbing into my chest, her hot breath pounding rhythmically against me as her warm tears ran down the front of my shirt.

I held on until Brittney ran out of sobs. She looked like hell, her clothes were half torn off her, her face was all banged up and bruised, she was dirty, and her hands were bound with heavy rope. She had obviously been through hell, but wasn't broken, her spirit still strong.

'Brit, baby, are you okay? Are you hurt?'

'I'm okay Tommy, I'll be fine now that you're here. How did you find me? How did you get in? How did you get past all the guards? And who's been doing all that shooting? Did you see that big bastard? He beat me up and nearly raped me – if you hadn't turned up when you did, he would have finished me off. It was awful, I was scared to death, I thought I was a goner. Oh, I'm so relieved to see you Tommy.'

'Bastard! Oh, baby, I'm sorry it took me so long to find you, I was so worried about you. I'm glad I got here in time.' I was jumping between relief at finding Brittney alive and anger at what they'd done to her. 'Let's get you covered up and then get the hell out of here. I'll explain everything later. We have to finish up in the warehouse first.'

I pulled out my enormous hunting knife, cut the ropes binding her hands together, took off my flak jacket and zipped it around her and then we headed off out of her prison. I picked up my axe handles on the way to the door, then paused as I remembered a critical detail. 'Hold on, where's Amy? Why isn't she with you?' I asked Brittney.

'Oh Tommy, it was terrible, we got separated. She got taken to Kiev. She's with that psycho Vladimir! We have to save her!' wailed Brittney in response.

'It's okay Brittney, of course we will. As soon as we get out of here, we'll go get Amy. She'll be alright.'

With Brittney now covered up and a bit more composed, I said, 'Viktor, this is Brittney. Brittney, meet Viktor.'

'We've met. A long, long time ago,' said Viktor cryptically with a mysterious smile as he looked into Brittney's eyes and shook hands with her. What was *that* all about?

'Uh, are you sure? I don't remember meeting you,' said Brittney.

'Well, you were very young my dear. I'm glad we found you, but disappointed we didn't find your mother as well.'

The mildly confused Brittney said, 'Thank you, Viktor. I'm pleased to meet you. I know how much you mean to Tommy and how much you helped him win his gold medal.'

'Viktor, what the hell are you talking about? How could you possibly have met Brittney before?' I asked.

'That's another long story, let's save it for later. Right now, we need to focus on what we're doing here,' he replied.

Shaking my head for the umpteenth time at the Viktor enigma, I decided to drop it and do my best to help us all stay alive for the next few minutes.

I was so glad that two of the most important people in my life could finally meet, albeit under less than ideal circumstances. Pleasantries over, we returned to the task at hand and stepped out of Brittney's cell and walked down the corridor.

Chaos reigned in the warehouse. We stepped out from our doorway and saw men running around randomly, heard shots ringing out, shouting voices and doors banging.

Suddenly one of Vladimir's men popped up in front of me and raised his gun at my head. Instinctively I reacted, instantly swinging up both my axe handles in an arc from either side of me, meeting at exactly the same time at each of the poor guy's ears. Cranium sandwich anyone? Kind of like a beetroot sandwich, except messier and without the bread. Serves him right for pointing a gun at me.

Brittney dropped down to the guy and picked up his gun. She expertly hefted it, checked the clip and the safety then cocked it ready to fire. I looked at her with raised eyebrows and said, 'Well, well, the things you learn about your girlfriend when you're in a life-threatening situation, hey?' She looked at me, shrugged her shoulders and turned her attention to the crowd of combatants.

'So who's who? I don't want to shoot the good guys,' she asked.

'We're the cool-looking ones with the black ninja outfits. The other guys don't have kick-ass uniforms like us,' I replied.

'Okay, good to know,' she said. 'What now?'

'What do you think, Viktor? Looks like the boys have got it pretty much under control now,' I said.

As he was about to respond, Brittney pointed to the opposite corner of the warehouse and said, 'What about Borys? That big bastard over there – he's the one who attacked me!'

'Too late, looks like we've missed the boat – he's outta here. He knows they're beat, so he's splitting. Don't worry, we're gonna get that asshole. I'm going to give him a massive beating for what he did to you,' I said, my blood boiling in anger as the man-mountain turned and headed out the door. Seconds later a spray of gravel hit the side of the shed as he peeled out of the carpark.

'We need to interrogate these men to find out where they're keeping Amy,' Viktor said.

'Yep, better make sure Uri's boys don't kill them all. These Cossacks are a bloodthirsty lot, aren't they? Glad they're on our side!' I said.

Just then I heard a commotion from above and spotted Uri up on a catwalk pointing a gun at someone, but he hadn't seen the guy behind him preparing to shoot. 'Uri look out behind you!' I yelled but could see it would be too late.

BOOM! A shot went off right beside me as my sweet innocent girlfriend with legs apart and arms extended out in front like an expert marksman had squeezed off a shot from 30 metres and hit the target right in the head, splattering his brains, blood and bits of skull against the wall behind him. I turned to her in admiration and said, 'Nice shot sweetie.' She hit me with a smile and batted her eyelids innocently at me.

The body dropped gracefully down from the catwalk as if in slow motion, hitting the floor with a sickening and altogether ungraceful thud. Uri gave a quick wave of thanks and made his way down the stairs, waving his captive ahead of him.

A corral of sorts was forming in the middle of the floor of the warehouse. We started making our way over when suddenly one more of Vladimir's men appeared from around a corner, swinging a punch at me. Working from muscle memory developed through years of training, I easily sidestepped the punch and then swung an axe handle down low, sweeping his feet out from under him and landing him flat on his back.

I reached down, grabbed him by the collar and dragged him over to the marshalling yard to join the rest of his clan. We quickly updated Uri, knowing we needed to act fast before the police turned up. Paying protection money only went so far – it didn't buy complete immunity from wild and crazy gunfights in the busiest port in the country.

Uri shouted out to the captive crew in Ukrainian and Viktor translated for me and Brittney, 'Uri is telling them that their operation in Odessa is officially shut down, with many dead or deserted, including their boss who left them for dead. He said he would let them go on the condition they never come back and tell us where the Kiev headquarters are, where they've taken the other woman.'

The motley crew looked at each other and then in silent agreement they nodded together. One spokesman called out to Uri and Viktor again translated, 'He says the location of their headquarters in Kiev is in a town called Glebovka, north of Kiev on the west bank of the Dnieper River just off the road to Chernobyl. It's the fourth driveway heading north past the Gintama-Briz Resort Hotel. It's a holiday area for rich Ukrainians with huge houses on big, secluded properties.'

After we took down the details of the Kiev base, Uri made one final announcement and the building emptied quickly as everyone scattered moments before the sound of sirens split the night air in the distance. The cops would find a heap of treasure in this lot – guns, ammunition, grenades, rocket launchers, you name it, there was some serious military hardware in here. Not to mention all the dead guys lying around the place. This little catastrophe would set Vladimir's operation back months, if not years, and cost him an awful lot of money. Poor little Vlad was going to be mighty pissed off about tonight's turn of events and I was damn happy about that.

Viktor, Brittney and I ran out of the building, jumped into Uri's car and sped off back to his place.

CHAPTER 53

There was an awful lot to catch up on back at Uri's home. We finished the night with a couple of stiff Vodkas and some of Babushka's sweet breads. There was a lot of planning to do if we were going to save Amy tomorrow.

'Uri, my brother, thank you so much for everything you did tonight. You saved Brittney from a horrible fate with Borys and returned her back to Tommy. It's a great relief to us. You've made us all extremely happy tonight. Thank you from the bottom of my heart. We owe you a great debt,' said Viktor.

'My old friend, there is no debt to repay. You are family, and family looks after each other, no matter what, when or where. I am glad I could help and like I said before, it's a win-win. We've been looking for an excuse to send that gang on their way and now it's done. Life on the docks can go back to normal.'

'Yes, thank you so much Uri. Words can't express how grateful we are for your help, when you didn't even know us,' I said, and Brittney nodded vigorously in agreement.

'You really are very welcome Tommy. Now I must thank *you* Brittney, for saving my life. You returned the favour, so we are even anyway,' said Uri.

'Yes, and what about that? I didn't know you could shoot, Brit,' I said. 'When did that happen and how did I not know this?'

'Well, Mom gave me a gun club membership for my sweet sixteen birthday. I used to love going down to the shooting range after school to squeeze off a few rounds. I didn't tell you because you told me how your dad died, and I knew how much you hated guns. I felt bad and didn't want to tell you that I actually *love* guns,' said Brittney.

'Fine. Since we're a couple, you can do the shooting for both of us.'

'Alright, let's all get some sleep,' said Uri. 'You can wash up in the main bathroom and I'll get some new clothes for Brittney from my daughter's old cupboard – you probably want more wardrobe choices than a bulletproof vest.'

'Thank you, Uri. Again. For everything,' said Brittney with a smile as she walked over to Uri and gave him a big hug and a kiss on both cheeks, eliciting a huge grin from the gruff old man. Then she turned and gave Viktor the same treatment, 'And thank you Viktor. You really are as wonderful as Tommy said.'

I took Brittney's hand and we wandered off to our room for a shower and some much-needed sleep. Plus, I knew the conversation that was coming up. I could tell that Brittney had wanted to ask, but the timing hadn't been right yet. I knew that as soon as we were alone, she would ask me about Chad, and I wasn't looking forward to breaking the news to her about his death.

After our shower we got into bed and lay on our side facing each other. She moved close, took a deep breath, looked me right in the eyes and said, 'Tommy, please tell me what happened to Chad.'

I paused briefly, wondering how to word my response but I knew that Brittney would just want to hear it straight. In a voice full of tenderness and the love I felt for her, I said, 'I'm so sorry baby, but Chad is gone. He didn't make it. He died right there on the mat.'

Brittney burst into tears and I wrapped her in a warm hug, drawing her close to me. Soon we were both sobbing. I hadn't been able to talk to anyone about Chad since he died, so I hadn't really mourned him until that moment with Brittney.

We eventually fell asleep in each other's arms as we wept into our pillows, wet with our tears of grief.

CHAPTER 54

I woke to the first rays of morning sun streaming in through the bedroom window, which somehow managed to get me right in the eyes like a solar homing beacon. Clearly the concept of curtains hadn't caught on everywhere in Ukraine. But still, I can think of worse ways to wake up, with Brittney still in my arms and sound asleep after the exhaustion of her past few days.

I carefully snuck out of bed. Well, as carefully as someone as enormous as me can sneak. I'm certainly no cat burglar but thankfully Brittney is a heavy sleeper and she stayed put once the mattress had recovered from my exit.

I got dressed and then as per my usual morning routine, I headed for the kitchen in search of food. The house was quiet, with the only movement being Uri's mother just starting her first stirrings in the kitchen. 'Good morning, Babushka,' I said with a smile and a pat on her shoulder. She returned the smile and gave my hand a squeeze. 'Can I help with breakfast?' I stupidly asked, even though I knew she didn't speak any English. She looked at me quizzically, so I resorted to sign language with props.

I grabbed a knife, a chopping board and a heavy skillet and made cutting motions and put the skillet on the stove, then held my hands out, raised my eyebrows and shrugged my shoulders. It was all I had, but it was enough – the question got through.

'Ah!' she said, in the apparently universal symbol of understanding, gave me another one of her gorgeous toothless grins and nodded her head. She went over to the pantry and pulled out a bunch of potatoes.

Spuds for breakfast – awesome! She handed me the peeler and set me to work.

We prepared the whole breakfast together in comfortable silence, only communicating when one of my tasks was finished and she assigned the next one. It took me back to the days of cooking with Mum in the kitchen at home and I realized how much I missed my mother and wanted to see her again. I couldn't wait until all this craziness was over and I could head back home for what would be the first time in two years.

Brittney finally surfaced bleary-eyed just as our breakfast preparations were complete. I gave her a kiss and said proudly, 'Good morning, honey. Look – Babushka and I made breakfast! I figured you would be pretty damn hungry after all that time locked up with no food.'

I wanted to make sure I got some food into Brittney to prepare her for the day ahead. It would not be easy rescuing Amy. Brittney would need all her strength for the task. I needed to keep her focused on her mother, who was still alive and desperately needed her right now, rather than be distracted by her brother, who was beyond help.

'Thanks, Tommy, I am actually starving right now.'

'Sit down and help yourself Brit, we've got a real feast laid out for you. I am so going to learn to cook Ukrainian when we get home, if this is the kind of breakfast they eat here!'

Viktor and Uri came in next and sat down, looking serious. It looked like it was time for some casual breakfast conversation of something like the impossible rescue of a loved one from a psychopathic killer in his headquarters near an exploded nuclear reactor, battling against men with deadly radiation weapons. Just another morning chat in Odessa, really.

Uri started the strategy session. 'You'll need to get Amy today. They'll be expecting you now, so there'll be no element of surprise to help this time. But there should be less of them now. From what I hear, Odessa was their main operation and we wiped out most of his men from there.

You'll need to get on the road soon – it's about a five-hour drive to Kiev. I'm sorry, but I can't give you as many men to help this time and unfortunately, I can't come either. We have many things we must take care of here after last night's activities. There will be visits from the police and customs inspectors who will no doubt want to stick a flashlight up my ass to see what I'm hiding in there. I can give you eight good men, but that's all. You can have my grandson Ilya; he will lead them.'

'Thank you, Uri, that's a great help. You've already done so much; we really appreciate your extra help. I'm sure that will be enough to do what we need to do.'

'I'll supply you with whatever weapons you need, of course. You can keep your guns from last night. Tommy, you seemed to like your axe handles, so you're welcome to keep those. We'll certainly need to find something special for Brittney. I'll let you choose something from my own private collection.'

'Awesome, thanks Uri!' was the muffled reply from Brittney, through a mouthful of buttermilk pancakes smothered in honey.

'Since you have less troops this time and stealth is no longer a factor, I'll tell Ilya to take some heavier firepower. We have some RPG's that he's been bugging me to let him shoot.'

'Rocket Propelled Grenades? Cool,' I chimed in, hoping to impress everyone with my knowledge of military acronyms, but apparently to no avail.

'Sorry Tommy, but that's not what it stands for. The Americans invented that term after the Russians came up with the weapon called Ruchnoy Protivotankovyy Granatomyot, or RPG, which actually means handheld anti-tank grenade launcher,' replied Uri. Guess I'd better stay out of the cool military talk.

'What about transport to Kiev?' asked Viktor.

'I recommend something anonymous-looking, that will blend into the crowd and won't stand out. You'll be driving in broad daylight and there's a chance there will be police roadblocks set up. Vladimir might even have scouts watching the roads for you. We have some old ZAZ Zaporozhets that we use regularly when we want to stay inconspicuous,' responded Uri.

'Zaz what? Is that a car?' I asked.

'Yes,' said Viktor. 'It was the Soviet version of the People's Car. Ukraine made millions of them. It's a rear engine, air-cooled car. Affordable but ugly, underpowered and tiny. Nobody in their right mind would use it for a rescue mission, it's perfect.' Viktor finished with a laugh. Lucky we're a bit mental then, I guess.

'Take four cars and split up a bit so you don't look like a convoy. Okay, I think that covers everything unless anyone can think of anything else?' said Uri.

'Nope, I think that's everything, thanks Uri,' said Viktor. 'As they say in the movies, *let's get ready to rumble.*'

'Okay Brittney, you come with me and check out my special gun collection. You obviously know how to use one, so you can take your pick.'

'Thanks Uri, I look forward to choosing which weapon I'm going to use to blow away those bastards who killed my brother,' said Brittney in a menacing tone, then she paused, looked over at me and said, 'You don't mind me getting a gun, do you Tommy?'

'No, of course not honey. Like I said, I don't mind you shooting, so long as I don't have to do it, and nobody shoots at me. Go pick out a nice one.'

I went back to the bedroom to pack and Brittney bounded in a few minutes later brandishing two particularly lethal looking weapons. 'Look! I got an Uzi sub machine gun! I've always wanted one of these. And a Glock pistol. Mom never let me have anything this cool.'

'Look at you, like a kid in a candy store. Unbelievable. Please tell me they're not loaded, and the safety is on.'

'Yes, it's fine. Don't be such a baby, I know what I'm doing. They're not going to go off unless I want them to.'

'Okay, okay. Are you ready to go?'

'Absolutely. Let's go save Mom from the Russian mafia!'

Now *there's* a phrase you don't hear every day.

CHAPTER 55

The drive to Kiev was uneventful. Viktor, Brittney and I were in one of the old Zaporozhets, which I've got to say made the Volkswagen beetle, the German People's Car, seem like a damn limousine in comparison. I had the pleasure of driving the little buzz-box all the way, wrestling the gearshift like a stick in a puddle and the steering wheel like something out of a Sherman tank.

The other eight members of our team were distributed in three other ZAZ's. We saw a few police cars on the way but had no trouble. We stopped in Kiev for a late lunch and some final planning and mapped out our approach. There were two ways into Vladimir's headquarters, so we decided to split up and approach from each direction just in case.

It was mid-afternoon when we approached Vladimir's property. We did a drive-by reconnaissance and discovered it was a big rural block of land with high fencing fronting the road and a huge iron gate bristling with security cameras. There was a large saloon car with heavily tinted windows parked behind the gate, presumably containing a couple of armed thugs. The enormous house was a long way back behind the front fence. A frontal assault on the gate looked like a dicey option. We knew we didn't have complete surprise on our side this time, but just a little bit of unexpectedness would be a good thing, if possible.

We checked the neighbouring land, but the side fencing into Vladimir's property was high and solid. Subtlety was not going to be easy. We got on the phone with Ilya and after a few minutes of brainstorming he paused and said, 'You know you want to see it. Let me show it to you. I guarantee it will work.'

'Okay, fine. Go ahead,' we responded in unison.

Ilya set up in an area across the road from Vladimir's gate, under cover of a small group of trees, hidden from view of the men in the car behind the gate. He crouched, took aim with the RPG and then let fly. With an almighty WHOOSH and a huge plume of smoke and flame pouring out behind it, the rocket grenade raced across the road to its target and exploded the heavy gate like it was nothing, creating a massive flaming eruption. The car behind the gate was washed in the fiery fallout from the explosion.

Straight after the impact, all four of our little Zaporozhets raced in through the open gate, buzzing like mosquitoes as we revved the guts out of the tiny engines. I looked in my mirror and saw the car behind take off in a cloud of dust, flying down the driveway after us – the RPG hadn't taken it out. The powerful car quickly gained on us and the occupants were soon firing out the window on our race to the house at breakneck speed. As soon as the gunfire started, all four cars peeled out like some crazy fan spreading out from the driveway, heading off onto the grass. The car behind could only choose one target to follow, which unfortunately was us.

I needed all the driving skills I had to keep us from getting run down by the speeding car behind. Dodging, weaving and swerving, I was revving the absolute hell out of the pissy little car and it was protesting mightily. We bumped and crashed and bounced over the uneven surface on a bone-jarring, teeth crunching wild ride. We managed to avoid getting shot, thanks to all my crazy manoeuvring, but stopping without getting wiped out would be a challenge.

'Okay, we're getting close to the house, get ready to get out!' I shouted over the noise and chaos that was the inside of our tiny car. 'I'm going to pull a handbrake turn – you two get ready to shoot those bastards!' I waited a couple of ticks and then violently turned the steering wheel with one hand and wrenched the handbrake with the other, pulling it so hard

I'm surprised it didn't snap off in my hand. We slewed sideways, off the grass and onto the gravel at the front of the house and leapt out, guns blazing. Viktor and Brittney laid out a hail of covering fire as we raced headlong around the back of the enormous garage that looked like it could swallow a whole fleet of cars.

As we reached the cover of the building, we regrouped with the rest of our team, who had made it around to the meeting point. Our pursuers now became the pursued, because they were in such an exposed position and under fire. They crunched their car into reverse and accelerated wildly backwards around to the other side of the house.

'Okay, we're in. Now for the hard part. Finding Amy without getting ourselves and her killed!' I said. 'What's the plan?' I figured Viktor and Ilya were the criminal masterminds of the group, so they should call the shots in this pressure situation.

'I say we leave one man to cover the front exit and one out the back to cover the rear, then the rest of us go inside,' said Ilya, taking command of his troops.

'Agreed,' grunted Viktor. 'Brittney, Tommy you two stay with me. We'll take upstairs, the rest of you take downstairs.'

'Done. Let's go,' responded Ilya.

We stepped out of the safety of our shielded position behind the garage and were instantly greeted with a spray of bullets at our feet! Not entirely unexpected, since we had announced our arrival quite dramatically. Still, not a very hospitable welcome. We hurriedly jumped back behind the garage.

Ilya peered around the corner and spotted a sniper poking his rifle barrel out an upstairs window. 'Okay, I see him. I'll take him out from here. The rest of you go around the back and go in the rear of the house.'

We didn't wait for further instruction and took off in the other direction. Apparently, there was no sniper coverage at the back of the house. Maybe Vladimir didn't have many troops here to back him up.

Then a staccato rattle of gunfire erupted from the back of the house! So much for getting my hopes up. The guy covering the back had simply had the sense to wait until we were in the open before taking a shot at us. But thankfully he must have been a cheap recruit because his aim sucked. He managed to miss all of us on his first round of shots.

Running at full speed Brittney raised her Uzi and opened fire on the upstairs window where the shots had come from. Steady as you like, she sprayed the area around the window with her machine gun until inevitably one of her bullets found their mark. Man, those Uzis were kick-ass! Like a scene out of an old wild west movie, a body tumbled out of the window like a floppy mannequin, dropped like a stone and hit the ground with a sickening thud. You don't get any deader than that.

A single shot rang out from the front of the house, followed soon after by a crash that sounded like a body falling on the porch near the front door. Seems Ilya got his man too. Things were going well.

We raced up the back steps on to the wide porch. Without breaking stride, I hunkered down like a line-backer and slammed my shoulder into the back door with the momentum of a charging bull. I smashed right through the door, peeling it back from the frame and sending huge splinters of wood flying in all directions. What I didn't know was there was one poor bastard waiting behind the door supposedly to protect against someone coming in the back, except he hadn't planned on quite such a violent entry. He was only a little guy and he got absolutely slammed when I burst through the door like a human battering ram. I sent him flying down the hall, then he continued sliding on his back, already unconscious. 'Knock, knock,' I said with a smile as I came to a stop.

Viktor and Brittney leapt past me, heading up the stairs, guns drawn and ready to fire. A shot rang out from above, whizzing past Brittney's head and sending splinters flying as the projectile buried itself deep in the ornate mahogany lining of the staircase. Brittney returned fire up the stairwell with her trusty Glock, but the shooter had retreated into one of the upstairs bedrooms.

Viktor ran up the stairs two at a time, wheeled around on the landing, heading for the bedroom. Obviously from the *shoot first, ask questions later* school, Viktor quickly raised his shotgun and buried two loads of shot into the door, then dropped and slid on his back, feet first, into what was left of the door. As he disappeared into the room, a shot rang out and a bullet flew out through the door right where Viktor's chest would have been and embedded itself in the side wall of the hallway. An instant later, Viktor from his lying position let fly again with another shotgun blast from point blank range that sent his victim flying up in the air and back into the wall behind him.

Silence followed the chaos, but only briefly. A creaky floorboard in the hallway behind us saved my life as one of Vladimir's soldiers took one step too many, his position betrayed by the noise from the shifting floor timber. In a flash I spun on my heel and wind-milled my arms around in a blur. As I whirled around, my eyes met my attacker's as my arm slammed against his outstretched hands holding the gun that had just been pointed at my head. I grabbed his hand as I went, turned it over and captured the wrist, bent it forward at right angles then continued my rotation, dropped my weight and slammed my free hand against his upper arm, locking his shoulder and applying a solid arm bar that forced him to the floor in a second. As his head hit the deck, I felt his shoulder pop out of its socket and his arm went limp as he cried out in pain. I finished him off with a strike to the side of the head, knocking him out cold.

Shots rang out downstairs as our troops cleaned up whoever was down there. No calls came from anyone about finding Amy.

We searched the rest of the upstairs rooms to clear the floor. Just in case Amy was in one of the rooms, we agreed we shouldn't continue Viktor's particularly violent method of opening doors, so we decided that

Viktor and Brittney would each take one side of the door while I kicked it in and then spun out of the way. The effect was overly dramatic on the first room, which was completely empty, but better to be safe than sorry.

The second room proved more of a challenge. I launched a good kick at the door, but my foot stopped with a thud. Clearly this was no ordinary door, it was steel lined and had a reinforced frame that would take more than a kick to get through it. We needed a key, so decided we should try and keep the next guy not only alive, but conscious, so we could question him about Amy.

The third unsearched room yielded more of a reward than the first and the second. One of Vladimir's troops got off a shot, but Brittney quickly returned fire and got him in the leg. He went down in pain and Viktor jumped in and disarmed him. I watched the door for any stragglers while Viktor questioned him in what sounded like Russian. Apparently, he wasn't particularly cooperative, so Viktor encouraged him to talk by grinding his shotgun muzzle into the bullet wound in the man's leg. First, he screamed in agony and then sang like a canary. When he was finished, Viktor silenced him with a single sharp blow from the butt of his shotgun across the side of his head.

'He's the man who was guarding Amy,' said Viktor. 'He's given me the key to the secure room. He said that when they heard the explosion at the front gate, Vladimir and Borys grabbed Amy and took off downstairs. We must have just missed them.'

We tore out of the room onto the landing, where I came face to face with a bull of a man running full speed down the hall at me. Straight away I knew what to do and funnily enough, even what to say. 'Are you afraid of flying?' I called out to the charging bull. He looked at me quizzically as I stayed in his path and then at the last possible second reached out both my arms, grabbed his jacket at the shoulders, laid back, dropped my weight and then slammed my right foot deep into his solar plexus, driving it in, up and then over my head as I laid down on the floor. His own momentum carried him onward and upward, continuing his headlong drive, with me just gently helping him on his way with a final thrust of my foot. His feet left the ground and he was now horizontal, doing a fair impression of a fat Superman as he went sailing perfectly through the upstairs window at the end of the hall, smashing through the glass as he went flying out into space in a flurry of glass shards and wood splinters, screaming as he flew. Gravity soon took over and arrested his forward momentum, sending him earthwards in a flailing panic of arms, legs and screaming until he was silenced forever when he landed with a crash, right through the windscreen of the huge, gleaming S500 Mercedes that had been innocently resting in the yard. I stood up, surveyed the scene and called out the window, 'Well, you should be!'

We took the key, opened the steel door and hurried in to check it out. 'I'll prop the door, so it doesn't close behind us and keep watch too. You guys see what you can find,' I said.

'She was here! They're the clothes she was wearing when they separated us,' said Brittney, pointing to the clothes in the corner.

'There's a message in the bathroom, written in lipstick on the mirror,' called Viktor. 'It says *Chernobyl*.'

Just then I heard through the now open window in the hallway what sounded like a big speedboat roar into life. I rushed over to the window, looked out and saw a large boatshed and dock on an *enormous* body of water that I hadn't noticed when I was down at ground level. Maybe I'd been too busy getting shot at to notice the scenery. The body of water was so big it looked like a huge lake but was in fact the Dnieper River, which ran right through Kiev and was one of the longest rivers in Europe. That map I'd bought was really paying off with my local knowledge.

Speeding away from the dock was a large launch, a *go-fast* boat, just like I'd seen on documentaries where smugglers used them to outrun the Coast Guard in the Caribbean Sea. I'm guessing it contained all three of our targets – Amy, Vladimir and Borys. 'Let's go!' I shouted and vaulted over the landing rail and onto the stairs, bolting down to the ground floor, with Brittney right behind me. Viktor called out from the landing, 'You two go ahead, I'm not as fast as I used to be. I'll look after things here. Go and get Amy!'

'Okay, call me later, I've still got the phone. But if something happens, let's meet back at Rodina Mat, the Motherland statue in Kiev, if either of us gets held up,' I yelled out behind me.

But then the hapless victim of my door-busting entry into the house completely screwed up our plan. He'd managed to regain consciousness while we were mucking around upstairs and he flicked out his leg just as Brittney was running past at full speed, sending her flying, sprawling on the floor. 'Ow! Son of a bitch! Goddamn it, I've hurt my ankle! Tommy, you go ahead, right now. I won't be able to run. Go get Mom!'

Torn between looking after my girlfriend and saving her mother, I took one last look at her and she waved me on, adamant that I should continue pursuit. 'Okay, bye! Love you!' I called out over my shoulder as I took off out the door. My last sight of Brittney was her launching a side kick with her good leg, catching her tripper right in the face, snapping his head back and sending him off to sleep again. That's my girl.

Legs pounding like battering rams, arms pumping like pistons, I was a very large machine running at full speed down the hill towards the river. Thankfully I was in peak physical condition and familiar with this kind of exertion. I had just competed in the Olympics a few days ago, after all. But it was a bloody long way to go at a full sprint. Breath rasping, lungs screaming and blood pumping, I finally reached the boathouse and could still hear the boat tearing up the river and see the last remnants of the ripples on the water from the wake of the big craft.

I desperately hoped there would be another boat in the shed, otherwise Amy would be gone, and our rescue efforts would be for nothing. As I rounded the corner of the boathouse, I crossed my fingers and my prayers were answered as I spotted another go-fast boat with the key in the ignition, presumably waiting for the remainder of Vladimir's gang who we'd waylaid back at the house.

Not one to look a gift horse in the mouth, I jumped in, turned the key and gunned the enormous triple outboards to life. I blasted the throttle and launched out of the boat shed like I'd been shot out of a cannon! The 1,000 horsepower that was bolted to the back of the fibreglass hull, reinforced with Kevlar and carbon fibre, certainly packed a mean punch. In a moment of lucidity, I had to admire Vladimir's taste in big boy's toys. Heading upriver, I set out in pursuit of Amy, although they had a big head start on me, so I wasn't convinced I was going to have much luck catching her, but still I had to try.

This boat is an absolute beast! I looked down at the speedo, and the needle just kept climbing and climbing, going around the dial until it maxed out at 150 km an hour. I was shitting bricks at this speed, feeling like all I needed was a bit of a wave and I would be a goner. But I guess they were designed for smuggler's runs across the seas and waves of the Caribbean, so they could cope with bigger water than a river. The minutes flew by and I chewed up the distance with the big outboards running flat out just on the redline, keeping the boat at top speed. Up ahead, I could still see a faint sign of ripples on the surface of the river, so figured I would just have to keep on going until something happened.

And then, something did.

Behind a rocky outcrop along the bank of the river I saw Vladimir's boat lying in wait for me, with Borys standing right up on the bow of the boat with a particularly nasty-looking weapon pointed right at me! I immediately cut the gas to wash off some speed (no brakes!) and turned the wheel as much as I dared at that velocity, sending the boat lurching crazily. Borys took a sighting on me and pulled the trigger on his enormous assault rifle, which launched at my boat what I was soon to learn was an explosive shell traveling at supersonic speed. His first shot missed, cannoning into the water just below me and to the side, exploding on impact and sending a spray of water 10 metres up in the air. Shit, that was close!

I slammed the throttle down full again and raced off into the middle of the river, with Vladimir in hot pursuit, gunning his engines. I looked over my shoulder and saw Borys taking aim at me again, so I tried some evasive action, which was not easy, because the high speed limited the magnitude of the turns. Struggling to retain control over my boat, I tried one last evasive manoeuvre, but it was useless. Borys pulled the trigger and let fly with another explosive shell, which this time found its mark, thankfully on the opposite side of the boat to me and down low at the water line. I bailed out just in time, launching myself overboard just as the explosive projectile ripped into the hull of my boat and blew it to smithereens.

The force of the blast slammed into me while I was still airborne from my jump, propelling me out and up with enormous force, pursued by the rapidly expanding surface of the fireball that used to be my boat. I probably would have thought it was pretty cool if I wasn't so close to death. My body became a crazy tumbling and whirling missile, still moving forward at boat speed of almost 150 km an hour but now also with angular momentum from the blast that had blown me out vertically and horizontally and had even sent me spinning head over heels into the bargain. I was like some crazy physics vector from high school, except the only answer this time was certain pain and potential death. Old Mr. Peebles, my science teacher from Kings Cross, never thought up this equation for us!

Finally, Earth's gravity won out and brought me back into its clutches. Man, this was going to hurt. Crash! I hit and bounced up off the surface, like some crazy skipping stone thrown by the hand of a playful giant. Up and down I went, flying and bouncing across the surface of the water, losing speed and height each time. I could tell I was about to dig in and go under, so I drew in a deep breath and tucked myself into a ball to reduce the chance of ripping off an arm or a leg. My many times of being dumped in the surf off my board had prepared me well for this moment.

Splat! Finally, I slowed down enough for the river to catch me in its watery embrace instead of allowing me to bounce along on the surface. I stuck hard, the inertia of the water grabbing me and bringing me to an almost immediate and very painful stop. After a few moments of submersion, I got my bearings, worked out which way was up and struck out for the surface. Big mistake.

As my head popped up out of the water, I heard an explosion instantly matched by a tracer bullet exploding into the water right beside my head. Bloody Borys was doing his best to finish me off! I ducked under again and bullets continued to come, tracing their deadly path through the water, leaving a trail of turbulence behind. I knew I was screwed unless I did something completely radical, so I quickly surfaced again, took a few fast, deep breaths to hyperventilate and oxygenate my blood, then took one final deep lungful of air until I felt like my chest was going to burst. Then I dived down, as deep as I could go, out of range of Borys' deadly firepower.

The adrenaline was still pounding in my system from my long sprint and the water pursuit, not to mention being launched out of an exploding boat at ludicrous speed and then being shot at for good measure. It wasn't easy, but I took myself back to my deep diving days, got my body and brain back in the zone, slowed my heart rate and convinced myself I had no need for air. My training remembered, I soon reached a peaceful calm and settled in for the wait, counting away the seconds.

The minutes ticked by in my peaceful underwater world. It was bloody cold, but I was used to the chill from my days of winter swimming and surfing at Bondi Beach, so that was no great shock to the system. I couldn't see much except for a dim light coming from the surface of the river, but my ears were the more important sense at this point. I was hoping to hear some action from Vladimir's launch.

Five minutes in, and I still felt reasonably comfortable. Then the noise I was straining to hear finally came, but instead of getting quieter as they receded into the distance, it got louder! They were coming closer, so close that they were right on top of me. I could see the bottom of the boat right on the surface above me. They traced slow circles, searching, searching, but seeing nothing. Six minutes turned into seven, then eight minutes and I was starting to get worried. I was approaching my maximum dive time and the boat was right above me.

Nine minutes ticked over, and my lungs were starting to burn, my brain was yelling for attention, clamouring for me to breathe, breathe, breathe! But I couldn't surface, not yet. I willed my brain into submission, knowing that I would be dead if I surfaced for air. Ten minutes came and now it seemed like every part of my body had joined in, every cell was starving for life-giving oxygen, but I continued my resistance.

Finally! Sweet relief came over me as I heard the engine roar fully into life, saw the rudder above me take a heading straight upriver and the triple props did their job, churning the water and sending the boat on its way. They'd finally given up on me, figuring one of the bullets must have found their mark, or I'd drowned, or both.

I fought the urge to break the surface for another thirty seconds until the vision and the sound of the boat receded into the distance upriver. I surfaced as gently and as quietly as I possibly could to avoid the risk of detection from the boat in the distance, but it was bloody hard to restrain myself from bursting out of the water like a whale breaching. I expelled all my dead air in a huge blast as I emptied my lungs and then immediately refilled as I gulped huge lungful after lungful of that glorious oxygen. Air never tasted so sweet, so pure and so cool. I don't think I've ever felt quite so alive, as my body's lifeblood was recharged with that most special of gases known to the scientists as O_2.

After the all-systems warning was heeded and my bodily demands were slowly satisfied for air, my brain started returning to normal function and I was able to take stock of my current situation. The conclusion? Deep shit. I was floating smack bang in the middle of the Kiev Sea, which was an enormous 12 kilometres across – so wide I couldn't even see the shore on either side of me! And I was in the middle of freaking *nowhere*, I had no transport and my phone would be as dead as a doornail after its extended immersion.

I struck out for shore, swimming strongly at the start but that strength soon faded. It took me forever to reach the shore, by which time I was completely exhausted. My feeling of sweet relief as my hands touched mud soon turned to horror as I looked up and saw two Ukrainian cops staring down at me, guns drawn and pointed at my head. *Goddamn it!*

'Hello Sir. Did you enjoy your swim? Your friend Vladimir called us and thought you might have got into some trouble, so he asked us to check up on you to make sure you're okay,' jeered one of them. Sarcasm somehow seems so much more annoying just after you've suffered a couple of near-death experiences. 'Actually, he thought you were dead and wanted us to look for your body in case your corpse floated on to shore. But since you appear to be quite alive, you can come back with us and we'll toss you in a cell for the night and then Borys can come and collect you tomorrow.'

Awesome.

CHAPTER 56

'Brittney, are you alright? Can you walk?' asked Viktor as he made his way down the stairs after the commotion of Tommy's exit.

'Yes, I think I can walk, but ballet is out of the question for a while.'

'Okay, we'd better regroup and get out of here. Tommy could be gone for a while. We'll call him later and work out where to meet up with him. With all the racket we've been making, the police will be here at any moment. I'll grab the guard from upstairs and bring him with us for questioning in case Tommy doesn't catch up with Vladimir.'

Viktor headed back upstairs and reappeared a moment later dragging the unconscious body of the guard he had knocked out earlier. He pulled him along the floor and down the stairs by the scruff of the neck as the man's feet beat out a steady thunk, thunk, thunk rhythm as they thudded down each of the steps.

Brittney called out to the rest of their gang, all of whom were thankfully alive although some were slightly the worse for wear. Ilya had been stabbed and two of the other men had been shot, but according to them this was nothing serious. 'These Cossacks sure are a tough bunch,' thought Brittney.

'Thank you again, Ilya for everything you've done. We couldn't have made it this far without your help,' said Viktor.

'Viktor, it has been our pleasure to fight alongside you,' replied Ilya. 'My grandfather used to speak of you when I was a boy, telling me stories of what you and he used to get up to. He always said you were the toughest man he knew. I believe him now that I have seen you in action for myself. I feel like I have now met the legend. I'm sorry but we can't continue any further on your mission. Kiev is as far as we can come; we need to get back to Odessa tonight. Our Hetman needs us after the mess at the docks. Plus, some of us could do with some medical attention,' he said with a half-smile / half-grimace as he clutched his side where he'd been stabbed.

'That's okay, I understand. And thanks again for everything you've done for us, and Uri of course. Let's grab the cars and get out of here,' said Viktor.

What had moments before been a stately manor in the countryside was now violated by the battle. Broken doors hung from their frames, windows were smashed, walls were riddled with bullet holes and the floors and grounds were littered with dead or unconscious bodies. The group left the carnage behind as they took off in their trusty Zaporozhets, which still started, despite all the abuse they had copped on the way into Vladimir's property. Even Tommy's car after all he had put it through cheerily sang its wheezy song as soon as Viktor turned the key and it spluttered into life.

They turned out onto the road in opposite directions and innocently went on their way, keeping well under the speed limit. They had made it out just in time, for they soon heard sirens wailing and saw police cars come flying in towards the scene of the carnage. The cops were in for a long night of investigations and questioning.

Groans emanated from the back seat of Viktor and Brittney's car as their captive started to come around after his concussion. Brittney pulled out her Glock, turned to face the back seat and levelled her gun at him. He blinked himself back into consciousness, saw the gun and nearly passed out again in fear and surprise. Once he'd recovered his composure he said, 'Don't worry, I'm not going to do anything stupid or try and escape. I like being alive too much for that. Except right now my head feels like I'm already dead and my leg is on fire. Why did you have to do that to me?'

'You deserved it for what you did to my Mom, you bastard!' spat Brittney.

'Alright, alright, calm down. I'll just sit here and be quiet,' he replied, closing his eyes and settling back in his seat.

'Good, you do that and make sure you don't bleed all over our car,' said Brittney as she tossed him an old rag from the floor of the car. 'Wrap that around your leg, it should stem the flow.'

'What do you think we should do, Viktor?' asked Brittney, feeling very lost now that she and Tommy had been separated so soon after their tearful reunion.

'Let's try and find somewhere to stay that's nice and quiet and out of the way where we can question the guard and lay low until we can contact Tommy. I think it's too early to try and call him yet, we'll give him another couple of hours. It's getting late now, so we should probably plan on spending the night somewhere around here.'

'Okay, that sounds like a good idea,' replied Brittney. 'There's a small town coming up ahead. Maybe someone there knows somewhere to stay.'

Viktor parked the old ZAZ in front of the tiny town's only store and went in to speak to the shopkeeper, coming out a few minutes later with a smile on his face and two bags bulging with food.

He jumped back in the car and said, 'There's a farmer down the road with a cottage on his property that he rents out; it's vacant right now.'

'Sounds perfect,' replied Brittney. 'Let's go.'

With pleasantries and money exchanged between Viktor and the farmer, all well away from the car and its potentially troublesome inhabitant, they made their way up the front steps and into the old stone cottage, which had clearly stood for hundreds of years.

'First things first,' said Viktor. 'Grab the zip ties and tape out of the bag and we'll make our guest comfortable.'

'Look, I told you, I'll cooperate with you, I'll tell you whatever you want to know. Vladimir is nothing to me. He's a pig and a cheapskate. He's not worth the trouble to try and torture anything out of me. Ask me whatever you like and then let me go, please! I won't be going to the cops and I sure won't be getting in touch with Vladimir. He'd probably kill me for being incompetent, the asshole.'

'Interesting. I'm seeing a common theme here. There seems to be a distinct lack of loyalty among Vladimir's men. You're not the first who's been ready to spill the beans on Vladimir at the slightest threat.'

'What can I say, the man is a nutcase and a lousy payer. What do you want to know?'

'Is the woman alive?'

'Yes, she's very much alive. She left kicking and screaming. Borys had to drag her out of the cell when she realized that you were coming through the gate. He slapped her around a bit until Vladimir told him not to damage his *bride*. I've seen Vladimir do some crazy things, but he's really lost it this time with this woman. What is it about her that he's suddenly so worked up about?'

'Never mind that. We want answers from you, not questions.'

'Okay, okay. What else do you want to know?'

'Was she treated okay? Did they hurt her?' asked Brittney.

'The worst thing she had to do was endure a dinner date with Vladimir, which I guess is a kind of torture. But other than that, she was treated alright. She had her own room, shower and fresh clothes and as far as I'm aware she wasn't beaten except for Borys at the end there when they took her away.'

'Where are they taking her?' asked Viktor.

'Well, you people have been particularly troublesome. Vladimir had three bases, but you took out the biggest one in Odessa and then the next biggest in Kiev, so he's retreated to the only one he's got left – the smallest one, near Chernobyl.'

'Where exactly is it? How do we find it?' asked Viktor.

'I'll need a map to show you. I've never been there, but I've seen where it is.'

Viktor went out and checked the glove box of the old car and found a touring map of Ukraine, yellowed with age, frayed along the edges and worn along the folds, but still serviceable. He laid it out in front of Vladimir's henchman, who very cooperatively pointed out the precise location of Vladimir's Chernobyl base, deep in the exclusion zone.

'What's the security like there? How many men does he have at his base?' continued Viktor.

'From what I hear, the security's not that great and he doesn't have many men up there, maybe only five or six.'

'What do they do up there? Why does he have a base so close to the nuclear plant?'

'Didn't you know? I thought that's why you must be after him. That's where he gets the Chernobylite. They extract it from a radioactive mass in the basement of Reactor 4 called the Elephant's Foot. That's what Vladimir and Borys used to kill that Olympic wrestler in Bucharest.'

Viktor quickly looked over at Brittney as the blood drained from her face and she collapsed on the floor in a heap.

CHAPTER 57

'Alright, alright, take it easy! Keep your shirt on. No need to get nasty,' I said to my dim-witted police guards. They looked like simpletons but at least always had the sense to keep me at gunpoint when I wasn't locked up because I could clearly beat the shit out of them both with one hand tied behind my back. Which I would just about need to do considering I was in handcuffs with my hands behind my back at this stage as they pushed me into my cell and clipped me with a whack from a nightstick on the way in.

I stumbled into my cell and they locked the heavy steel door behind me. 'Come here, put your hands through the hatch,' snapped one of the guards. I walked over to the door, turned around and did as instructed. Blessed relief! They removed my handcuffs, which I have to say from first experience were not a lot of fun to be wearing. They'd been bloody tight around my big wrists and had cut off the blood circulation to my hands, which were now completely numb. I quickly rubbed and massaged my wrists and hands, working the blood flow back into them and trying to regain some feeling after I got through the painful pins-and-needles phase.

'Goodnight, pretty-boy,' sneered the smartass guard through the hatch. 'Hey, I saw you on TV a few days ago. Your shiny gold medal won't help you in here. You belong to Borys now. He's looking forward to seeing you in the morning.' Then he shut the hatch and flicked out the lights, swamping me in complete and utter blackness.

I'd lost track of time by now, but I knew it was night-time. It had been a huge day of monumental effort and I was completely exhausted, desperate for rest. I collapsed on the wooden plank hanging off the wall that was masquerading as a bed and was fast asleep in a matter of seconds.

CHAPTER 58

'Brittney, take your time, wake up slowly. How do you feel? Are you alright?' asked Viktor.

'I don't know. How did I end up here?' said Brittney.

'You fainted and I carried you to the bed.'

'Oh God, Chad! Vladimir killed Chad! And now he has Mom! Why is he doing this to us? I don't understand Where's Tommy and why haven't we heard from him? We don't even know if he's alive or dead. Oh Viktor, why is this all happening?' wailed Brittney as she burst into tears.

'Vladimir is a violent, brutal and crazy man. There is no logic or reason to what he is doing or what he has done. But the feelings driving Vladimir are very deep, they go back 20 years and even further to his childhood with his brother Nikolai.'

'Yes, I know about Nikolai. He's my father. Mom told me all about it when we were locked up in Odessa together. She said it was horrible, that Nikolai used to beat her, rape her and almost killed her more than once, all when she was still just a teenager. She said it was only because a man named Pasha saved her and helped her escape that we survived and had the life we had in New York.'

'Yes, things were extremely difficult for your mother. She lived in constant fear for her life and the safety of you and your brother.'

'What? What do you mean? How do you know? And what did you mean earlier when you said that we'd met before?'

Viktor took a deep breath and said, 'Valentina, I knew your mother 20 years ago, since before you and Anatoly were born. I was there when she met your father for the first time. I helped her and protected her from Nikolai's brutality as much as I could. Like you, I go by a different name now than the one I was born with. I am Pasha.'

Brittney was silent, unable to say a word in response to this stunning piece of information. A fresh set of tears welled in Brittney's eyes, her lips started quivering and she wordlessly sat up on the bed, reached out her arms to Viktor and hugged him in silent thanks.

Viktor was moved beyond words. His mind lurched back to that fateful day when he helped the desperate Tatiana and her children escape from Nikolai. Then, inevitably, he was drawn to the next day when he lost his darling Katerina. So many times, he had replayed those events back in his mind, like a silent projector flashing past his eyes. He had questioned his actions and wondered if he had taken a different course whether Katerina would still be alive today; with them sharing the idyllic life they pictured so vividly for each other.

But in this moment, as the weeping Brittney wordlessly clutched him in an embrace of thanks for her life and those of her mother and brother, Viktor knew without a shadow of doubt that he had done the right thing. If not for him, Tatiana would surely have been dead by now and her children more likely than not would have been turned into monsters like their father because of his abuse. Viktor had saved three lives that day. Unfortunately, he had also lost one life and ruptured his own.

Viktor reflected on the teachings of his Zen masters and the role of Karma in his own life. He had done horrible deeds, many violent acts in his life that upset the balance of his Chi, his life force, which he had spent the last 20 years trying to rebalance, to gain peace. The new path of his life started that day when he helped Tatiana and now, in this moment he knew deep down in his heart and soul that he had made the right choice in saving those lives. He knew that Katerina would have wanted this life for him.

'Thank you, Pasha. Thank you for saving us. Thank you for giving our family our lives. Thank you for *my* life,' whispered Brittney into the warmth of Viktor's strong embrace.

Brittney had always longed for a father. She had not had adult male influences in her life, no father, no uncles, no grandfathers. These moments shared with Viktor had a tremendous impact on Brittney, right to her core. A deep bond was forged between Brittney and Viktor in that one embrace.

Finally, her emotions spent, after what seemed to them both an eternity, Brittney pulled away from Viktor and they both wiped the tears from their face.

'What happened to you? Why did you need to change your name? And how did you end up in Sydney and being with Tommy?'

'I was severely injured and suffered a great loss because of a car bomb that was ordered by Vladimir. My darling wife Katerina was killed in the explosion and I very nearly died.'

Brittney gasped in shock and said, 'No! Because of what you did for Mom? Does that mean it was our fault?'

'No, no, my dear, that wasn't the reason at all. Vladimir killed his brother and took over his criminal business and tried to kill me because he thought I was loyal to Nikolai and would fight against Vladimir. He simply saw the opportunity that your mother's escape presented and chose that moment to strike. After the explosion, a good friend of mine – a doctor named Dmitri, saved me. He changed my name from Pasha to Viktor and smuggled me out of Chechnya to Japan. After a few years there while I recovered from my horrible injuries, I moved to Australia, which is where I met Tommy. Dmitri was the doctor who also helped your mother escape.'

'Really? It sounds like I owe him a great debt, helping to save both my mother and the man who saved her.'

'He was happy to help me. I saved his life many years ago when we were just kids, so he owed me a life debt that he was glad to repay.'

'It's amazing how everyone is connected and intertwined in all this,' said Brittney. 'Across three countries and 20 years, we're all connected and brought to this moment and convergence of events where each depends on the other.'

'Yes, I think it was my destiny to save your mother that day, so you could meet Tommy and I could be here right now, talking to you and helping save your mother once again.'

'Hmm… maybe you're right. I've never been a believer in fate or destiny, I've always thought we make our own way in life, that we are defined by our actions, that nothing is pre-ordained. But the very fact that you and I are standing here together talking after what you did for me all those years ago is making me question my beliefs about fate. Do you believe that Tommy and I were meant to be together? Are meant for each other?'

'I don't know about that Brittney, but what I do know is that I've never seen a couple so perfectly matched, so suited to each other and who are so good together. I don't know if you were *meant* for each other, but I definitely believe you should be together.'

'You know Viktor, I really love Tommy. A lot. I don't know if he knows just how much.'

'I'm sure he knows Brittney, and I know he loves you a great deal too.'

'Do you think he's okay? I wonder why he hasn't called yet; it's late.'

'I'm sure Tommy's fine, he's probably just been held up somewhere, or his phone died.'

'I just hope it's not him that's died!' said Brittney fiercely.

'Sorry, bad choice of words. Forget I said that. How about we try and call him now and if we can't get through, we'll try again in the morning and then if we still can't get through to him then we'll go to Rodina Mat.'

'Yes, please,' sniffed Brittney.

Viktor tried Tommy's number, but the line was dead.

CHAPTER 59

I woke sometime in the night, prodded by my subconscious to work out how the hell I was going to get out of this cell. Clearly my Lizard brain, the ancient part responsible for primitive survival instincts and the fight or flight reflex, figured I'd had enough rest and wanted me to get on with surviving. Everything hinged on the next few hours. Brittney and Viktor would be worried about me, waiting for me and with no clue where I was or even if I were alive or dead. Then of course there was Amy to rescue. Plus, if Borys came for me, I would be in real trouble. I had to do something and do it *fast*.

My brain whirred through the possibilities and settled on a plan that had a good chance of success. I felt my way around the walls until I found the toilet in the corner and took a piss as part of the bodily preparation for my next move, then laid down in what I figured was about the centre of the floor.

I took myself back to my Zen training with Viktor that he learned from his masters in the Japanese temples. I closed my eyes, emptied my mind, focused inward and progressively slowed my breathing and my heart rate. Soon, I was barely conscious and completely still, appearing on first impression to be well and truly dead. I settled in for the wait.

I lose sense of time when I meditate like this, so I have no idea how long it took before my brain registered the lights flickering into life. I heard noises as the guard opened the inspection hatch in the door to check on me and heard him call out to his partner.

There was much animated discussion behind the door of my cell as the guards deliberated about what to do with me. Clearly, they were concerned. With my very shallow, slow breathing, there was no visible rise and fall of my chest. My heart rate and metabolism flickered when I heard the heavy sound of steel on steel as the keys clanged, then the lock turned, and the door swung open. Slowly and cautiously the guards entered. I could tell by the sound of footsteps that one guard approached me, presumably with the other one hanging back and guarding me. My metabolism flickered again, preparing me for action.

The guard knelt beside me, put his finger on my neck to check for a pulse and brought his face down inches from mine to check for signs of breath.

NOW! My brain snapped into hyper-drive and my eyes suddenly flew open like a corpse rising from the dead. My right hand flew all the way around behind the guard's head, cupped his chin and then with a quick pull I wrenched my right hand back around, taking his head with it, his body progressively following the spin of the head, the neck, then the shoulders, the torso, the hips and the legs. I moved my right arm and applied the choke hold around his neck, holding him helpless. He was stretched out full length on his back on top of me, shielding me from the guard with the gun. It had all happened so fast that the guard hadn't had time to react. One minute I was dead, the next I had complete control over his partner and left him without a shot.

'Drop the gun or I'll snap his neck like a chicken! Do it!' I yelled to the standing guard, the one with the smart mouth from the night before. I knew I had to work fast, and that shock and awe were my main weapons right now. Wide-eyed and panicked, the guard dropped his gun and kicked it over towards me.

'Good. Smart move,' I said. Still with the choke hold applied to the first guard, I stood up, dragging my prisoner with me, and then frog marched him over to the other guard, who had backed himself into a corner. Subtlety was most definitely not the order of the day; speed and efficiency were required. With that in mind, I maintained the choke hold with my right arm, then snapped out my left hand, grabbed the other guy by the throat and in one swift move smashed his head back against the solid brick wall behind him, then unleashed a massive kick, smashing him square in the balls and then tossed him to the ground like the garbage that he was.

'How do your nuts feel about my gold medal now, smartass?' I said to the crumpled mess on the floor.

'What about me?' stammered the remaining guard, who I still held in my grip.

'I've decided I'll let you go,' I replied.

'Thank you, thank you,' he said.

'Sorry, only choking. Time for sleep,' I said as I applied the choke hold completely, putting him out cold in a few seconds and then dropped him on the floor too, right beside his mate.

I quickly grabbed the cell keys, peered out the door to the thankfully empty corridor, shut the door and locked it behind me, then turned out the lights for good measure. I noticed dawn's early light coming in through a window in the corridor and hoped that the police day shift wasn't too early. I spotted the exit from the cells area out to the lobby, quickly headed down there and looked out through the viewing panel in the steel door. Again, there was no sign of any other cops at this early hour, but I figured there must be someone around somewhere, so decided to head for the emergency exit rather than out through the main entrance.

I made my way out into what looked like an impound yard with a few cars scattered around. Just what I needed – wheels! I checked the booth, grabbed a set of keys with a remote then walked quickly into the yard pressing the unlock button. When the key's partner winked its lights at me in greeting, I jumped in and slowly drove out of the yard to the end of the driveway at a locked gate. I still had the guard's keys on me, so jumped out of the car and on the fourth try managed to unlock the gate and calmly drove out of the lot. Thankfully, it was only a small police station in a quiet backwater, so security had been relatively slack, making for what turned out to be quite a straightforward escape for someone of my skills.

I was getting the hang of this mayhem business.

CHAPTER 60

Viktor and Brittney woke at the crack of dawn. Desperate for news of Tommy, Brittney grabbed the phone and called Tommy's number before she'd even got out of bed. Still the line was dead, no response.

'Damn it! Why won't he answer? We have to go to the meeting point Viktor; I can't stand being here any longer,' said Brittney.

'You're right, Brittney, but let's have some breakfast first. We've got a big day ahead of us and we don't know when we'll be able to eat next.'

'Alright, but let's make it quick and then hit the road.'

'Uh, excuse me,' came a voice from the corner. 'But what do you plan to do with me? I'm still tied up, you know.'

'I know. We'll let you go when we leave, which is more than you deserve,' replied Viktor.

CHAPTER 61

Next time I pick a rendezvous point, I'll make sure it's not so damn far away. Although in my defence, Rodina Mat, the Motherland Monument, was about the only landmark I could think of in Kiev at the time since I was in a full sprint in pursuit of a departing speedboat. So, I guess I should be thankful that I had the presence of mind to think of anything at all. But it was a much longer drive from the police station to our meeting point than I'd intended.

My stolen car from the police impound lot was doing the job nicely and seemed reliable enough. I just hoped the petrol in the tank would get me there, since I didn't have enough cash on me for fuel, let alone breakfast, which was now a pressing need. All I had were a few coins in my pocket, which wouldn't get me far.

Distance issues aside, Rodina Mat was a damn good choice for a meeting place, since it was such a significant landmark. A 62m tall stainless-steel statue waving a 16m long sword on top of a hill is kind of hard to miss.

I just made it to the museum district in Kiev, running on fumes before my car finally died, leaving me just a short walk through the gardens along the bank of the Dnieper River, a horrible reminder of yesterday's marathon swim. My arms and shoulders gave an involuntary shudder at the reminder of that hellish exertion in the river.

It was still early in the morning, with not much action in the city apart from a few keen exercisers in the park. I pulled what few Ukrainian Hryvnia coins I had out of my pocket and decided I would see what I could find to eat while I waited for Brittney and Viktor. I found a coffee shop and managed to negotiate a trade of my coins for some Sosysky, the breakfast sausage I had cooked with my new favourite old woman, Uri's Babushka. It was nowhere near enough, but it tasted bloody good. Hopefully, the others would turn up soon and we could sort out the money situation.

I wandered over to the monument, gazing up at its brilliance as the morning sun caught the gigantic shiny sword pointing skyward.

I settled down on a seat at the base of the statue to wait for my gang to rendezvous. Thankfully, I didn't have to wait long, as it seemed they were as eager to see me as I was them. In less than an hour, they turned up in the trusty old ZAZ and I don't think I've ever been happier to see anyone, ever, as two of the three most important people in my life appeared from around the corner.

'Brittney, I'm so glad to see you!' I shouted as she limped over to me and I wrapped her up in a huge hug and kissed her deeply. 'Getting you back after being away for so long and then losing you again so soon was a nightmare! Let's stick together from now on, hey?'

'Tommy! I'm so happy to see you; I was so worried about you! I thought maybe you were dead when we didn't hear from you and couldn't get through on your phone,' said Brittney, who had put her palms on both my cheeks and was kissing every part of my face.

'Plenty of tries, but nobody's killed me yet. I'm still causing havoc out there,' I said, then turned to Viktor. 'Hi Viktor, I'm glad to see you again too. Are you guys okay?'

'Yes, we're fine,' replied Brittney. 'My ankle's not too bad, I can walk fine, it's just a bit sore. But no running for me for a few days.'

'What about you?' asked Viktor. 'Are you okay? Since you don't have Amy with you, I take it you weren't able to catch up with them?'

'Well, you're right in one sense. That is, I don't have Amy. But unfortunately, I did catch up with them. Or rather, they hid behind a section of bank jutting out into the river and blasted the shit out of me with an explosive shell that blew my boat to smithereens! Luckily, I was thrown clear but Borys kept shooting at me, so I went on a long dive, staying under for more than ten minutes.'

'What? Ten minutes! How the hell did you manage that?' asked Brittney, astonished.

'Looks like you're not the only one in this relationship with surprises, Brit. You can thank Viktor for that one, with all his Zen training. When I was young, I used the breathing techniques that Viktor taught me and extended it to diving. I used to practice seeing how long I could stay under. It's amazing what having your life threatened with certain death can do to your personal best time.'

'What happened then? How did you get away?' asked Viktor.

'Well, because I stayed under so long, they finally buggered off, so I surfaced, but it was like I was in the middle of the goddamn ocean! Man, that Dnieper River is huge. I reckon I had about a five-kilometre swim, which took me more than two hours. I was completely stuffed when I finally reached the shore.'

'And then you found somewhere to stay the night and then made your way here?' asked Brittney.

'I guess you could say that; I kind of got arrested. Borys had two cops on his payroll, so ordered them to come and look for my body in the river around about where they left me. But they spotted me swimming and then lay in wait for me on the bank, guns drawn. There was nothing I could do.'

'So, then what?'

'They took me back to the cop shop and tossed me in the drunk tank for the night.'

'What are you talking about? Cop shop? Drunk tank? What do you mean?' asked Brittney.

'Sorry, I mean they took me to the police station and locked me up in the cells for the night. I was completely shagged after the huge day, so

I just collapsed on the bed, exhausted and passed out to sleep straight away.'

'You spent the night locked up in a jail cell? How the hell did you escape?' asked Brittney.

'Again, kudos goes to Viktor, his training saved me again,' I said, with a nod towards Viktor. 'Remember that training we used to do, where we slowed down our breathing and our heart rate? I got so good at it, I looked like I was dead. Mum used to hate it when I did it at home, it used to really freak her out. So, I laid out on the floor, pretending to be dead and when the guards came in I took out those pricks, locked them in the cells, pinched a car from the impound yard and now here I am with you guys. What's for breakfast?'

Viktor laughed and said, 'Alright, that sounds like quite an adventure. Let's go get you fed, and we'll tell you what we've been up to and plan our next move.'

Cashed up once again thanks to Viktor's stash, I filled my belly while they filled my ears with what they'd been up to. I was stoked to hear that they'd managed to find out where Vladimir had taken Amy. I'd been concerned that my failed boat chase had been our only chance to recover Amy.

It was also good news to find out that Vladimir's troop numbers were running low because our two attacks had taken out a lot of his soldiers and that this last target was his only remaining bolt hole. After Chernobyl, he had nowhere left to run. But it would still be tough to take out Vladimir and recover Amy safely. There were only three of us now and we had still had Borys to contend with, along with the remaining members of Vladimir's team.

The most astonishing news was what Vladimir was up to, extracting Chernobylite and injecting it or shooting it into people, confirming beyond doubt that he had been the one responsible for Chad's death.

It was only a couple of hours drive to Chernobyl and we wanted to get there as quickly as possible, because Amy had had to spend a whole night with Vladimir and Borys doing God knows what to her, so we checked our gear, jumped in the old ZAZ and headed north out of Kiev on the road to Chernobyl, the last stop on our mission to save Amy.

CHAPTER 62

The exclusion zone around Chernobyl was a desolate wasteland of abandoned buildings. A triumph of Soviet-era planning, the once thriving model city of Pripyat and the smaller town of Chernobyl were hurriedly evacuated shortly after the reactor explosion. The temporary evacuation soon morphed into abandonment, with time estimates before resettlement could be considered safe for human occupation being some 20,000 years.

Entire hospitals, schools, theatres, sports halls, apartment buildings and swimming pools remained, abandoned and unchanged for decades. Acres upon acres of wooded forest were stripped by the fallout, the remnants now pumping out its own radiation. Pripyat even included a fairground with carousels, bumper cars and a huge Ferris wheel, completed just days before the disaster but destined never to take passengers, the grand opening usurped by an event of much greater significance.

Facilities within the exclusion zone were not limited to those associated with human habitation. At the height of the Cold War, the Soviets developed the *Duga* over-the-horizon-radar system as part of their anti-ballistic missile early warning system and built a Duga installation in Chernobyl. Known by NATO as the Steel Yard or colloquially as the Russian Woodpecker for the sharp, repetitive tapping noise it produced over radar, the Duga systems were extremely powerful and caused havoc with commercial broadcasts, aviation systems and amateur radio enthusiasts. The Duga array in Chernobyl was huge, a leviathan steel structure soaring 150 metres up out of the earth and stretching 700 metres wide, with a weight of over 14,000 tons.

The Chernobyl nuclear disaster rendered the Duga radar facility useless, an anachronism of Cold War history like so many Soviet military facilities around the world, abandoned and left to decay.

They say one man's trash is another man's treasure. To Vladimir, the Duga facility was worth salvaging – he saw potential where others saw nothing. Through his military contacts and a request for a Research Project, he paid a sum that the State Emergency Service of Ukraine, responsible for the administration and control of the exclusion zone, were only too happy to accept. With that, Vladimir had control of Duga, representing an ideal base for his operation. Located only a few kilometres away from the Chernobyl nuclear plant and the source of his Chernobylite, Duga was ideally located for his purposes.

The main hurdle for Vladimir was gaining unfettered access to the Chernobyl plant, away from the prying eyes of security patrols. The answer laid in simple brilliance and the utilization of freely available resources left abandoned in the exclusion zone, untouched for years. With knowledge, resourcefulness and application, old mining and tunnelling equipment was resurrected and used to construct a tunnel 2.5 metres in diameter, high enough to stand up in and just wide enough to drive a small car through.

The tunnel extended from the Duga station all the way to the basement of Reactor 4 in the Chernobyl plant. Lurking in the bowels of the nuclear reactor was the Elephant's Foot; one of the most dangerous objects on Earth and the source of the deadly Chernobylite. Decades after its formation, the Elephant's Foot was still a source of lethal radiation, emitting levels up to 10,000 roentgens per hour, equivalent to over four and a half million chest x-rays. Just a few minutes of direct exposure to the Elephant's Foot would be fatal, with death from radiation poisoning a guaranteed outcome.

CHAPTER 63

Borys was behind the wheel with Vladimir riding shotgun and Amy in the back seat, bound and gagged with doors locked and hidden behind dark tinted windows. They had spent the night before at Vladimir's house in Strakholissya on the west bank of the Dnieper River just outside the exclusion zone. Borys had pulled their go-fast boat into their private river port attached to the house. Tired after the attack on their Kiev base and subsequent escape, Vladimir decided that they would spend the night in the house before going to their Chernobyl base early the next morning.

It was just a short drive from Vladimir's house at Strakholissya to the main checkpoint entering the exclusion zone. Borys flashed their Duga permit to get them through security and into the zone. Another short drive brought them to their Duga base of operations. Borys nodded with approval at the armed guard standing at the entrance, pleased to see that they had some security forces remaining after the rest of their troops had been decimated.

Vladimir and Borys exited the vehicle with Amy in tow, struggling against their hold but to no avail. They entered the building and were greeted by Aleksei, Vladimir's chief scientist. 'Aleksei, my friend, it is good to see you. First things first, do you have somewhere we can put this?' said Vladimir, with a nod of his head to Amy.

'You can put her in the storeroom; it has a strong door,' said Aleksei.

'Thanks,' grunted Borys and tossed Amy in the room indicated, still bound and gagged.

With Amy out of the way, Vladimir continued, 'So, Aleksei, how is the progress coming along?'

'Excellent Vladimir, all is well. Our first shipment just left this morning, in a truck on its way to Odessa. Production has been high, and we sent our first 5,000 units in that shipment. I confirmed the order and the payment has been made into your account. We will be ready to ship the next batch of 5,000 units next week. We have enough Chernobylite stockpiled to produce another 10,000 units after that, which will be enough to fulfil all our current orders. The human trial a few days ago was a spectacular success. All went precisely according to plan.'

'Are there any problems?'

'Well, the outstanding success of the human trial created a difficulty which, while not unexpected, is still a challenge. A nuclear team was called in to investigate the death of our test subject and they identified the source of the radiation as Chernobylite. The authorities have locked down the plant, cutting off external access and putting all work on hold. We still have secret access to the basement via our tunnel, but there is some increased risk of discovery, so it is prudent to suspend extraction activity for a while. But it has no impact on our current operations, because we have been extracting for months and have built up a good stockpile of source material.'

'Excellent work, Aleksei. We have had some difficulties on the operations side. Unfortunately, our test subject had family and friends with him, who have proven to be unexpectedly resourceful in pursuit of us. The woman is the boy's mother, Tatiana.'

'What happened in Odessa and Kiev? Is there any danger to us here in Chernobyl?' asked Aleksei.

'Odessa was bad,' replied Vladimir. 'Our entire organization was wiped out, a lot of our men died, and the rest deserted us, the scum. We were attacked by a bunch of mad Cossacks, one of the old gangs on the docks. I don't know how Tatiana's people managed to get help from the Cossacks, but I did not anticipate this move, it was very unexpected. We lost a full shipment of weapons to an extremely important client. The fallout from the battle was too big even for our high-level police protection. It will take us some time to get back on our feet and re-establish operations from a new facility.'

'Kiev was bad also,' chimed in Borys. 'We thought we would be safe there, but someone must have talked, given away our location. A group turned up to our Kiev base and took out most of our men. Idiots! Vladimir and I got away on the boat with the woman, spent the night at the house last night and then came straight here this morning.'

'As for risk to our base here,' said Vladimir, 'I don't think we have too much to worry about. There were only two men who knew the exact location of this facility and they were loyal to me, so it's unlikely they will inform our pursuers where we are based.'

'Nevertheless, we should prepare just in case,' said Borys. 'How many men do we have here, Aleksei?'

'We have eight men, they all assist with extraction, processing, manufacturing, packing, maintenance and security. Counting us three, we make 11 in total.'

'Are the men capable?' asked Borys.

'Well, they can all handle a gun, but most of them are just glorified labourers, certainly not soldiers.'

'Alright, just in case, I suggest we increase our security presence and reduce our manufacturing for a few days until we're sure things have settled down.'

'Agreed,' said Vladimir. 'Double the guard out the front and make sure the remaining men inside are ready for what might come.'

'I will instruct the men now,' said the ever-efficient Aleksei and left the room accompanied by Borys to supervise the security arrangements.

Vladimir entered the storeroom, which represented yet another prison cell for Amy. She fired a malevolent glare at him as he entered, angrily gesturing at him to remove her gag and bindings. Vladimir pulled out his gun and waved it at Amy, saying, 'Alright, I'm going to untie you,

I don't want you to be uncomfortable. But don't do anything stupid. I don't want to have to shoot you or tie you up again.'

Amy seemed resigned to her fate as Vladimir removed her bindings and gag, knowing that she could not escape on her own and would need to wait for help, to hope that it would come. She had been shocked to see Tommy on the boat yesterday and then was devastated to witness his death at the hand of Borys. She was desperate for news of Brittney but was filled with hope after the action in Kiev and their hasty escape. Someone was obviously trying to rescue her, and she hoped with all her heart that Brittney was behind it all.

Amy decided to bide her time and try to remain placid and cooperative with Vladimir so she could strike out at just the right time. Vladimir held the gun on her with a watchful eye while he cut the heavy-duty plastic zip ties from her wrists and removed the gag that had been stuffed in and taped over her mouth, then gave her a much-needed drink of water.

Once Amy's mouth could function again, she said, 'So what exactly do you hope to achieve by kidnapping me? I'm still not sure I understand.'

'But Tatiana, isn't it obvious? I want us to be a family; I want us to be married. You see, I didn't want you before because you were so young. But now you have matured so much, like a fine wine, that I'm ready for us to be together.'

Amy felt the bile rise in her throat in disgust at the prospect of being with this deluded psychopath. What was he thinking? How had he possibly gotten this idea into his head? 'But Vladimir, we hardly know each other. How can we possibly be together?'

'We share a common bond, Tatiana; a strong one. We both had to escape Nikolai. You were strong enough to do it in your way, which we I admire greatly. I chose a rather different path, but one with a similar outcome.'

Amy's eyes narrowed as she studied Vladimir for more of a sign of what he was alluding to. 'I don't understand, what do you mean?'

'I've never told anyone this Tatiana, but since we are going to be together, I feel I should tell you the truth. You, more than anyone, will understand.'

Vladimir paused and Amy held her breath in anticipation.

'I killed Nikolai, I pulled the trigger, his own brother.' A deep exhalation of air accompanied the confession, which hung heavily in the room.

Amy was stunned, silent. Vladimir waited expectantly for some response from her, seemingly even a gesture of thanks. Slowly she said, 'But why, Vladimir? How *could* you? Your own brother?'

'Surely you understand, Tatiana! You know what he was like. What he used to do to you! He was the privileged one, the lucky one, always getting what he wanted, the spoilt one, the loved one. He had the power and the respect of his men but what did I have? Nothing! Some *scraps* from his table!' Vladimir by this stage was shouting his responses, his voice rising with every syllable, face turning purple with rage.

Amy knew she had to do something to stop the volcano erupting. She had seen this kind of thing too many times before not to know what was coming next if she wasn't careful. 'I'm sorry, Vladimir. Of course, I understand what you mean and why you did it, why you *had* to do it. We're all better off without Nikolai.'

Amy's placating words had the desired effect and Vladimir's rage receded. 'Rest now, my dear, I must check on preparations out there. Once you've shown that I can trust you, I'll let you out and we can start our life together under more appropriate conditions.' He smiled, leaned in close to Amy and kissed her on the cheek. It was all she could do not to recoil in horror at his touch. The revulsion caused a hot flush in her face, a clenching of her jaw and a tense rigidity through her whole body.

'I'll check in on you later,' said Vladimir as he turned and headed out the door, locking it firmly behind him. As the door closed, Amy was overcome by a violent shudder of her whole body and an involuntary cry of, 'Ugh... what a foul, disgusting asshole of a scumbag! What is it with the men in this insane family?'

CHAPTER 64

The road north out of Kiev was initially busy but the traffic thinned out more and more as we approached Chernobyl. I was in my customary position behind the wheel and we made good time. We'd been running over plans between us, but it was clear that we needed more information. This was our last chance to rescue Amy. We knew where she was but had no idea how to get to her. She was deep in the Chernobyl exclusion zone, which was a subject we knew nothing about.

We stopped at the last town before the exclusion zone entry checkpoint, pulling up outside the general store. Viktor went in to see what he could find out about the exclusion zone, the level of security and how best to get in. He took the map in with him with our target marked on it, to pinpoint where we needed to get to.

Viktor came out of the store with a big smile on his face, clearly having gathered some good intelligence. 'We're in luck,' he said, as he slid into the car. 'Apparently, Chernobyl is now a popular and active tourist destination!'

'What! Who would be stupid enough to turn a radioactive wasteland into a tourist attraction? More to the point, who the hell would want to go there anyway?' I asked, stunned at this bit of news.

Viktor shrugged and said, 'Where there's a need, someone will fill the market. Apparently, they call it *dark tourism*, where people go and see places associated with death and suffering. People started sneaking into the zone unsupervised, so the authorities felt they should have some control and make some money too, so they legalized it and licensed the operators. The store owner has a relationship with one of the tour operators, who runs trips from Kiev. He said he can arrange for the bus to stop here on the way through and pick us up. We go through the checkpoint as tourists, then sneak away from the group at the first stop, going the rest of the way on foot. I showed him our target and he said it's a radar facility called Duga; a huge steel structure, we can't miss it.'

'Does the tour stop at this Duga facility?' I asked.

'The shop owner said it's not on the tour anymore. Up until a few months ago, they used to stop there and look around, but the tour operators were banned, prohibited from stopping there. He said there's a scheduled stop not far from there, so when we sneak off, we won't have far to go on foot.'

'What about the tour operator? Won't they stop and look for us if we don't get back on the bus?'

'He said it's not that uncommon for people to wander off because they want to look at something in more detail. To prevent inconvenience to the whole group, the operator has a policy of waiting no more than 15 minutes, then they just call security and they send out a patrol to pick up the stragglers, when they have time. It sounds like it doesn't set off too many alarm bells. It seems that security is not too tight in the zone.'

'Sounds good. What about all our gear? We've got a lot of tools of death and destruction in the boot of our little ZAZ, which we need to take with us.'

'That's okay, we have some good bags. We can hide the stuff in the middle of the bags and wrap clothes and food around them. It's highly unlikely that we'll be searched.'

'Love your work, Viktor. Sounds like a good plan. What do you think, babe?' I asked Brittney, who had been listening intently.

'I'm in – let's do it!' replied Brittney without a moment's hesitation. 'What time is the bus due?' she asked.

'We've got half an hour until the bus gets here. That will give us plenty of time to get our gear ready,' said Viktor.

'Sweet! Let's get organized,' I said, jumping out of the car and round the back.

Bags packed? Check. Adrenaline pumping? Check. I had my knife in its sheath strapped to my thigh down my pants, Viktor and Brittney had their pistols jammed down the front of their pants and the rest of our gear was in a backpack each. We were all set. Unfortunately, my trusty axe handles wouldn't be coming with me because they were just a bit too conspicuous.

The tour bus cruised down the main street, the door opened, and we stepped up, showing our tickets to the driver on the way through and took our seats. After just a few minutes we saw what our guide informed us was the Dytyatky checkpoint on the border of the exclusion zone. This was our only potential barrier to entry, but it turned out that hiding in plain sight was a good strategy. The border guard came on the bus, gave us all a bored cursory glance like he'd seen it all before and sent us on our way.

We kept a close eye on our map and soon saw our target in the distance – a huge steel structure that was visible for miles around! Our tour guide pointed it out to us as a note of interest but said that unfortunately we couldn't visit it up close because of some 'stupid new rule from the bureaucrats in Kiev' and that we could only look at it from a distance. We travelled up a series of dirt roads and were let out of the bus at a good vantage point to see the Duga radar array. All the tourists piled off the bus and milled around like sheep, trying to get the best views and photo spots. Our little gang of three moved away from all the other tourists and then when our guide's attention was occupied fiddling around with his phone, we quietly snuck off into the trees.

After a couple of minutes, we heard voices calling out urging everyone back on the bus, quickly followed by shouts in the distance as they started looking for us. But we were long gone by this stage, well on our way to Vladimir's last base and refuge.

We only had to walk for about 30 minutes, which was just as well because Brittney's ankle started playing up towards the end. We slowed down as we got close, making sure not to break cover. We peered out through the trees and got our first close-up view of this thing. It was absolutely *gigantic* – one of the most enormous structures I'd ever seen! It looked like about 15 buildings side by side, each 50 stories high. The Soviets didn't muck around in the Cold War – this was some serious shit.

As our eyes grew accustomed to the scale of the radar array, our focus was then drawn to a more human scale, down to the building at the base of the steel antenna structure. We spotted two armed guards standing by the door and a black SUV parked out front. This certainly looked like Vladimir's Chernobyl base, but we felt we should wait for confirmation before we started killing people just in case they happened to be regular Ukrainians guarding something else.

We soon found our confirmation when I felt a surge of anger as the front door of the building opened and the huge, menacing figure of Borys appeared for a moment and then headed back inside. This was it! Amy must be inside somewhere. Our final mission was at hand.

Viktor pulled his little binoculars out of his bag and examined the scene more closely and reported, 'Okay, we have the two out the front plus Borys and Vladimir. I can see three more men inside through the glass, so that's at least seven men, maybe more. We need to be careful.'

'Agreed. We shouldn't go for a full-on frontal attack like Kiev here. We don't have the firepower, or the backup,' I said. One thing that might possibly work in our favour was the guards didn't look like professional soldiers. The way they stood and handled their weapons, they didn't seem like they really knew what they were doing and weren't particularly alert. Then one of them even lit a cigarette! At least being surrounded by the ever-present radiation inside the Chernobyl exclusion zone, this was probably one of the only places in the world where smoking was unlikely to appreciably increase your risk of getting cancer.

Viktor, looking thoughtful, said, 'We need a diversion; I think it should be a big one. I've got some C-4 plastic explosive in my bag that Uri gave me as a parting gift; he said I should use it for old time's sake. This looks like the perfect opportunity.'

'What do you want to blow up?' I asked. He simply smiled and turned to look at the gargantuan steel radar array towering above us.

'That? Are you out of your tiny mind, Viktor? It's enormous!'

'I don't mean *all* of it. Just the end bit. Just enough to make a lot of noise and scare the pants off the men inside, make them think there are more of us here than there really is, and that we're better armed than we are. Trust me, I know what I'm doing, I've blown up lots of stuff before in my previous life.'

Shaking my head in dismay at this latest revelation from my peaceful old Zen master, I shrugged my shoulders and said, 'Fine, if you want to relive your youth and blow shit up, go ahead. What's the plan after the diversion happens?'

'I'll shoot the two guards just as we blow the Duga array, then Brittney and I will pick off more men as they come running out the door. Then we all head inside to finish off the rest of them and grab Amy. Simple.'

'Hmm… I guess that could work. You're the boss and we're on your home turf, plus I don't have any other brilliant ideas, so I guess we should just go with that crazy plan. What do you think Brit?' I said. We were gambling with her life and that of her mother, so she had a right to be involved in these decisions.

'If Viktor says he can do it and that's the best plan, then I say we go for it,' replied Brittney. That's my girl – always up for action. If there was a violent way to get something done, it seemed she would choose it every time.

Viktor opened his bag and I peered in. It looked like something out of a terrorist's orientation kit, with sinister grey blocks of pliable plastic explosive, detonators and wires. The security guard at the checkpoint would have had a freaking brain aneurism on the spot if he'd checked Viktor's bag on the bus. Viktor removed what he didn't need from the bag and headed off into the forest, leaving us standing guard in case there was any movement at the base.

Brittney and I settled down to wait for Viktor to return, keeping our vigil on Vladimir's base. About half an hour later, Viktor returned, trailing a long line of sinister-looking red wire, feeding it out behind him. He had a spring in his step, like he was a young man again, about to get into trouble. 'Okay, we're all set to blow,' he said. 'We should spread out, so it looks like there's more of us. Brittney, you stay here with the detonator. I'll move over there and shoot the two guards; I'll use the silencer to keep the noise down, so we get maximum effect when the Duga blows. As soon as both guards drop, you push the button on the detonator.'

'You mean I get to blow some shit up? Cool!' said Brittney, eyes wide with excitement.

'Tommy, you go down there around the side of the building and take out anyone who comes running around the corner,' continued Viktor.

'Okay, got it,' I replied.

Brittney looked at me with concern and said, 'Whatever happens Tommy, promise me you'll be careful. There'll be lots of bullets flying, so make sure you stay safe, okay? I love you.' Then she planted a big wet kiss firmly on my lips.

'I love you too, honey. Now you promise me you'll be careful too. There'll be some big guys here, including Borys, so make sure you don't take on too much, alright?'

'Okay, I promise. I've got my Glock and I'm not afraid to use it!'

Viktor said, 'Alright, let's go. Everybody be careful. Be alert and ready for anything. Amy's life depends on us and what we do in the next few minutes.'

Great, thanks Viktor. No pressure.

I crept around the tree line to flank the guards and took my position around the side of the building. I looked over at Viktor and saw him take aim with his pistol, which somehow looked even more menacing with the long silencer on it.

Viktor squeezed the trigger in quick succession. Two spits of noise pierced the quiet and the guards dropped one after another, both down with head shots. Viktor was clearly a cool hand at this kind of thing.

I looked over at Brittney and saw her stab her finger down on the detonator. It took some time for the signal to reach its target and for just a brief second, I thought maybe it was a dud. But then, all *hell* broke loose! Four massive explosions; BOOM, BOOM, BOOM, BOOM, splintered the air and cascaded around me as the separate explosions combined into one gigantic fireball that shot 30 metres up in the air. It was like Armageddon!

It was all too much for the old structure, which had been rusting and decaying in the radioactive, toxic environment with no care or maintenance for more than 30 years. As the effects of the blast receded, I looked up at the monstrous structure and saw it slowly buckle and move, almost like it was coming to life, trying to pull itself out of its roots, but only succeeding in twisting itself into a falling, crazy mess of steel and wire. The creaks and groans turned to roars and metal screams of a deafening pitch as huge steel members tore at each other, bolts snapped, and welds sheared in one gigantic metal cluster-fuck.

Finally, one end of the gigantic structure, a section that looked more than 150 metres high and 50 metres wide gave way completely and toppled over, crashing down towards the earth, finally coming to rest with an ear-splitting crash.

Overkill? Nah.

CHAPTER 65

Viktor's mayhem certainly had the desired effect. Two men came tearing out the doors of the Duga building, yelling for the downed guards. One of the men fell just a few steps after getting out the door, shot by Viktor or Brittney, I couldn't tell who. The time for silencers was past; now the shots rang out in full volume and bullets zinged off the wall of the building. The remaining target eluded the shots and ran towards my corner of the building, gun drawn and yelling at the top of his lungs. I waited for him in my hidden position around the corner, then suddenly shot out my arm in a savage clothesline with the full weight of my shoulder and body behind it.

The poor guy looked like he'd run full speed into a low-hanging tree branch! The top half of his body stopped dead, but the bottom half kept going, his legs flying crazily up into the air, spinning him up to horizontal, then dropping like a log flat on his back from two metres up in the air. He hit the ground with a nauseating thud, gasping for air, so I put him out of his misery and knocked him out cold by pile-driving an elbow into his face. Then I grabbed his gun and tossed it into the forest.

We'd taken out four guys with relative ease and the chaos of the Duga array explosion had the desired effect, so I figured it was time to make our way into the building. We would need to do it sometime, and it seemed best to do it now before they bunkered themselves in. I grabbed a grenade out of my pack, pulled the pin and rolled it along the front of the building, where it came to rest perfectly just outside the doors. I retreated around the corner of the building just as it detonated with an almighty roar, raining fire and smashing the doors off their hinges.

I ran to the door, crouched down low and crawled my way through the smoke, closely followed by Viktor and Brittney. The grenade explosion had taken out the main lights, so the room was now lit only by the dim green glow of emergency lighting, creating an eerie fluorescence through the clouds of smoke from the blast.

I stuck my hand down my pants and carefully extracted my lethal hunting cutlass. At well over 30 centimetres long, it suited my size to a tee. Being a country boy, even though I hated guns, I'd played with my fair share of knives, but I have to admit I'd never plunged one into a human before, so I was pretty daunted at the prospect of what might come. Turns out I didn't have to wait long to find out.

One of Vladimir's men appeared out of nowhere and raised his gun right at me. Working on reflex, I threw up my left forearm to block the gun, which went off, sending a shot flying up into the ceiling. With my right hand I plunged my knife in an upwards thrust entering under his rib cage, penetrating deep and piercing his heart. I stabbed upwards so hard I lifted the guy off the floor, his feet quivering and shaking as they dangled beneath him.

I dumped the lifeless body back to the floor, allowing my knife to slide out as he fell off it. I felt a twinge of remorse as I saw the look of shock on his face, but took comfort from the certain knowledge that this bastard wouldn't have hesitated for one second to put a bullet in me, plus he was actively involved in the activity with Chernobylite at this terrorist base, which therefore meant he was somewhat responsible for Chad's death. I wiped my enormous knife and bloody hand on his clothes and looked around for more targets.

I glanced over to the opposite side of the room and noticed Brittney was in full flight. She spun around like a whirling dervish and got vertical at the same time and unleashed a frightening turning roundhouse kick that copped her hapless opponent right on the side of the head, the full force of Brittney's 360 degree rotation rendering him unconscious before he hit the floor. Viktor was doing well too – he had one guy already on the floor with blood spurting from a wound in his neck. What a mess.

Attention back on me and my surroundings, I was alert for anything coming my way, which was just as well, because a man was levelling his gun at me. I dived to the floor, narrowly avoiding the shot he fired, and as I did, I swung both my feet around in a huge arc, chopping him off at the knees with a textbook foot sweep. Simple but effective.

The guy came crashing down to the floor. I couldn't help myself; I was so pissed off at getting shot at that I picked the guy up off the floor, still groaning, pressed him up above my head, spun him around in a helicopter move and letting out a primal roar, threw him against the wall, the slam knocking him senseless. Overly dramatic, perhaps, but certainly satisfying.

Then the big guns came out. I knew it would happen soon enough; Borys appeared on the other side of the room. Oddly, I noticed the top button of his pants was still undone, suggesting he might have been taking a dump when all the action hit. Whatever the reason, I was thankful for the delay. My stomach churned as I saw him head towards Brittney, with a murderous look on his face, snarling at her, 'I told you I'd get you for what you did to me, you bitch! I'll hear you scream before this is over!'

Brittney let loose with a roundhouse to his shoulder, but Borys swatted it away like he might a pesky fly. He was too tall for Brittney to get in a head kick and too strong to be affected by anything else. She tried a front kick to his stomach but that bounced off and then a lightning left, right, left combination of punches to his face. Borys roared like a bull, grabbed Brittney's hand and smashed his fist straight into her face! 'Brittney!' I yelled as she dropped like a stone, her body completely limp.

'AARRGGHHH!!!!!' I roared and charged towards Borys, head down, shoulder in and arms out to wrap around Borys' huge frame. I got in a few fast steps and built up a good amount of momentum and then gathered him up in my mad charge. His enormous bulk lifted off the floor and we went flying into a door, slamming it back on its hinges. I recovered first and jumped on top of him, raining wild punches down on his face. I had never truly wanted to kill anyone in my life before, but now after what Borys had just done to Brittney, I had the blood lust. A red film washed over my eyes and I literally saw red as I flung crazed haymaker punches, forgetting all my training in my rage at the beast beneath me.

Borys copped some punishment from my attack, but through his own years of training he had the presence of mind to stay alert and saw an opening in my frenzied punches. He quickly raised his hands to protect his face and then caught my left hand in a vice-like grip and applied a fierce wrist lock, the strongest I had ever felt. He twisted and applied pressure in just the right measure and at just the right angle, forcing me to twist my body along with my wrist, flipping me off him. He quickly got to his feet, shook himself off and looked at me with the biggest sneer possible.

'Is that all you've got?' he snarled. 'This is going to be too easy. I could shoot you now, but that would be too quick. You need to suffer for everything you've done. Plus, I want you to see what I'm going to do to your little girlfriend over there. She's got spirit, but I'll soon knock that out of her.'

Finally, my training kicked in. I calmed myself, slowed my breathing and focused. Time for combat mode. Just like on the mat, but deadlier and with a lot more moves that would get me expelled from any Judo school. With my heightened awareness, I glanced over at Brittney and noticed she was still breathing, with a steady rise and fall of her chest. Viktor too, was doing fine, holding his own with the rest of the men. All I had to worry about was right in front of me. Borys was all I needed to focus on.

'Okay, time to stop playing. Let's rumble. You're big, I'll give you that.

But like they say, the bigger they are, the harder they fall, right?' sneered Borys.

'Yeah that's what they say. But I say the dumber they are, the harder I kick their ass! And you're about the dumbest bastard I've ever seen, Borys,' I responded, with a sneer of my own. I really had grown to hate this prick in a very short space of time.

Borys was clearly a boxer, a street fighter more comfortable with his fists than his feet. He equalled my reach and was certainly a tough matchup for me, the toughest I'd ever had. My Olympic gold medal match just a few days before had been until then the most important fight of my life, but that paled into insignificance compared to the bout that was now before me.

Despite his size, Borys moved quickly, with good foot speed. He danced around and started throwing testing left jabs at me, which I blocked comfortably. Then he followed one of his jabs up with a blindingly fast right hook that caught me by surprise, landing a glancing blow on my left cheek. Shit, that bloody hurt! Need to be more careful.

I stepped back from Borys' next punch combinations, saw an opening when he was slightly off-balance and launched a short, sharp front kick right up into his solar plexus. 'Oomph!' came the rush of air as I got him right in the guts. His head dipped involuntarily as he struggled to recover his breath, so I followed in quickly with a solid left cross right to his jaw.

Angry now at the unexpected blows he had just copped, Borys stepped back for a moment and took stock of the situation and of me, realizing he would need to be a bit more cautious.

Borys stepped in again, with the same left jab / right hook combo he had laid out before. Ready this time, when he launched his big right hand, I rotated and stepped in close to his raised arm, dropped my weight in a crouch and raised both my forearms in a solid block. I then trapped his extended right arm under my left armpit and smashed my right elbow into the side of his face, snapping his head back and splitting his right eyelid.

Borys roared in a fit of extreme anger and fought to free his right arm, which I still held captive. Then he did something clever, rather unexpectedly. Instead of trying to pull his arm away out of my grip, he left it there and rotated the rest of his body right around the back of me, swung his left arm around and captured me in a bear hug! I hadn't really anticipated what appeared to be his signature move, because he really locked it in tight. He got a good grip and absolutely put the squeeze on me. I could feel his hot breath puffing on my neck as he strained with all his considerable power to crush the life right out of me, the strain increasing the blood flow from his eye so much that I could feel it squirting onto my shoulder.

Borys really had me good in this crushing bear hug. My breath got shallower, I started seeing stars and was on the verge of passing out, realizing that it would soon all be over.

CHAPTER 66

'Get off me, you freak!' shouted Amy.

Vladimir had wrestled her down to the floor and planted his knee on her chest. He quickly bound her hands with zip ties once again and dragged her up to her feet.

'What are you doing? Where are we going?'

'We're getting out of here Tatiana. We're going for a drive down the tunnel and then we'll escape from the other end. But I don't think I want to hear you whining all the way, so it's time for some peace again.' Vladimir whipped a gag out of his pocket and tied it around her mouth.

He peered out the slightly open door to make sure the coast was clear, then snuck out down the hall past his chief scientist Aleksei, who was cowering in his lab. Vladimir gave him a cursory glance as he went past the open doorway and said, 'I'm getting her out of here. You and Borys make sure you take care of this place. I'll come back later when everything has settled down.'

Vladimir was not known for open confrontation; he worked in the shadows and dealt in whispers, not shouts. He was an especially dangerous kind of coward, one you didn't want to turn your back on, as his brother and nephew could attest. There was simply too much heat in this situation, and he wanted out, to escape with *my Tatiana*, as Vladimir's deluded mind now thought of Amy.

Vladimir's gang had two tunnel cars, the ever-popular small Ukrainian cars that had already served Viktor and Tommy so well. He bundled Amy into the ZAZ, locked the doors, pulled out his gun and pointed it to the side, right at Amy's head. 'One move that I don't like, and I'll blow your head off,' said Vladimir. 'I won't like it and I don't want to do it, but I will if I have to. No funny business, just sit there quietly.'

Amy didn't doubt for a second that Vladimir would follow through on his threat, so decided to wait for a better opportunity of escape and sat motionless, staring out the windscreen at the long, dimly lit tunnel ahead of her. She could just make out dots of light in a long, straight line disappearing into the distance.

Vladimir slipped the car into gear and headed off down the tunnel.

Back at the base, Viktor had been busy. He was just finishing off the last of Vladimir's soldiers, whom he had dispatched in a variety of manners, both armed and unarmed. He was covered in blood as he pounded the last unfortunate thug into submission, who collapsed like a drunk down to the floor. Viktor looked up from his battle just as the taillights of the ZAZ disappeared into the tunnel and figured that Vladimir and Amy must be in there. Then he glanced over at Tommy caught in Borys' bear hug, and Brittney lying unconscious on the floor.

Things were not looking good. But then they got a whole lot worse.

As Viktor's attention was distracted by the plight of his comrades, he felt a fierce sting in his neck and knew instantly it must be a Chernobylite dart. He looked over at the chief scientist in his lab coat, who was lowering the air gun with a smug, self-satisfied sneer on his face. Both men knew that he had just dealt Viktor a death blow. Whilst not as immediate as a bullet, the outcome was just as certain.

In a panic, Viktor grabbed his neck but could feel nothing. The deadly radioactive sliver was already inside him. His life now had an expiry date in the near future; his stomach dropped, and he let out a huge sigh. The sliver would already be on its way somewhere in his body and he had no time to get medical help to remove it before it did too much damage. Plus, there were friends to save and men to kill. First one on the kill list was that mad scientist.

Viktor shot the lab coated geek a murderous glare and strode the few steps across to the other side of the room. He reached out his left hand and grabbed the scientist by the throat, squeezed hard and slammed the back of the man's head against the wall. A broad smile of victory cracked the scientist's lips as he said through choking breath, 'It doesn't matter what you do to me, you fool! I'll be dead in a few days anyway and so will you! And our shipment of 5,000 units is already on its way – there's nothing you can do to stop it!'

'Tell me where it's going!' ordered Viktor as he tightened his grip on the scientist's throat.

'Forget it! There is nothing you can do to me that will make me tell you where that shipment is. I'll be dead soon enough when my cancer finally takes me, so you can't threaten me with anything. My Chernobylite will be used by freedom fighters to punish those that laid waste to my motherland and poisoned me with their radiation. Their message will be heard loud and clear across the globe. You lose!'

'Wrong! You lose,' said Viktor as he calmly squeezed the life out of the scientist, choking the man who had just killed him. Aleksei's eyes bulged, his face went purple and his arms flailed about down by his sides as Viktor kept squeezing and squeezing, crushing his windpipe and cutting off all supply of air and blood. Finally, the twitching stopped, and the chief scientist of destruction was well and truly dead, but not before he had seen his creation of horror come to fruition when the shipment had left the facility that morning.

As he looked over to the other side of the room, Viktor saw Tommy about to escape from Borys' grip and Brittney start to stir, so he figured they would be okay and could help each other out. Tatiana needed him again, so many years after that first time. He also knew he must finish Vladimir; he simply could not let him escape. Decision made, Viktor ran over to the other tunnel car, jumped in, turned the key that was kept in the ignition and tore off down the tunnel in a cloud of dust.

CHAPTER 67

'Snap out of it! Wake up! Get your shit together!' Man, my lizard brain could be annoying sometimes, especially when it was so insistent about trying to save my life. I came back to my senses from the brink of unconsciousness and went back to the dojo, to a drill I'd practiced thousands of times. I could even hear Viktor's soft voice instructing me as I went through every step of my defensive manoeuvre.

Suddenly I dropped all my considerable weight straight down at the same time as I violently thrust my arms out and then up by my sides as I dropped. Continuing the sudden but fluid movement, I stomped my left foot down hard, raking the shin behind me with the side of my boot and then slamming it down hard on the top of Borys' foot. With knees now bent and bear hug broken, the stomach behind me was exposed to the full force of the right elbow that I jack-hammered back in hard, then swung my fist down in an arc, pivoting on his stomach and smashed him right in the balls with my fist. Reversing the vertical arc, I then swung a back fist straight up into Borys' face, pounding him in the mouth; his upper and lower lip immediately gushed a fountain of blood.

I stepped back out in front of Borys, turned and saw him doubled over in pain from the combination I had just unleashed on him. I launched my right foot straight up with a stiff, straight leg almost all the way up to my right shoulder and then brought down a mighty axe kick straight on top of his head. Borys went down like the sack of shit that he was, driving his face into the floor to demolish what was left of his features after Brittney had broken his nose yesterday and I had just finished off what was left.

Borys lay still and silent after the epic battle. He was done. It was over! I looked over for Viktor but there was no sign of him. I could hear a car fading away and saw a set of red taillights receding in the distance down the tunnel.

I swung around to check on Brittney – she was stirring! She was okay, thank Christ. I rushed over to her side, knelt and cradled her head in my hands as she slowly came around. 'Brittney, babe, are you alright?' I asked, fear in my voice, hoping she would be okay.

'Oh God, I feel terrible! What happened to me? I can't remember anything,' she replied as she put her hand up to her face and felt her left eye, which was already puffed and closing. 'God, what must I look like?'

'I hate to say this babe, but you look like shit. Borys punched you right in the face, the bastard. But I fixed him up, he's out cold over there behind me on the floor.'

Brittney glanced over my shoulder and then before I could even comprehend what was happening, she pulled out her Glock in a blindingly fast, fluent movement and blasted off three shots into the bloody head of Borys, who had somehow come around much quicker than I thought and was raising his gun at my back, ready to fire. A split-second later and we would have been history.

'Tommy! How many action movies have you seen? Don't you know to always make sure you move the gun away from the guy who you think is knocked out but wakes up just at the last minute?' she scolded me.

'Nah. That's what I have you for Brit, to do the gun thing,' I replied and kissed her. 'I'm so glad that you're alright, we're alright. I was so worried about you after Borys punched you like that, the bastard.'

'Me too Tommy, I'm glad we got rid of that animal,' said Brittney and then with a start, exclaimed, 'Where's Viktor? And Mom? We've got to find them!'

'I don't know. Let's go have a look.' We walked over towards the tunnel, keeping an eye out for any more attackers, but it seemed like they were all accounted for. We saw what looked like a crumpled white coat lying on the floor and then realized it contained the wasted body of a man, who judging by the lab coat was a scientist associated with Vladimir's dark Chernobylite scheme.

We looked in a room off to the side of the main central space and could see what looked like the cut-off remains of heavy zip ties. 'Looks like Amy might have been held in here,' I said. 'There's no sign of anyone else and we haven't seen Vladimir yet, so it looks like he's taken off with her again. A few minutes ago, I saw the taillights of a car heading down the tunnel, so I guess Viktor took off after them. Let's do the same, we'll see if we can find some transport.'

Luckily, we hit pay-dirt after a quick search of the big workshop yielded a quad bike. I jumped on, started it up and Brittney climbed on the back. We headed off into the dim light of the tunnel, apprehensive about what was ahead and knowing that we were going deeper into Chernobyl territory and subjecting our bodies to God knows what unseen damage from the high radiation levels.

CHAPTER 68

The car ahead was travelling quickly, but Viktor was the more desperate driver of the two, and quickly gained ground in his pursuit of Vladimir and Amy. The tunnel was narrow, the walls closed in tight around the car and the sparsely located lights shone dimly in a steady sequence down the tunnel. The red taillights in the distance got steadily bigger and brighter as Viktor closed the gap between the cars. Viktor was desperate to catch Vladimir before he could steal Amy away forever. His life had come full-circle and he knew he had to do whatever it took to save her.

Viktor could see the end of the narrow tunnel approaching in a bright wash of light up ahead as it opened out into a large chamber. He changed down a gear and floored the accelerator, putting on a final burst of speed, catching up just as Vladimir exited the tunnel out to the chamber. Viktor went wide and slammed on the brakes, skidding to a stop between Vladimir's car and one of the two exit doors out of the chamber. He glanced over at the other car just in time to see Vladimir with his gun levelled right at him, ready to squeeze the trigger just a couple of metres away from him.

Instinctively, Viktor dropped down across the front seat. The gun fired and a bullet smashed its way through both the front windows. Viktor reached out his foot to the passenger side door handle, pressed it down and then hurriedly slid feet first backwards out of the car, landing in a low crouching position on the ground. He drew his gun, stayed low and crept around the back of the car to try and get to Amy.

Viktor heard a car door creak open and peered over the windowsill of the car. He could just see Vladimir's outline as he pulled Amy out of the car and started to wrap his arm around her neck, raising the gun towards her temple. She would soon be his shield; he had to work fast!

'Careful!' called out Vladimir, 'Don't try anything or I'll put a bullet right in her pretty little head!'

Viktor dropped down onto his stomach, peered under the car and could just make out Vladimir's feet planted firmly on the other side of the car, along with Amy's struggling lower limbs. He could make the shot if he was careful and got an opportunity with Amy clear enough from Vladimir. He levelled his pistol, took careful aim and waited. Thankfully, Amy quickly obliged as she angrily shoved Vladimir with her shoulder. The few inches of space it gave Viktor as Vladimir shifted his weight was just enough. Viktor squeezed the trigger and the bullet exploded out of the gun, racing away from him on its journey under the car. The bullet just clipped its target, wounding Vladimir's ankle enough to cause extreme pain but unfortunately not great damage.

Viktor's shot was enough to give Amy the edge she needed. With another heave of her shoulder she ducked out of Vladimir's grip and ran around behind the car. Vladimir screamed in pain, rage and frustration and got off a shot that just missed Amy, the bullet slamming into the body of the car beside her.

Realizing that his position of power had not only eroded but completely evaporated, Vladimir decided to make a run for the exit across the other side of the room, even though there was one right behind him. Clearly the furthest exit was a better escape path than the closer one. Vladimir took off towards the door, firing shots as he went. Viktor quickly returned fire from his position of cover behind the car. None of Viktor's shots found their target, but it was enough to stop Vladimir in his tracks and turn him back from his run to the exit. Vladimir was close to being pinned down in the corner, so he took the only option open to him and in a split-second decision he bolted for the nearer exit door, turned the handle and ran through the opening.

As the door swung closed behind Vladimir, Viktor made a similar quick decision, jumped up from behind the car and ran to the door, calling out behind him, 'Amy, you stay here. Whatever you do, don't follow me! Wait for the others. If they don't turn up, go back down the tunnel and find them.'

By this stage Amy had managed to pull the gag out of her mouth and called out, 'Okay, I'll stay here, I guess. But who are you? How do you know my name? And why are you helping me?' Her question fell on deaf ears.

Viktor pushed the door and grunted as he felt the unexpected weight of the extremely heavy door. Clearly it had some heavy-duty shielding built into it. He was surprised to find a second door immediately behind the first. He went through that also and discovered it was a door of an old steel cupboard. Vladimir's workers had hidden the secret access to their tunnel in a disused piece of furniture to avoid discovery, a ploy that had proved extremely effective over their months of Chernobylite extraction. On the other side of the door, Viktor found a metal bar and jammed it hard up under the door handle in case someone tried to follow them. He didn't want any of his friends in this place – he sensed he was now inside the building housing the remains of Reactor 4 of the Chernobyl nuclear power plant, the scene of a radioactive disaster and destruction on a scale never before seen in human history.

Viktor knew he was doomed from the Chernobylite sliver inside him and had nothing to lose. He was determined to take out Vladimir, no matter how much more it shortened his already reduced lifespan.

It was deathly quiet inside the reactor building and dimly lit by low level lights. Viktor heard footsteps receding in the distance, pulled out his torch, quickly flicked it on and saw a shape disappearing around a corner, so set off in pursuit. As his light scanned the room cutting through the gloom, Viktor realized he was standing inside the famous sarcophagus that had been put in place to bury the radioactive contents under a mountain of concrete in the months after the explosion and then again with a new construction decades later to protect the crumbling edifice of the first hasty construction.

As he was running through the reactor hall in hot pursuit of his quarry, Viktor couldn't help but imagine that Hades, the ancient Greek God of death and king of the underworld, would have felt right at home here. And he pictured the fear, the terror and the bravery of the Ukrainian firemen who were first on scene and marched into certain death to do what needed to be done to stop the reactor flames and contain the meltdown in an effort to minimize the fallout and destruction wrought by the nuclear fire. And now, so many years later, when to most of the world's population, the Chernobyl disaster was relegated to just another chapter in a history book, here he was, running through a radioactive kill zone in pursuit of a madman.

Viktor rounded the corner at full speed and was shocked to feel a bullet zing past his face and smash into the concrete wall behind him, blasting exploding fragments of masonry into the air and his face. Vladimir had been lying in wait down at the end of the corridor and had taken a shot as soon as he spotted Viktor. Working solely on instinct, Viktor dropped down to the floor and returned fire, narrowly missing Vladimir but spooking him enough to send him running down the stairs coming off the side of the corridor.

Having gained valuable distance on his adversary, Viktor leapt to his feet and continued the charge. This time, when he reached the stairway, he quickly poked his gun around the corner and sprayed three shots down the stairs, then followed through. In the beam of his torchlight, Viktor noted the signs warning of the deadly radiation hazard and strict instructions to wear protective clothing. He wryly noted that his lightweight pants and jumper hardly qualified as protection against the hard radiation that he was sure was already wreaking irreparable cellular damage on his body.

Viktor continued down, following the noise of Vladimir's path. Until now, the immediate threat and spectre of death represented by Viktor and his gun had been more daunting to Vladimir than the long-term death represented by Chernobyl and its radiation. However, Vladimir finally reached a point of equilibrium where the two threats appeared similar in magnitude. He had spotted a sign in his path indicating that he had now reached the basement and Vladimir knew from photos and information gathered from his chief scientist and his robots that the infamous Elephant's Foot was around the next turn in the corridor. He had to turn back!

Vladimir hugged the wall, slinking along the corridor back towards the stair exit and Viktor's impending arrival. He heard Viktor's approach, took aim and waited. But Viktor was prepared – instead of running out of the stairwell standing, he slid out feet first on his back. Vladimir squeezed off one shot, but it went high. Viktor squeezed off one too, but it went wide. Now standing still and both looking directly at each other, they took a second for a better aim and both depressed the trigger on their handguns at the same time.

Two muted clicks were the only sound played out in the empty corridor, as both combatants had emptied their clip seconds before. Viktor was first to act as he leapt to his feet, charged towards Vladimir and while still a full three metres away from his target, leapt into the air, turned on his side and extended his right foot in a perfect flying side kick. Vladimir was transfixed, held immobile as the scene unfolded before him, almost in slow-motion. More accustomed to deploying human weapons to do the fighting for him, Vladimir was not made for such close-quarters combat.

Viktor's flying sidekick landed squarely in Vladimir's chest, blasting him down the corridor flat on his back, stunned, breathless and unable to move. Viktor quickly followed up with a vicious punch straight into Vladimir's face, instantly bringing forth a gush of blood from a lip burst apart from the force of the crushing blow between teeth and knuckle.

Viktor quickly formulated a plan and looked around for what he needed to help him carry it out. A quick search of some rooms off the corridor yielded a coil of wire that would suit his needs perfectly. He quickly ran back down the corridor to the groaning Vladimir, dragged him to his feet and applied a wrist lock, forcing Vladimir's hands up behind his back.

Viktor then marched Vladimir along the corridor towards the Elephant's Foot, the so-called *Monster in Chernobyl's Basement*.

'What are you doing? Stop!' shouted Vladimir in a panic as he came to his senses and realized where they were headed and what Viktor was planning to do. 'You're not just killing me; you're killing yourself too. You're mad!'

'I'm already dead. Your scientist made sure of that when he shot me in the neck with your Chernobylite. I'm just taking matters into my own hands, accelerating the process a bit and going out on my own terms. I've decided to do the world a favour by taking you out at the same time.'

'But why? Why are you doing this to me?' pleaded Vladimir, now bordering on the edge of hysteria as they continued their inexorable march towards the Elephant's Foot. 'Why have you been chasing me all this time? What did I ever do to you?'

'You really don't remember, do you? Have I changed that much in the past 20 years, *Vladimir*?' said Viktor. He paused the marching, pushed Vladimir up against the wall, grabbed him by the throat and leaned in close, just a few inches from Vladimir's face and then turned the torch light on himself. The result presented a ghoulish visage to the stricken Vladimir, with no trace yet of recognition.

'What are you talking about? Do I know you?' stammered Vladimir.

'Think Vladimir, think. Cast your foul mind back 20 years.'

'What is this? Revenge for Nikolai?'

'Ha! Nothing could be further from the truth, you fool. Look harder!'

shouted Viktor as he got even closer to Vladimir. 'I'll give you a clue. You killed someone who was incredibly special to me, a beautiful soul who had nothing but good in her heart. She meant the world to me. She died in a car bomb explosion that was arranged by you and very nearly killed me in the process.' Viktor's final words turned quiet and menacing as he got even closer to Vladimir, breath hot on his face.

'Aaarrrgghhhh!!!' screamed Vladimir as the waves of realization and understanding came crashing down on him. 'Pasha? But how is that possible? You *died*!'

'Not all of me died, Vladimir. Part of me did die in that car bomb when you took my wife Katerina from me. But the rest of me survived and here I am about to end your life, something I clearly should have done many years ago. While I was recovering from that terrible day, I made a commitment to the memory of Katerina that I would live a good life and forsake revenge against you, her killer. But when I discovered you had killed your nephew and kidnapped Tatiana and her daughter; I knew what I must do.'

Vladimir started struggling against Viktor's iron grip around his throat. Viktor calmly drew back his fist and again smashed it straight into Vladimir's face, knocking him senseless once more and adding more blood to the rapidly spreading mess. He dragged Vladimir's limp form along the corridor and around the final corner. The huge, menacing lump that was the Elephant's Foot, an intensely radioactive mass formed decades ago during the reactor meltdown, was still there, a liquid fall frozen in time, radioactive lava in suspended animation – *Chernobylite*.

There was evidence of much activity around the Elephant's Foot, including scuffs and scrapes around the base from the robots, holes drilled in its surface and dust particles flowing down its sides. But the main body of the Chernobylite was still well and truly there, steadily pumping out its deadly radiation dose as it would for millennia, unless of course some other criminal lunatic started mining it again.

The air itself seemed charged, reacting to the unseen blasts of high-energy particles bombarding everything in their path. The temperature around the mass was high due to the heat emanating from the radiation source. Viktor registered a metallic taste in his mouth, surely a result of the high-energy radiation. Viktor knew his life was close to an end, he just needed to give Vladimir a fitting send-off. He heaved up Vladimir's limp form and tossed him like a rag doll onto the evil-looking mass. He stretched Vladimir out on his back, his body laid out over the Elephant's Foot.

Viktor uncoiled the wire loop he had retrieved, understanding that the binding itself would be highly radioactive after many years in this environment. Quickly, expertly, he bound Vladimir firmly into position, stringing him out tightly over the surface of the Foot, body arched back and stretched over the mass. Arms, legs, chest and neck were bound tightly. There would be no escape for Vladimir. He would suffer the same terrible fate he had dreamt up and inflicted on Chad and had been prepared to do the same for so many others.

Stepping back with a satisfied smile, Viktor surveyed his handiwork. Vladimir was trussed like a freakish Christmas turkey on a whole different kind of oven. A groan emanated from the imprisoned body and small twitches soon turned to wild convulsions as Vladimir realized where he was and struggled to escape. Like a wolf caught in a trap who would chew off its own leg to escape, Vladimir struggled wildly in an erratic attack of movement, oblivious to the tight wire cutting through his skin, sending rivulets of blood running down over the surface of the radioactive mass beneath him.

'PASHA!' he screamed violently. 'Let me go! Don't leave me like this! Put a bullet in me or something, but don't make me die like an animal, shitting and pissing and bleeding from every hole!'

'This is only what you deserve Vladimir, for everything you have done over your despicable life; not just to me, but to so many others. The world will be a better place without you in it. Your life has been like some hideous virus smearing and infecting those around you with your debased filth. It's time for the cure, and its name is Uranium-235. Don't worry, it gets right in and works fast.'

Task completed, Viktor turned on his heel and strode down the corridor and up the stairs, back to check on Amy.

CHAPTER 69

After our long journey down the narrow, dark tunnel, we came tearing into a large, bright chamber. There were two cars skewed across the floor, clearly ditched in a hurry. There were no people in sight.

We jumped off the quad bike and Brittney apprehensively called out, 'Mom?'

'Brittney!' shouted Amy as she appeared from her hiding place behind the car. 'Oh my god, Brittney, I'm so happy to see you! I was wondering if I would ever see you again.' She ran over to Brittney and threw her bound hands over Brittney's head, grabbing her in a fierce embrace.

The two women burst into tears and were soon sobbing, overcome with relief at finding each other again. I stayed quiet, knowing the close bond of mother and daughter needed time to reconnect. Finally, the hug ended, and Amy leaned back, taking her daughter's tear-stained face in her hands, looked deep in her eyes and said, 'Oh Brittney, I love you so much. Thank you for surviving and coming to get me.' Then she kissed her delicately on the lips.

'I'm so glad you're okay Mom, I was so worried about you with that psycho Vladimir. Every time we got close; he took you away again. Are you okay? Are you hurt?'

'I'm fine, nothing serious,' replied Amy. 'I'm sure you look much worse than I do. What happened to you?'

'Goddamn Borys, the crazy bastard, punched me in the face a couple times, among other things. But I paid him back in spades. He's got a few of my bullets in him now, the prick,' Brittney said proudly.

'Good! I'm glad he got what he deserved; he was a nasty piece of work,' said Amy. Then she turned and saw me and said, 'Tommy! I'm sorry, I was so busy with Brittney, I didn't even notice you. Come here and give me a hug.'

I stepped over, pulled out my knife, cut Amy's wrist bindings and then wrapped her up in a big hug.

'Thank you, Tommy, thank you for saving Brittney and coming to get me,' said Amy, getting up on her tiptoes and kissing me on the cheek. 'I was sure you died out on that boat, I'm so happy to see you still alive.'

'I'm pretty happy to still be alive too Amy, but it sure was bloody close out there on the river,' I replied.

Then there was a heavy silence as Amy turned and looked at Brittney, who had tears welling in her eyes.

Amy walked over to Brittney, took both her hands in hers and said, 'It's Chad, isn't it, Brit? He's gone.'

'Oh Mom, I'm so sorry, but yes, he's gone. Vladimir and Borys killed him.'

There was no shock on Amy's face. It seemed that deep down she knew that Chad was already gone. She had been holding on to a faint glimmer of hope but finally learned the truth. Brittney took Amy in her arms and they cried quietly together, grieving for the loss of a truly wonderful son and brother.

After a few minutes, I moved over to them both, put a hand on Amy's shoulder and said, 'I'm so sorry Amy, I can't believe he's gone. I keep expecting him to show up somewhere and just say hello. He was my best friend, a beautiful human being. I really miss him.' Tears started running down my cheeks as Amy put her arms around my waist and hugged me again.

Then suddenly our collective grieving was interrupted by a loud TAP, TAP, TAP! It was like the sound of a bird pecking against a window. I looked over towards the corner of the room and saw a door with a small, heavy glass pane in it and saw a knuckle rapping on the glass. What the hell? It must be Viktor! I'd forgotten all about Viktor and Vladimir after finding Amy.

'Viktor! Is that you?' I called out as I ran to the door. 'Are you alright?'

Viktor pointed to his ears, indicating he couldn't hear me. I tried the door handle, but he mouthed the word, 'No' from the other side of the door and shook his head vigorously. Clearly, he didn't want me in there with him. He raised his finger up to glass level and pointed across to the side of the door. I looked over and saw an intercom there, presumably put there so the workers could communicate between what I assumed was the extremely radioactive zone (where Viktor was standing) and the 'safe' zone, or more accurately the 'not-quite-so-deadly-but-still-highly-radioactive' zone (where I was).

I pushed the button on the intercom pad and said 'Does this work? Can you hear me, Viktor?'

His response crackled through the tinny speaker, 'Yes, I can hear you fine, Tommy. Are you okay? Did you find Amy? Is Brittney alright?'

'Yes, we're all here and we're all fine. Here they are,' I replied as the girls came into view and waved and smiled at Viktor through the glass.

'What about Borys? Did you finish him off?' asked Viktor.

'Well, sort of. I beat him down and then Brittney finished him off with a couple of shots. He's dead, he won't be coming after us.'

'That's good,' replied Viktor with a nod.

'What about Vladimir?'

'Dying as we speak,' he said with a smile. 'He should just about be a radioactive barbeque by now. I strung him up with steel wire and laid him out over the Elephant's Foot.'

'Good. I'm glad to hear it's the end of that bastard. Is that Elephant's Foot the source of the Chernobylite?'

'Yes, it's a big radioactive mass in the basement under Reactor 4. It's an extremely deadly and creepy looking thing. You can see the dust around it, leftovers from where they've been mining it.'

The next question was more difficult and even though I thought I knew the answer, I still had to ask. 'Um, Viktor, why are you still in there? Why won't you come out? Is the door broken?' I asked hopefully.

'Well, I jammed the door so you couldn't come in Tommy, I didn't want you in here, it's too dangerous. Plus, I'm too radioactive now, I'd make you sick.'

'What did you do, Viktor?' I asked, my voice trembling. I was grateful to feel the warmth of Brittney's hand slip into mine and to feel Amy's hand as she put it on my shoulder.

'I chased Vladimir in here. He was getting away and I couldn't let that happen. He had to pay for what he's done.'

'No, Viktor, you're killing yourself! Getting revenge on Vladimir wasn't worth that! You should have let him go.'

'It's okay, Tommy. I know I'm dead already. That damn scientist shot me with Chernobylite back at Duga. I would have been dead in a couple of days anyway, there was nothing I could do about it. I just sped things up a bit.'

I was stunned into silence; I couldn't speak, with the knowledge that my second father would soon be dead, a mere ten years after my first. It was too much for me to bear.

Amy stepped up to the glass and looked through it with intent, studying the man on the other side of the door. After a long pause she asked in a quivering voice, 'Pasha? Is that you?'

'Yes, Tatiana, it is me. It's Pasha.'

'Oh my God, Pasha! It is you! I thought you were dead! How did you survive?'

'It's a long story; I told Brittney the whole thing, there's no time to tell you now, she can fill you in.'

'I, I don't know what to say,' stuttered Amy. 'Except, thank you. Thank you again from the bottom of my heart for saving me, for saving my children and giving us a wonderful life together.'

'You are very welcome, Tatiana. Very welcome.'

Viktor looked back at me and said, 'I'm sorry Tommy, but we don't have much time. There's something extremely important that needs to be taken care of. Thousands of lives depend on it.'

'What do you mean? Isn't this over yet? What else could there possibly be?'

'The first shipment of Chernobylite left Duga this morning, just before we arrived. There are 5,000 units on board. You need to stop that truck. Most likely it will be going to the port at Odessa. You must get someone to set up roadblocks and stop the shipment. You need to get out of here now. Drive back down the tunnel to Duga, the guards should be there by now to investigate our little diversion. Explain what's happened and convince them to help you. You *must* stop that truck!'

'But Viktor, what about you? We can't just leave you here alone in that hellhole!'

'Tommy, it's okay, I'm ready to go, it's time. It is my destiny; our fates, yours and mine, have been intertwined for the last twenty years. If I hadn't saved Tatiana and her children from that lunatic Nikolai all those years ago, you would never have met Chad and found such a good friend. You would never have met Brittney and fallen in love. Now here we are, come full circle and I am twice the man I was back then. Now I have the power, the knowledge, the heart and the commitment to do what had to be done and to do it properly. I gladly sacrifice myself to rid the world of the scum that is Vladimir Zhukov. I gladly pay the ultimate price to eliminate that poison. It is my chance to repay my debt to the Universe, to balance the ledger to try and right the terrible wrongs that I did in my early days. It is my Karma and I am ready to be reunited with my darling Katerina. I have lived far too long without her.'

Finally comprehending Viktor's motivation for his actions, I could do nothing but shrug my shoulders, nod my head, give thanks and say goodbye to my friend, my mentor, my teacher. 'Thank you, Viktor, for the man that you are and for everything you have done for me. Thank you for saving Brittney and Amy and Chad all those years ago. Thank you for taking a scared little boy under your wing and teaching him to be a man. I would not be who I am today without you in my life. Thank you for giving me the strength to live again after my father died. Thank you for all you've taught me, both on the mat and off. You mean everything to me.'

'Thank you, Tommy for those words. I'm so proud of you, proud of the man you've become and what you've achieved. I never had children of my own, but I am very proud to call you my Son. Katerina would have loved you and she would have been so proud of you too.'

Like some clichéd movie moment, I put my hand up to the glass, desperate for some semblance of contact with the man who meant so much to me. Viktor did the same from the other side of the glass and we shared a moment as I looked deep into his eyes, which were wet with tears, just like mine.

'Goodbye Viktor, my father.'

'Goodbye Tommy, my son.'

CHAPTER 70

Viktor turned away from the door and made his way back into the chamber of death. He walked slowly across the floor of the reactor building, taking in the gloomy surroundings as he moved. Down the stairs into the depths he went, feeling ready to vomit as the effects of the astronomical radiation dose he had suffered started to make their presence felt.

As he walked, he pulled the gun out from the top of his pants and reached into his pocket for his spare clip, calmly reloading his gun as he walked.

Rounding the corner, he saw the sinister mound of Chernobylite for what he knew would be the last time. Sprawled over the top of the Elephant's Foot was the contorted body of Vladimir, clearly dead already. True to Vladimir's own prediction, shit and piss was running out of his pants and blood was running from his eyes, nose, mouth and ears. His face was twisted in a mask of horror with skin stretched tight, pain and trauma frozen on his face forever.

Viktor looked on, morbidly fascinated at the scene before him and said to the corpse, 'Finally, I have my revenge, Vladimir, you bastard. I didn't do this to you in Katerina's name, because she wouldn't want that. I did it for me and for Tommy, Brittney, Amy and especially for Chad. You got everything you deserved; except I just wish I had done it sooner.'

Satisfied that Vladimir was most certainly dead and had suffered to the extreme in the process, Viktor turned and walked away. He didn't want to be near Vladimir, down in a dungeon, when he ended his life. He walked up the stairs and out onto the reactor floor, feeling an odd kind of physical connection with the reactor, knowing he had a piece of it inside him and knowing that they were both a relic of history, past their prime. It seemed somehow fitting that he should say goodbye to the world in the shadow of this monolith.

After 20 years of living as Viktor, in his final moments Pasha reclaimed his lost identity as he prepared to once again be with his Katerina. Pasha lifted the gun, tilted his head back and put the soothing cold steel of the muzzle against his throat under the chin.

With a sigh and a calm feeling of sweet relief, Pasha pulled the trigger and instantly descended into darkness, his only companion the ghostly remnants of the gunshot reverberating around the giant echo chamber, slowly dying away into silence.

CHAPTER 71

The trip down the tunnel had been quiet, our three hearts heavy with the loss of Viktor.

I drove slowly out into the Duga station and we were immediately faced with eight very confused and angry guards, all pointing their guns directly at us. I slowly brought the car to a stop and we all put our hands up in the air inside the car. 'Brittney, leave your gun in here and I'll leave my knife. We don't want to spook these guys,' I said.

Slowly we got ourselves out of the car, hands still very much in the air. 'Can anyone speak English?' I asked hopefully.

'A few of us do,' replied a heavyset guard in a thickly accented voice. 'As the ranking officer here, I will handle this. Who are you and what are you doing here?'

'Well, that's a long story and I will explain it to you soon, but right now we have something very urgent that we need to deal with. Come with me and I'll show you something.'

Three guards stayed covering Brittney and Amy, and four other guards accompanied me and my English communicator to the production room. With more confidence than I felt, I walked into the room, picked up a package of the very sinister looking black and yellow Chernobylite slivers and said, 'Someone has been extracting Chernobylite from the basement of the reactor building and making it into weapons.'

The eyes of the slack-jawed guards widened at this incredulous piece of information.

'There's a huge shipment of this deadly stuff driving along a

Ukrainian highway somewhere as we speak – it left here this morning. Do you keep records of the vehicles that go through your checkpoint? Maybe you can track it from that,' I said.

There was a lot of confusion on the guard's face, as he looked very dubious about my explanation. It seemed my fear they wouldn't believe my story was well founded.

'How do we know it's not *you* that made these Chernobylite weapons?' sneered a particularly unpleasant looking guard. 'You have no proof of what you say. There are a lot of dead bodies here and nobody to confirm your story.'

'Um, yeah, sorry about the mess,' I said as I looked around at the bodies strewn around the room, knowing there were more outside, not to mention the fact that we'd blown up a major piece of real estate on their private property.

'How do we know you won't try the same on us?' said the guard.

'Are you *serious*? How the hell could I do anything to you guys, with all the firepower you're holding?' I replied.

'Let's get you back to the gatehouse and introduce you to my superior officer and then take it from there,' said the first guard.

We quietly climbed into the troop transport and headed off to the gatehouse, feeling like prisoners again. The adrenaline was wearing off by this stage and exhaustion was taking over. Sitting in the back seat, I was holding Brittney's hand and she was holding Amy's. 'We'll be fine, don't worry girls, we'll be fine,' I said, trying to sound reassuring but not quite feeling it. We stopped at the gatehouse and were shown into a room and heard the door lock behind us, imprisoned once again.

Our new cell was drab and grey with no windows, lit by a solitary dim light bulb dangling from the centre of the ceiling. The only additions were a small plastic table and three flimsy plastic chairs. Something told me I exceeded the safe working load of that poor excuse for a piece of furniture, so I didn't risk parking my heavy frame on it.

A few minutes into our incarceration, we heard a key turn in the lock and the unpleasant guard from the Duga confrontation came in, furtively glancing back into the corridor as he shut the door behind him. As soon as he entered the room, he drew his gun and pointed it straight at us! I instinctively stepped in front of Brittney and Amy, spreading my arms out to my sides to shepherd them behind me.

'Where is Vladimir?' the guard hissed. 'What have you done with him?'

'What! How do you know Vladimir?' I asked, stunned at the audacity of this guard and the extensive reach of Vladimir's network.

'Never mind that!' snapped the guard. 'Where is he? He promised he would look after me and pay my way out of this radioactive hell hole.'

'Last I heard, he was tied up on an elephant, well actually, its foot,' I responded, frustrated that Vladimir's influence was still functioning, reaching out from beyond his radioactive tomb.

'What do you mean? Tell me where he is!' said the guard as he wildly waved his gun at us, voice rising in intensity.

'Sorry to be the one to break the news to you pal, but Vladimir is dead. He's frying somewhere in the bowels of Reactor 4. It's over. Give it up!'

'BASTARD!' shouted the guard as he raised his gun and levelled it at my head. Shit, this was not good. We were in a room with no escape, no cover and no time to make a strong move on this lunatic. I decided on a desperate move with little chance of success, figuring that anything was better than nothing. I reached out my right foot towards the chair nearest me and swiftly kicked it right at the guard, just as his finger started squeezing the trigger. He paused his shot and swatted away the chair like the nothing it was, smiled and took fresh aim.

'STOP!' blared a voice in our cell. 'Drop your weapon!' Our attacker looked up and around the room in a panic, eyes wide and gun waving, trying to work out where the sound was coming from. I pushed Brittney and Amy down to the floor behind me and rushed the guard, taking advantage of the distraction. He turned to me at the last second as he noticed my movement, but it was too late. I was on him in a flash, his gun still waving up at the ceiling.

I slammed my shoulder into him and grabbed him around the waist. Hit with the full force of all my weight and the momentum gained in my three steps across the room, the guard's feet left the floor as I stood up to my full height and continued my run across the room. Two more steps brought me to the wall and SMASH! I pounded his body into the wall like a Mack truck and felt the compression of his body as he absorbed the impact, squashing him like a bug on a windscreen. Crack, crack went two ribs as the compression reached its limit. I stepped back and he slid down the wall all the way to the floor.

A bunch of keys rattled in the lock, so I backed away over to the opposite corner of the room, again shielding Brittney and Amy from whatever was coming.

The first guard, our English translator, entered the room, breathless. 'Are you okay?' he asked.

'Who the hell was that guy? He was working with the psycho that was mining the Chernobylite!' I said in a huff.

'We know that now. We had our suspicions about his motives but hadn't been able to confirm it until now. Only a few people knew that this room was recently wired with a hidden camera, microphone and speaker. We thought he might try something, so we stayed back and watched and sure enough, he made his move.'

'Gee, thanks for the heads-up. You used us as bait to catch your stinking fish!'

'Sorry, but it was the only way we could work out who was telling the truth – you or him. We were keeping a close eye on everything and it all worked out okay, nobody got hurt. Well, except for him of course,' he said with a nod to the groaning, crumpled body on the floor.

'So now do you believe us?' I asked.

'Yes, we know you weren't working with, what name did he call him – Vladimir?'

'Good. Now can we stop pissing around and get out of here so we can stop that shipment?'

'Yes. We'll have a look at the records of the vehicle movements. We'll have the registration number noted and we'll have it on video too.'

This was a bit more like the cooperation I was hoping for from the guards. I guess they, more than anyone, wouldn't want bits of the nuclear waste they were supposedly guarding being shot around all over the place, knowing it could be traced back to the source.

'Please let me introduce myself. I am Mykhail,' said the guard.

'I'm Tommy, pleased to meet you,' I replied and shook his hand.

Mykhail led us out of the cell to a much more comfortable lounge area that had an actual couch to sit on. 'Please make yourselves comfortable, I will be back soon.'

We all felt much better being out of our cell, free to walk around and without anyone poking a gun at us, which was encouraging.

A few minutes later our new friend reappeared, this time with an imposing character in full dress uniform. 'Tommy, this is our Captain of the Guard,' said Mykhail.

'Pleased to meet you, Captain,' I said and extended my hand. A name was clearly not necessary for this man, who appeared to go by title alone.

After a brief handshake, the Captain said, 'It seems you have done us a great service. We have contacted the police and given them the registration number and description of the truck. They have mobilized all available resources and set up roadblocks on all the possible routes out of here. Thank you.'

We sat down with the Captain and ran through the whole explanation of the last few days, all the way from the start at the Olympics to the grisly end in Chernobyl, with Vladimir and Viktor dying inside the nuclear plant. When I finally finished my story, the Captain, who had clearly been listening intently and thinking hard as it went on, said, 'Well, Tommy, that's quite a story. Thank you. From us here at Chernobyl and from the whole of Ukraine, thank you. You have done us a great service. *However*, nobody can ever know. You were never here. Justice has been done. The man who did this to us and killed your friend is dead.'

'I understand,' I said, certainly not wanting any glory out of all this. I was more than happy for this story to be buried. 'What about Pasha?'

'He is a local hero. Our internal police report will say it was him, and only him, who did all this. We cannot have international visitors linked to this. Nobody needs to know about any of you, it will just create unnecessary panic and chaos.'

'What about the police? Will they be okay with all this? We kind of created a bit of a mess in Odessa and Kiev, which I guess they are still trying to sort out.'

'Yes, the police agree also. They too are grateful for your help, but do not want any publicity about this. They also pass on their thanks for weeding out the crooked police members in Kiev.'

'My pleasure. I'm glad they found those two scumbags,' I replied. 'So, the cops are happy to just let us go?'

'Yes, there will be no charges against you. How could there be if you were never here? We will arrange for you to get back into Romania, retrieve your passports and make your own way home, as if nothing happened here. From what you said, there is no record of you entering Ukraine, so there doesn't need to be any record of you leaving it. But we need to move quickly. We don't want anyone poking around asking questions and connecting you three with anything. We'll get you out of the country tonight. You can eat and shower here and change into fresh clothes from the storeroom. We'll leave soon and get you across the border in just a few hours, then drop you in Bucharest.'

This was just way too surreal.

CHAPTER 72

The old clunker of a lorry bounced and clattered its way along the highway from Chernobyl down to Odessa, the driver paying no heed to the sensitivity of his cargo. There were boxes upon boxes of Chernobylite slivers and air pistols stacked inside the back of the truck. Unfortunately, the men hired by Vladimir were not particularly experienced or diligent package handlers, so the integrity of the boxes in the back of the truck was soon breached by the constant jolting and banging of the crates in the back. An old, frayed hold-down strap succumbed to the strain and snapped under the load of one highway bounce too many.

A large box containing 64 packs of Chernobylite slivers, finally free from its bindings, shimmied its way along the top of the packing crate. Another bounce sent the box sliding off the edge and it dropped down to the tray of the truck. The box split open, spreading the contents across the floor of the truck tray.

Bump after bump pounded the truck suspension that had ceased to function years before, continuing the jolting journey of the packages in the back, sliding closer and closer to the edge of the tray and the roadway beneath. Finally, one last pothole finished the job.

Four packages, each containing four Chernobylite slivers, fell out through a hole in the lorry's canvas siding and bounced to a stop along the highway as the truck receded into the distance.

Minutes after the slivers had escaped their transport, a police roadblock startled the driver as he rounded a bend on the highway heading into Kiev. The driver slammed on the brakes and quickly turned the wheel to avoid the roadblock but was immediately thwarted by the police car that appeared out of a narrow side street behind him. The lorry was boxed in with nowhere to go.

As far as the police were concerned, all the Chernobylite was safe.

CHAPTER 73

True to his word, the Captain hurried us out of Ukraine without a minute's delay. There was no trouble at the border crossing and no questions asked. We drove through the night and into the next day, sleeping much of the way and the rest of the time replaying in our minds the madness of the last few days.

On the way to Bucharest we got in touch with George, who was still in town. He picked us up from the Captain, who promptly turned around and started the long drive back to Chernobyl, content that the potential publicity crisis had been averted.

We had nothing except the clothes on our back. Thankfully, George was well set up in Bucharest with a car, money and accommodation. He took us all back to his hotel suite and sorted out beds for us.

It blew my tiny mind; incredibly, the Olympics were still running as if nothing had happened! There had been some disturbance around Chad's death, but that had since been explained away by the Romanian spin doctors as a virus. We all agreed it was best to leave the story as it was. None of us wanted to stir up any trouble and didn't want to create a media circus that wouldn't help anyone.

We went to my dorm in the Olympic Village where I retrieved my luggage, complete with passport, papers and gold medal and sadly picked up Chad's belongings too. Brittney and Amy retrieved their luggage from their hotel, and we all went over to George's suite, none of us wanting to let any of the others out of our sight. We got room service and then crashed for the night, exhausted.

The next morning was perhaps the most bizarre of the whole weird experience. Pretending everything was normal, I attended the closing ceremony of the Olympic Games, marching along with my fellow team members and explaining away my absence as having gone on a days-long bender celebrating my gold medal and mourning Chad.

All the members of the American and Australian teams wore black armbands as a symbol of respect for our fallen friend.

In a touching show of respect for Chad, he was posthumously awarded an Olympic silver medal during the Closing Ceremony, which was proudly accepted by Amy.

We flew out of Romania the next day, vowing never to return.

CHAPTER 74

The church was packed to the rafters – standing room only. People had come from far and wide to farewell Chad at his memorial service. School friends, college buddies, work colleagues, teammates, fellow competitors, Olympic officials, media staff and more had streamed into the cavernous space as soon as the doors were flung open. People were left out in the foyer, forced to watch the proceedings on remote monitors and listen over loudspeakers. The turnout was testament to Chad and the lives he had touched over the course of his all-too-brief time on the planet.

I nervously approached the lectern, settled myself and then raised my head to face the throng. I extracted the ratty notepaper from my pocket and studied the chicken scratchings that I had scrawled a lifetime ago in a rundown flea-bitten hotel in remote Romania, when I was tired, desperate and alone, feeling the deepest depths of my loss for Chad. I drew in a deep breath and delivered my eulogy, as promised.

I managed to keep myself together just long enough to deliver my speech and then broke down on the way back to my seat alongside Brittney and Amy. The other speeches passed in a blur, but I know it was a good send-off. It was a fitting tribute to a wonderful young man, taken way before his time.

After the service, when all the guests had paid their respects to Amy and Brittney, the three of us went back to Amy's apartment. It was my last night in New York before I had to leave the country, my student visa being no longer valid. I would have to apply for a green card in order to come back and live in the States and just hope for a positive outcome. This meant Brittney and I would soon be apart for an extended period.

Still, we had managed a long-distance relationship before, and we would do so again until I could somehow make my way to L.A. to be with Brittney. Only this time, the distance was much further and the time difference more challenging, but we knew we could do it.

I hugged Amy goodnight and then Brittney and I went off to bed for our final night together for who knew how long.

At least I would be seeing Mum again soon. I was flying out in the morning back to Sydney, to a life that seemed so alien after my last four years in the States, not to mention the Olympics, Chad, Amy and especially Brittney. The thought of Kings Cross without Viktor just didn't seem right at all.

As I boarded my flight the next day, I closed a big chapter of my life and couldn't help wondering what on earth was in store for the next one. I seriously had no idea.

CHAPTER 75

I'd landed back in Sydney a few days before. It had been weird living back in the tiny apartment with Mum at Judy's club after the last four years of freedom, living in my dorm room at college. Mum had been so glad to see me that she broke down and cried when I made my way through the gate at the airport. I must admit I let loose some waterworks of my own – I really needed my mum after all the chaos and emotion of the previous couple of weeks.

The day after I landed, Mum and I had gotten straight to work organizing Viktor's memorial service. It was important to give him a good send-off and for his students to know that he was gone, since Viktor hadn't had time to do any more than stick a note on the door of his Judo school before he left, stating that classes were cancelled until further notice.

Viktor's dojo was jam-packed full of all his students, friends and parents of students. There had to be over 300 people in the dojo. It was a great testament to Viktor's contribution to the community that so many people wanted to pay their respects.

I made my way to the front of the training hall, turned and faced the assembly and without saying anything, I leaned forward at the waist, making a deep bow. In profound silence, every single person in the dojo returned the bow in unison, showing their respect for their much-loved and sorely missed friend and teacher.

I took a deep breath and prepared to begin my second eulogy in just over a week. First, I'd had to say goodbye to my best friend, and now to my mentor, teacher, master, friend and surrogate father. I'm not much for prayer, but I did send one upstairs at that moment, desperately hoping that this would be the last funeral speech I would need to deliver for many years to come.

I started my speech shakily in a quivering voice, full of emotion. 'Thank you everyone for coming along today. Viktor would have been incredibly happy to see so many of you here. It means a great deal to me that you are all here to say goodbye to Viktor, who truly was a great man. As many of you know, I was very close to Viktor. I was extremely proud to call him my second father and I'm happy to say he was proud to call me the son he never had.

'Many years ago, Viktor took a scared little boy under his wing. He cared for me, protected me and taught me how to be a man. He gave me the strength I needed to survive the loss of my father, to recover from my despair and to reclaim my life. I dedicate the Olympic gold medal that I'm wearing around my neck to Viktor and the contribution he made to me and the impact he had on my life.'

I paused, took another few deep breaths, and looked over at Mum, who gave me a smile and a nod, letting me know as always that she was there for me in love and support, giving me the strength to continue. 'All of us knew Viktor was a great teacher, but did any of us really know Viktor the man? He was very private and never shared any of the history of his life before Australia. He hadn't even shared the story of his life with me, and we were close and spent a great deal of time with each other. In our last days together, I had the privilege of learning about some of Viktor's past and how he came to be in Australia and was able to have such a positive impact on all our lives.

'Viktor was so much more than just a teacher. In my darkest hour, I called for help and Viktor came running to my aid, without hesitation. He was an incredibly special man who rescued me after a personal tragedy. In that process I got to know much more of the man who meant so much to me. He grew up in a tough neighbourhood in Odessa in

Ukraine and then moved to Chechnya in Russia as a young man. There he was drawn into the web of an evil tyrant who ran a criminal empire. Viktor risked his life to rescue a young woman and her two infant children, but he paid a high price for his courage when his wife was killed and he himself almost died. After years of recovery from his injuries, Viktor finally found his peace and was able to put his traumatic past behind him. That's when he came to Australia and started his Judo school.'

There were shocked looks and murmurs around the dojo as people absorbed this information about Viktor.

'Viktor came to help me in Romania after the death of my best friend, which had affected me very deeply. He and I spent a few days together and he really helped me get back on my feet. Sadly, he succumbed to a sudden illness that took his life way too quickly. But I take comfort in the fact that he was in his homeland when he died. It seemed to make him happy that he was there when the end came. Viktor's desire to live a good life and help people made him a great contributor to his community, and for that we honour him today. Let us now share a silent moment of reflection as we each remember Viktor in our own way.'

The silence that followed was initially sombre, but soon turned to smiles and nods as people thought of Viktor and the positive impact he had made on their lives and the good times they had shared together.

I broke the quiet and proceeded with my final goodbye. 'Viktor, you meant the world to me and I will be forever grateful for all that you have done for me. You helped make me the man I am today, and you saved my life more than once. I will miss you more than words can express. Goodbye, my friend, my teacher, my father.'

I gave one final, deep bow of respect for Viktor and then returned to the mat and a very welcome hug from Mum.

The service continued with two other speeches, followed by the obligatory sandwiches, chocolate biscuits, tea and coffee until finally

Mum and I were the only ones left, cleaning up the dojo. 'What's going to happen with Viktor's school? What about his students?' she asked.

'One of his senior assistants has decided to take over the school,' I replied. 'He's a black belt who's been with Viktor for years and said he's willing to take it on and make a go of it. He knows he has big shoes to fill, but I think he'll do a good job – he's a good man. I said I would come whenever I can and help him with the classes. It will be good for me to stay connected to Viktor through this school, which he started from nothing and meant so much to him.'

'That's good Son, I'm glad you can still be involved, I think it's important for you and for everyone here. You did such a good job with the eulogy, it was perfect. How are you feeling now?'

'I feel hollow, completely empty, like an old shell on the beach with nothing inside but distant noise. I can't believe I lost both Chad and Viktor, two of the most important people in my life, in the space of a week. I feel so *lost*.'

Mum reached up and put her hands on each side of my face, pulled me down to her and slowly and gently kissed away the tears that were by now streaming down my cheeks, just like she used to when I was a kid.

'I'm sorry, Tommy. It's so cruel that at the moment of your greatest triumph, when you finally achieved your goal after so much hard work, that the joy of that moment was stolen from you by the deaths of those so close to you. But always remember they will live on through your memory, just like your father does to this day. And never forget your achievement, your gold medal and what that meant to Viktor and Chad.'

'Thanks Mum. You always know just what to say to make me feel better. I love you.'

'I love you too, Tommy.'

In that moment I felt a desperate yearning, a crushing need to be with Brittney. She was so far away, back at college on the other side of the world, in a country where I was no longer allowed to live.

CHERNOBYLITE

'Mum?'

'Yes, love?'

'I miss Brittney.'

'I know Son, I know.'

EPILOGUE

'Hey Babe, how are you?' I said to Brittney, from home in Sydney to her on the other side of the world.

'Hi Tommy, I'm awesome, it's so good to hear your voice!' came the excited response. 'I've only got a minute, we're just about to head out the door.'

'That's cool, I just wanted to say a quick hello and see how your visit's going. Is it all working out alright? How's your Mum? It must be pretty confronting for her after all these years, going back home for the first time.'

'It's going great – Chechnya is amazing! My grandparents are so sweet. It's fantastic to meet them. For my whole life it's just been me, Mom and Chad, just the three of us. It's really comforting to know that I have more family. I just wish they could have met Chad,' said Brittney with the inevitable emotional edge creeping into her voice, the sense of loss and grief still so raw.

'You got over there pretty quick. Did Amy already know where her parents were?'

'Yes, she said she looked for them a while back and found out where they were. She wanted to keep an eye on them and make sure they were still alive and doing okay. The trigger for her was being back in the region, so close to where she grew up, and of course with all the trauma of her past now dead and buried, there was nothing standing in her way to reconnect with her parents. I'm so glad she did Tommy, it's wonderful!'

'That's great Brit, I'm so glad the trip is working out well, and it's so good to talk to you.'

'Thank you, Tommy, I'm really happy that we made the trip. Sorry, but I need to go now, we're going to visit some of Grandma's friends. Love you. Bye.'

'Love you too, Brit. Have a good day. See you.'

The conversation was short and sweet, but left me feeling good, knowing that Brittney was doing well and was getting to know more of her history and her new-found family. The familiar ache I felt when I wasn't with Brittney returned and I knew with absolute certainty that she was the love of my life and that we had to find some way to be together.

Then the phone burst out an unexpected ring that brought me back from my daydreaming. I hit the answer button and brought the phone to my ear.

'Hello? Is that Thomas Taylor?' rang out a woman's high-pitched voice in a strong American accent.

'Yep. This is Tommy. Who's this?'

'Tommy! I'm so glad I tracked you down! We must meet. I need to see you. Can you get on a plane and be in L.A. by Friday?'

'What? Why? Who is this?' I said, confused.

'Sorry, I'm getting ahead of myself. My name's Suzie and I'm a casting director in Hollywood. A professor of yours from film school just showed me your Little Bo Peep performance from college and then showed me a video of you winning a gold medal at the Olympics. Honey, you've got the look, the body and the talent to make it in the movies. We want you to audition for a part in our next movie. We'll pay for you to come out here, of course.'

'Gee let me think about that for a microsecond! Hell, yeah! Email me the details, buy me a ticket and I'm there,' I replied. We swapped details and then I hung up the phone, set to burst out of my skin.

'Mum!' I shouted. 'Guess what! I'm going to Hollywood, baby!'

'What? That's amazing Tommy! But you've only been back for two weeks.'

'I know, sorry Mum, but the movies are calling. I've got it all worked out – I'll slam dunk the audition and get the part, then I'll be able to live in the States again, close to Brittney in L.A.'

'Tommy, that's wonderful. Of course, you have to go. You'll be incredible, I know.'

'Thanks Mum. I'm going to be a star and make a wad of cash, enough so you won't have to work anymore. Maybe you can buy a share of the club from Judy if you want. Hey, maybe you can come out to L.A. with me! You can see some of the world, live somewhere new, it'll be awesome! Anyway, I need to go do something now, so I'll see you later. Love you.'

As I took off out the door, Mum just shook her head and smiled just like back in the day.

I jumped in the car, made a quick call, drove across town and then climbed out at my destination, bursting with excitement.

'G'day mate, glad I finally tracked you down. Took a bit of work, but the classic car club was pretty helpful,' I said to the man waiting in his driveway.

'Yeah, I'm glad you found me too, mate. Here she is, just like the day my dad bought it off your mum.'

There it was! My dad's old bright orange Torana SLR 5000. It was just like I remembered it ten long years ago; like reconnecting with Dad.

'Yep, that's definitely the car and I definitely want to buy it. I don't have all the money yet, but I will soon. I'm about to get a new job. Can I just put down a deposit today?' I asked hopefully.

'Sure mate, that's fine. I'm not in any hurry. My dad died recently, and we talked about how good it would be to get it back to the original owner. Take your time.'

'Thanks heaps mate, you're an absolute champion! This really means a lot to me.' We shook hands to seal the deal and said our farewells.

I climbed back in my car, took a couple of deep breaths and had a moment of reflection. Things were going to be alright. I pictured my 12-year-old self, lying in the back of my dad's ute just before he died and the words that I said that day came back to me like it was yesterday.

Life doesn't get any better than this.

THE END

ABOUT THE AUTHOR

Mike Dowsett lives in Melbourne, Australia with his wife Liz; they are the proud parents of three adult sons. Mike's other titles include his business book *Engineer Your Business* along with fictional works *Killer Addiction* and *Odessa*. You can find out more about these and Mike at www.mikedowsett.com

www.ingramcontent.com/pod-product-compliance
Lightning Source LLC
Chambersburg PA
CBHW030231120726
47903CB00005B/1441